PRAISE FOR CHRISTINE NOLFI

Treasure Me

"This zesty novel is rife with witty dialogue and well-drawn characters."
—*Publishers Weekly* for the Amazon Breakthrough Novel Awards

"A riveting read for those who enjoy adventure fiction, highly recommended."
—Susan Bethany, *The Midwest Book Review*

Second Chance Grill

"Nolfi writes with a richness of heart that is incredibly endearing."
—Renee Fountain, *Book Fetish*

"An emotionally moving contemporary novel about the power that relationships have to transform lives."
—Susan Bethany, *The Midwest Book Review*

The Impossible Wish

"You'll fall in love with Nolfi's quirky and slightly irreverent characters. The conclusion is guaranteed to warm your heart."
—Bette Lee Crosby, *USA Today* bestselling author

"Fast, fun, and fresh, filled with colorful characters—*The Impossible Wish* delivers the heartfelt entertainment Nolfi's readers have come to love!"
—Toby Neal, author of the bestselling Lei Crime series

The Tree of Everlasting Knowledge

"A novel of remarkable, rare substance."

—Casee Marie, *Literary Inklings*

"Poignant and powerful, *The Tree of Everlasting Knowledge* is as much a saga of learning how to survive, heal, and forgive as it is a chilling crime story, unforgettable to the very end."

—Margaret Lane, *The Midwest Book Review*

Sweet Lake

ALSO BY CHRISTINE NOLFI

The Liberty Series

Second Chance Grill (Book 1)

Treasure Me (Book 2)

The Impossible Wish (Book 3)

Four Wishes (Book 4)

The Tree of Everlasting Knowledge (Book 5)

The Dream You Make

Heavenscribe: Part One

Heavenscribe: Part Two

Heavenscribe: Part Three

The Shell Keeper (Kindle Worlds Novella)

The Shell Seeker (Kindle Worlds Novella)

Sweet Lake

A Novel

CHRISTINE NOLFI

LAKE UNION
PUBLISHING

Published by Lake Union, Seattle

www.apub.com

Amazon, the Amazon logo, and Lake Union are trademarks of Amazon.com, Inc., or its affiliates.

ISBN-13: 9781503942516
ISBN-10: 1503942511

Cover design by Rachel Adam

Printed in the United States of America

For Patricia, Leslie, Stacy, Laurel, and Thomas
and the history we share

Chapter 1

Coconuts bouncing down a bowling lane.

Linnie Wayfair woke with a start. She peered through the semidarkness in a vain attempt to locate the disturbance. No, coconuts weren't the source of the sharp rattling. She didn't stow tropical fruit in her suite—or own a bowling alley, for that matter.

Wincing, she glanced at the ceiling. Bats in the attic?

Problems galore plagued an inn the size of the Wayfair. Problems multiplied when half of the rooms were shut tight, the air inside growing stale and the four-poster beds lying naked, the Italian linens and the velvet bedspreads packed away. As for the attic, raccoons never waited for an invitation. Bats were also savvy party crashers.

In autumn when Ohio's temperatures plummeted, Linnie patrolled the attic in her brother's old football helmet and the wool topcoat her father hadn't taken to Florida. Neither of her close friends volunteered for the missions. Since she didn't believe in conscription, she went up by herself armed with a steel garbage lid, a flashlight, and an oversize broom that would make a witch proud. When claws skittered or the flapping of invisible wings zoomed by, she always contemplated adding her brother's old BB gun to the arsenal.

The thought never led to action. She didn't have the heart to harm any critter.

Please, not bats. Outside shadows caressed the rolling hills. Farther off, fingers of daylight glittered on Sweet Lake's teal-blue surface. Linnie was about to pass the sound off as nothing when the rattling started again.

From the corridor Jada Brooks padded in with her 'fro bouncing and her slippers smacking the floor. "What *is* that?"

The Wayfair's pastry chef and second-in-command wore yoga pants and a heavy jersey. Despite summer's arrival, the neglected south wing usually remained chilly until noon. Linnie grabbed her robe from the chaise lounge in a corner of the suite.

"I'm not sure," she replied, cinching the belt.

Jada gave out a mock shiver. "Not more bats." Her chestnut-colored eyes rounded. Then she glanced at the ceiling. "Should I wake Cat?"

"To do what?" Linnie ducked beneath the bed, found her slippers. "Cat doesn't like vermin any more than you do. Let her sleep."

"It's June, not October. If the bats have come early, I'm not going upstairs with you."

"You never go upstairs with me."

"Well, I'm not starting now."

"There aren't bats nesting in the eaves." More rattling, and Linnie perked her ears. "The sound's coming from the lake."

They went downstairs to investigate. Behind the reception desk Mr. Uchida dozed, the carnation pinned to his lapel wilting. His light snoring carried across an area more closely resembling a living room than an austere hotel lobby, with tapestry chairs and thickly cushioned couches. Above the lobby, the main portion of the inn remained blissfully silent.

Linnie said, "Whatever's going on, it hasn't woken our guests." Only the murmured conversation of the morning kitchen staff drifted into the lobby.

Jada frowned. "Do you think . . . ?"

"Oh, I hope not."

"They usually give us fair warning."

Linnie's irritation gained speed. "*Usually,*" she repeated, fearing the worst. "If they've broken the rule, I will not be amused."

"Relax. Maybe they're holding a ceremony to place good vibes around the Wayfair. It *is* the beginning of the tourist season. We can use the help."

"I don't need their help." She wasn't foolish enough to rely on a group of nutty women to make magical charms in hopes of increasing the inn's reservations. "They're supposed to give me notice before holding a meeting on the beach. If they're here out of a misplaced desire to help, they should've given me a heads-up."

Jada glanced at the clock above the dozing Mr. Uchida's head. "Stop worrying. It's barely dawn. They aren't dancing around naked."

"And you're sure because . . . ?" Given the recent fiasco, she wouldn't put anything past the Sweet Lake Sirens.

Last month, newlyweds honeymooning at the Wayfair had decided to take a midnight stroll around the lake's dancing blue waters. On the beach, the Sweet Lake Sirens were holding an impromptu meeting. The women, mostly middle-aged or older, had imbibed too many of the mojitos that were a Mendoza family staple. One of the members, certain she'd lost all feminine allure, bemoaned her husband's golf obsession and lack of sexual interest since his retirement.

Frances Dufour, the group's oldest member, had arrived at the perfect—and perfectly silly—solution.

During daylight hours, Frances wore a variety of sedate dresses to highlight calves as shapely at the age of seventy-four as they'd been in her twenties. In summer months, she carried a parasol with a design of lilies stamped on the fabric. The care and maintenance of her alabaster skin was a particular obsession, and one that put her at odds with her closest friend and rival, Cat's mother, Silvia Mendoza.

For her part, once summer's glorious heat descended on the town, Silvia changed her calendar, choosing only to meet with clients at her accounting firm in the morning hours. This left afternoons free to languidly bronze her skin on the shores of Sweet Lake. The hedonistic pursuit, as well as her flamboyant daywear and abundance of jewelry, provided the spark for many a squabble with Frances. Of course, there were other deeper reasons for the blend of animosity and devotion governing their relationship.

Unfortunately for the newlyweds strolling beneath the waxing moon, Frances had brought along a tin box of embroidery thread to the meeting. She announced that the Sirens could help their troubled comrade by donning the fabric of the natural world. When the newlyweds stumbled across them, the Sirens were sitting naked in the moonlight sewing bikinis out of maple leaves.

The couple, scarred by an eyeful of mature woman flesh, had checked out of the inn the next morning.

The memory propelled Linnie across the lobby. Wandering the grounds in pj's wasn't standard operating procedure for her or Jada, but what choice was there? Better to drive the Sirens from the beach before any of the guests awoke. With only half of the rooms booked, she didn't need more cancellations.

Outside, a peaceful silence cocooned the veranda that wrapped three sides of the inn. Flowerbeds in need of upkeep dotted each side of the stone walkway. The Wayfair perched on the highest point in the area, and Linnie resisted the pull of gravity as they hurried downward to the lake that shared the town's name.

The golden sands of the beach rested in shadow. She spotted a cluster of the Sweet Lake Sirens huddled in a circle.

"Great. Just great." She counted ten women. "Are the others coming?"

Jada surveyed the group. "Doubtful. The rest are getting ready for work or readying kids for summer camp."

Pulling off her slippers, Linnie marched across the sand. Several of the women paused from the ritual to stare at her solemnly.

"What's up?" she asked, taking care to wipe the amusement from her face.

On their heads, the women wore headbands threaded with hot-pink and sapphire-blue feathers. The colors were undoubtedly symbolic—pink for womanly virtue perhaps, and blue for wisdom. The group shook rattles fashioned from gourds. Zigzags of paint on the gourds resembled African art. The design was probably something Frances had discovered in a fashion magazine.

The eldest of the Sirens held Linnie in an unblinking stare. Jada stepped back, away from the intense scrutiny.

"Melinda Petronia Wayfair," Frances intoned, "your latent wisdom has drawn you to the Siren's call. Welcome to our circle."

"You were expecting me?" A first, since the Sirens only allowed members at their meetings.

"By hearing the call, you have proven yourself worthy."

Linnie crossed her arms. "For Pete's sake, Frances. It's a miracle half of my guests didn't hear the racket. Will you stop already?"

Apparently the wrong reply because Frances shook the colorful gourd beneath Linnie's nose with more vigor, as if her exertions might bring the response she desired. "The Siren's call offers you protection from the danger ahead."

Danger? A nasty twinge of fear zapped Linnie's stomach. She brushed it off. The only danger she faced was a return to the near bankruptcy that had plagued the Wayfair for the last seven years.

"Next time you want to wake me at dawn, send an invitation," she snapped. "I won't RSVP."

Silvia leapt forward, giving her rattle a shake. Whereas Frances was tall and slender, the co-leader of the Sirens was shorter and more robust, a voluptuous fireball with flowing hair nearly as long as Cat's. Like everyone else, Linnie preferred to avoid Silvia's temperamental outbursts. She also secretly admired Cat's mother—the aging process had softened, but not destroyed, her sex appeal.

Her eyes drifting shut, Silvia rolled her head back and forth. "Submit to our wisdom! The longer you wait for our protection, the stronger he grows. Submit now!"

"Who's growing stronger?" Another bad response, since she didn't really care.

Eyes still shut, Silvia murmured, "I cannot say more until events unfold."

Linnie blew out a stream of air. "Go home already. Fine by me if you keep the mystery to yourself since I can't deal with your antics before my first cup of joe." Approaching, she took a gander at Silvia's face in the greyish light. "Of all the silly . . . what's with the eye makeup?" Her lids were covered with greasy blue shadow, and dots of orange lipstick arched beneath her brows. "If I were checking LinkedIn for a new CPA, you would *not* receive my call."

The insult yanked Silvia from her pseudo-trance. "How can we lend protection if you won't heed our wisdom? The peril is great."

"Yeah? If I can't raise the occupancy rate at the inn, I'm in peril. Other than that, I'm doing fine without your early-morning voodoo."

"Do not take these matters lightly. Let us protect you!"

Frances breezed forward. "Take your kettle off boil, Silvia. Are you *still* taking potions? Sixty-five is too old for hormone replacement therapy."

A debatable point, Linnie mused. At times, half-moon bruises that looked suspiciously like hickeys appeared on Silvia's body. Hidden behind an ebony curl near her ear, on a bronzed thigh as she sunbathed—no one in Sweet Lake doubted passion lurked in the Mendoza marriage.

There wasn't time this morning to contemplate Silvia's fortunate status. The two Sirens began arguing. This left their comrades frowning with confusion, their feather crowns growing floppy in the rising humidity.

Jada pulled her out of earshot. "Shouldn't we find out why they think you're in danger?" Thanks to the Sirens' bizarre warnings, her caramel-colored skin had taken on an unmistakable ashen hue. "Maybe one of the Sirens had a prophetic dream about you or the inn."

"No, thanks." Clearly Jada was buying into their silliness.

"You really should make them tell you."

"And risk encouraging them? Not on your life. They'll stuff my slippers with dried herbs or insist on hanging trinkets around the inn." Linnie waved a hand at the group. "Wrap up the meeting and clear the beach, will you? I don't want my guests put off their breakfasts if they see you out here. And for heaven's sake, stop rattling the gourds. This is a vacation town. You'll wake everyone."

༄

Frances pressed a hand to her overexcited heart. The dawn ritual hadn't produced the intended result, a mishap for which she bore responsibility. The Sirens wouldn't have intervened without her insistence they demonstrate solidarity on what would prove a most trying day. Once the mail arrived at the inn, Linnie was in for a shock.

Helping the young was always a delicate affair. It was easy to overstep or provide counsel without an invitation. Steering a woman toward the discovery of her inner strength was even more difficult in a case such as Linnie's. Although she'd never voiced the opinion directly, Frances was certain she viewed the Sirens as a group of addle-headed women. A common misperception, given Linnie's youth.

Most women were blind to their feminine power until they'd overcome great obstacles. The sudden loss of a cherished job, steering children through the treacherous teenage years, divorce or enduring the death of a loved one, which practically amounted to the same thing— any event capable of breaking a woman could break her open instead, to reveal her true beauty and power.

Such a test now confronted Linnie.

"This has not worked out as intended," Frances murmured as the girl stalked away.

Once she'd left the beach with Jada at her side, Frances nodded to her comrades. One by one, the women lowered their rattles. Distress passed from one face to the next like a virus. There wasn't a woman among them who wouldn't meditate for long hours to conjure positive vibes to guard Linnie.

Silvia, clearly in a funk, spun toward the rolling waves of the lake. The surf bubbled around her toes as she brooded in privacy. Behind the beach, the rising sun painted the forest with rosy light.

Penelope Riddle landed her rheumy gaze on Frances. "What should we do now?" She adjusted her eyeglasses on her perspiring nose.

The owlish proprietor of Gift of Garb, the consignment shop in town, looked ready to weep. All of the Sirens were fond of Linnie, but Penelope was an especially sensitive creature.

Needing to comfort her, Frances said, "We'll continue to surround Linnie with positive thoughts."

"Shouldn't we have told her about the letter from her brother?"

"Certainly not. It wouldn't please her to learn we've been checking her mail." The Sirens had taken a vote, with the majority deciding it was best to keep Linnie in the dark. "If she's faced with a crisis, we'll find a way to intervene."

Behind her thick glasses, Penelope's eyes watered. "I wish we knew what the letter contained. I hate the mystery of not knowing." Her son, the mail carrier for the route that included the inn, had called his mother the moment the suspicious missive reached the post office.

"At least your boy alerted us to the letter's arrival. Kind of him to wait until today to make delivery." Frances had requested the delay, allowing the Sirens to gather before the letter reached Linnie's hands.

"What does it matter? Linnie refused our help."

"She may have a change of heart."

"Don't hold your breath. She's awfully mad." Penelope sniffled. "How can we help if she's angry at us?"

"She'll calm down. Then we'll see." The reassurance didn't stop a tear from escaping the corner of Penelope's eye. Her distress brought Frances to a decision, and she quickly added, "Rest assured, she's already receiving help. Silvia and I are seeing to it."

Penelope brushed the tear away. "You are? How?"

Silvia, eavesdropping from the water's edge, sent an impatient look. "Frances, we agreed to keep our plans secret. Why blab to the others?"

"We made no such agreement."

"We did!"

"Be sensible. How does one keep a party under wraps?"

"Stop hedging. I'm referring to the deposit for the party and you know it."

The disclosure sent a rustle of discontent through the group. The women followed their valiant leaders without question, but they didn't like being out of the loop. Silvia was typically spouting off without thought of their feelings.

Determined to smooth their ruffled feathers, Frances motioned the women closer. "We've talked Linnie into opening the ballroom for Silvia and Marco's anniversary party," she explained. "Remember all the lovely events held there years ago?"

Tilda Lyons, a petite woman with cinnamon-colored hair, shimmied her shoulders with glee. "I loved the autumn dance Linnie's parents used to hold. The most romantic affair of the year."

Penelope nodded in agreement. "Me too."

The waltz down memory lane brought a glower from Ruth Kenefsky. Petite like Tilda, the retired police dispatcher wore her stark white hair in braids around her weathered face. "I didn't care for the dance," she remarked in a voice as gravelly as a man's. "Too many drunks wandering the streets afterward and couples carrying on in Sweet Lake Circle. If you're gonna have sex, you ought to do it indoors."

"Useful advice," Frances murmured, needing to steer the conversation back to high ground. "Perhaps we'll see the dance reinstated. After we made a deposit for the anniversary party, Linnie hired a painter. He's already finished in the ballroom. I hear the new paint is quite pretty— an ivory shade with a hint of pink."

Tilda caught the gaffe. "You contributed to the deposit?" The forty-ish realtor had a deplorable habit of ferreting out uncomfortable facts. "Awfully nice of you."

The comment brought Silvia near. "Yes, Tilda. She paid half of the deposit for my party. I didn't want her money."

The allusion to her wealth brought Frances discomfort. She thought of the Sirens as her sisters—or, more precisely, her sister warriors in the defense of goodness and beauty. If the group also secretly dispensed charity and brought lonely hearts together on the sly, all the better. Most of all, she strived to keep the Sirens in harmony. Nothing spawned division more quickly than a conversation about personal wealth.

Smoothing over the impasse, she informed Tilda, "I insisted on pitching in. Silvia and Marco weren't planning a large party—certainly not one large enough to fill the ballroom. They were kind to agree with my plan."

Tilda caught on fast. "You're hoping to encourage Linnie to hold other events?"

"If she does, she'll gain the confidence to restore the Wayfair completely. Sometimes we must take the smallest step before finding the courage to leap."

"Frances, you do more to help Sweet Lake than anyone else. If you get Linnie to fix up the inn, you'll become an absolute miracle worker."

An overstatement, but the remark pleased Frances. She did feel a special responsibility. Aiding the struggling town was the best way to honor her late husband's memory and to show gratitude for all the material blessings she'd received in her long and mostly happy life.

Silvia frowned. "If you want to help Linnie, you should've let me steam open the letter. I'm not saying the party is a bad idea, but the girl has bigger problems."

"Honestly. How would you react if we read *your* mail?"

"If I'd received a missive from a scoundrel, I wouldn't care."

They'd argued the finer points of mail tampering a dozen times. If left to her own devices, Silvia would've strong-armed Penelope's son into letting her slip inside the post office after hours. She would've pried into half the incoming mail before the younger Sirens wrestled her to the ground.

Shuddering at the thought, Frances said, "We're Sirens, not petty criminals. We don't break into buildings, public or private. Or commit mail fraud."

"You and your unbending rules." Silvia stomped her foot. "We had a good reason for sneaking into the post office. We didn't, and now Linnie faces danger without a hint of what she's up against."

"Must you resort to high drama? Even if you had steamed open the letter, then what?"

"We'd know why he's bothering Linnie!"

"We'll know soon enough."

Unfortunately, there was no telling if Freddie intended to disrupt the world Linnie was intent on saving. Success wasn't guaranteed, and she didn't need more upsets.

Masking her concern, Frances slid the feather crown from her head. Wayfair ingenuity had created the town she loved. A Wayfair had opened the first trading post clear back in 1822. The first lumber mill and the streets carved from the dense forest, the first mayor and the mansion that became one of Ohio's most historic inns—the ambition of Linnie's forebears had molded each success. Yet contrary to popular opinion, Frances believed the family had experienced more bitterness than sweet.

If more bitterness lay on the horizon, Linnie deserved better. The only Wayfair left in town, she wore her family's tattered fame with grace.

On the hill above the lake, her tawny hair swirled in the breeze. Reaching the inn, she ascended the steps of the veranda. Soon the mail would arrive on her doorstep. Would she read the letter with rage or calm?

Frances prayed for the latter.

Chapter 2

Cat stormed into the ballroom with hell's fury in her eyes.

On a ladder beneath the chandelier, Linnie fought for balance. The mail had arrived at the front desk, allowing her high-strung friend to pluck out the most unsavory letter. Another bill from the plumber? A shockingly high estimate to sand and varnish the neglected flooring in the Sunshine Room?

Why even *think* about reopening more guest rooms or the moth-balled south wing? Dreams were for suckers. It would serve her right if the Wayfair's hospitality manager held something awful in her fist.

Perspiration beaded on Linnie's cheeks. More love letters from the IRS she didn't need.

The ladder joggled, and she let out a shriek. Down below, Jada let go of the rails.

She planted her hands over her eyes. "Girl, I'm asking you nicely to go away." She peered at Cat between two fingers. "I'm in no mood for Greek tragedy."

"This can't wait." Cat's wavy brown hair swished across her back as she waved the letter madly. "Of all the despicable, detestable . . . I'm so angry I could scream."

"Keep your anger to yourself. Upset Linnie and she'll crawl back into her hole. Let's wait until lunchtime to read the mail. I have marble-toffee cheesecake chilling in the fridge."

"I'm all for self-medicating with sugar during a normal tragedy. Won't work. This is *bad*."

Feigning calm, Linnie climbed down the ladder. "Cat, take a chill pill." Then she regarded Jada, nervously plucking at the tight curls crowning her head. Cat's suggestion of doom was getting to her. "What do you mean, I'll crawl back into my hole?"

"She means you're gutless," Cat offered. "Nothing like your distinguished ancestors. They carved this town right out of the Ohio wilderness."

"They were fortified by whiskey. Not really a fair comparison." Her treacherous friends exchanged an amused glance, and Linnie thrust her palm out. "Give me the letter. Whatever the problem, I'll deal with it."

Jada was faster. Air *whooshed* from her lips as she snatched the envelope. "No wonder the Sirens wanted to protect you. It's from your brother," she growled. "How dare he!"

"Freddie sent the letter?" A nasty bucket of fear poured into Linnie's belly. "How did Frances and the others . . ."

She stopped in midsentence. *Ozzie Riddle.* Penelope's son worked the mail route that included the Wayfair. Did the dutiful son clue his mother in?

She was trying to work it out as Cat said, "I knew we were in for bad luck. Last week I dreamt Sweet Lake was built on quicksand and sinking fast. Then last night I dreamt the town had sunk clear down. Nothing was left, not even a rooftop sticking out of the mud. There was a pig standing in Sweet Lake Circle and it looked mean. I woke up screaming."

For precisely four seconds, Jada stared at her. She asked, "Have you been eating barbecue?"

"No, I haven't been eating barbecue!"

"Tamales at bedtime, anything like that?"

Cat threw her arms in the air. "A devilish pig has nothing to do with food. Can't you see a premonition staring you in the face? I dreamt about the pig, and now look what's in the mail. We're staring at doom."

"An evil pig represents doom? You're a fruitcake."

A squabble about the evil pig ensued. Linnie pulled a rag from the pocket of her coveralls to swab her perspiring cheeks. Several deep breaths didn't manage to slow her pulse.

Noting her distress, Jada stopped arguing with Cat. "Take a few more breaths." She understood how much Linnie hated surprises.

"Make her sit down," Cat suggested.

"I don't want to sit down. Give me some space, both of you."

Ignoring the command, Jada slung an arm across Linnie's shoulder. Cat also moved in. Together they held the letter at arm's length.

Linnie's attention landed on the return address. *San Fernando, California.* The gravity beneath her feet loosened.

Jada tightened her hold. "Should we call your parents?"

Shrugging free, Linnie slumped to the floor. "Absolutely not." Conversations with her parents were stilted at best. More importantly, she hated to upset them. "Look what Freddie's last caper did to my father. He's never fully recovered from the stroke. I'm not putting his health at risk."

"We leave them in the dark? Sure that's a good idea?"

"Until we know what this is about."

"Open the letter and we'll know."

"Give me a sec, okay?"

"Do the yogic breathing." Jada demonstrated, her lips pursing. *"Hmmm."*

A wheezing gasp popped from Linnie's throat. "Nope. Not working." What if Freddie showed up in Sweet Lake? She'd removed his name from the bank accounts, but he *did* have rights. "How 'bout this? Later I'll see what my brother wants." Like in the next century.

Cat muttered, "Gutless."

Elbowing her in the ribs, Jada said, "I hate how badly your family was hurt. Why is Freddie bothering you after all this time? You've been through enough."

"Not just me—the whole town."

They'd all paid dearly. Sweet Lake was a mere shadow of the vibrant tourist center that once drew visitors from throughout the Midwest to enjoy the mineral-fed lake and lush forests. Once the Wayfair shuttered half of the rooms and tourism dwindled, local business closures followed—including the bakery Jada had built singlehandedly and the special events company Cat had opened with a small inheritance from her grandparents. Next? The gift shop closed. Then the Eggs Up diner and the sports equipment store turned out the lights. Half of Sweet Lake Circle now stood empty, the buildings growing moss and the windows streaked with grime. If not for the few remaining establishments, like the law office and the landscape firm owned by the determined Kettering brothers, the circle would resemble a ghost town.

The tragedy in Linnie's family had led directly to all the suffering. Although she battled overwhelming guilt, she refused to give up. She didn't possess her father's bold personality or her grandfather's insatiable drive, but she was a Wayfair. Even if she never healed from the betrayal, she'd keep moving forward—for her own good and the town's. If it took a lifetime, she'd return Sweet Lake to prosperity.

Breaking the gloomy silence, Jada said, "Maybe we're overreacting. What if you're holding an apology note? Seven years too late, but maybe Freddie sent one. You don't have to reply."

"I don't intend to." Pinpricks of pain scattered across her heart. Fighting off the depressing emotion, she added, "He's dead to me. There's nothing he can say to mend our relationship."

Cat shifted from foot to foot. "Jada, you don't think he's coming here, do you?"

"To risk a public flogging? He wouldn't dare."

Linnie looked up sharply. "Most of the town has forgotten my brother exists. They don't have the facts on why the inn lost business. My father kept a lid on the specifics." He'd especially worried about the inn's staff learning the truth and a blow to morale worsening the situation.

"Your closest friends have all the details," Jada pointed out. "Don't forget, taking the money wasn't his only bad move."

"She's right," Cat agreed. "Freddie never had any sense. If he shows up now, we're the least of his worries. Unlikely he'll figure it out. Does whatever he wants without thought of the consequences."

Jada grunted. "That's putting it mildly."

Rising, Linnie stuffed the letter in her pocket. With pride she regarded the ballroom. If Freddie's note contained nothing but bad news, she'd survive.

Sure, her friends regarded her with worry, but she wasn't as faint-hearted as they imagined. Hadn't she found the courage to begin refurbishing the ballroom? Silvia wanted to host her anniversary party here, and the deposit she'd made was incentive enough to proceed. Still, the gamble took every shred of Linnie's thin optimism.

She'd checked and rechecked the P&L statements, taking care not to make a rash decision. The Wayfair didn't merely support her and a scaled-down staff. Thanks to the stream of checks mailed to Florida every month, her parents were also doing fine in Tampa. Although her relationship with them was strained, there wasn't a decision she made without taking their welfare into consideration.

The sharp scent of paint spiked the air. Next week the parquet flooring would receive a thorough cleaning. Despite her naturally reticent nature, Linnie had managed to ruthlessly negotiate an affordable price from a floor cleaning service in Columbus.

Well, she'd signed the contract. Jada had negotiated the price.

Pulling herself together, she reached for the bucket of sudsy water. She went back up the ladder trailing bubbles from the rag she'd neglected to squeeze out.

Jada's brows hit her hairline. "You're back on the cleaning spree? Aren't you curious what Freddie has to say?"

"At the moment, no. We have work to do." Reaching for a crystal teardrop dangling from the chandelier, Linnie expelled an impatient sigh. "Are you helping or not?"

❧

Nodding to his secretary, Daniel Kettering strode out of his law office swinging his brown-bag lunch.

The balmy June temperatures were too much of a lure to consider dining indoors. The maple trees dotting Sweet Lake Circle rustled pleasantly in the breeze, and the traffic around the circle was light. Dashing across to one of the many picnic tables, he did a second take.

His younger brother and niece occupied a table. Crumbs framed their mouths. PB&Js, Daniel surmised, noticing the dab of peanut butter on the frothy tutu that was part of Fancy's summer garb. The five-year-old was frilly in the extreme, with a bedroom chock-full of baby dolls and a closet crammed full with dress-up clothes. Princess outfits were a favorite.

Beyond the pair, his dog raced across the grass. Puddles leapt skyward to make a perfect catch. Trotting back, the mutt dropped the Frisbee in Philip's lap.

Tossing the toy aside, Philip said, "Don't blame me. Fancy insisted on bringing your mongrel with us. We'll take him back to your house in a while."

"Good. I have back-to-back meetings until six." As the only legal counsel in a thirty-mile radius, Daniel handled everything from estate planning to divorce proceedings.

Fancy hopped up and threw herself into his arms. "We had to save Puddles," she informed him in her faint, singsong voice. "He gets lonely when you go to the low office."

"Law office, buttercup."

"Okay." Her cornflower-blue eyes grew serious. "Do you have brownies? Daddy promised to bring some of Jada's. He doesn't have any."

The comment put Daniel on alert. It wasn't like Jada to send his brother from the inn without a box of her delectable baked goods. Which meant Philip hadn't gone to the inn as planned.

Masking his unease, he held up his sack lunch for Fancy's inspection. "I have a ham-and-swiss and an apple. Want some?"

"What else do you have?"

"That's it."

She wrinkled her nose, and her father said, "Honey, why don't you play with Puddles? I need to talk to Uncle Daniel."

"Me first." She pulled on Daniel's pant leg, urging him to bend down. When they were eye to eye, she whispered, "Can I look to be sure?"

He opened the bag. "Where's the trust? Honest, no brownies." At her disappointment, he added, "If I had one, I wouldn't even ask you to split it with me."

"Okay."

She ran off with her lemon-colored hair snapping in the breeze. Puddles, which Daniel suspected was the curious offspring of a standard poodle and Chewbacca from *Star Wars*, sprinted to meet her in the center of the grass.

He slid onto the picnic bench. "You didn't go?" Unwrapping the sandwich, he bit with relish.

Philip grimaced. "She canceled."

"Linnie canceled the meeting about the new landscape?"

"Got a call from Cat telling me not to come."

"That's unusual. Why didn't you hear directly from Linnie?"

"Cat didn't explain. Just delivered the news, then hung up." Philip raked his hand through his hair. "Talk about a disappointment. I'm counting on the work. The rhododendrons are set for delivery, and I thought Linnie would spring for the azaleas too."

"The inn does need to improve curb appeal." Like everything else at the Wayfair, general maintenance took a hit seven years ago. "Odd for Linnie to put you off when you've been mapping out the improvements for weeks."

Nor did cancelling at the last minute make sense. Linnie was conscientious to a fault. She delighted returning visitors with questions about their families or favorite hobbies. She never forgot an employee's birthday, and she sent holiday cards to nearly everyone in town. She wouldn't put Philip off without a good reason.

His brother continued. "There's something wrong at the inn. Daisy from housekeeping was at the drugstore. She said Jada looks like she could spit fire. Cat was crying."

"That's not good."

"Think the landscaping job's canceled?"

Daniel tossed down the sandwich. "Don't jump to conclusions. Linnie has been thinking about upgrading the grounds for years." The boxwood lining the inn's golden sandstone exterior was overgrown, a real eyesore.

The reassurance didn't assuage his brother's doubt. "I wouldn't be so sure. The way Daisy was talking, they're dealing with a crisis up there."

"What sort of crisis?"

Not financial—Linnie's careful management was working its magic. If she harbored a fault, it was a fear of moving too quickly. Any number of banks would grant the Wayfair a line of credit. Bank loans too. The inn's cautious manager couldn't stomach risk.

"Something about a letter," Philip said. "Came in today's mail."

What sort of correspondence would make coolheaded Jada furious and urge Cat to bring on the waterworks? Worried now, Daniel absently watched Fancy racing between picnic tables with Puddles on her heels.

He asked, "What about Linnie? She's also upset?"

"No idea." Philip drummed his thumbs on the table. "I asked Daisy if she knew the contents of the letter. She didn't." He stopped drumming, looked up. "Think I should call? Try to reschedule?"

"In a day or two. If there's a problem, give Linnie time to sort it out. She loves the designs. You've spent weeks revising sketches, coming up with the perfect combination of plant stock."

Philip gestured at the empty buildings on the other side of the circle. "Bro, you're confident I won't join their ranks?"

From behind, an elegant voice said, "Personally I'm *not* confident any business in town is safe."

Together, they turned to their unexpected visitor. Shutting her sun parasol, Frances ducked into the shade. She didn't usually barge into conversations, and Daniel suspected there was a good reason for the intrusion.

"I'm sorry, Philip." She perched beside his brother on the bench. "The letter isn't good news." Daniel caught the distress in her eyes as she regarded him. "Freddie wrote to his sister."

The news took him aback. "He has the gall to bother her, after the mess he caused?"

"I suspect he views the past differently than the rest of us."

"Doubtful he thinks about the pain he caused." Frowning, Daniel stared through the dappled shade at a point that didn't exist. Irritation followed as he considered the cautious attempts Linnie was making to put her world back together. "She's been through enough. Her father's stroke could've killed him, and Treat sure wasn't happy about retirement. Linnie wasn't happy about taking over either."

"Treat and Sarah never prepared her for the responsibilities of running the Wayfair," Frances agreed. "Their greatest ambition was for their daughter to marry and give them grandchildren. The fools. She's smarter than they guessed. All the attention they showered on Freddie, as if she wasn't half as talented."

"She's damn talented," Daniel shot back, a defensive tone coloring his words. It bothered him how fully Linnie's parents underestimated her. "She's done a good job breathing life back into the place. An impossible feat for most people, yet she's making headway. Look at the mess she had with the IRS. All taken care of."

"If Freddie doesn't tamper in her affairs, she'll experience true success. Not overnight. But with enough hard work, she'll have the inn back to capacity bookings."

"If she succeeds, those tourism dollars will rebuild the town." He glanced at Frances swiftly. "You believe Freddie's on his way back?"

"I do. And if he causes more trouble, the Wayfair may not survive."

The pronouncement sent worry across his brother's face. Daniel, a more stubborn adversary, refused to buy into the gloomy statement.

"You're speculating," he told Frances. "I'll wager Freddie's happy in California. No reason for him to set foot in Ohio. You're guessing at his intentions."

"Hardly."

She seemed about to add something else. Her hesitation, more than her dire predictions, sent unease through Daniel.

"How can you guess at Freddie's plans?" he demanded. "Are you getting this from a crystal ball?"

"I don't have a crystal ball, nor do I need one. Isn't it obvious? The letter is his calling card."

Daniel chewed this over. "Even if you're correct, Linnie's older now," he finally said. "Mature. He won't walk over her a second time."

"I agree she's proven herself an accomplished businesswoman, but she's still fragile. All the shops that closed . . . She isn't responsible, but she does carry tremendous guilt. Look at how she's cared for Jada since the bakery closed, and Cat since her event planning business went under. She's given them new jobs at the inn and free lodgings in the south wing." In quiet reflection Frances ran her fingers down her sun parasol before adding, "If Freddie throws the Wayfair back in peril, what then? Or do you believe she'll win singlehandedly once again?"

A challenge, and Daniel's emotions tumbled before it. "She's better prepared now precisely because she's older. She won't let him undo all her hard work."

He said the last of it with thin conviction. When Linnie's world broke apart, his respect for her ability to navigate her own path had encouraged him to stand by. Blunting his better instincts, he'd let her fight alone.

It was an error he sorely regretted.

Unease shifted through Daniel. If Frances was correct, would he make the same mistake again?

Chapter 3

With a grunt, Linnie hauled herself from the tranquility of sleep. An uncomfortable weight pressed down on her thighs.

Bleary-eyed, she regarded the woman roosting on her like a vulture. Tall, slender, Jada was a good four inches taller and quite a bit stronger. She also possessed a stubborn streak that beat Linnie's handily.

"Jada, we're too old for slumber parties. What are you doing in my room?"

"Little Miss Faint Heart, you are not going back to sleep." Jada dropped the full weight of her athletic body on her prisoner. "You've worn through the last thread of my patience."

"Get off!"

"Only if you promise."

The inference was as subtle as a two-by-four. "That's blackmail," Linnie growled. "Totally unlike you."

"As if I care. It's been twenty-four hours. Open the letter."

"No." Pushing free, Linnie got out of bed.

"You act like you've been sitting shiva for years, which I'd forgive if you were Jewish. You can deal with whatever Freddie has to say."

Although it was early summer, the air held a chill. A typical occurrence, since the heating and cooling units in the south wing were shot. Even so, the three-story wing boasted some of the prettiest views of the lake and the sweep of pine, maple, and oak trees in the forest beyond.

The guest rooms were among the largest at the inn, with individual sitting rooms, where business tycoons in ages past had enjoyed a late-night brandy in front of the licking flames of the fireplace.

Shrugging into her robe, Linnie stalked to the dresser. Last night she'd tossed down the letter with the unrealistic hope that gnomes would run off with it while she slept. Or she'd awaken to discover the correspondence had never existed in the first place. Either solution would've met with her approval since she didn't have the strength to deal with Freddie. Their relationship had gone south clear back in childhood.

Certain there was no way to fix it now, she stuffed the letter into her pocket.

Jada tracked her movements with ill-concealed frustration. "Girl, you've got to screw your head on straight. Pretending he isn't reaching out won't make the letter go away. What if he's writing about something important, like he needs a kidney transplant?"

"Stop exaggerating. Freddie's never been sick a day in his life."

"Not true. Remember when we were in eighth grade? Your brother almost missed his high school graduation. Running a fever, bedridden for days—your Mom was frantic."

"Jada, you're a ninny. Freddie wasn't sick. Just another one of his great performances. You *know* why he was skipping school."

At last Jada's neurons fired. "Oh. Right. That was the spring your parents hired the young tart from Tennessee."

"Are you kidding? She was forty years old if she was a day." The woman had arrived with an impressive résumé in hotel management. Other more enviable resources trumped her human resource skills, including an hourglass shape and a Southern drawl capable of ensnaring willing suitors. Considering, Linnie added, "I never blamed her. Freddie didn't require much encouragement in the sexual arena. My parents were furious when they found Mr. On-Death's-Door camped out in her bed."

"He's probably still Playmate of the Year." Jada paused in dreamy reflection. "We all had a crush on him. Our mothers did too."

"None of you had an ounce of sense." *Coffee.* There was a chance of surviving the conversation with a heart-thumping jolt of caffeine. She risked a glance at her friend, lounging on the bed in thermal long johns and the silly zebra slippers Linnie had bought her as a joke gift last Christmas. "Fix your hair, will you? You look like Jimi Hendrix."

Rolling her eyes, Jada flopped down on the pillow.

"If you insist on rousting me at dawn's first light, we might as well eat," Linnie remarked in a more agreeable tone. Her stomach rumbled. "Will you make apple pancakes? I'll chop up the walnuts." Excessive calories were the perfect complement to caffeine overload.

"You want a batch of my special pancakes? Here's the deal. I'm never making them again if you keep acting like a pigheaded fool."

"Keep pigs out of this. Cat's dream is still giving me the willies."

"Speaking of Cat, she talked to her mother last night. The Sirens have another meeting scheduled."

"Don't tell me they're back at the lake."

"They went to Sweet Lake Circle. They're showering you and the town with protective vibes."

"They're blowing this out of proportion."

"Cat believes they'll protect us, burn incense around town, or make charms to hang around the Wayfair. I'd hold out for divine intervention, but it might take too long. Trouble this bad, the Sirens are the only solution."

Linnie ditched the irritation and located her common sense. "Enough with the old woman voodoo. Is there someone I can bribe to get them to stop? At the very least this will disrupt the planning for the anniversary party."

"Don't underestimate the Sirens. They're not as silly as you think."

Right. "If you won't make breakfast, then I'm getting dressed. I should go over the numbers before Philip arrives. I'd like him to start on the new plantings ASAP. I hope he doesn't need a bulldozer to remove the boxwood." The racket would irritate guests, but the spindly old shrubs were seven feet tall.

"Relax. We canceled for you. Cat made the call."

She halted in the center of the suite. "Why cancel my appointment with our favorite landscape architect? We took a vote at the last employee meeting. Everyone agreed to a hold on wage increases so we can start sprucing up the place." The nearly unanimous vote had been heartwarming. Sure, a few of the women in housekeeping were fuming—if Linnie was moving forward, they preferred to send the ancient washers and dryers to meet their maker.

"Linnie, the meeting was yesterday."

"Why didn't you remind me?"

Jada gave a look implying she was dealing with a dunce. "Gosh, let's see. You climbed the ladder, cleaned the chandelier for ten seconds, and came back down. You flew out of the ballroom so quickly I couldn't find you for hours. I would've sent out hound dogs, but we don't have any."

Fair enough. Her brother's attempt to make contact was a more difficult blow than anticipated. A long walk in the forest had provided the best remedy.

"I'm sorry I took off." The disappearing act had clearly rattled Jada. When she smiled, Linnie added, "I hope Philip isn't upset. All those weeks coming up with designs free of charge. The work means a lot to him."

"He'll forgive you."

She stepped toward the bathroom, hesitated. "I don't have anything on my calendar this morning. I'll run down to Sweet Lake Circle, see if Philip has time to chat. Have any fresh brownies in the kitchen?"

Jada laughed. "Fancy will be delighted. I'll pack a box."

∼๑

At the bickering outside, Daniel stopped pouring kibble into the dog bowl.

Puddles bounded into the living room behind him. Together, man and beast watched the gaggle of Sirens marching down Orchard Lane. In the lead Frances and Silvia batted each other with dried gourds on sticks. The weapons appeared less life threatening than the insults they lobbed.

Amused, he returned to the kitchen to feed Puddles and finish breakfast. Since time immemorial, women had met up at the lake or in the circle during odd hours. None of the men in town understood why grown women chose to stick feathers in their hair or cavort in chilly waters beneath the moon. Before the town's decline, several of the Sirens had sold handmade jewelry at the now-defunct gift shop. The earrings and necklaces were fashioned with the shells of freshwater mollusks washed up on Sweet Lake's beach and pretty rocks scavenged in the forest.

In Daniel's estimation, the group was harmless. The primary, if unspoken, reason to join the Sweet Lake Sirens seemed obvious. Entry gave a woman the perfect excuse to drink too many of Silvia's delicious mojitos and complain about a husband, living or dead.

He nursed his coffee as his dog made short work of the kibble. Why were the Sirens meeting this morning? Hopefully Frances's prediction about Freddie returning was off base. Linnie had enough responsibilities without dealing with her brother.

His phone buzzed.

Philip skipped the pleasantries. "I can't tell if Fancy's getting sick."

"Temp?" Daniel eyed Puddles. The beast rooted for crumbs by the fridge and eyed him back.

"Cool as a cucumber. Says her tummy hurts, though."

"What about her ears?" Fancy had a history of earaches.

A pause, then, "Says her ears don't hurt."

Puddles butted him in the thigh, prodding Daniel to grab the croissant still warm from the microwave. "Does she want to spend the day at summer camp?" he asked, flinging the croissant into the air.

Muffled conversation, then, "She'd like your esteemed opinion, Counselor."

Daniel took a last swig from his cup. "I don't think she wants to go. You're up at the Dufour place this morning?" Frances owned a beaut of a colonial on Highland. His brother was planting a new rose bed in back, complete with an arbor.

"Supposed to be there in fifteen minutes. I have a meeting out of town afterward. Bidding on a landscape job for a new office park near the highway." Philip hesitated before adding, "Scaring up a babysitter will take half an hour."

"Call me when you have someone lined up, and tell Fancy I'll pick her up by three o'clock." He was in court later this morning, then drawing up a will for a family in town. A light day.

"Thanks, bro. Expect me no later than dinnertime."

His brother was about to hang up when Daniel heard himself say, "Any word from Linnie?"

A mistake. Puddles, his matted snout hunting the linoleum for a second croissant, abandoned the search and dropped onto his haunches. He gave out a moan so intense, his master got a visual of Fancy having a rare tantrum in public.

Philip whistled, impressed. "Man, what's with the dog?"

"Forgot to feed him," he lied. Mortified, he wafted the box of croissants beneath the traitor's snout. Puddles continued moaning. Daniel spilled the entire box onto the floor.

"Sounds bad. Do mutts get cavities?"

"They have teeth just like us. So, yeah. I guess they do."

"Should you take him to the vet?"

"No." *Maybe.* In between moans, Puddles made short work of a dozen croissants. Was it okay to give antacids to a dog?

Philip chuckled. "If you decide to take him in, Fancy won't mind tagging along. Just don't let her see anything small and furry. I don't have your dedication to animal welfare. She's been jonesing for a bunny rabbit."

"All right."

He let Puddles out one last time before fetching his briefcase. From the picture window, the goofy beast, tongue lolling and floppy ears twitching, watched him stride down Orchard for the short walk to Sweet Lake Circle. Some people were cut out for the frenetic energy of the city, the miles of concrete, and the relationships that bubbled up like champagne but dissipated just as quickly. Daniel wasn't one of them. After law school, he'd tried a short stint at a firm in New York City. He'd missed the crickets bringing in the night.

Upon his return to open the town's only law office, Frances had brought him bouquets of honeysuckle for a week straight. She understood how much he longed to inhale the cloying sweetness.

On the circle, his brother's landscaping company stood directly next to the law office. He discovered Linnie jiggling the doorknob of Unity Design.

"Good morning." Daniel offered a cordial smile.

Beaming, she regarded him. "Hey, pal."

Inwardly he cringed at the sobriquet. "My brother's not in." *Pal*, a depressing indication of his buddy status.

"He needs a receptionist." She held out a carton tied with pink ribbons. "Brownies, for Fancy. There's enough for you and Philip, too."

"Great." He took the box. "Should I tell him you stopped by?"

Linnie rubbed her lips together. She looked tired, her hazel eyes puffy. She had on one of her quirky getups, exercise pants and a top big enough to cover Daniel's frame. Presumably the top was meant to hide the attractive curves she possessed in abundance. Luckily it didn't quite do the trick.

He tried again. "Want some java? Kay isn't in yet, but I can scare up a pot." Among the many things he had in common with Linnie was an inability to get the pistons firing without a morning fix. They were both addicted to coffee in its various guises—hot, iced, flavoring ice cream—no doubt they'd both purchase coffee-flavored cereal if such a thing existed.

Relief warmed her face. "You don't mind? Actually, I could use some advice."

"Always happy to help," he said, leading her through the lobby and into a ballet they'd long mastered: Linnie storming into his office after the Wayfair's bank accounts were cleaned out, seeking advice on pressing charges; Linnie dissolving in his arms at the hospital, needing reassurance her father would live. The daunting task of assuming control of the inn at the tender age of twenty-five—how he'd find her past midnight in the circle, flung out across the top of a picnic table like a kid making snow angels, her tawny hair tumbling around her shoulders.

The idea of carrying on the family legacy terrified her, a legacy carried only by Wayfair men—until her sudden promotion.

Back then, she'd yelled at the heavens for hours or until exhaustion took hold. When her eyes grew sleepy, Daniel walked her back to her car, her fingers held in his like a gift he yearned to keep.

Dismissing the memory, he waited as she studied the walls in his office, inspecting photos she knew by heart. She was wound up, rolling forward on the toes of her tennis shoes. The effort failed to make her a scant inch taller.

Locating a neutral starter, he said, "Rumor has it you and Jada are fixing up the ballroom."

She fell back on her heels, her attention stubbornly trained on the photos. "Not just us. I hired a painter. Finished early this week. You'll have to stop by—the walls used to be that dull grey, remember? I chose an off-white hue with a touch of pink at the base." Pausing at a photo of Fancy on her first day of kindergarten, she added, "We're having an event in the ballroom."

"That's news." Like everyone else, Daniel held out hope she'd reopen the shuttered portions of the Wayfair.

"The Mendozas are celebrating their fortieth," she said. "We have less than three weeks to get our acts together. You'll get an invitation. Silvia's inviting most of the town."

"Looking forward to it." He let the silence wind out. Finally he plunged in, asking, "Is this a new start? The inn used to do a healthy trade in weddings. Services by the lake, receptions in the ballroom— Linnie, the economy is improving. You can take out ads in bridal mags, drop off flyers at the local churches and the temple."

"Maybe."

"Destination weddings are a profitable sideline. Worth looking into." The comment pressed lines into her forehead, and he held up his hand in apology. "Just an idea."

"Right." She puffed out her cheeks. The endearing tic made her look like a blowfish. "Cat and Jada think I'm gutless. Do you agree?"

"I think you've been through a lot."

"There's nothing wrong with slow and steady. Rome wasn't built in a day."

"Sure."

At last she settled on the leather couch.

Taking his time, he went out to grab the coffee. There was no point in pushing Linnie. She'd take the next step, or she'd pull back and let the ballroom grow a new layer of dust. Daniel prayed for the former. The grand functions her parents had overseen were a cherished part of Sweet Lake's history. Linnie had shone at the countless events, her glossy hair drawn up on her head, the low-cut gowns she'd worn, even as a teenager, showing off too much bosom. She'd never been the prettiest girl in town, but she'd been the most vibrant.

Returning, he was relieved to find the delicate lines smoothed from her brow. "Sugar, extra cream." Seating himself, he handed over the cup.

A polite sip, and then she resolutely set the cup down. She pulled out the letter he knew was the source of her anxiety.

With a smack, it dropped to the coffee table. A familiar, scratchy cursive ran across the cover. Daniel placed his untouched cup aside.

"So it's true. Your crazy brother wrote to you."

"You aren't surprised." A statement, not a question.

Immediately he cleared up the mystery. "I ran into Frances on the circle. She told me. I'd hoped she got her facts wrong."

"I'm worse. I'd hoped gnomes would run off with the letter while I slept."

"Not likely." The flap was unbroken. "You don't intend to see what Freddie has to say?"

The query curved her spine. "What if he . . . wants something from me?"

Years of legal work had taught Daniel to recognize the omission of relevant facts. "Simple," he replied, wondering what she was hiding. "If he comes looking for a handout, tell him no."

"What if he's in trouble?"

"Then he's in trouble. Happens all the time."

"I hate him for taking the money, but what if I . . . I don't know, feel compelled to help? Play rescuer because his health's bad, do something stupid?"

The admission lifted his brows. "You care about Freddie? That's a switch. I thought you wanted him flayed and his entrails scattered before wild dogs." Despite the fetching confusion in her eyes, Daniel grinned. "Or was it wolves? I have trouble keeping track of the punishments you devise for your brother."

She lifted her shoulders to her ears, another mannerism he particularly liked. "Daniel, I wish I could switch with you. What did I *do* to deserve this curse? Why didn't I get your brother?"

The soliloquy, uttered repeatedly through the years, was now a longstanding joke between them.

"Philip's also a pain," he shot back, playing along. "Here's a fun fact. He still can't throw anything together except burgers and fries. Okay, he's also figured out how to fling pizza in the oven, but Italian doesn't agree with Fancy. Too much red sauce and she sounds like a pop gun. I should charge for catering."

"Good thing he lives nearby. Makes the catering easier."

"I guess it's all right. I mean, what would I do with the leftovers?" The allusion to his single status was a blunder—no matter how much he wanted Linnie, he didn't want her pity. Deftly, he got back on track. "Bottom line. You can open the letter or throw it away. If Freddie needs help, you're under no obligation to aid and abet his current foolishness, whatever it is."

"I'm off the hook?"

"You were never on the hook in the first place. If his health is bad, he should drink less and cut down on the ladies. Not that he will. Men like Freddie don't change. However, he probably doesn't require financial assistance. I'm not a fan of B movies, at least not those featuring vampires in space, but I have the impression he's doing quite well."

"Bad Seed Productions is earning a profit? No way."

"Guess again—this is the era of YouTube and Netflix. *Film Cut* magazine even did a feature on Freddie. He's doing all right. Better than all right."

She laughed. "Stop Googling him. I gave up the habit for my thirtieth birthday, a big present to myself. Two years now, and I don't have the least curiosity. Why don't you follow suit?"

"Checking Google is the best way to protect you." He let his attention linger for as long as he dared. The familiar hunger drove through his blood. The beauty mark a hair's breadth from her mouth was a particular obsession. Cutting off the appraisal, he reconsidered the admission. "You don't mind, do you?"

"Of course not." Darting past his defenses, she leaned in, landing a smack on his cheek. His thermostat soared. "You're the best, Daniel." She got up to leave.

"Linnie?"

She paused by the door. "Yeah?"

"What's the verdict?"

"About reading the letter? Still undecided."

His throat tightened. "You've got to stop living your life on the fence."

After his last appointment, Daniel picked Fancy up at the babysitter. The impromptu meeting with Linnie had left him blue, and he was glad for the diversion of little-girl laughter. They took Puddles for a walk on the north side of the lake, far from the revelry of the inn's vacationing guests and the possibility of running into the Wayfair's pretty manager. When he returned his niece to Philip at six o'clock, he was sinking beneath exhaustion unrelated to the work left at the office.

The life he imagined held Linnie at its center. He still coveted the dream. Yet he was now aware of the elusive quality of wishing for a relationship that may never grow from friendship to love. Life didn't always work out as planned.

It wasn't yet ten o'clock, but he'd given up watching any of the shows he'd downloaded from Amazon or surfing through sports tweets on Twitter.

Puddles, a more determined optimist, leapt onto the king-size bed. The dog made hairpin turns, knocking pillows to the floor. The ritual never gained the intended result, and Daniel shooed him off. He'd reached to extinguish the light when the doorbell rang.

Pulling on jeans and a T-shirt, he came to a decision. If Linnie was on the front stoop seeking more assurances, he'd handle it. No, he wouldn't land a kiss sure to tattoo her senses. He'd never take the plunge without an invitation.

But he *would* open the damn letter.

Satisfied with the plan, he strode through the living room, smoothing his hair into place. As he swung the door open, the greeting he'd rehearsed melted away. His mind emptied out.

On the doorstep, Freddie Wayfair offered a grin.

Chapter 4

Slack-jawed, Daniel regarded the heir apparent who'd run off with stolen cash and ill-formed dreams seven years ago. Beneath Freddie's chin, a cravat of crimson silk wagged.

He looked like John Waters. If he went much more rakish, people would wonder which side of his bread he buttered.

"Daniel, it's been too long!"

Not long enough, he mused. The last time he'd been foolish enough to hang out with Linnie's brother, they'd been home on break from their respective colleges. The lucky bastard, who'd received a Mustang convertible for his twenty-first birthday, corralled Daniel into a road trip.

On the adventure in Cincinnati, Freddie left the keys inside his new car. The thief who took the Mustang from the parking lot of Cheetah's Strip Joint zoomed away in a haze of burnt rubber. Afterward, Freddie continued to race through his father's money and soon forgot the event at the strip joint.

Unlike the forgiving Wayfairs, Daniel's parents were livid. He was nearing his thirties before his mother's eyes stopped hurling thunderbolts at the mention of Sweet Lake's most disgraced son.

Freddie peeked behind Daniel's bulk. "Planning to ask me in?"

"Wasn't my first impulse." He leaned against the doorjamb. "Why are you here? You're supposed to be in California filming trash. What is it this time, *Werewolves on Mars*? Or have you moved on to slasher flicks?"

Freddie's blue eyes blazed. "My studio doesn't produce gore. Bad Seed has built a strong brand of genre-blended films. We have a substantial following in Asia and South America." With ease, he slipped into patent curiosity. "I'm disappointed with my sister. Didn't she mention my arrival? I assumed you were still close."

"Are you joking? She received your letter yesterday."

"Ah." Freddie nodded, a sage philosopher overdressed for the occasion. "Did I forget to snail mail in a timely manner? I would've preferred to call or send e-mail."

"Why didn't you?"

"Her number's a state secret, and she's reported my e-mail as spam."

"Smart girl." Puddles bounded up, and Daniel grabbed the beast by the collar.

"What's this?" Distaste sprinted through Freddie's eyes. "Does it bite?"

"For you, he'll make an exception."

"Lock up the monster, will you?" The filmmaker breezed past and into the living room. "I wouldn't have come if this weren't important. Can you at least hear me out?"

Indecision caught Daniel by the throat. He should've pressed Linnie to open the letter in his office. If she'd known her brother planned to reappear, she would've left town in a hurry.

How to proceed? There was no telling what trouble Freddie planned to rain down on her life.

A more pragmatic thought intruded. Given Freddie's track record, wasn't it best he'd dropped by here first?

Needing to protect her, Daniel came to an uneasy decision.

Shooing Puddles into the backyard, he returned with his game face on. Cordiality was a nonstarter. He waited for Freddie to explain.

Beneath the smooth John Waters impersonation, Linnie's brother seemed upset. He cut grooves across the carpet, assessing the bookcase of legal tomes, pausing to study the painting of the lake hanging above the couch. At length, he noticed the wet bar at the end of the room. He took down a glass and poured two fingers of Smirnoff.

"I need your help, Counselor." He downed the liquor, then looked to Daniel expectantly.

"For what? A lawsuit against your studio? Get a lawyer based in California."

"Bad Seed isn't under threat. I need legal counsel in Ohio."

"And you have the nerve to ask me for representation?" The brush-fire igniting in Daniel's chest threatened to burn through his composure. "Do you have any idea how much you've hurt Linnie?"

Freddie rolled his eyes. "I suppose you'd like to tell me."

"Yeah, I would. If you're curious, I was disappointed when your parents stopped her from notifying the police. I sure don't understand why they covered up the facts. You shouldn't be filming schlock movies in California—you should be serving time. Why your parents let you get away with cleaning out the Wayfair's accounts is beyond logic."

"Play fair, Daniel. All the family accounts were linked, personal and business. I didn't take every dime. There were extenuating circumstances."

"Circumstances brought on by you. What if your father had died? It wouldn't hold water in court, but those of us aware of what you'd done would've considered you guilty of negligent homicide."

The latter put a gratifying dent in Freddie's bravado. "Taking the money was an impulsive act," he admitted. "I didn't mean to hurt my parents or Linnie. Dad had investments, a dozen places to pull cash. How could I know he'd have a stroke five months after I left and need money for a thousand co-pays?"

"Plus an early retirement, which your sister continues to support. She walks around in old shoes but never forgets to send the monthly stipend."

"She supports our parents? I wasn't aware." Freddie glanced at his empty glass. Licking his lips, he managed to plant his attention on his Italian loafers. "I didn't mean to saddle her with the inn. She was so carefree, and I thought . . ." Frowning, he looked up. "I don't know what I thought."

The stab at an apology sure as hell didn't suffice. Daniel had never shaken the memory of Linnie on the day she'd packed her parents off for Florida. She remained chipper while helping her father into the taxi. She blanketed her hollow-eyed mother with kisses. Friends and neighbors were there to see the elder Wayfairs off—Jada, Cat, and most of the Sirens, with tearstained cheeks.

After the taxi drove off, Linnie gave a rousing speech to the staff about how nothing would change, how the inn would continue to prosper. Her closest friends and Daniel already knew the Wayfair's finances were a house of cards, rendering her speech heartbreaking to behold. Once the staff got back to work, she disappeared.

Linnie had shut herself inside the office that had belonged to her father one short day earlier. The dank scent of tobacco left behind by the former occupant lingered among the stacks of paperwork unattended for too many weeks. On a corner of the desk, a printout of the names of each employee bore Linnie's careful script in the margins. Within days, she would let half of them go.

Daniel had found her behind Treat Wayfair's imposing desk, sobbing into her hands.

Like the letter he should've insisted she open, the day her parents left represented a missed opportunity. During the intervening years, he'd replayed that fateful day with regret. He should've told Linnie she wasn't alone, that she'd never spend another day alone if she'd have him.

Stung by the memory, he told Freddie, "Here's an idea. Want to clean up your mess? Start by paying back every cent, with interest. Linnie has only recently begun taking steps to refurbish the inn. Given all the work she's done to keep the place afloat, she deserves to succeed."

"I will," Freddie quietly replied. "I swear it."

The promise was startling. Tamping down his ire, Daniel floundered. Trusting the man before him was dangerous. Freddie was capable of manipulating them all.

Daniel scrubbed his palms across his cheeks. "Let me get this straight. You've returned to make amends with your sister?"

"In part. And only if you'll help me with another matter." Uncharacteristic remorse flickered through Freddie's expression. Instantly the emotion disappeared. "First, I need an assurance you'll respect the attorney-client privilege. Nothing we discuss gets back to my sister or anyone else in town. Agreed?"

Daniel suffered the uneasy notion he was dancing with the devil. "I help, and you'll make things right?"

"If you don't trust me, I'll put it in writing."

"I'll draft the agreement first thing tomorrow."

Freddie released a short laugh. "Fine, Counselor." The merriment didn't reach his eyes. "Afterward, I'll have you contact the boy's family."

"What boy?"

"A starstruck kid. He wanted to work in the industry."

"Employee of yours?"

"Bryce didn't have the qualifications. Several actors on my last film paid him under the table to run errands. I should've thrown him off the lot, but he did have an eagerness to please. So I let him stay."

"Sounds like you made a mistake."

"The accident didn't happen on the lot. Don't ask me to take responsibility."

An unexpected revelation, and Daniel rocked back on his heels. "He was injured?" Freddie nodded, and despite his reluctance to help,

Daniel found himself sorting through the legal ramifications. "Even if he wasn't an employee, you're not in the clear. He can sue your production company."

"He won't sue."

Now it was Daniel's turn to laugh. "I've always thought of you as a lot of things, but naïve isn't one of them."

"You don't understand."

"Got that right. Care to explain?"

"Bryce thinks of me as . . ." His voice drifting off, Freddie walked to the foyer. Apparently the turn in the conversation bothered him.

Trying to fit the pieces together, Daniel followed. "Thinks of you as what?"

"Never mind. It's not important. What *does* matter is Bryce's reluctance to accept my help. He's too proud."

"What do you expect me to do?"

"Persuade his parents. We can agree you *are* persuasive in all matters—except one." A taunt glittered in Freddie's eyes. "Why is that? You have the finesse of a politician. You can talk anyone into anything. Why is my sister immune to your persuasions?"

A direct assault, and Daniel's heart seized. "We're close friends. Leave it at that."

A cruel sort of amusement played with Freddie's lips. "You've never told her how you feel? Astonishing."

Daniel wiped the emotion from his face. "Here's the thing," he replied with rigid calm. "The carefree Linnie you remember? She died when you dropped your responsibilities on her shoulders. When she wasn't letting members of the staff go—a process that gave her hives for months—she was busy getting your parents settled in Florida. She doesn't date. Doesn't take time off, doesn't laugh much—and Lord knows I miss her laughter. Fixing *your* mess consumes her days." The intensity seeping into his voice brought him to a stop. In a more professional tone, he said, "I need the details of Bryce's accident and an understanding of how you'd like to help him."

"Let's cover the details tomorrow." Wearily, Freddie glanced at his watch. "Long flight. I have to find somewhere to stay. When should I drop by your office?"

Snapping out a time, Daniel brought the meeting to a close. His guest walked out the door, and he shut his eyes tight.

Why promise to keep Linnie in the dark? Attorney-client privilege notwithstanding, it was a decision he was sure to regret.

On the cedar deck outside the Sunshine Room, guests sipped drinks beneath star-studded skies. The kitchen staff was finishing for the night, and Linnie had let all but two of the waitresses leave. Behind the canopied bar, the bartender and his assistant would serve drinks until midnight or the last guests returned to their rooms, whichever came first.

The Wayfair drew families and couples seeking rejuvenation in the rural setting. The days saw many of them out on the lake enjoying water sports or trekking the paths in the woods. By nightfall, most of the guests were spent and rarely stayed up late. As the inn's manager, Linnie usually remained downstairs until the bar staff prepared to leave. Tonight her sedate linen dress seemed more constricting than usual, her black pumps too tight. Ascending the stairwell to the south wing, she decided to change into tights and a lightweight sweater.

Leaving her suite, she caught the murmur of Jada's and Cat's voices. She stuck her head into Cat's room. On the bed, a variety of trinkets surrounded them.

The crisp scent of lavender tickled Linnie's nose. There were other more subtle scents—marjoram, rosemary, and a hint of pungent clove. She picked up a small bundle of herbs tied with simple twine. Pink feathers stuck out from beneath.

"The answer is no." She cast a look of disapproval on her pajama-clad friends. "Jada, if I'd known you were up here celebrating craft day, I would've asked you to help the staff close up the kitchen. Cat, you could've stuck around to help the waitresses. We still have guests outside looking for refills."

Cat flicked a curtain of glossy hair over her shoulder. "What choice do we have?" she retorted. "Mami has the Sirens making amulets for us to wear, but we can't wait for them to finish. I'm not going to sleep until I'm sure we've protected the grounds. I'm tired of having nightmares."

"And your mother wants you to hang this stuff around the Wayfair?" Silvia was a crack accountant, but her superstitions made no sense.

"She says it'll help."

"Well, she's nuts." Unfortunately, Frances also believed herbs were useful for the most unlikely problems, like keeping Freddie from stepping inside town. No doubt they'd scared Silvia's husband out of the Mendoza kitchen while they devised silly remedies.

"Linnie, there's nothing wrong with insurance."

"Spiritual insurance? Cat—no. If you and Jada are determined to hang this stuff around your necks, that's as far as it goes. I'm not having my guests find herbs dangling from doorknobs or sprinkled underfoot."

"You're gutless *and* shortsighted."

"Because I don't want charms littering the inn? Freddie isn't coming back!"

Jada, whose nervous gestures were fast returning her curls to the Jimi Hendrix style, leapt off the bed. "Have it your way," she said, coming nose to nose. "Want us to stop with the superstition? Then read the letter. If Freddie's merely trying to open the lines of communication, I'm going to bed. The herbs are bothering my sinuses."

"I meant to open it at Daniel's office," Linnie revealed. "Honest, I did."

"You were at his office?"

"This morning."

"Did he know you were coming?"

"I ran into him when I tried to look in on Philip at Unity Design." Several hours later, she'd reached Philip by phone. He was thrilled she'd accepted the job quote, promising to begin work on the new landscaping in the morning. "I caught Daniel on the way to his office. He offered coffee, so I went inside."

"But still you chickened out." Her voice softening, Jada added, "Honestly, girl. Why drag our favorite attorney into this, especially if you have no intention of reading the letter? Now Daniel will worry. Isn't it enough having your closest friends and the Sirens at wit's end?"

"As if Daniel needs incentive to worry about Linnie," Cat added. "His favorite pastime."

Jada shook her head. "Nope. Not even close. Daniel's favorite pastime? Pining away for her. A weaker man would admit defeat and find someone else. Of course, I can't imagine Daniel looking at anyone else."

The turn of the conversation filled Linnie with discomfort. She sank onto the side of the bed.

Cat said, "He's only had eyes for Linnie since she was a teenager. Not that she would've noticed him back then. Too tame. Interesting how the good boys turn into the great men."

"Stop it, both of you." Linnie flopped onto her back. "I didn't ask Daniel for advice to lead him on. He's an attorney, remember? I wanted his feedback in case Freddie had written about . . . forget it."

Cat thumped her on the thigh. "Gutless, shortsighted, *and* stupid. We're not concerned about you leading Daniel on. We're concerned you'll never lead that big, beautiful man to your bed. What are you waiting for? Get your groove on, babe. Jada and I will happily clear out of the south wing. Take as long as you need to have your way with him."

The risqué suggestion stirred the yearning Linnie was adept at suppressing. Warmth pooled in her belly alongside the uncomfortable reservations so familiar she could recite them in her sleep. Managing the inn demanded every waking hour. They'd only recently erased the red from the books. It was a long way from breakeven to profitability. As for relationships, they took time to nurture and grow.

For the foreseeable future, time was in short supply.

A bigger concern? Her long-buried guilt. Cat's assessment was accurate—she hadn't taken notice of Daniel's attentions until her irresponsible brother opened a trapdoor beneath her world. The easygoing life she'd led disappeared overnight, and Daniel became her rock. Taking their relationship to its logical conclusion wasn't smart until time became available for a real commitment. He deserved nothing less.

And if he didn't wait around? She despised the risk. If he found someone else, she'd do her best to feel happy for him.

Approaching, Jada smiled. "We're not coming down on you."

"Speak for yourself. Cat is coming down on me. Little Miss Sassy."

Cat thumped her again. "Got that right. You and Daniel should be married by now, with a bunch of kids racing around the Wayfair. Ditch all the reasons why you don't have time for romance, and remember your eggs. Want them to shrivel like raisins? Wait much longer to let him know you're interested and they will."

"Hey! I've only got two years on you. Worry about your own eggs."

"You think I don't?"

"I think you spend too much time worrying about my reproductive chances when you ought to find a man for yourself."

"As if I'm not looking." Cat yanked up her pajama top. "Stay frisky, girls," she said, addressing her navel. "When the right man comes along, I promise to grab on and not let go."

Jada sent a warning look. To Linnie, she said, "You'll never muster up the courage to open Freddie's letter alone. Read it now. If you faint, I'll catch you."

"You'd better."

Resigned to the decision, Linnie fetched the letter. Her pulse bounced like a rubber ball as she tore open the envelope.

Hello Sugarpop,

In June I'm in Ohio on business. Short stay. Shall we meet for lunch? I promise not to order dessert if you'll spare me the complaints about the latest diet failure. I'm mystified as to why you bother. Would baby seals appeal without the extra padding?

I hope this letter finds you less hostile toward your legendary brother.

Freddie

She grimaced at the opener—*Sugarpop.* To this day, her mother continued to use the humiliating nickname. Freddie knew how much she despised it.

Business. So he wasn't in town for a social visit. A no-brainer, since he didn't have a friend east of the Mississippi.

Everyone who'd suffered the misfortune of knowing him well wanted him jailed or strung up. The Sweet Lake Sirens wanted him dead. Thanks to record-breaking YouTube views, Freddie had launched Bad Seed Productions after stealthily filming the Sirens during a midnight soiree involving too many of Silvia's mojitos. In the video, he'd wisely blurred their faces—an obvious choice, since the Sirens never would've signed consent forms. If they'd caught him lurking in the bushes, they would've beaten him senseless.

If he came back now, he was cruisin' for a bruisin'. They'd never forgiven him for sending glimpses of their breasts into cyberspace.

Reading from over her shoulder, Cat said, "You don't look like a baby seal. Your brother's a meanie."

"There's a news flash." Absently Linnie stared at the ceiling, thinking. "He's coming for business. What business?"

Knitting her fingers in her lap, Jada said, "Show this to Daniel immediately. If there's anything to worry about, he should be in the loop. I mean, if Freddie thinks he can stake a claim . . ."

Worry extinguished her voice, forcing Linnie to supply, "He's not crazy enough to interfere. After seven years? My parents would stop him."

"You're positive?"

"I guess."

Was she? Linnie's heart skipped a beat.

Jada regarded her with misgiving. "Wayfairs and their sons," she muttered. "You ought to put your foot down, tell your parents enough is enough. Make them do the right thing."

Cat looked from one to the other. "Mind cluing me in? I have no idea what you're talking about."

Of course she didn't. Nor would Jada have a clue if not for Linnie's incredibly difficult twenty-sixth year. In a moment of weakness, she'd spilled the details about the inheritance her parents had drawn up. At least she'd dropped the embarrassing facts on Jada, who'd guard a secret from invading Huns. No one else in town knew the truth, not even Daniel. Discussing the inheritance was humiliating, and Linnie spent as little time thinking about it as possible.

The pregnant silence brought Cat to full attention. "Well? I'm waiting. If this is like the blood oaths we took as kids, go on. Prick my finger. Just disinfect the needle first."

Jada stuck her hand deep into her curls. "We can't tell you. No offense."

"Offense taken. Why can't you tell me?"

"Because we're not your only best friends. You'll blab."

"If I shouldn't tell Mami, just say so."

"Cat, you'd discuss the details of your sex life with your mother. Icky." Jada reconsidered. "Not that you have a sex life."

"As if we're not all virgin queens." Cat wrinkled her nose. "Well, sort of. We're die-hard abstainers by default."

Linnie blew out a breath of frustration. "Shut up about sex already," she said, pulling her friend into a sitting position before she belted out a Latino ballad about finding love. Cat's search for the perfect hunk of testosterone was her life's pursuit. "If we explain, you can't blab. You'll swear not to mention this to your mother. It would take all of ten seconds for her to share the news with the Sirens. Swear it."

Her brown eyes dancing, Cat made an X over her heart.

Linnie's tongue stuck to the roof of her mouth. Her lips went as dry as the Sahara.

On the exhale, she blurted, "I don't own the Wayfair." She hesitated, gauging Cat's reaction. None so far, which wasn't necessarily a good thing. "I mean, I don't own it entirely. After my parents got settled into retirement, well . . ."

"Geez, Linnie—*what?*"

Continuing proved difficult. Burying the hurt, she made herself say, "My parents transferred ownership of the Wayfair. After my dad's stroke, they decided they shouldn't delay. I guess they were mulling over the transfer for a long time. So they left the inn to both me and Freddie. Get it? The thieving rat bastard who's my brother is a fifty percent owner of the inn. Even though he stole from the accounts, my parents still gave him half of the inheritance."

"*Whaa-at?*"

"The transfer went through a year after they moved to Florida. Freddie was long gone by then."

"Why didn't they cut him out of the will? He nearly bankrupted the inn!"

Linnie sank into silence, and Jada muttered, "Wayfairs and their sons. I'll never understand the stupid tradition."

Cat's golden skin took on decidedly grey tones. "What if he's coming back to push you out?" she asked Linnie.

"My brother has no interest in taking over. He hates the inn, always did. 'Swabbing down floors and dining with the unwashed masses' he called it."

"I don't care what he called it. You don't have a handle on his intentions. The Wayfair wasn't much of a prize when you were fighting off the IRS, but now? You're turning the place around. If I were a thieving, philandering, no-good narcissist, this is *exactly* when I'd make my grand entrance."

The observation placed a chill on the suite. In shared gloom, the women contemplated the havoc Freddie was capable of inflicting on their cherished inn.

Jada was the first to awaken from a near-catatonic fear of the consequences. Chin tipped at a haughty angle, she swept from the room. She returned with Linnie's purse.

"No more hiding in a hole." She handed the purse over. "Drive to Daniel's house and have him read the letter. If Freddie's about to stake a claim or plans another run through your bank accounts, you need legal muscle on your side."

"And boxing gloves," Cat added. "Big ones."

The lurid possibilities made Linnie desperate for consolation.

Viennese Dobos torte.

She'd tiptoe downstairs, grab the dessert Jada had concocted this afternoon, and lock herself in her suite. There was also strawberry swirl cheesecake resting nicely in the fridge. After a sugar OD, she'd burn the letter. If her brother turned up, she'd fake amnesia, pretend she'd never seen him before in her life.

"Oh no you don't." Jada hauled her to her feet. "You're not crawling into your burrow with any of my desserts. Snap out of it! Tell Daniel. He'll draw a road map for survival."

Linnie tamped down her cravings and one perfectly acceptable daydream. "What about my nasty habit of leading him on, as you guys put it?"

"We can't solve that. Ignore Daniel for months, and nothing changes. He'll still love you."

"Get your facts straight. He doesn't love me. He has a crush." More than she deserved, actually.

Refusing to argue the point, Jada pushed her out the door. "Go, before you have second thoughts. He probably hasn't gone to bed yet." Linnie was about to spout an objection, and Jada added, "Don't worry about the guests or closing down the Sunshine Room. We'll deal with it."

"You're sure about this?"

In one voice, the women shouted, "Yes!"

Linnie wasn't sure about trusting their judgment. She sailed out of the Wayfair on a wave of apprehension.

Moonlight washed the empty streets in a cold glow. From the forest an owl's hoot floated on the breeze. Rounding Sweet Lake Circle, she realized she'd left her cell in the pocket of her work dress. Hopefully the unplanned visit wouldn't rouse Daniel from sleep.

At the stop sign midway down Orchard Lane, she brought the Honda to a rolling stop. Daniel's low-slung ranch house, three doors up, was on the right. A quick glance in the rearview mirror confirmed she'd run her fingers through her hair a thousand times. Scrambling for her purse, she dug around for a brush.

She'd angled the mirror close when the crack of a door slamming brought her head up. A man in a yellow suit descended the steps in front of Daniel's place. She threw the car into park.

Not just any man.

Freddie. The sight snatched her breath away.

And just like that, the trapdoor again popped open beneath her world.

Chapter 5

In a cloud of exhaust, Freddie's car disappeared.

How much time passed before Linnie's brain blinked on once more was difficult to assess. Fifteen minutes? Distressing thoughts followed. Her brother, sauntering to his car with smug superiority. Daniel, conspiring with the enemy.

The inn, under fire. Bankruptcy. Ruin.

Lou's Ice Cream Shop.

The sugar shack lay five miles outside town. Was it too late for a cone with sprinkles?

A horn blared, snapping her jaw shut. A truck swerved around her car.

The pock-faced kid at the wheel hung his head out. "What's wrong with you, lady? It's a stop sign, not your garage."

The kid sped off, trailing gas fumes and the last of Linnie's pride.

She was done for. Somehow Freddie had maneuvered into Daniel's life. She hadn't caught an inkling of their association. Why didn't her old pal come clean this morning? Was he mixed up in her brother's mysterious business in Ohio? Freddie had looked downright merry.

Anger knotted Linnie's heart. Needing answers, she flew past the stop sign and toward the ranch house.

The neatly mown lawn nestled in darkness. The porch light was off. She marched through the shadows with the awkward gait of a mummy, hands outstretched.

She tripped while ascending the steps, jerked upright, and started pounding on the door.

Muttered cursing from inside. Daniel flung the door wide.

She hurtled past and nearly fell over Puddles. She had more than thirty pounds on the pooch and could've done serious damage. She stowed her anger to crouch for a sloppy smooch. Gratified, the dog began running the Indy 500 around her legs.

Next she zeroed in on Daniel. Tapping into anger was preferable to acknowledging the hurt bubbling up inside her. From the looks of it, he needed Valium. His sandy-brown hair stuck up from his scalp like a porcupine's quills. The five o'clock shadow rimming his square chin was dark enough for midnight, which wasn't a bad thing. Oddly, he wore an apron dusted with flour.

"What are you doing?" she asked.

"Baking. Chocolate chip." He swiped at the flour marring his face, adding a thicker dab of white. "Couldn't sleep."

"Who bakes on a work night?" The timer dinged, and she stalked to the kitchen with Puddles on her tail. Over her shoulder, she shouted, "Why are you consorting with the enemy? For that matter, why is the enemy in Sweet Lake?"

"Wait a second. You saw Freddie?"

"From a safe distance."

"Cool down, okay? I didn't know he'd stop by. I sure as hell didn't know he was in town."

"Oh, really? That's not how it looks from the cheap seats." She found a potholder, removed the cookie sheet from the oven. The scent of chocolate bloomed in the air. Leave it to Daniel to bake cookies as delectable as Jada's. The man was nothing if not precise. "Here's an easy question. Why did my brother leave your house grinning like a Cheshire cat?"

"He self-medicates, fantasizes about women, is planning his next schlock movie—how should I know?"

"Is he back in trouble? Let me guess. In between films, he's robbing banks?"

"With your brother, anything's possible."

"Don't you dare make light of this. My worst nightmare just strolled back into town, and the first thing he does is pay you a visit. It doesn't look good, pal."

"Linnie—"

Puddles dropped onto his haunches. The mutt lifted his snout to howl like a wolf on the prairie.

She arched a brow. "What's wrong with your fur baby?"

"Cavities."

"He howls all the time. Might be something more. Get him to a vet."

"Later."

Daniel shooed the whimpering beast into the yard. He returned with his grey eyes softening. The cheap ploy filled her belly with warmth.

He started across the room but stopped, her expression warding him off. "Listen, I'm as shocked by Freddie's appearance as you," he said. "I was in bed when he dropped by. No call, no advance warning. You have to believe me."

"Like that's easy to accomplish." She pried a cookie from the pan and bit down. "Why was he here?" Singeing her lower lip, she flinched.

Daniel looked at her helplessly. "I can't say."

Her appetite fleeing, she tossed down the rest of it. "Can't or won't?"

"Both. I'm sorry."

In all their years of friendship, they'd never argued. Not one serious disagreement, not even a raised voice. They were perilously close now.

"I thought I could trust you," she said, and her voice broke. The hurt she'd tried to keep at bay washed over her.

His eyes beseeched hers. "You *can* trust me. Always."

"You're working for Freddie?"

"Essentially."

"Legal work for Bad Seed?"

"I'm not at liberty to say."

Another swipe at his porcupine hair, and the pain centering in her chest deepened to unbearable. Daniel was the most ethical man she knew. She relied on him completely, although she'd never told him outright. How could Freddie get him to handle legal work?

Therein lay the problem. Freddie breezed through life getting exactly what he wanted. She wasn't even sure she could trust Jada and Cat around him. When they were all in their twenties, her friends had trailed behind Freddie with mindless adoration. His charisma was blinding, a terrible force.

He'd taken enough. She refused to surrender Daniel.

A remarkable defiance carried her across the room. Daniel had a good six inches on her, but she approached quickly, taking him off guard. Straining to cup her hands around his neck, she steered his head downward. She lifted her lips to his before he might resist. She brought every feminine wile she possessed to bear as she captured his mouth, luring him in with a playful flick of her tongue, arching her breasts against the wall of his chest.

Making the first move was bold in the extreme, but she was too hurt to let her natural reticence get in the way. Taking charge was exhilarating, proof of a power she hadn't known she possessed. But her elation fled as Daniel's initial shock retreated and he wrapped his arms around her. With devastating tenderness he returned her ardor, his mouth coasting over hers.

She was no longer in control, no longer making a point about whose side he should take in the war of the Wayfairs. Daniel took possession of the kiss, channeling a decade's worth of yearning against her lips.

The simple message she'd meant to send went devastatingly awry. A groan erupted from his throat. He lifted her slightly off the floor, making her heart somersault with pleasure. With strength and grace, he maneuvered her back across the room. She went fluid with desire as he pressed her against the counter.

He ground his hips against hers, taking her arms and draping them over his shoulders, opening the generous curves of her body to his slow, thorough caresses. The moment hung suspended out of time. His hands were everywhere, tangling in her shoulder-length hair, flirting with the edges of her breasts, skimming down her back as if he were testing the limits of his self-control. Cupping her bottom, he repositioned her with a hungry moan that spiked passion in her blood. Spinning, she became dimly aware he'd broken off the kiss to nibble on her neck. He murmured her name with a reverence a man less consumed would reserve for prayer.

When she began responding with hungry caresses, he let her go. His skin flushed, he stepped back. Daniel was a man with a respect for limits. She was vaguely aware he'd crossed a self-imposed line.

The air bristled with electricity. Enough voltage pinged between them to light up Las Vegas. Outside, Puddles barked at the moon.

Daniel was the first to land his senses on terra firma. "Why did you kiss me?" he demanded.

A lazy sort of luxury made Linnie's brain hazy. She shook her head to clear it, latching on to her anger. "Got me," she snapped. Anger was a better option than considering how she'd altered their friendship without weighing the consequences. "I've had a strange day."

"So you thought you'd cap it off by playing the seductress? Here's the thing about rules. Change them, and someone might beat you at your game."

"What's that supposed to mean?"

"You're an adult. Figure it out."

She yanked open the drawer beside his sink, grabbed a baggie. "No, thanks. I have bigger fish to fry." She dropped three cookies inside. "Should I buy a shotgun and run you and my brother out of town? Seeing as you've become fast friends?"

"This is unbelievable. You're still mad?" Glaring, he got his breathing under control. "After what just happened?"

"You betcha."

"Hold on. Let's cool down, talk this through."

"Not on your life, pal."

"I'm not your pal." His mouth curved at a rakish angle. "Not anymore."

The suggestive comment started her head spinning again. She sagged slightly against the counter.

She was still searching for a suitable retort when he added, "Go home, Linnie." His gaze took a leisurely stroll from her forehead to her toes, igniting tiny fires. "If you don't, I'll have you stripped down to your skin in five seconds flat."

Shocked by the strength in the challenge, she searched for her voice.

"I'm going," she replied, swerving past him before she changed her mind.

Chapter 6

Finishing her morning coffee, Linnie walked to the veranda's railing and breathed in the fragrance of honeysuckle. The sweet scent had always proved calming. After last night at Daniel's house, she needed the restorative powers more than usual.

This morning the honeysuckle blended with the faint scent of yesterday's suntan lotion left behind by the vacationers staying at the inn. Some of the early risers were already dining in the Sunshine Room or readying their families for a day at the beach. Her emotions settling, Linnie went back inside and descended the steps to the basement.

The two youngest maids on staff, Daisy Kane and Carol Rhodes, folded sheets before the row of industrial-size dryers.

"Almost finished?" she asked them. "I need help in the ballroom."

Daisy, a strawberry blonde with an excitable nature, gave a cheerful thumbs-up. "Sure thing. The waiters have the tables back in place?"

The waitstaff had removed twenty round folding tables from storage in preparation for the Mendozas' anniversary party. "Chairs too," Linnie supplied. "Everything's covered with dust. We'll wash it all down."

After folding the last sheet, the girls followed her back to the main floor. The pleasant sounds of conversation drifted from the Sunshine Room. June was always a good month, and eighteen rooms were booked. In two weeks, the remaining rooms would have occupants during the weekend of Silvia and Marco's anniversary bash. They'd invited friends and family from as far away as Cleveland.

With the maids' help, Linnie carried buckets of soapy water into the ballroom. The walls no longer carried the tang of fresh paint, and the addition of furniture made the cavernous space more inviting. The waitstaff had arranged tables at one end, leaving the portion of the ballroom closer to the dais open for dancing. The two large chandeliers, one at each end, sparkled from the careful attention that Linnie and Jada had given them.

Carol, a quiet, slender girl, surveyed the tables before them. "Where should we start?" she asked Linnie.

"Why don't you and Daisy begin near the dance floor? I'll work on the tables here. We'll meet in the middle."

"All right."

Linnie dunked her hands into the warm water, squeezed out the rag. After little sleep, her heart still swam with confusion. Last night she'd started something with Daniel without thinking it through.

She'd ended something too. The unpleasant fact of his association with her brother, an association Daniel refused to clarify, had dissolved a once-easygoing friendship.

For several years now, Linnie had recognized the mutual attraction. Yet she'd taken the companionship for granted. Daniel never pushed, never demanded. His attentions were a comfortable part of her routine, as unchanging as the golden sandstone of the Wayfair. Daniel was just as solid—precise, but also predictable. What she hadn't understood were the strong, swift currents running beneath the edifice of his life.

Nor did she understand enduring passion with any confidence.

The best years of her youth had been spent learning to manage the Wayfair. She'd traded the pleasures of early adulthood for a family legacy, and long hours learning the basics of accounting with

Silvia's help. In the kitchen, the cook taught her a system to inventory perishables. The maître d' schooled her in fine wines. There was time for little else. The shallow relationships of her early twenties, before Freddie upended her world, were no more capable of offering instruction on how to proceed with Daniel than cartoons might teach her Japanese.

"Look who's up with the robins. Need help?" Jada, dressed in jeans, reached for a rag. "I can put off baking for another hour."

Linnie dismissed her dreary thoughts. "Help's always welcome. Thanks."

"Philip's outside with his crew. Said they'll try to dig out the monster boxwood by hand. If it's a no-go, they'll have to use the backhoe."

Daniel's brother had promised to keep the noise to a minimum. "If any guests complain, let's serve free dessert tonight."

Jada murmured her assent. Then she asked, "Headache gone?"

Linnie bit her lower lip. Rarely did she lie to anyone, let alone Jada. It was time to come clean.

"I didn't have a headache last night. I wasn't ready to go into the details." She paused a beat. "Freddie's here, in Sweet Lake. I saw him leaving Daniel's house."

Jada dropped the rag into the bucket. "Why do I have the feeling there's more bad news?"

"Because there is. He's hired Daniel. For what, is up for grabs. Daniel wouldn't elaborate."

"Impossible. He'd never handle legal work for your brother."

"Believe it." A stone lodged in Linnie's heart. "Plus I did something without thinking first. We started arguing, and I kissed Daniel. One of those crazy, stupid impulses. I can't explain what happened next."

"Well, try!"

"He sure wasn't himself. He was . . . into it." The memory of his large, hard body pressing her against the counter put spots of black in her vision. A sampling of the pleasure he'd given once again glided through her limbs. Running from the intoxicating sensation, she added, "He was nothing like the stable man we all know and love. Now I can't get him out of my head. The worst part? I'm really hurt because he's a turncoat."

The news bounced off Jada. Slowly she pulled out a chair and sat. "Thanks to your parents, you aren't the only one with a stake in the Wayfair," she said warily. "What if Freddie's planning to wrest control from you?"

"God, I hope not."

"Daniel always has your best interests in mind. What if he offered to renegotiate the contract to ensure you get a fair deal? It's not like he can stop Freddie from making a claim. He can do his best to protect you."

The stone in Linnie's heart became a torment. "I don't care if Daniel thinks he's on the side of the angels. If he's helping Freddie, he's betrayed me."

"And you kissed him."

Linnie flopped into a chair. "I was so angry. I didn't stop to consider how good I'd feel. He totally bowled me over. I didn't know he had it in him."

"You're nuts. He *is* a man. Hot-blooded and happy to share."

"All these years, and he's never made a pass."

"Linnie, work consumes your whole life. The only social outings you allow are the occasional movie with Cat and me. Daniel's been waiting forever. He wants you to stop making your family legacy the center of the universe and start living. I mean, face it. You've never given him much in the way of a green light."

"He's not getting one now," she snapped, and immediately cringed. That wasn't the signal she'd given him last night. "Why is he consorting with the enemy?"

Jada's dark gaze held compassion. "That isn't what's really bothering you. You're miserable because you finally lit the match. What were you expecting? Girl, you've been in love with Daniel for years."

The opportunity to disagree wasn't forthcoming. Outside the Wayfair, angry voices rang out. Daisy and Carol, finished at the third table, shot to the windows. Someone was getting ready for a brawl.

Linnie and Jada ran into the hallway and through the lobby.

On the wide sweep of lawn, Daniel's younger brother came at Freddie with fists raised. No one gave much thought to Kettering height and strength, or the way Daniel and Philip towered over any crowd. They were solidly built, unassuming men—friendly and low-key unless provoked.

Now Philip's easygoing nature melted beneath the fury in his eyes. His crew crowded behind him, the planting project momentarily forgotten. They were ready to fight.

Crossing the veranda, Linnie raced down the steps. Predictably, Freddie was too foolish to run for cover.

"Philip, stop!" She leapt before him. He didn't possess a cool head like Daniel and was prepared to land a punch. "He's not worth it."

Freddie chuckled. "Sugarpop, I'm worth ten times more than you. Hasn't anyone pointed out that filmmaking is profitable?"

Philip glanced at her, then lowered his fists. "If you're rich, pay her back what you owe her," he growled. "Then clear out."

"Clear out? The Wayfair is my second home. I've missed the grande dame."

Philip looked to Linnie. "What's he talking about?"

Freddie supplied, "I'm co-owner of the inn."

"Bullshit."

"All true. Go on. Ask her."

"He's telling the truth." Gently, she steered Philip back another step. He'd curled his fingers, an indication his temper wasn't yet under control. "We own the Wayfair fifty-fifty. Sadly."

The information didn't immediately register with Philip. When it did, he took her by the shoulders and set her behind his back. His desire to protect her, coming on the heels of Daniel's betrayal, clouded her vision with tears. On the verge of crying, she sucked in air.

A glance over his shoulder, and the signs of her anguish proved Philip's undoing. "You own half of Linnie's inn?" he asked Freddie. "Congratulations."

The blow he landed sent his opponent flying. Freddie careened to the grass with a thud.

Incredibly, he rose with a snarl. He was also a tall man, but he didn't have the muscle of the Kettering brothers. Daniel was slightly larger, but only a fool would tangle with Philip. Especially now, as he strode near with the ferocity of a lion.

"Try it." Freddie lurched forward. "Hit me again, and I'll sue." Blood oozed from the gash in his chin. Angrily, he brushed it away. "Want to lose your company? I'll bankrupt you with lawsuits."

"Like you nearly bankrupted your kid sister? You're a bastard. What are you doing here?"

"Paying a visit."

"She doesn't want to see you." Philip hesitated, turned to Linnie. He surveyed the tears catching on her lashes. "You want him off the premises, right?"

With effort, she swallowed. "Right."

"I'm leaving." Freddie adjusted his tie, a maroon silk with streaks of canary yellow running through the cloth. Regarding her, he added, "Put your gorilla on a leash. I'm busy for the rest of the day, but I'll drop by tomorrow." He looked at his watch. "I don't want to be late for my meeting with Daniel."

Philip laughed with disbelief. "You're seeing my brother? Why? Need a shiner to go with the chin?"

"I've hired him."

"Like hell."

"I have." Jingling his car keys, Freddie watched the color seep from his adversary's face. Satisfied, he regarded Linnie. "Explain to the gorilla, Sugarpop. I really must go."

Wordlessly, she clasped Philip's cold fingers to lead him toward the inn.

⁓

The princess waved her sparkly wand.

Setting down his briefcase, Daniel offered a weary smile. Why his five-year-old niece was playing on the floor beside his secretary's desk proved too complex a question for his addled mind. On a normal day, her appearance wouldn't disturb him.

Today was anything but normal.

Last night he'd received little in the way of shut-eye. At dawn, exhaustion overtook him and he'd slept through the alarm. He'd still be down for the count if the heavy dog breaths across his face hadn't rousted him from an arousing dream about the kiss he'd shared with Linnie. He awoke in a miserable state of longing.

Cracking open his lids, he found Puddles reclined on the opposite pillow, the beast's close-set eyes regarding him like those of a long-suffering spouse.

His trip to Ohio Republic to open the bank account took longer than expected. Daniel was left with the disagreeable sensation of standing behind the eight ball at the start of the workday.

Apparently the conclusion wasn't his alone.

Behind rectangular eyeglasses of cobalt blue, his secretary regarded him closely. On the fast approach to her sixties, there wasn't much Kay Harnett missed. Of medium height with a linebacker's build, she ran the law office with smooth efficiency. Already she'd filled the place with the aroma of freshly brewed coffee. The silver-haired grandmother of three had also pulled open the bottom drawer of her desk. Inside were toys and art supplies, Fancy's private stash.

His niece hopped up from where she'd scattered coloring books and fat crayons by Kay's feet. "Uncle Daniel!" Wand still waving, she scampered forward. "I told Daddy I don't want to go to summer camp today."

"Seems like you've given up on summer camp." A real problem, since his younger brother didn't have a babysitter on standby 24/7.

"I don't like boys."

"The boys at camp?"

She leaned against his knees, pinioning him with a long-lashed gaze. "They put worms in their pockets." The puffy sleeves of her princess costume lifted in tandem with her revulsion. "I saw 'em. After they were squished. Andy McFee said he'd put them on my hamburger bun."

He scooped up her sparrow's body. "Andy isn't much of a gentleman. Did you inform him you prefer catsup?"

"You're silly." She pressed her nose to his. "Can I stay at the low office? Mrs. Harnett says it's okay."

"Law office, buttercup." Out of habit, he pressed a palm to her silky brow. "How's your tummy today?"

"Hungry."

With bemusement he shook his head. No doubt Philip put out nothing but toast for breakfast. In fairness, Linnie had invited him to start work on the new foundation plantings.

Which left the issue of famished royalty up for grabs. There wasn't time to head back to the house to let Fancy root through his kitchen for a meal suitable for a princess.

Coming to the rescue, Kay retrieved a packet of instant oatmeal from yet another drawer. "Fancy, we'll make this to hold you for now. Perhaps your uncle will let me take you to the inn for an early lunch."

"Can we see my daddy when we go?"

"Just for a moment. I'm sure he's up to his armpits in dirt.", To Daniel, Kay said, "After Fancy and I dine at the Wayfair, I'll call around, find someone to babysit."

"Good deal. I have an interesting meeting this afternoon." He set his niece down. She raced back to the coloring books. "A one o'clock appointment with a new client."

"Anyone I know?"

"Freddie Wayfair. I need to draft a contract before he arrives."

His secretary absorbed the news with thinning lips. "The demon seed is in town?"

"Unfortunately."

"He's been gone for years. I was under the impression we were rid of him permanently."

"Someone forgot to erase Sweet Lake from the map." Daniel thought of something else. "I may also be out of town for several days."

"Business for the Wayfairs' tarnished golden boy?" With misgiving Kay read the answer in her employer's gaze. "Don't worry about Puddles. I'll call my husband to prepare him for the invasion. Does the beast still slip pot roasts off counters? There *are* limits to my hospitality."

He chuckled. "Face it, Kay. You love Puddles as much as I do."

"Adorable as his owner, and perhaps a bit wiser." Driving the point home, she asked, "When your new client arrives, should I offer tea, coffee, or arsenic?"

"Surprise me."

"Here's a better idea. Why don't I take my time with Fancy at lunch? You deal with Freddie on your own."

"Probably for the best." She'd struggle to maintain a civil tone.

She regarded Fancy, belly down at her feet, coloring with single-minded intensity. Satisfied she wasn't listening, Kay said, "Now everything makes sense. I was curious why you look like a visitor to the seventh circle of hell." Lowering her voice further, she added, "Did you have the sense to ask him to park behind the building? The fewer people aware of his arrival the better. Can you imagine if the Sirens find out? Having one's breasts flashing through cyberspace is not a happy circumstance."

"You mean a film of one's breasts."

"As if it makes a difference to women of a certain age."

Searching for the exit to the conversation, he said, "I have Freddie's number. Will you do the honors?"

"If I must. How long is he staying in Sweet Lake?"

"Not long. At least I hope. Do you pray? I could use extra chits in heaven."

"You're on your own, son." Kay hesitated. "What about Linnie?"

"She knows Freddie's here."

"She's aware he has an appointment with you?"

Daniel winced. "Oh yeah." How to gain her forgiveness was a distinct problem. Groveling wasn't his style, and last night's moment in his kitchen had changed the calculus of their relationship. Were a dozen red roses in order? Two dozen?

Kay assessed the dismay furrowing his brow. "The eighth circle of hell," she murmured. "Be careful, Daniel."

Too late, he mused. Given the deal he'd struck with Freddie, he was in hell for the foreseeable future.

"Hold my calls." He strode toward his office. "I need to get going on the contract."

Throughout the morning, he worked with grim concentration. Linnie remained in his mind like background noise, a subtle hum of yearning beneath the more pragmatic demands of writing an airtight contract. The sweetness of her lips, the feel of her feminine body pressed willingly to his—he'd almost lost control. Fueled by her rash invitation, he'd considered taking her right there in the kitchen. The need, bottled up for too long, ran hot in his veins.

When she flung herself into his arms, why didn't he stop her then? *Simple,* he reflected, completing the contract and setting it aside. Even if he'd guessed her intentions, he wouldn't have refused. He couldn't have refused. For more years than he cared to count, he'd been waiting to hold her in his arms.

Several minutes before noon, Kay left with Fancy. At one on the dot, Daniel went to check the small lobby at the front of the office.

With satisfaction he noted his client, dressed in a suit of yellow pinstripe, was on time. He did a second take. A bruise purpled Freddie's chin.

"Nice." Daniel tapped his own chin. "Catching up with old friends?"

"Like a high school reunion with more rage."

Freddie didn't elaborate, which suited Daniel fine. "This way."

In the office, he waved his client into the chair before the desk. Seating himself, he slid the contract across.

"You'll make a good faith deposit into this account," he began. "Ten thousand dollars, which I'll return to Linnie. You then have until July thirty-first to deposit the full amount, plus interest. You have six weeks to get all the funds in order."

Freddie took the contract, read quickly. "I won't need six weeks."

"Fine," Daniel replied coolly, masking his astonishment. The total amount was triple what he'd squirreled away for retirement. "Sign here."

The contract sealed, Freddie pressed on without preamble. "As I mentioned last night, Bryce Reed worked under the table for the talent on my last film. Now home with his parents in Medina." He handed over the address. "I offered to help after the accident. He was embarrassed and refused."

"How old is Bryce?"

"Twenty-one going on fourteen."

Like the average boy on the verge of manhood, Daniel mused. "How does a youth from Ohio land in California?"

"Business schools."

"What?"

A nearly imperceptible tremor ran up Freddie's wrist. He lowered his hand to his lap.

The conversation came at a cost, which was unexpected—and intriguing.

"Business schools," he repeated with mild impatience. "I'm contacted frequently. Entrepreneur builds a film studio through Internet marketing, finds success overseas—I can't speak at every university, though I do visit schools in Ohio when time permits. Bryce was a student at Ohio State. After my talk, he bombarded my e-mail with pleas for a job. He showed up at one of our shooting locations with enough passion to lasso the moon."

"Like Jimmy Stewart in *It's a Wonderful Life*?" He'd forgotten Freddie's prodigious ability for citing old films. From junior high onward, he'd been incapable of concentrating on studies. But he'd always possessed the uncanny ability to spout lines from scripts dating back to the 1930s.

"Yes, but in place of Mary, our impetuous youth loved cinema. Passionately and without reservation."

"Like you." The observation left a chilly silence, and Daniel asked, "To clarify, he wasn't formally on your payroll?"

"Only handling errands for the talent under the table. I should've put a stop to it."

"Tell me about the accident."

The question hung in the air for an uncomfortable moment. Daniel got the impression of another bill coming due as Freddie toyed with the gold cufflinks on the blindingly white shirt. Striking how he'd chosen a life behind the camera. Linnie took after the pleasantly featured and darker-haired Wayfairs. Freddie had improved on his mother's blonde glamour, transmuting the resemblance into a striking presence with movie-star allure.

"You have to understand filmmaking." He smoothed down his tie as he gathered his thoughts. "My production company attracts all types.

We don't have the budget of a big studio, and the majority of the crew is young. A lucky few invest several years at a place like Bad Seed before moving on."

"Makes sense."

"The average camera operator, assistant, or gaffer never receives the call from a major studio. They stay on. Others find less promising forms of amusement."

"Gaffer?" The term was unfamiliar.

"In charge of lighting."

"The accident . . . the result of a less promising form of amusement?"

"Bryce fell in with some of the older members of my crew, techs and camera operators. Most had given up on landing in Hollywood. I should've fired the lot of them. Our production schedule is hectic, but even so, I sensed the rumblings. The discontent." He paused, holding Daniel in a meaningful stare. "You're made of stronger stuff. Pining away for my sister, never making a move—do you ever want to drown at the bottom of a bottle?"

The question took aim at Daniel's heart. The prick of intense pain, and he heard himself say, "Bryce's accident was the result of drinking?" Under no circumstances would he discuss Linnie or his feelings for her. He wouldn't give her brother the satisfaction.

"Drinking and drugs, after a particularly long day of filming. A group of the men were stoned and stupid. Bryce tagged along. Someone got the idea to set off fireworks."

"While they were stoned? That's crazy."

"The boy got too close. Second-degree burns on his face." Freddie lowered his attention to his lap. "More serious damage to his eyes. Might be permanent."

"He's now blind?" The possibility sickened Daniel.

"The Devlin Eye Institute in Cleveland may be able to save his eyesight. With a cornea graft or a transplant—I don't understand the specifics. But I will pay. You'll assure Bryce's parents I'll cover all expenses."

Daniel reached for a pad, jotted a note. "Isn't he covered by their insurance? They may only require help with out-of-pocket costs. If they have an eighty-twenty plan, there's a cap on expenses."

"They removed Bryce from coverage when he ran off to California." Freddie shrugged. "I doubt it matters. Blue-collar family, barely getting by—their insurance wouldn't have been enough. Would've spent years digging out from under co-pays."

"And you're offering to cover the entire cost? Even though you have no legal obligation?"

Which begged the question: What would compel Freddie to open his checkbook? He thought only of himself. Helping the less fortunate wasn't in his DNA. A shallow man, he was a cheap rhinestone compared to Linnie's diamond-bright depths.

Or so Daniel thought until his client spoke again.

"I'll cover everything," Freddie insisted, his voice thick with emotion. "The cost is immaterial."

Mystified, Daniel tossed his pen down. It was none of his affair. Yet he couldn't keep the curiosity at bay.

"May I ask why you're willing to help at all?"

Chapter 7

Freddie's threat to return the following day never materialized. Nor was he spotted in town the day afterward. Gossip traveled quickly in a town the size of Sweet Lake, and everyone Linnie asked assured her that Freddie was gone—at least for the time being.

As Cat filled the table in the meeting room with to-do lists for her parents' anniversary bash, Linnie wondered about his whereabouts. According to Philip, Daniel was out of town for an unspecified period. He'd left without explanation and wasn't answering his brother's calls. Was he on a trip with Freddie?

The meeting room, situated in a narrow hallway near the inn's noisy kitchen, was a favorite haunt. Floor-to-ceiling cherry wood paneling carried the luster of an expensive jewelry box. The carpet sported a whimsical design of teal peacocks cavorting amid peach-colored flowers. Long ago, female guests had enjoyed teatime in the cozy room while their husbands took part in turkey shoots in the forest or filled the Wayfair's veranda with cigar smoke in the late afternoon.

Not until the 1980s, when Sarah and Treat Wayfair accidentally broke the family tradition of bearing a single male heir, did Sarah claim the room for her own. The wood paneling muffled the sounds of guests coming and going and lent a respite from Treat's manic energy. In relative peace, Linnie's mother spent blissful hours on the pale-pink couch or at the cherry wood table knitting scarves, throw blankets, and the occasional nubby sweater.

Elbows on the table, Jada studied the proposed menu of hors d'oeuvres. "Your parents will spring for shrimp cocktail?" she asked Cat. "They've invited nearly two hundred guests."

"Not a problem. They'd like to celebrate their fortieth in style."

"You're talking twenty-five pounds of shrimp, give or take."

"Let's err on the side of caution. Plan on thirty pounds."

"We still have to tally the liquor bill, desserts, band, and extra waitstaff." Jada's voice revealed doubt. "This is beginning to resemble a wedding reception."

Cat's golden-hued cheeks took on a fierce tint. "We're not skimping on the menu. This is what Mami wants." Closing down the debate, she turned to Linnie. "Did you get the seafood quote from our supplier? I need the final cost."

The task had slipped Linnie's mind. "I'm sorry," she said. "I'll call today."

Impatience rippled through Cat's eyes. "We're prepping the first major party at the Wayfair in almost a decade. Stop worrying about Freddie. So he's disappeared. Good riddance, I say."

"He's not gone for good," Jada muttered. She landed a sympathetic gaze on Linnie. "When he does make another appearance, what's the game plan?"

On the table, a pencil hid beneath the paperwork. Rolling it free, Linnie began chewing on the soft middle.

Obviously Jada hoped she'd demand the return of all monies taken seven years ago. Linnie deserved an equitable resolution. Yet the need didn't match the message in her heart. Fantasizing about ways to confront Freddie had been easy when she'd believed he'd never set foot in Sweet Lake again. She'd certainly never expected to protect him from an all-out brawl with Philip on the front lawn of the Wayfair.

Since then, she wasn't accosted by reflections on her brother as a sophisticated man brimming with arrogance. She was dogged by images of a much younger Freddie, the wild boy of the woods.

He nearly failed every year of school, his textbooks left out in the rain or forgotten on the beach. Although four years younger, she learned to organize his life, quietly slipping into his room at sunup to unearth his book bag from beneath heaps of clothes on the floor. She'd wake him before their father burst in.

Linnie, so much like her father, instinctively knew how to shield her brother from the laser-like intensity of Treat's morning rituals. *Wayfairs aren't sleepyheads—get a move on.* Freddie would place his narrow feet on the floor, dizzy as a drunk, as Linnie displayed his neatly packed book bag for their father's inspection.

Jada removed the pencil from between Linnie's teeth. "Well?" she asked quietly. "What's the plan?"

"The next time Freddie drops by, I'll ask for the money."

"Good. It's time he settled up."

The tacit approval didn't buoy her spirits. "What if we've been looking at this the wrong way?"

"I'm not following."

"Freddie did have Dad's permission to access all the accounts. What if my brother didn't exactly steal the money?"

In quiet moments, she'd always wondered about his deeper motives. It was easy to assume his shallow nature drove every decision he made—and his self-centeredness did come into play. But as she took in the outrage glistening in Cat's eyes and Jada's confusion, she again circled around to an uncomfortable truth. Her understanding of Freddie was flimsy at best. How to guess his true motives with any confidence?

Warding off her friends' protests, she held up her hands. "Sure, he wired thousands of dollars to a California bank account we didn't know existed. I'm not denying the facts. What if he was just looking for the fastest way out?"

"Out of what?" Jada demanded.

"Ohio, our parents' disappointment, the family legacy—all of the above."

Cat sputtered, "You're excusing his actions?"

"I'm saying he didn't consider how much he'd hurt the rest of us. Dad's stroke, the inn nearly going under—Freddie didn't mean to cause a catastrophe. He just wanted to leave. Being Freddie, he didn't stop to consider the consequences."

Jada's eyes flashed. "He thought only of himself."

"Sure, but he thought our parents had money to spare. After the film of the Sirens got all those hits on YouTube, he found his calling, something he did well. He'd failed at everything else."

Except women, Linnie mused. He'd successfully romanced dozens of willing lovers. He dumped them just as quickly. On the surface, his cruelty seemed another example of a shallow nature. But she also wondered if a lonely childhood had taught him to mistrust deep relationships.

She was still mulling it over as Jada said, "Linnie, he wasn't a child. Freddie cleaned out the accounts when he was twenty-nine. Old enough to know better—and see the mess he left behind. Come to think of it, why didn't he start paying you back once Bad Seed got off the ground?"

"Maybe he tried. It's not like I'd take his calls. Back then I was so hurt by how he'd betrayed us, so angry. I didn't want to hear his voice."

"Fair enough. Then why didn't he put a check in the mail? He didn't need you to accept an apology to set things right."

"Injured pride?"

"Avarice has my vote."

"You're wrong. Our parents managed to forgive him. I didn't." A sudden discomfort swept through Linnie. "I still don't. He'll never admit as much, but he cares about my opinion. Reason enough to hold off on paying me back."

The words were barely out when another fragment from the past twisted her heart. Freddie's hair tangled with leaves, his shirt torn from a solitary trek in the forest, where he'd been working on the tree house he'd built singlehandedly. Was the memory one of the countless times her mother sent her to fetch him? He appeared late on every occasion, trudging past the guests milling on the veranda, head lowered as Mr. Uchida called out a greeting from the front desk. Linnie had inherited their parents' uncanny sense of time. Wake her in the wee hours of the morning, and she'd know the precise minute. Freddie easily confused 6:00 a.m. for 6:00 p.m.

She caught her friends exchanging worried glances. Jada told her, "Be reasonable. This is *not* the time to feel compassion for your brother. We don't have an inkling of his true motives. Never forget he's an opportunist. I'm still waiting for him to come clean about the concert tickets that disappeared from your bedroom our freshman year of high school."

Linnie shrugged. "He was born with sticky fingers. Doesn't mean he's here to cause more trouble."

"Get real. Some people don't have a good side. Whatever his motives, he'd better not turn your world upside down. Not again."

Jada paused as familiar voices grew in intensity outside the meeting room. Delight lit Cat's features.

Linnie groaned.

Silvia and Frances burst inside. Frances was dressed in a typically sedate dress. Silvia's heavy gold bangles jingled as she propelled her shorter, more voluptuous body to the head of the table. She wore apple-green capris and a hot-pink shirt with a plunging neckline.

"Is there any truth to the rumors?" Cat's mother appeared too furious to await a reply. "That icy crone, McCready, said the most awful thing when I stopped by the drugstore to get a prescription. She insists Freddie went into Daniel's law firm through the back door."

"Today?" Linnie flinched at the hopeful notes in her voice. If her brother was back, perhaps Daniel was too.

Freddie she could do without. Daniel she missed terribly.

Silvia swung around, the bangles singing out. "Three days ago," she supplied. "McCready saw him park in the back lot. Is it true? Freddie's in town?"

$$\sim\!\!9$$

The question floated between the women like a dank odor. Gleaning the truth in Linnie's eyes, Frances lifted a hand to her throat. So her prediction was correct. The letter was Freddie's calling card.

There was no stopping trouble, but so soon? She gripped the edge of the table as her precarious blood pressure dropped. It was unconscionable for Linnie's brother to show up right after sending the letter. The rules of etiquette dictated one wait at least several days after writing before storming the unsuspecting town. She couldn't direct the Sirens to make enough charms or summon enough positive energy on such short notice.

"Where are my smelling salts?" she murmured.

Silvia darted her a fiery glance. "Get a grip, Frances. I forbid you to faint."

She met the rebuff with a dignified stare. "Can't you see I'm in distress?"

"I can see, and I don't care. We must get to the bottom of this."

Oddly, the rebuke steadied her pulse. "Silvia, when your dander's up, you display the warmth of a Russian winter." Frances made a mental note to stock her friend's cupboards with more soothing valerian root and chamomile teas. Evidently Silvia had run out. "How does Marco put up with your tantrums?"

"I'd explain, but there are children present. And one of those children better start talking." The hot-tempered Siren narrowed her sights on Linnie.

Her ire threw a chill on the room. Moscow in January, compliments of the Siren most apt to follow her temper into the melee and damn the consequences. Frances cherished their long and enduring friendship, but no aspect of Silvia's personality caused more grief. Life's most precarious moments needed time to unfold and find resolution. The lesson was lost on Silvia. She jumped into every fray with her blood up and her voice unforgiving.

Which described the present situation as she asked Linnie, "Why was your brother in Daniel's office?"

Frances pitied the girl, cringing beneath the misdirected fury. "Daniel is helping him with legal work," Linnie replied. "I'm not sure if the work involves the film company or a personal matter. Honestly, I don't have the details."

"Daniel won't explain?"

"Since when do lawyers reveal confidential information?"

"Nonsense. He's your *close* friend," Silvia replied, with special emphasis on *close*.

"He doesn't share confidential information—even if it concerns my brother."

Sensing an opportunity, Frances eased into a chair. Guiding the young took finesse and sensitivity. Linnie and her peers managed to ping electrons across the planet and furthered social equality with more gusto than any preceding generation. Their texting abilities astonished. There wasn't a monkey alive capable of peeling a banana faster than a young person could text.

Yet in matters of *amour*, the young rarely found bliss without a road map. If Linnie needed a push in the right direction, Frances refused to miss an opportunity to help.

"Have you tried persuading Daniel?" she asked. "I don't give a hoot about the man's ethics. This is war."

Threads of color crept up the girl's neck. "I can't make him explain why he's helping my brother. Our friendship doesn't obligate him to spill the details."

The admission didn't surprise. Before the girl's parents retired, Frances was a frequent dinner guest at the Wayfair table. She recalled Sarah's constant prodding of her daughter, the subtle criticisms that stole Linnie's confidence.

"You should consider if you're underestimating your ability to sway Daniel," Frances said, hoping to heal the wounds of doubt Linnie carried. "Why, you're lovely. Your skin is so creamy it practically glows, and your eyes have always reminded me of butterflies, so large and long lashed. Why wouldn't he bring you into his confidence?"

The compliments missed their mark. "Get real." Linnie wrinkled her nose. "Women don't bat their eyes at men. Not in this century."

"Perhaps not, but here's an idea. Have you used every means at your disposal? He is a man, after all."

Cat, latching on to the query's subtext, jumped in. "Use your brain, girlfriend. Frances is asking if you have lingerie. You know—the big guns." She tapped a polished nail on her chin. "Oh, right. Your wardrobe consists of boring work outfits. You couldn't lure a man to spill his secrets if your life depended on it."

"Hey!"

Silvia stared the lot of them into silence. "So what do we have?" she muttered, pacing before the table like a flamboyant bird. "The devil's spawn is stirring up trouble. He has Daniel in his clutches. We need to get to the bottom of this, but Linnie can't perform the seduction required to make Daniel roll over. Not to put too fine a point on it, she hasn't connected with her femininity since she rode on the back of a Harley with—" Silvia turned to her daughter. "What was his name?"

"Butch," Cat piped up. "Butch on a bike. Don't you love the symmetry? Not much rattling around upstairs, but he *was* a hot body."

Linnie pressed her forehead to the table. "Let's not rehash my youth. I don't have the strength."

"Find it." Peeling the girl's forehead from the table, Frances smiled reassuringly. "If there's anyone who can bring down the admirably high wall of Daniel's principles, you're the woman for the job. He's smitten. Unleash your power. And use your breasts."

Caught up in the moment, she patted Linnie's bosom with grand-motherly approval. Given the girl's endowments, she'd have Daniel singing out his secrets in no time. "If you can't recall how to take a man down, the Sirens will lend suggestions."

Linnie's chair squeaked in protest as she moved out of reach. "Frances, I don't need your help!"

"Between us, we have more than a century of experience." Fearing she'd gone too far, Frances lowered her hands to her lap. "You'd do well to memorize a chapter from our playbook."

"Lessons in seduction, compliments of the Sirens. What a great idea." Rising, Linnie marched to the door. From over her shoulder, she added, "During the next full moon, I'll haul my ass down to the beach for the primer."

She dashed out, depriving Frances of the opportunity to apologize. In her wake, the other women exchanged worried glances.

Silvia was the first to speak. "Did you have to get hands-y?"

"I wasn't being hands-y. Can't you recognize affection when you see it?"

"If you need something to cuddle, get a dog. By the way, it's one thing to follow your natural mothering instincts, quite another to invade a woman's personal space. I'm sure Linnie figured you'd next outline the more delightful reasons to practice Kegel exercises or stuff her bra with herbs."

Mentioning Kegel exercises *had* been on the agenda. "Oh, be still," Frances muttered. She felt bad enough about botching the attempt to help.

Gratitude eased her disappointment when Jada cleared her throat. Pulling Silvia into a chair, she waved a hand at the lists for the anniversary bash. She resembled a game show host enticing Cat's mother toward door number two.

Glad to have escaped, Linnie slumped against the wall. A playbook on love? Admittedly she'd skipped dating for eons, but she didn't need help from the Sirens. Not that she had any intention of seducing Daniel for mercenary gain—or plain old fun.

Still, she'd been curt with Frances, who might have strange ideas about feminine wisdom, but did possess a wealth of kindness. The local humane society relied on her largess, and children in town never skipped the Dufour residence on Halloween. In lieu of loading kids up with sugar, Frances baked tray after tray of the best granola bars in three counties.

Aware she'd treated the Siren badly, Linnie wavered. Go back inside and apologize?

The opportunity vanished as Daisy rushed into the hallway. The maid looked like a finch high on stimulants.

The clatter of pots from the kitchen, and a waiter hurried past with a tray for the Sunshine Room. Daisy threw herself against the wall.

"What is it?" Linnie demanded. The girl's springs were wound far too tightly.

"Better get to the lobby."

A disgruntled guest? Linnie dashed through the hallway and into the back portion of the lobby's seating area. In her haste, she crashed into Mr. Uchida.

The collision popped the natty carnation from his lapel. The flower bounced across the floor. She bent to retrieve it, but he caught her by the shoulders. A salvo of incomprehensible Japanese spilled from his mouth.

She broke free. "English, please!"

"Your brother has more luggage than a Kardashian. His goons demanded the key to the largest suite!"

A more detailed explanation wasn't necessary. A fizzy excitement spiraled through the lobby.

Guests in animated groupings awaited the appearance of a celebrity. A false, and understandable, impression—outside, a white limousine sparkled in the sun. Two men, each larger than a refrigerator, placed suitcases in a growing pile by the front desk.

Near the luggage, a girl with spiky orange hair stalked in a ferocious circle. She growled into the headset clamped to one bluish-white cheek. Linnie's eyes widened. The skirt plastered across the girl's thighs wasn't really a skirt. More like a skimpy headband with steel rivets.

Out front, Philip stood with his landscaping crew. They were slick cheeked from hours of toiling in the sun. Each man wore an expression of disgust as the chauffeur walked past them to open the door for his client. With a wave of his hand, Philip led his men back to work.

Freddie danced up the steps. He entered the lobby with the joie de vivre of an actor receiving his third Academy Award.

"No autographs, please!" He winked at a matron stationed by the desk.

Linnie came forward. "He's no one special," she told the woman. She blocked Freddie's path. "What are you doing?"

"Checking in."

"No way."

"Corner suite, second floor," he blithely informed her. "I've taken smaller rooms for my staff. I do hope the Wi-Fi is up to date. Can't hold online meetings if it's on the blink."

"Wait. No." At the commotion, several of the waitresses from the Sunshine Room tiptoed into the lobby, as did a twentyish kid on the kitchen staff. Flashing her most confident smile, Linnie told them, "There's nothing going on—just people checking in. Back to work, everyone."

The employees returned to their duties.

She pushed her brother toward the wall, whispering, "You aren't staying here. Your boxing match the other day on the front lawn? Jada had to concoct a story about you and Philip being on the outs since high school."

"How odd." Her brother toyed with the silk cravat at his throat. "What was the story?"

What does it matter? "Something about vying for the same cheerleader, and Philip's still upset."

"An old canard. Besides, he was a freshman during my senior year. Unlikely we'd compete for the same woman. Couldn't Jada come up with something more creative?"

"Forget the story! Freddie, my employees aren't aware I'd like to run you out of town. They don't need to see the boss arguing with her long-lost brother. Bad for morale."

Glee danced in Freddie's eyes. "The staff assumes we get along?"

"Why wouldn't they? You took off, and the rest of us went on with our lives. Lots of people lost their jobs thanks to you. The ones who didn't just want to earn a paycheck. They couldn't care less about you."

"The prodigal son, lost to the sands of time. I'm not sure how to feel about this. I'd looked forward to burnishing my foul reputation."

A predictable response from a megalomaniac. "Don't confuse the staff's disinterest with the reception you'll receive from people who knew you well. If the Sirens find out you're in town? They'll string you up by the short hairs. I'll watch."

"As if I'm afraid of a bunch of middle-aged women." He stepped around her. "Now, go away. I'd like to retire to my room."

"You're not staying here!"

Smirking, he patted her cheek. "Why don't you run along, find a cupcake to soothe your nerves? Sugar *is* your drug of choice."

She dug around for a rejoinder. As she did, the girl with orange hair flipped the bird. Then the girl marched up the stairwell.

A popping started in Linnie's ears.

Bad timing for a brain aneurism.

Curbing her fury, she rounded on Freddie. "You're not creating party central here. Get out. Now."

"Calm down. I don't care to see a member of my own race getting above herself."

The quote was familiar. "*Guess Who's Coming to Dinner?*" she guessed. "I'd put out the welcome mat if you were Sidney Poitier. You aren't. Go back to California where you belong."

"Why, Sugarpop, you're becoming unhinged." Devilry lit in his eyes. "Does this mean you haven't missed me?"

Climbing out of the car, Daniel took stock of the street. Small homes, average neighborhood. Laughter peppered the air, a gift from kids out on summer break. By the house on the corner, two boys in shorts took aim at a third with a blast of water from a gardening hose. The third kid sprinted left. The arcing stream of water tossed diamonds through the sunlight. Safe from the line of fire, the kid twirled with the abandon of unencumbered youth.

Beside the Reeds' front steps, scarlet geraniums beckoned. They bobbed vibrant heads from a flowerbox the size of a postage stamp.

Daniel prided himself on punctuality, but he was late. Two days of discussions at the Devlin Institute had worn his nerves thin. He'd met with billing supervisors and the surgeon tasked with performing Bryce Reed's upcoming cornea transplant. He'd quizzed enough accounting personnel to make their names a collective blur. There was still no exact dollar amount for the tests, surgery, and subsequent care Bryce required.

Best guess, Freddie was looking to write a check well past six figures.

"Mr. Kettering? I'm Janis, Bryce's mother."

A bashful wave, and the woman trotted down the steps. Petite, plump, in a lavender sweater and a billowy skirt. She appeared delighted by his arrival.

Daniel took her offered hand, shook gently. "Mr. Wayfair isn't joining us. He sends his regrets. He hopes to meet you and Mr. Reed soon."

A polite fabrication. They'd driven to Cleveland in Daniel's car. Then Freddie ditched him at the Devlin Institute. At the last minute, he changed his mind about going on to Medina to meet the Reeds. It was a safe bet he'd flown back to Sweet Lake.

"Oh, that's too bad. I was looking forward to meeting him. Gale was too, but he was called into work. Second shift at the factory over on Millridge." Janis led the way into a house thickly scented with sugar. Catching Daniel's frown, she explained, "The start of canning season. I've been putting up jellies."

"My mother used to can in the summer. Smells delicious."

The comment sent her hands into the air. "Where are my manners? Would you like something to eat? A slice of pie?"

"A glass of water would be great." Since the night with Linnie, his appetite was on sabbatical. At Devlin in Cleveland, on the drive to Medina—he'd nearly called her a dozen times. To say what, he wasn't sure.

"One glass of water coming right up."

She left him in a living room not much larger than the flowerbed out front. The faded plaid couch gave the impression of a garage sale find. The flat-screen TV wasn't large, but appeared new. Daniel stepped past a recliner that was faded like the couch. The wall behind was naked, with the exception of a family photo in an oak frame.

Janis and Gale Reed, surrounded by four boys with cookie-cutter snub noses and pointed jaws. The family stared directly at the camera with pride and a hint of mischief. Only the oldest boy, his eyes large and filled with stardust, hung his attention on something out of view.

Bryce Reed.

Returning with a tall glass, Janis peered toward the narrow hallway. "Bryce, get on out here. Mr. Wayfair's lawyer is waiting to meet you." Handing the water over, she ushered Daniel into the recliner. When he'd seated himself, she added, "The trio is up at the community pool. Eli next door took 'em. Eli works third shift at the factory. Said he didn't mind getting them out of my hair."

"The trio?"

"My three younger boys. Bryce is the oldest by five years. That's him, in the photograph there. Every family gets one dreamer, right?"

"Probably," Daniel agreed. Philip, in his family. Freddie in the Wayfairs'. Privately he ticked off something else he had in common with Linnie. They were both more responsible than the other sibling. He wondered if they'd find more happiness if they understood the knack of living impulsively.

Her skirt billowing, Janis sat on the couch. Head cocked, she squinted at the hallway. "Bryce, c'mon!" She lowered her voice. "A twenty-one-year-old does *not* want Mama's help. Took a week or so before he memorized the house. Lots of cussing while he did—my husband would've grounded him for a month, hearing those words. We agreed our boy had been punished enough."

She dug around for another smile, but her mouth twitched. Moved by her effort to ward off despair, Daniel said, "I can't imagine what this has been like for you and your husband."

A terrible gratitude nested in her eyes. "Yes . . . just awful. Bryce running off to California, scaring us half to death. Then the call about the accident."

"Mr. Wayfair called?"

"No, no—some nice woman at the hospital in San Fernando. I don't think Mr. Wayfair heard about the accident until Bryce didn't show up at the studio. Those men who set off the fireworks are in jail now."

"They pleaded down to six months." Freddie had given him the basics. After a pause, he asked, "Did you fly out to get your son?"

"Mr. Wayfair took care of everything. What a kind man. One of his assistants flew back with Bryce. All of the stuff in Bryce's apartment? Mr. Wayfair packed everything up personally. Sent all those boxes first class with the sweetest note."

A bizarre revelation. Freddie, a kind man? That he'd written a sympathetic note after packing an injured boy's apartment was even more difficult to grasp.

Processing the information would have to wait. The light tapping of a cane announced Bryce's arrival.

Although Daniel didn't have children of his own, the sight stirred every fatherly instinct he possessed. Thick gauze hid the boy's damaged eyes. He was taller than expected, with wide shoulders not yet muscled like a man's. The loose jeans draping his lanky frame probably had fit before chance and tragedy stripped him of his sight.

"I've got a seat waiting for you," his mother prodded, sparing his pride. Following her voice, Bryce shuffled to the couch. Steering him down, she added, "Now, don't be disappointed. Mr. Wayfair isn't here. Over in your daddy's chair is Mr. Kettering. He's the lawyer helping us get you into the Devlin Institute."

Bryce propped the cane against his thigh. "I'm glad Mr. Wayfair didn't come. He's done enough."

"He's happy to help," Daniel offered. It felt awkward, engaging the boy as he attempted to locate their guest by sound alone. "How are you doing? Ready for the surgery?"

"I guess so. Dad thinks I shouldn't get my hopes up."

Janis opened her mouth to refute the claim. No words came.

Rescuing her, Daniel said, "Nothing wrong with optimism. I spoke with your surgeon personally. You'll meet him yourself in a couple days. He's confident you'll regain sight to your right eye."

The boy rubbed his knuckles with a careless thumb. "Not my left?" Tiny pearls of blood surfaced on the damaged skin.

The sight jolted Daniel with a memory of Linnie when she'd been little older than Bryce. "The surgeon will try to save the sight in both eyes," he murmured, recalling the week after she'd fired half of the staff. She'd rubbed her knuckles raw. He'd purchased a jar of petroleum jelly, warning it wouldn't look good if she bled in front of guests.

Brushing away the painful memory, he added, "When your parents take you up to the institute, ask all the questions you'd like. Your primary doctor has already sent your medical records. The more you know going in, the less frightening you'll find the entire process."

Bryce took this in with troubled calm. His Adam's apple bobbed in his throat. Beneath clumps of shaggy hair, red welts framed his cheekbones. Was he drunk on the night of the accident? Too far under the influence to step away from the sizzling danger of the bottle rockets?

Suddenly he said, "Can I ask you a question, Mr. Kettering?"

"Anything."

"Is Mr. Wayfair mad?"

The question floated, unbound. Janis smoothed an imagined crease from her skirt. Caught off guard, Daniel puzzled over the boy's meaning.

Filling the void he'd created, Bryce stammered, "At me, I mean. For making him spend a bunch of money. He doesn't have to. I didn't ask for his help."

"He knows you wouldn't have asked, son."

The compassion seeping into his voice was a blunder. Beneath the gauze, the boy's features grew taut, his mouth drawing into a rigid line. Not a boy, Daniel reminded himself. Bryce Reed was an adult. Daniel pitied him for all he might lose.

Sullenly, Bryce said, "He doesn't owe me anything. What I did was stupid. He shouldn't pay for my mistakes."

His mother gripped his knee. "Mr. Wayfair wants to help!"

She landed her attention on Daniel, the desperation she telegraphed bounding past her son's pride. The chance for her son to regain his eyesight. A winning lottery ticket in the form of a generous filmmaker.

The permanent blindness awaiting Bryce if his pride trumped common sense.

Coming to her aid, Daniel repeated his client's desire to spare no expense. He spent long minutes detailing the groundbreaking techniques pioneered at Devlin. Wrapping up, he promised to answer any questions that might arise, day or night. To both mother and son, he handed a business card.

On the highway, the sun painted the horizon crimson. Loosening his tie, Daniel allowed his mind to drift. Meeting Bryce was more disturbing than anticipated. The techniques pioneered at Devlin were superior. Still, there was no guarantee they'd work in this instance. Despite Freddie's largess, Bryce might spend a lifetime in darkness. It was a cruel punishment for one foolish mistake.

Daniel's cell phone buzzed.

Philip wasted no time laying on the recriminations. "What the hell, bro?" he snapped. "I was getting ready to send out an APB."

"I've been busy."

"Where are you?"

He squinted at the exit sign streaming past. "North of Columbus. Heading back now."

"You're hours away."

The statement carried worry, putting him on alert. "Does it matter?"

"Why do you think I left so many messages?" Philip paused for emphasis. "Here's something I'll bet you didn't know. Your new client owns half of Linnie's inn."

The announcement sent the car skidding. Daniel righted the wheel before he crashed into a Ford pickup.

"Bro, you hear me?"

"I heard you. You're sure about this?"

An unnecessary question. Thumbing through his phone, he found Linnie's number.

Disgust carried Frances into the kitchen.

At the stove, the Sirens' frenzied co-leader stirred three large, bubbling pots with abandon. Across her shoulders, Silvia's thick black hair frizzed in clumps. Tendrils of steam spiraled around her face, beading perspiration on every inch of available skin.

Which was a lot of skin. Given the kitchen's sauna-like temps, she'd dressed for warfare planning in shorts and a halter top.

Frances hung her purse on a hook by the door, far from the craft items scattered on the counters. More items were heaped before the women seated around the kitchen table.

She lowered her hands to her hips. "Silvia, are you completely unhinged? This is crazier than the suggestion we break into the post office to read Freddie's letter before Linnie received it. You aren't really going through with this, are you?"

"You know damn well I am."

"You can't!" This madness went against everything the Sirens believed. Searching for the means to calm her friend down, she added, "We're meant to use our collective energies for good, never for ill. Before you take this any further, let's at least talk. Or we can hold a meeting with the full membership and put it to a vote."

Silvia's wooden spoon clattered from one pot to the next. "You want a democracy? Run for office. Enough of our members agree to make the plan feasible." She waved a hand at the women clustered around the table. "If you refuse to participate, no one cares."

"Have you stopped to consider Linnie?"

"Have you? I'm not the one who got hands-y with her." Silvia grabbed a dishcloth and swabbed her face. "Offering a Sirens' primer on sex and patting her boobs—she's not exactly happy with you."

"Yes, and she still hasn't forgiven us for the unfortunate night when the newlyweds found us on the beach." Frances hadn't forgiven herself either—stitching bathing suits out of leaves *had* been her idea. Desperate, she searched for more reasons to bring her friend back to her senses. "What about the guests staying at the Wayfair? If you carry out this madness, they'll see you. You're willing to risk harming Linnie's business?"

"We'll come and go before anyone notices."

On the counter, Frances noticed a pile of dangerously sharpened sticks. "You aren't planning to harm him, are you?" She shivered. There were many things she could stand, but the sight of blood wasn't one of them.

"Don't get your panties in a twist. We'll merely scare him, and good." Silvia peered into a pot, then added another block of wax. "Go home, will you? Add a shot of whiskey to your chamomile tea and climb into bed."

From the kitchen table, Norah Webb spoke up. "I'm with Silvia. Ten minutes of torment is exactly what he deserves."

The Siren, a runway model in her youth and now in her early sixties, had buried four husbands. A terrible round of luck, but her long hair paired with the black outfits she favored led children in Sweet Lake to believe she was a witch. Ridiculously, the rumor found believers among several of the town's women, all of whom had lobbied unsuccessfully for entry into the Sirens. Sour grapes, really—the unlucky Norah had married one man after another with an unreliable ticker.

Frances sighed. Storming the inn wouldn't help her comrade's already blackened reputation.

A point she made before adding, "You should all stop and think about the message you're sending. Act like crazed warriors, and you'll undo all our good work. This behavior is far beyond our code of conduct."

Tilda, sorting tiny brass bells into piles, looked up nervously. "Silvia, maybe she's right. Can't we find a nicer way to punish him?"

"What do you suggest? A box of chocolates and a slap on the wrist? Keep your dizzy opinions to yourself."

"I'm just saying . . ."

Silvia tossed more wax into the pots. "Show some pluck, will you? Retribution should be fast, fierce—and never nice!"

The outburst started Penelope's lips quivering. "Hear the Siren's call and give kindness in secret," she murmured, slumping deep in her chair. "We're miles from the mantra now."

"You are," Frances agreed, sensing a chip in the wall of rage Silvia had deftly constructed among their peers. She regarded Mr. Uchida's older sister, now retired from the elementary school. "Think of all the good work we've done. Thanks to Yume's marvelous suggestion, we've managed to anonymously fund summer camp for dozens of local children." Yume smiled, and Frances added, "A kindness done in secret, and one for which I'm particularly proud."

"Seven kids this year," Penelope agreed.

"Yes, and what about your latest idea? It was grand."

"You mean 'love among the ancients'?"

"Who can deny the energy we channeled gave pitiful Ralph Euchanhofer the impetus to woo Kelly O'Neill?" Scooting their wheelchairs together whenever the Sirens visited the retirement center had surely helped, but it seemed wise to give the sensitive Penelope all the credit. "Look at them now. Eating meals together, playing checkers every night. Such bliss. Ralph's even stopped spitting at the nurses."

Behind her thick glasses, Penelope's eyes brightened. "Here's an idea. We should concentrate our energies on making Linnie fall in love with Daniel. Wouldn't they have the prettiest kids?"

Frances beamed. "Let's make your suggestion the first item of business at our next meeting." She cast her attention across the others with mild reproach. "Bringing lovers together is a better use of our energies than resorting to retribution and low impulses. We're Sirens. We have a duty to let generosity of heart guide our pursuits."

With her spoon, Silvia smacked the counter. "Oh, will you all shut up? I don't care about our mantra or making people fall in love. Not tonight." Heaving the first pot from the stove, she plodded across the room. "We still have to assemble the weapons and work out tactics. Lynnette, Kathryn, Biddy—go through the sticks and make sure they're all sharp. And get waxed paper from the drawer over there. I don't want to scrape wax off my table for a week straight. Norah, get the string."

Frances uttered an objection. The words faded beneath the sounds of shuffling feet as the women leapt into action.

Penelope asked, "What about me and Tilda?"

"You'll help with assembly." Silvia returned to the stove. "Get moving. I don't want to be here all night."

Frances hurried after her. "Please, Silvia. Don't do this. It's madness."

She succumbed to defeat as the fiery Siren, pretending her ears didn't function, grabbed the second pot and stalked past.

Chapter 8

The gentle push on her shoulder rocketed Linnie from her dreams. Groggy, she focused on the shadowy presence beside the bed. Jada, in an oversize T-shirt.

"What's happened? Freddie hasn't started a fire, has he?" Since checking in this afternoon, he'd flirted with every female employee of childbearing age and turned the Sunshine Room into a karaoke bar.

"He's in his suite."

"Lock him in, keep an eye on the door. I'm going back to sleep."

"It's Daniel, on my cell. Says you aren't picking up your messages."

"Only because I've misplaced my phone." She'd hurled the device at her brother's head before storming upstairs to bed. Tomorrow she'd dig around the shrubs behind the Sunshine Room.

"Worry about your phone later. Daniel sounds upset." Jada tossed her cell onto the bed and strode out.

"Linnie?"

She peered at the clock. "Daniel, it's one a.m. Call me tomorrow."

"I've been leaving messages for hours. Meet me at the beach."

"Now?"

"No, next Tuesday for dinner," he replied acidly. He did sound upset. "Yes, now."

"Making peace with gooey s'mores by campfire? Don't waste your time. I can't fight with you this week. I have previous commitments."

The rebuff only hardened his tone. "Fifteen minutes," he said. "Be there."

He hung up, leaving her no choice but to pull on jeans and run a brush through her hair. She left the suite and reconsidered. Marching back inside, she went to work with toothpaste and mouthwash. A touch of mascara and a hint of blush completed the regimen.

She was furious with the man. All the more reason not to play fair. What had Frances suggested this afternoon?

This is war.

If Daniel assumed he'd beat her at the new game they were playing, he'd miscalculated. Yanking open dresser drawers, she dug out tighter jeans. The coup de grâce? A strappy bra and a low-cut tank top.

At the front desk, Mr. Uchida clacked away at the computer. The rose in his lapel was shedding petals down the front of his rumpled blazer, and his stubby black hair stood on end. He looked like a terrier in a thunderstorm. A logical conclusion, since the whirlwind of Freddie's entourage had kept him jumping all night.

By some miracle, the inn rested in a peaceful stillness. Freddie, assuming he was still awake, was either kicking back alone or continuing the drinking spree with female guests in his suite. A night of martinis would knock down most adults. Not Freddie. Cast iron had nothing on his liver.

The moon rode high above the humid night. Barefoot, Linnie hurried down the steep incline guided by the silvery light. Crickets sang a melody to summer. On the beach Daniel wove a path beside glittering waters.

He got straight to the point. "Freddie owns half of the inn?"

The blunt opener took her off guard. "Doesn't your client share everything with you?" she countered.

"Oh, sure. He gives me access to his financials, his darkest secrets—did I mention we're pledging the same fraternity?" Daniel flashed a look of irritation. "Philip dropped the bomb while I was driving back to Sweet Lake. I nearly drove into a ditch."

The part about a near-accident zinged her heart. She was peeved at the man but didn't want him injured.

Regrouping, she asked, "Why do you care about my brother's stake in the Wayfair?"

"I'm not interested beyond the impact on you. Are you under the impression I want Freddie playing havoc with your life? And for the record, I care that you didn't trust me with your secrets. We're good friends. Why didn't you tell me?"

No answer to that, and she risked a quick appraisal. Frustration brimmed in his wide-set eyes. Another jolt of emotion, and she tried to discount how attractive he looked in the moonlight. Unshaven, in a soft T-shirt and faded jeans. The man wore a suit with panache, but the casual look increased his sexual appeal by miles.

"Hard to say why I never brought it up," she lied, thinking, *Disappointment, humiliation—take your pick.*

"Of all the things not to mention, this one's the winner." He rolled his shoulders, the irritation rising off him like steam. "Guess what? If I'd known in advance, I could've put my foot on Freddie's throat when I drew up the contract."

"What contract?"

He threw his attention on the surf. "Forget it."

"Gosh, who's the one keeping secrets?"

"The lawyer with an unfortunate obligation to his client."

"Yeah? Is he the same guy who's supposed to be my true-blue friend?"

The salvo wheeled his attention back to her. The intensity of his appraisal stirred the hunger she'd done her best to disregard since his mysterious departure from Sweet Lake. He took his time studying her, the strong, unvoiced emotion brewing in his eyes.

At last he said, "I will explain. Once your brother gives the go-ahead, you'll have all the details."

"How nice. Freddie's in the driver's seat. Like taking a drive in the country with a lunatic at the wheel. What are we, unwilling passengers?"

"Not for much longer."

Daniel angled his shoulders forward. He thwarted the urge to step closer, the reason for his hesitancy clear. Their fleeting moments of passion had destroyed the easy camaraderie they'd once enjoyed. In its place a heavy awareness bloomed.

The surf rolled gently to the beach. The lulling melody sharpened Linnie's senses as the mutual attraction put them in an uneasy orbit around each other.

She was acutely conscious of each emotion flickering across Daniel's face. Regret, recrimination, annoyance—she'd never seen him this unsettled. The loose purchase he kept on his emotions was oddly thrilling. At his sides his hands wavered; then he pressed them flat to his thighs. Her hunger intensified.

He wanted to touch her. He was doing everything in his power to squelch the impulse.

She took the step closer he denied himself. "You've been gone for two days," she said, vying for the upper hand. "Where were you?"

"Cleveland, Medina—stop changing the subject. Why didn't you tell me about your brother's stake in the inn?"

"I'm really not sure."

"Linnie, I can tell when you're holding back. You do this thing with your cheeks."

"What thing?"

He stroked the soft indentation in her right cheek. "With your dimples." Quickly he returned his hand to his side. "They dance whenever you're holding back."

The prospect of Daniel reading her so easily was unnerving. "They do not." Whatever happened to the mysteries of the feminine heart?

"They're dancing now." His eyes beckoned her nearer. "I need the truth."

She'd arrived at the strong, sturdy wall of his chest. Gaze averted, she breathed him in. He smelled of the outdoors, of leaves and the green of summer, with a subtle musky note underneath. Why did his scent calm her mind and not her body? Desire skittered her pulse.

She hazarded a glance. "Who likes to discuss their greatest defeats?" The memories pressed down, a heavy burden. "My parents decided to leave the inn to me and Freddie equally. How do you prepare for a blow you don't see coming? Like a fist aimed in the dark."

"You should've seen it coming."

The comment was uncharacteristically harsh. "How so?"

"The legendary fortune of the Wayfairs. How they bear only one child per generation, and always produce a son." His eyes softened. "Until you came along and tinkered with the master plan."

"Who cares about a master plan? After what Freddie did, my parents should've broken off contact. I assumed they'd written him out of their will. Who wouldn't? They did stop speaking to him for about a year, no longer. Everything went back to normal."

"They forgave so quickly?" Indignation laced Daniel's voice. "One year?"

"Hey, I was just as shocked. I'd call Florida to see how my parents were doing, and my mother would slide in updates about Freddie's life in California. I didn't know how to react. Mostly I'd change the subject or keep the call short. But I knew she was hoping I'd patch things up with him too."

The pain of betrayal increased, knitting tightly against the yearning for Daniel's embrace. The need for his reassurances—for more than friendly comfort—threatened her poise. But like her parents, Daniel played both sides. He wanted her to believe he had her best interests at heart.

He was working for Freddie.

Daniel smoothed her hair, apparently sensing the private battle she waged. He seemed fascinated by the task. Pride begged her to move out of reach. Exhaling a ragged breath, he outlined the sensitive skin of her ear with the lightest touch. The sheer pleasure of his touch rooted her on the sands.

Another fluid expression, and he came to a decision. Without seeking permission, he folded her into his arms. She went to him stiffly, her arms locked at her sides.

"When did your parents transfer ownership?" In a show of tenderness, he lowered his chin on her head.

"A year after Freddie left, maybe a little longer. I can't remember the exact date." The heavy beat of his heart resounded in her ears. Her eyes drifting shut, she rested her cheek on the rising warmth of his chest. "My father called, said he'd made some decisions. Told me to look for the paperwork in the mail. Short call, with no explanation."

"They handed over half of the inn without insisting Freddie return the money?"

"They didn't want to lose their son."

"What about the harm to their daughter?" The breeze ruffled Daniel's hair, swirling around the silence growing between them. When it became clear she'd give no reply, anger peppered his voice. "Back then, if I'd had a clue they'd let him off the hook, I would've called your parents. Made them listen to reason, convinced them to make you the sole owner of the inn. There's so much I could've done."

Her anger at him wasn't enough to squelch the bolt of pleasure his conviction sent through her. "What makes you think I'd let you fight my battles?" She let her hands find purchase around his hips.

"Because I'd do a better job protecting you."

"I'm not a child. I can protect myself."

"Not against your parents you can't. They're good people, but they walk right over you. I don't care about their ideas of Wayfair tradition and proud male heirs. *You're* the heir. I would've fought for what's yours."

The raw confidence of the statement nearly destroyed their tentative embrace. In his arms, she grew rigid.

Daniel refused to let go. He held on, held her close with the power of his affection. Was it any wonder her emotions were more fragile than the foam in the surf? She'd grown up with wealth and privilege—and the poverty of second-class status. In a thousand subtle ways her parents had telegraphed a destructive lesson. By virtue of her gender, she wasn't valuable. She wasn't precious like her self-serving brother.

Latching on to his sorrow, Daniel looked out over the lake. Moonlight frosted the waters a milky white. His thoughts were just as opaque, a muddle of confusion and regret.

By helping Freddie, he'd failed her in a fundamental way. He'd proven himself no more trustworthy than her family.

A situation he intended to remedy.

"Linnie, please hear me out." He balanced her chin on his thumb, searching for the means to open her heart. At last her eyes lifted, giving him the impetus to plow on. "This isn't how I wanted to begin our relationship. I spent too many years waiting for you, waiting for our lives to calm down so we'd begin. I can't undo past mistakes. I can swear I'll use all my power to sway Freddie."

"Sway him to do what?"

"If he won't let you buy his shares outright, I'll ensure he remains a silent partner. You have my promise."

Mischief combined with the amusement darting beneath thick lashes. "Who says we're in a relationship?"

That was all she'd heard? "I do," he replied gruffly. The mirth in her eyes nicked his pride. "I'm done waiting. I want you. Assuming you don't object, I plan to keep you."

Mulling this over, she lowered her mouth to the thumb he'd balanced beneath her chin. "I have a say in this? What a relief."

The sensation of her moist lips brushing across the rough pad of skin stoked the need rising in him. "Stop playing games. I'm serious."

"I've always thought of you as consistent. Are you also stubborn?"

"Only when I have everything at stake."

To drive the point home, he captured her mouth. He meant to contain the kiss, to drink her in, then let her go. The intention crumbled when she sank against him. The taste of her intoxicated him.

The self-discipline used to guide his life unspooled. Daniel allowed his reckless hands to range across her back.

Lost in her taste and the quivering welcome of her body, he coaxed her down onto the sands. For the briefest moment her lashes fluttered. Then she relaxed beneath him, her hands smoothing down the arch of his spine, spurring him on, her caresses becoming bolder. Careful to keep the bulk of his weight on his elbows, he broke off the kiss to drag his mouth across the silken skin of her forehead before lingering on the beauty mark painted beside her mouth. Every inch of her face was open to his affection, every velvety inch of her throat.

His self-control fading, he kissed her again. Then her thighs shifted temptingly beneath his. It was enough to drag him back to his senses.

Regrouping, he said, "Should I do this properly? Ask you out to dinner?"

The confusion ebbed in her eyes, replaced by an impish spark. "You got me down on the sand to make your big move? I'll give you points. This strategy is more interesting than the standard text message."

"I'd never ask you out with a text. A call, definitely." He couldn't temper the eagerness filling his voice. "What do you say? The best place in town's the Wayfair. The cuisine's great, but we should go farther afield. Drive out of Sweet Lake, have an adventure."

"You're really asking me out?" She pushed lightly on his shoulder. "Your timing needs work."

"You felt differently three seconds ago."

"Only because your kissing ability exceeds anything I'd imagined."

The compliment nearly eroded his resolve not to take her right here on the sands. An issue no longer in play as her features tensed, altering the mood. With frustration he rose. She allowed him to guide her to her feet.

Undeterred, he asked, "Should I ask when your brother leaves?"

"*If* he leaves."

"There's nothing holding him to Ohio, not even the Wayfair." He nearly fumbled by mentioning Bryce and the upcoming surgery. "His business here concludes soon."

"I hope you're right. Even if you are, I can't have a dalliance while you're working behind enemy lines."

"A dalliance?" Planting himself in her path, he fought to maintain a light tone. "Linnie, I'm not waiting until we're old and grey. Something always gets in the way. We deserve a chance to see where this leads." He dipped his face into her hair. "Why do you always smell so good?"

On tiptoes, she brushed her nose across his. "Soap," she teased. "The miracle cure."

He felt relief when he caught her fingers and she held on. "I want to make love to you," he told her, swallowing down his pride. "We can't take our relationship backward. What we had never would've been enough. You agree, don't you?"

The query loosed a sigh from her lips. "I do. But I can't think about this until everything's back to normal. Then we'll see."

He hooked a curl behind her ear. "Not the answer I'd prefer." Moonlight caught in the vibrant depths of her eyes. Her allure was enough to have him rethinking attorney-client privilege.

Breaking the interlude, she asked, "Have an idea when Freddie will vacate my inn?"

Daniel rocked back on his heels. "Freddie's staying at the inn?"

On the inn's second floor, the thick, greenish glass of the windows caught the morning light. It was nearing lunchtime, but Freddie had yet to make an appearance. Linnie needed to muster her courage and confront him about the money.

Ignoring the work piled on her desk, she'd allowed her worries to carry her out of her office and past the Sunshine Room. The back deck was blessedly empty. She appraised the acres she owned equally with her brother. Opportunity had spilled all of this at her feet. Once she'd despised the gift, viewing it like a millstone.

Was opportunity visiting her life once more?

Clasping the deck's railing, she let the memory of Daniel's kiss glide through her senses. He'd waited for opportunity, a vexing spirit, to reveal the proper time to begin a courtship. He wanted to start now, but she needed to resolve the problems with her brother first. How to do so wasn't entirely obvious.

"Miss Wayfair?"

She shook off her musings. "Daisy. Hello." The bubbly maid wasn't in uniform. "Coming in for your shift?"

"I'm off today." The girl fussed with her hair. "Mind if I ask you something?"

"Go ahead."

"Is your brother filming in Ohio? I played Juliet in high school. My biggest role—so far, anyway." She toyed with the buttons of her ivory blouse. "If he's hiring, I'd love to audition. Can I try out for a small role? I'll work hard."

"I'm sure you were wonderful in your high school play." Needing to let the girl down gently, she added, "Unfortunately, you'll have to wait for your screen test. My brother isn't filming here. In fact, he's leaving soon."

"You're sure?"

"I hope so."

Disappointment framed Daisy's mouth. "I guess the Sirens are out of luck too. They just went up to his room. I thought they were here to audition—"

Linnie never heard the rest. She sprinted from the deck.

The Sirens weren't here to audition. They'd come for blood.

Chapter 9

Frances opened her arms wide in a failed attempt to block the stamped-ing women.

She'd been trying to cool tempers since last night's meeting for battle planning at Silvia's house. During the intervening hours, she'd begged and cajoled, and spoken with most of the Sirens personally. Although a heartening number of the women had agreed not to come, the others remained firmly in Silvia's camp.

Deaf to her plea, Silvia charged toward the suite. Her warrior's cry echoed down the corridor. Frances risked whiplash as her attention ranged down the corridor then up again, taking in the doors to the other guest rooms. Thankfully none flew open. On such a temperate summer day, Linnie's guests were already down at the beach.

Her relief switched to shock as the others pushed her aside.

She careened into the wall. "This is no way to conduct ourselves!"

Her objection merely quickened their strides.

The cluster of simmering women invaded the suite. They were met by the orange-haired girl in Freddie's entourage. She let out a high-pitched shriek that went right through Frances's molars. Cradling her jaw, she heard something crash to the floor.

She rushed in, an unwilling witness to a skirmish of the mentally unhinged.

Splitting into two groups, her comrades wrested the tactical advantage from Freddie and his startled minions. Desperate for escape, the besieged filmmaker jogged left, then right. Frances nearly pitied him as awareness of his impending capture rippled across his face.

Then he made the foolish decision to leap onto the four-poster bed. A cheer went up as a group of Sirens cornered him.

They began poking at his feet with sticks artfully decorated with silver glitter and gold paint. Tiny sleigh bells hung from the glitzy weapons—a pièce de résistance Silvia had insisted they add during the late-night meeting. By midnight the Mendoza kitchen was a mess of glitter and wax, and Frances had given up on talking Silvia out of the plan.

Now the bells jingled with fury as Freddie attempted to bat the women away. Distressed by the melee, Frances pressed her hand to her heart.

Penelope Riddle, in her haste to reach the bed, bumped into her angry general. Silvia's left shoe rocketed high into the air. It landed out of sight with a bang as Penelope threw the upper half of her body across the bedspread. Heaving and grunting, she lunged unsuccessfully for Freddie's legs.

Beneath her skirt, something popped. She froze, belly down.

At the other end of the lavishly appointed suite, the second group cornered his bodyguards. Sirens pelted their quarry with herbs fashioned into waxy, pea-size balls. Despite her disgust at the Sirens' lack of decorum, Frances silently gave Silvia points for ingenuity. She'd melted the bars of wax with a jug of honey, making the balls easy to mold and rather sticky. They also smelled good. After Frances gave up on bringing Silvia to her senses, she couldn't resist tossing in a handful of peppermint.

Not that the men under attack seemed delighted with the scent. They shrank back with fear. A waxy bullet went astray, hitting a slender woman partially hidden behind the drapes. She gave out a bloodcurdling scream.

The evidence of her terror galvanized the giant oafs. Grabbing her, they fled into the corridor. Freddie's assistant with the snippy disposition, Miss Orange Hair, shot out behind the others.

They'd barely gone when Linnie rushed into the suite. "What is going on in here?" She slammed the door behind them.

Her appearance froze the angry warriors. Briefly Frances closed her eyes to concentrate on bringing her blood pressure back within normal limits. She opened them in time to glimpse Silvia pushing her way to the front of the crowd, the stick in her fist jangling.

Frances said, "Cool your jets, Silvia. Haven't you engaged in enough silliness for one day?"

At the criticism, Silvia slashed her stick through the air. "Why did you come? You ought to side with us."

"I *am* on your side. I just want you to calm down."

"No way. We let sleeping dogs lie before Treat and Sarah left Sweet Lake for retirement. They're gone now, and he shouldn't have come back."

"It's unlikely he returned with the intention of bringing you to full froth." Seven years gone, and Silvia continued to view the video as a personal affront.

From atop the mattress, Freddie piped up. "Thank you for pointing out the obvious, Frances. I never meant to inflame Silvia by posting the video on YouTube."

"Don't mistake my words, young man." She regarded him with disgust. "I'm not defending you."

On a corner of the bed, Penelope flailed helplessly. Her muffled cries brought statuesque Norah Webb forward, allowing Frances to snatch the jingling weapon from her fist. Together they hefted Penelope to her feet. The quivering Siren's lacy slip hung askew. She began whimpering, and Frances whispered soothing words. If this nonsense went much further, they'd all surrender the last of their dignity.

Having calmed her embarrassed comrade, Frances wheeled on the others. "We're Sirens, not hooligans. All of you *will* stop this insanity at once." Linnie glanced at her with gratitude, but Silvia muttered choice words. "Silvia—you too. We're all furious with Freddie, but we don't wish him harm. At least not in the physical realm." On the spiritual plane, he'd get his comeuppance in good time.

"Speak for yourself." Reaching across the bed, Silvia made a clumsy jab at his ankles. He leapt out of range, banging into the headboard. "The video has been out for years. I shudder to think how many people have viewed it."

"Your faces were blurred. Your anonymity is safe."

"What about the damage to my psyche?" She made another jab at her quarry.

With desperation Freddie looked to his sister. "Send them away!" He appeared convinced his attackers would draw blood, and the sticks *were* sharp. "I can't abide having my room overrun by unhinged women."

A grin threatened to overtake Linnie's mouth. "Your video, your problem."

"That was ages ago!"

"Doesn't mean they forgive you."

"Of all the—my YouTube fame is long past. Get them out of here!"

Penelope's raspy breaths accented his protests. Frances regarded the poor woman, slouching against the wall. A pity about her damaged slip—she'd dressed stylishly for battle in an emerald-green dress and fake pearls.

Steering her into a chair, Frances broke into the argument. "Freddie, I have a solution," she said, recalling the superb idea she'd mulled over this morning. "Thanks to your YouTube fame, you received the funding to launch your film company."

"Debatable, but what's your point?"

"The Sirens are in no small way responsible for your success. Give some thought to the prospect of bad karma following you around for the rest of your life. No different than physics, if you catch my meaning. Every action brings a reaction, especially on the spiritual plane."

Freddie bristled. "Frances, I do believe the hounds of senility are baying at your window. What are you trying to say?"

"Give us a cut of your next picture," she said, relishing the surprise leaping onto his face. "Bad karma's a bitch. I advise you to steer clear."

From behind her spectacles, Penelope blinked rapidly. "He'll give us money?"

Freddie wheezed an indignant breath. "I'll do nothing of the sort."

"If you don't, I shall wash my hands of this affair," Frances replied, lacing her voice with venom.

"Idle threats."

"In lieu of today's attack, my comrades were thinking about slathering your body with honey and hog-tying you in the woods. It *is* summer. They would've hung you upside down by the biggest wasp's nest in the area." A tall tale if there ever was one, and she experienced delight when the scoundrel's eyes widened. "Care to guess who talked them out of the plan?"

Beside her, Silvia stomped her unclad foot. "What good is money? I want my breasts rescued from cyberspace!"

Freddie gave a pitying look. "Perhaps we *should* discuss a payout."

"A payout for our pain and suffering—and you'll also repay your sister," Frances replied. "She's waited ages for you to make amends."

"Sounds great," Linnie agreed.

He hopped off the bed, taking care to keep his distance. "I suppose it is time to settle my debts." Even in boxer shorts and an Ohio State jersey, his loose-limbed beauty drew appreciative glances from the few Sirens who still had working ovaries.

Tilda especially was entranced. Pointedly Frances cleared her throat, and the realtor pulled her attention from Freddie.

His sister sent him a cynical glance. "You're back in Ohio to settle old debts? Talk about a first."

"New debts, old debts, and one especially poignant debt," he supplied, and Frances wondered at his meaning.

"I don't believe you."

"As if anyone ever does." He pulled on a purple robe luxurious enough for royalty. "The most misunderstood hero of my generation."

Silvia fished around in the pocket of her blazer. "You're nobody's hero," she informed him. "You're a demon. Go back to hell. Leave Sweet Lake in peace."

"Why is everyone intent on booting me out?"

She tossed a handful of foul-smelling herbs at his feet. "You need to ask?"

"Fine, Silvia. I'll leave Sweet Lake in obscurity. Are you satisfied?"

"Not even a little."

Frances steered her temperamental comrade aside. There were more lucrative ways for him to make amends.

"Three percent will do the trick," she told him.

"What?"

"You'll pay the Sirens gross points on your next film. Three percent." The money wouldn't mollify Silvia, but some of the women lived from one paycheck to the next. Frances had never experienced the lack of money, but she despised how a deficit of funds weighed on the others. Satisfied with her quick thinking, she added, "The time has come to settle up, young man."

"Are you deranged? I'll do nothing of the sort!"

"You'll also grant us access to all financials, pre- and post-production. Keeping an eye on the books is the only way to stop you from monkey business."

Freddie looked at her with disbelief. "You're demanding access to *all* financials?"

"You'll put our agreement in writing." The thrill of conquest squared her shoulders.

"What about my breasts?" Silvia, hunting for her missing shoe, looked up with outrage. "They're worth infinitely more than money. Why, they're out there floating around in cyberspace."

In vain Frances searched for her patience. "Silvia, you're sixty-five. I'll wager your breasts have *not* found their way to a porn site."

Freddie shooed the twittering flock toward the door. "Frances, I'll have Daniel draw up the papers you require. Now, if you lovely women don't mind, I must dress. I have an online meeting with my crew in less than an hour."

Mildly pacified, the women shuffled out. The door clicked shut behind them.

Linnie studied him closely. "Will you keep your promise to Silvia and leave? I'm partial to Sweet Lake's obscurity."

"She didn't press for an exact date."

"Freddie—"

"I'll leave, all right? Not soon, however. Circumstances force me to stay longer."

The news was disheartening. "You'll continue staying at my inn?" A vision of all-night frat parties jarred her temples.

"*Our* inn." He reached for the pack of cigarettes on the antique bureau, lit one. Smoke curled around his head. "As for the other matter? If you're about to ask, don't bother."

The implication was obvious. "I'm not asking," she said, pouring steel into her jelly spine. The effort wicked the moisture from her mouth, but she soldiered on. "I'm telling you to do the right thing."

"As if I'd know how."

"Then make this the first. Sell your shares of the Wayfair. I'll pay—gladly."

On a smirk, he nodded at her cheap dress and old pumps. "From the looks of it, you're barely earning enough to keep the lights on. Do you equip guests with flashlights when you hand out room keys?"

"I'll use the money you owe me and talk to the bank about a loan. If that doesn't cover the price of your shares, I'll borrow the rest from friends." An embarrassing prospect, but she *was* desperate.

He waltzed toward the sitting room trailing plumes of smoke. Putting her anger in a fist hold, she followed.

"Here's a novel idea," she said, taking care to blunt the anger in her voice. "Let's try five minutes of the truth. I'm sure you're unfamiliar with the game, but you might like it." She paused for effect. "Why did you come back?"

"Linnie, we were never close. I'm not about to share the reason for my visit."

"You aren't here to patch things up?" she asked, hating the hopeful notes in her voice.

He exhaled a stream of smoke. "Why bother? Your opinion of me is apparent."

"Have you at least apologized to Mom and Dad?"

"How original." He crushed the cigarette in the ashtray by his elbow. "Some advice, Sugarpop. If you and Daniel insist on working the same script, don't use the same lines."

"Daniel asked if you'd apologized to Mom and Dad?" The revelation lent a boost to her spirits. Nice to learn he'd gone to bat for her parents.

"He stole from your script while we drove to Cleveland. Nothing like redundancy to bore the audience."

"Freddie, this isn't a film. This is real life—the place where your actions have real consequences. You took most of the operating capital from the Wayfair's accounts. Dad's stroke was just a few months later. Can't you connect the dots?" She hesitated, struck by the nervous twitch in his fingers as he lit another cigarette. Apparently the rebuke was having an impact. The prospect compelled her to ask, "Why did Daniel accompany you to Cleveland? I still have trouble believing he's working for you."

"Must you insist on asking questions I won't answer?"

"Maybe I'm crazy enough to think you'll play the honesty card for the first time in your life. Grow a conscience. People do change."

"What a curious theory." He drew heavily on the cigarette, exhaled. "I've never seen it happen. Does it involve a bunny materializing from a hat?"

"Magic isn't required, but fortitude doesn't hurt. You can't see how other people evolve since you lack the talent." If his actions hurt the rest of the family, he didn't care.

Wisps of smoke floated around his head like a nesting of grey snakes. *Purgatory,* Linnie thought with sudden insight. For reasons still hidden, he'd put himself in a netherworld of regret. He'd never change, but a private sorrow haunted his eyes.

Which led to a curious observation. A host of unknown people inhabited the world he'd built in California. If an event in his life held the power to make him uneasy, was there someone he *did* care about?

Catching her appraisal, he blew smoke rings with feigned calm. "My turn," he said. "I was under the impression you inherited all the brains. Linnie with the perfect grades and the spotless presentation. Was I mistaken?"

The reference to their childhood brought unexpected sympathy. "Oh, Freddie. There's more to life than book learning. Look at all you've achieved."

The kindness she offered merely hardened his gaze. "Poor Linnie," he mused. "You're missing the point."

"Which is?"

"Are you suffering the delusion I have the authority to sell my shares? What makes you think I can?"

Incredulity brought harsh laughter from her throat. "Gosh, I don't know. Because they're yours?"

"When Mom and Dad gifted you this wreck of a mansion, did you read the contract they sent? I assume we both received copies in the mail."

A sickly sensation pooled in her stomach. "Of course I did." In truth she'd only read the first pages.

"The entire contract? Every last section of legalese?" When she looked away, he added, "Have you discussed buying me out with our parents?"

"I will," she promised, sensing defeat. Something was wrong. The arrogance returned to her brother's eyes, a cruel glint of triumph. Too quickly, she added, "They'll back me up. I've turned the place around, proven I deserve to become the sole owner. Why wouldn't Mom and Dad agree?"

"Sugarpop, you really are a fool. What you want and what's written in the contract doesn't match." Bringing himself forward on the chaise lounge, he held her gaze like a challenge. "Rest assured, I won't take over anytime soon. I love California. Frankly, I'm happy to let you do all the work. When I retire, your time at the helm will end."

Indignation brought her to her feet. "Who's living under a delusion? I've sweated every decision needed to stop the inn from being shuttered. You left me in a terrible pinch, and I hated you—hated everything you'd dumped on me. I'll never let you take it away."

Panting, she brought the tirade to a halt. Air strained against her lungs. The room spun in nausea-inducing waves, but she managed to plant her feet. When her vision came back into focus, she discovered a cruel delight lifting the corners of Freddie's mouth.

"And to think I was joking," he murmured. "You haven't read the contract."

Nursing private thoughts, he walked to the door. With a sideways glance, he delivered the parting shot.

"We're fifty-fifty partners, Linnie," he assured her. "But only until I buy you out."

Chapter 10

Mr. Uchida placed the frosty glass of iced tea at her elbow. "Freddie will be down in a moment."

"Thank you for ringing his room." Frances nodded at the glass. "And for bringing a refreshment." Waiting on guests wasn't part of Mr. Uchida's job description, and she appreciated the kindness. After the events in Freddie's suite, she was parched.

At the front of the veranda, a couple in swimsuits knelt before their young daughter. The mother dabbed sunblock on the child while the father slipped the girl's feet into sandals. The tasks completed, the family trotted down the steps.

They left behind a welcome silence. Nestled in the veranda's far corner, Frances lifted the glass to her lips.

Her thoughts drifting, she recalled the inn during its heyday, and the town that prospered in its shadow. Until cancer took him away, her beloved Archibald had worked tirelessly mapping out new subdivisions for the homes he built, the cottage-style dwellings suitable for a tourist town and the larger homes, like the colonial where she still lived. She'd always been grateful her beautiful soul mate had ascended to a better world before tragedy struck the town.

Now, if she strolled the streets behind the circle, she witnessed disrepair, the paint peeling from dwellings her husband had lovingly erected.

Sweet Lake was dying. People talked about Linnie righting the ship, but Frances questioned their optimism. Only recently had the girl brought the inn from the brink of bankruptcy. If she faltered, if her brother got in the way, the town stood to lose more than the inn.

Freddie appeared, his hair neatly combed. He'd dressed in a navy sport coat and ivory-colored pants. Frances patted the seat beside hers on the wicker couch. He chose instead the chair opposite.

"I've agreed to your terms. What now?" He peered over the veranda at the rolling hills. "Where are the others?"

"I've sent them home," Frances assured him. "I wanted to speak to you in private."

"Why do I have the sense you're about to impart advice?"

"Because I've known you since you were in short pants, and you do need my guidance."

He crossed his legs with mild impatience. "Go on."

Happy to teach him patience, she took a dainty sip of the tea. Frustration overrode the compassion she'd always harbored for him. Such a talented soul, yet Freddie was perverse and unyielding. The spitting image of his mother, but the hardening of his mouth reminded her of Treat.

"For however long you plan to stay in Sweet Lake, I suggest you tread lightly." She took another sip of her drink, allowing the suggestion to sink in. "The Sirens aren't the only ones upset by your homecoming."

"Sweet Lake isn't my home." Freddie shifted in his chair. "Nor do I understand why anyone else is upset."

Frances stilled him with a look. "You're blind to the harm you've caused." She'd always had a soft spot for him, which put a note of compassion in her voice. "The video is a minor infraction compared to the pain you've caused many others. The inn has suffered, but not nearly as much as the people who lost their jobs. They aren't aware you're to blame. But your appearance brings up memories of a difficult time in Sweet Lake."

"A bit of an exaggeration, Frances."

"Look around. The Wayfair now employs half the original staff. Some of the people let go are still out of work, seven years on."

The observation sent his attention across the empty veranda. In his throat, his Adam's apple twitched.

He said, "I never meant to throw people out of work."

"But you did. If not for Linnie's diligence, the damage would be even greater."

She let the observation linger between them, certain her words would rouse his conscience from deep slumber. Oh, Freddie liked causing havoc and alienating the people who loved him best. He enjoyed leaving the impression he never looked back, never gave a moment's thought to the pain scattered in his wake. Frances wasn't fooled.

When it seemed he couldn't bear another second of her scrutiny, he said, "You're laying on the guilt awfully thick. Are you looking for a confession? Then yes, my actions had unintentional results."

"They still do."

"Fine—so they do. I didn't come back to force more people out of work, or whatever you think."

"I haven't a clue why you're in Sweet Lake. I would like to emphasize your need to tread carefully. Some of the old wounds haven't healed. Don't reopen them."

He squirmed like a child caught misbehaving. "What do you want from me? I can't give everyone in town points on my next movie, if you're implying as much."

She relished the first signs of conscience wavering in his expression. "I'm not," she replied.

"Thank God for small miracles. I can't fund the town. I will try to do something nice for the remaining staff before I leave."

"Good idea. I doubt your sister can afford to give raises often. Any small kindness on your part will help."

Her approval seemed to placate him, and he glanced at his watch. No doubt he wanted to bring the conversation to an end. Frances let him stew for a long minute, aware that his respect for her, an inconvenience at the moment, kept him rooted in place. During Freddie's childhood, his mother, Sarah, was among her closest friends. Back then Freddie's antics caused Sarah worry—and nosebleeds, migraines, and more than a few tears. Through it all, Frances had counseled restraint. A creative child like Freddie needed time to find his path.

On a few dreadful occasions, she'd argued with Treat about being too hard on the boy. Those disagreements never brought the intended result, and Treat continued to push his son to become something he was not.

Her bond with the family allowed her to reach beneath the hard shell of Freddie's pose. "Why do you continue tormenting your sister? She loves you. More than you think."

He laughed in derision. "On this point you're wrong."

"Withholding forgiveness isn't the same as withholding love."

"I beg to differ."

There was no reason to debate the point. While Freddie remained in Sweet Lake, the possibility existed of healing the rift.

Choosing her parting words with care, she asked, "Is that why you're pretending an interest in the Wayfair? Your sister expects your worst behavior, and you'd hate to disappoint?"

Daniel finished the call from the Devlin Institute. According to Dr. Eriksson, Bryce Reed's first appointment with the medical team had gone well. Surgery was scheduled for next week.

Daniel was still on the outs with Linnie, but at least the decision to represent Freddie was bearing fruit. Soon Bryce would regain sight in at least his right eye. Would the cornea graft take in his left? During the call, Eriksson conveyed no guarantees. The surgeon remained optimistic that his patient would regain full vision. For Daniel, the chance at full sight was enough.

He walked into the other room to share the good news with Kay.

She eyed him appraisingly. "You look absolutely buoyant," she said. "A nice change of pace. Lately you've been a study in gloom."

"I do feel good."

"Then I hope this tidbit doesn't yank you from the clouds."

"Do you mean the Stillwell divorce? I've already scheduled their first appointment." He hated divorce cases. "Duke cornered me last week in the circle. Says it's an amicable split."

"I'm not talking about the Stillwells, although I do feel sorry for them. While you were catching up on work, the Sirens stopped by. They're up in arms about Freddie."

"Tell me something I don't know."

Kay angled her chin. "All right, I will. Among other reasons for the visit, they wanted to offer moral support."

"For me, or you?"

Immediately he wished to recall the question. For Kay, obviously. From her desk she withdrew a wreath of willow branches and honeysuckle.

Placing the wreath on her head, she struck a jaunty pose. "What do you think? Do I resemble a garden nymph?"

She looked silly, an opinion not worth sharing. "I wasn't aware you'd joined the Sirens," he said. "I was under the impression you didn't condone their superstitions or late-night revelries down by the lake."

"I continue to resist their repeated invitations." Enjoying herself, Kay adjusted the wreath. "I haven't been pursued this hard since my husband slipped love letters beneath the door of my college dorm room. Quite a thrill."

The romantic suggestion quickened Daniel's blood. How much longer would he have to wait for Linnie to recognize they were already in a relationship? She wouldn't quickly forgive him for helping Freddie, but he had every intention of wearing her down. Love letters, chocolates—could he convince her to join him on a short vacation to Miami? Keeping her naked for days sure got his vote.

Voices drifted in from the reception area. Energetic barking and an impatient command followed. Evidently Philip wasn't succeeding in getting Puddles to calm down. Fancy's laughter added to the chorus.

Breaking ranks, Fancy dashed in and threw herself into Daniel's arms. Puddles, straining his leash, dragged Philip to Kay's desk. With curiosity Daniel noted the storm clouds banking in his brother's eyes.

"Bro, we need to talk." Philip took a biscuit from the jar on the desk and lofted it into the air. Puddles leapt, taking perfect aim. "Representing Freddie in whatever legal mess he's in—you should've steered clear. It's a dumb move."

"I'm not representing him in a lawsuit." Daniel gave Fancy a peck on the cheek before lowering her to the ground. "Can the public flogging wait? I'm busy."

"No, you're not," Kay put in. "Philip, he's yours for the next thirty minutes. He'll work on the contract when he gets back."

Daniel, on his knees receiving sloppy kisses from the beast, looked up with confusion. "What contract?"

"Frances and the other Sirens strong-armed Freddie into giving them a percentage of his next film. They're trusting you to ensure they get every dime coming to them."

Philip whistled softly. "Freddie's toast. Nothing more dangerous than a bunch of middle-aged women. Add wisdom to seething hormones and nobody's safe."

Daniel's estimation of the Sirens grew. "Kay, how did they pull this off?"

"They were armed."

Philip opened a drawer in her desk, handed his daughter a cookie. "Silvia owns a gun?" he asked. "I can't imagine Frances armed with anything but good manners."

Kay sniffed. "Hardly. They came at Freddie with sticks. They frightened him sufficiently to receive three percent of his next movie. Frances made the deal."

Philip looked visibly impressed. "Fill me in on the details when we get back." He glanced at Daniel with less goodwill. "C'mon. You have some explaining to do."

In the circle, the local Girl Scout troop had set up tables for face painting. They were raising money for the annual camping trip held each September. Fancy's eyes lit with excitement. Philip pressed five dollars into her palm.

"Stay where I can see you," he instructed. "I'll be at the picnic tables with Uncle Daniel."

Fancy hopped up and down. "Can Puddles come with me?"

Daniel nodded. "Don't let the Brownies paint his face. I'll never get the muck out of his fur."

She raced away with Puddles barking in pursuit.

Once they were out of earshot, Philip let the anger seep onto his face. "Why the hell are you working for Freddie? I'd guess he's blackmailing you, but you don't have a dark past. What gives?"

"This isn't blackmail. I agreed to offer my services."

"Why did you agree?"

"Seemed the best way to help Linnie." His affection for her had made him rush in without full knowledge of the situation. "At the time, I didn't know he owned fifty percent of the inn. If I had, I would've played my cards differently."

"So he's manipulating you."

He thought of Bryce and the chance for regained eyesight. "Even if Freddie is using me for some other purpose, I don't regret the decision. The matter I'm handling on his behalf . . . he's doing something good."

"Freddie's bad news. He's incapable of doing anything good."

"Normally I'd agree. Not this time." Across the circle, Fancy perched on a stool. One of the Girl Scouts dabbed eye shadow on her lids. "Don't ask for the specifics. Freddie is helping someone—and the help *is* needed."

His brother absorbed the vague explanation with impatience. "Assuming I buy your story, which I don't, what about Linnie? You're good friends. How's she taking the news you're handling legal work for her brother?"

Suddenly drained, Daniel took a seat at the nearest picnic table. Under different circumstances, the comment would amuse. After all these years, his brother still didn't understand the true nature of his feelings for Linnie. Did the rest of Sweet Lake also believe he viewed her as merely a friend? Surely not Jada or Cat. At times Daniel caught them regarding him with pity and sweet understanding.

"Linnie's angry," he admitted. Philip prepared to hurl another volley, and he held up his hand. "Hold on, will you? I can't reveal my business with Freddie. I will tell you this much. I'm working in trade. He promised to return the money if I handled the other matter."

"You take care of a legal matter, and he pays her back?"

"She'll have all the money soon." At the doubt lowering Philip's brows, he added, "I wrote an airtight contract, which he signed without hesitation. If he reneges on the deal, I'll go after Bad Seed Productions. Believe me, I'll win."

"She knows about the deal you've struck?"

"Freddie insisted on complete secrecy."

"That's great. Have you guessed *why* he doesn't want her clued in? What better way to drive a wedge in your friendship—a permanent wedge. By the time she discovers what's really going on, she might never forgive you." Philip released a hollow laugh. "I have to give Freddie points. He's manipulated you perfectly."

Daniel resisted the cynical analysis. "You're reading too much into this," he shot back, worried by his brother's prediction. If the present situation destroyed his chances with Linnie, he'd never forgive himself. "What does he gain by driving a wedge between me and Linnie?"

"Don't waste your time searching for a plausible reason." His brother kicked a stone hidden in the grass, his frustration palpable. "Freddie enjoys making trouble. Plain and simple. It's what unhappy people do."

Daniel began arguing the point. His voice died as his attention strayed across the street.

Freddie stepped out of the law office with two large men. Apparently Kay had explained where to find her employer. Leaving his bodyguards standing before the office like a wall of muscle, he weaved through traffic to reach the circle.

"Philip, what an unpleasant surprise." He motioned to the men. "Don't try anything funny. I've brought protection."

Beneath his breath, Philip muttered, "Wimp."

"Don't you have some dirt to dig? Please leave."

Philip curled his fingers into fists. "Care to make me?"

Daniel blocked his brother from approaching. "Who are they? Linebackers for the Cleveland Browns?" He did a second take. Each man held a box in his arms.

"They're bodyguards from a firm in Columbus."

"You don't need them." He stared pointedly at his brother. "Philip is leaving."

Tension pulled the air taut. "Right." Philip's neck corded with fury.

To Daniel's relief, he marched off. Puddles raced across the grass to meet him.

Daniel was equally furious. Unlike his brother, he took care to hide the strong emotion.

A ruse no longer required as he turned on his client.

"I want the facts," he growled, "and no lies. I'm sick of being played."

Freddie's eyes rounded. "When have I lied to you?"

"The night you showed up at my house. Why didn't you mention your stake in the Wayfair?"

For a split second, Freddie seemed taken aback. "I assumed you knew." Quickly he read the consternation on Daniel's face. A malicious little smile threatened to overtake his mouth. "My parents transferred ownership years ago. Is it possible my sister failed to mention we're co-owners of the inn?"

Sick-hearted, Daniel fell back on his heels. God help him—Freddie wasn't playacting. He'd come to an obvious conclusion. There were precious few secrets between two people as close as Daniel and Linnie. Only this time, there was a secret—one too important not to share.

Freddie regarded him with false sympathy. "A word to the wise. If the woman you love doesn't share pertinent facts, turn a deaf ear to the wedding bells."

The jibe nearly ate through his composure. "If I'd known, I wouldn't have agreed to play intermediary with the Reed family," he said, forcing a level of calm into his voice. Cede to anger, and he'd give Freddie the upper hand. "What Linnie did or didn't do is immaterial. You should've laid out the facts when you requested my help."

"As if it matters now. You *are* my legal representative. I'm grateful for your services. Devlin wouldn't have scheduled Bryce's surgery so quickly without your involvement."

The compliment didn't placate him. "Will you sell your shares to Linnie? They're worthless to you."

"Will you give Philip a stake in your law firm?"

"He's no more interested in practicing law than you are in running an inn."

"Do you know what interests me?" With evident pride Freddie smoothed the lapels of his blazer. "The inn carries my family name. For over a century, a Wayfair has been at the helm. A *male* heir."

Something about his insistence didn't ring true. Why give a damn about a family legacy? Bad Seed Productions provided the sort of income Daniel never hoped to achieve in a small town. Not that he wished to trade places. Freddie lived well, but beneath the arrogance, he seemed unhappy.

It was time to call his bluff. "Let me get this straight. You're planning to close your film studio to claim your inheritance? Not much of a trade-off."

Freddie stared at him as placidly as a sphinx. "My ambitions are my affair. Not yours, Counselor."

The attempt to arrive at his true motives proved maddening. Philip was correct. Freddie's actions weren't governed by logic. He resembled a disenchanted teenager driven to foment chaos at every opportunity.

Daniel inked his voice with deadly calm. "Then let me disclose my ambitions. You won't gain control of the inn. Not now, not ever. Linnie will fight you—with my help. We'll drag you through so many lawsuits you'll end up making schlock movies from inside Ohio courtrooms. Better tell your crew in California to carry on without you. They won't be seeing much of the boss."

"How chivalrous. Ready to defend my sister's honor at the slightest provocation. Are you vying for sainthood?"

Freddie wasn't about to give up a lucrative film studio to carry on the family tradition. He'd implied as much. He *did* relish the distress he caused Linnie. If she believed he was intent on gaining control, the narrow confidence she'd recently mastered would disappear like mist.

Another consideration? A man who'd amassed wealth might easily crave more. Greed fired the ambitions of many rich men. Was this a simple grab for more cash? Unsure of the true motive, Daniel silently tallied his personal assets.

"How's this? I'll buy you out," he said, naming a price. If the offer put Linnie in the clear, he'd gladly make the sacrifice. "Give me several days. I'll put the cash together before the week's out."

Freddie blinked. "You're serious."

"Of course."

"Assuming I could sell, what would you do with the shares?"

The answer was simple. "Gift them to Linnie."

More blinking, and the muscles in Freddie's throat worked. Softly he said, "You do love my sister."

With all my heart. Daniel said, "Do we have a deal?"

"We do not." Despite the refusal, Freddie's gaze lost its dull sheen of arrogance. Rallying, he doused his voice with acid. "I must admit I'm impressed. Saint Daniel, alive and well in small-town USA."

"Go to hell."

"In time." He peered across the circle to the men he'd left crisping in the sun. "The contract you insisted I sign? I've fulfilled my obligation."

"You wired the ten thousand?" It was the good faith deposit on the money owed.

Freddie smiled. "Even better."

Chapter 11

Jada's expression required no interpretation. She thought Linnie was a shoo-in for dunce of the year.

They were locked together inside Linnie's office with the contract spread out between them. Ten pages in length, it was written in dense legalese by the Gaylord & Simms law firm of Tampa.

"I just don't get it," Jada muttered. "You signed this years ago. Who signs without reading the entire document? Granted, you weren't very organized back then. But you've had your act together for a long time now."

"I meant to dig through this a million times," Linnie hedged, reaching for another slice of German chocolate cake. Count on the thoughtful Jada to bring dessert to a secret meeting.

Jada slapped her hand away. "Why didn't you read every last sentence?"

"Give me a break. I've been pulling seventy-hour workweeks since my twenties. Haven't you ever put something off long enough to forget the task entirely?"

"Not a contract forcing me to share half my life's work with my deadbeat brother!"

"Well, I was hurt. I wasn't sure I could keep the Wayfair from going under. Brooding over my parents' decision made me so depressed, I wanted to give up. The better solution? Forget about the contract and hope Freddie stayed in California forever."

"So you tossed the contract into a drawer? That's about as dumb as it gets."

"C'mon, Jada. I didn't know about the clause. Besides, Freddie was long gone. No one thought he'd ever come back. I didn't think he'd show the slightest interest in claiming his stake. Why would he? Bad Seed Productions is a rousing success. He's built a new life in San Fernando on the backs of weird aliens from strange planets and vampires jumping into time machines."

"Has he demanded a salary?"

Linnie's stomach clenched. "Can he?"

Jada's ebony gaze flashed. "Gee, I don't know. Check the contract to find out."

"You and I would never take advantage of a hardworking sib, but Freddie's made of weaker metal. He's aluminum—no." Linnie stared longingly at the cake. "He's from another section of the periodic table. Rubber, maybe."

"Rubber isn't on the periodic table. Shut up. I'm reading."

"Not anymore. Give me the contract." She took the pages and dug in.

Freed of the task, Jada stared absently into space. "There's always greed. Maybe Freddie's itchin' for a new thrill."

"Shut up. I'm reading."

"Hurry up, pokey."

Turning to page seven, Linnie slowly gleaned the contents. Nearing the bottom of the page, she said, "Nothing here states he must work at the inn. Assuming I understand this correctly, he *can* demand compensation." Her stomach did a nasty flip. If forced to pay a monthly stipend, there was no choice but to fire someone on staff. "I don't care if greed holds the allure of ten bimbos trailing after him on a Friday night. If he asks, I'll refuse." The prospect of putting any of her employees out of work was unthinkable.

"Talk to Daniel. He'll find a solution."

"No can do."

"Why not?"

"Whenever I run into him lately, I end up in his arms. I'd blame Daniel, but I've been using the same tricks on him." She studied her palms. "Do I have blisters on my hands? I like playing with fire."

The disclosure nabbed Jada's complete attention. "Gosh, Linnie. I can think of worse fates than falling in love." Mischief twinkled in her eyes. "How far have you taken this? I won't use baseball metaphors, but you know what I mean."

"Not *that* far."

"What's stopping you?"

A list of reasons came immediately to mind. "For starters, I wasn't prepared for my feelings to deepen this quickly. I've been independent for a long time. It's scary to discover how much I need Daniel. Then there's the inn, which consumes my days. How can I fit a romance into the agenda? And let's not forget the issue of Daniel representing my brother. I wish he'd sought my approval before choosing to help Freddie out. Too late now, but a heads-up would've been nice."

"You don't think their business involves the Wayfair, do you?"

"No, there's another reason for Freddie's visit." She recalled his puzzling comment about paying karmic debts. "Whatever drew him back to Ohio doesn't relate to the family business. I have the sense . . . well, that he felt obligated to come back. If he feels an obligation, he cares about someone. Which would be a first. Besides, Daniel is too decent to get involved in something underhanded. He must believe Freddie is doing something good."

Jada smiled encouragingly. "Looks like you're running out of excuses to put a damper on romance with Mr. Perfect."

Count on Jada to tap into her deepest feelings. For decades now, she'd been Linnie's touchstone.

The first time Linnie met the woman destined to become her best friend she'd cartwheeled from the swing set during the third graders' recess, landing face down in the grass. Children flocked around her, laughing at her. Jada, newly arrived to Sweet Lake, pushed everyone back.

Crouching beside Linnie, she'd said, "Don't let them see you cry. I fall down too. I get right back up."

The fond memory of a childhood lesson in courage urged Linnie to admit, "Coming up with a dozen excuses is a lot easier than the alternative. The truth? I'm not sure I'm ready for the type of relationship Daniel has in mind."

"He *is* playing for keeps."

"How does that work? We marry, have a family?" Agitated, she rose from the table. Cutting a path across the Persian carpet, she considered the challenges she'd faced since her parents moved to Florida. "Don't get me wrong. I want all the white-picket-fence dreams. But I was so angry when everything went south and I was forced to take charge. Now? I've fallen in love with the ghosts whispering through the rooms and the creaky old floorboards. I love every block of sandstone my ancestors dug from the fields to build this place."

Jada's eyes softened with understanding. "Who says you can't have a successful business and the perfect marriage?"

"I can—someday. Not now." She paused at the bay window overlooking the incline of lawn and a section of the beach. A glorious June day, and guests were out on the sands. Others swam in the lake with their children, carefree vacationers without a worry to burden them. "How can I expect Daniel to understand we'll need to take it slow? If we go too far, too fast, we'll consummate our relationship."

"Serious relationships *do* become intimate. What's the big deal?"

"If I take our relationship to the next level, he'll start talking about marriage. He'll beg me to set a date in a matter of months. We're not kids. He's been waiting a long time."

"Stop jumping to conclusions. Why not talk to him?"

An option she'd considered then discarded just as quickly. Was there anything worth saying that wouldn't hurt him? Or come across as holding him at arm's length—which she didn't want to do.

"If we have a sit-down, he'll get the impression I care more about my job than him. He'll think I'm drumming up excuses or that I'm too invested in the Wayfair to give romance a fair shot." An ache of longing centered in her chest, but she forced herself on. "I do care about him. Deeply. I've never felt this way about a man before."

"Then give him the benefit of the doubt. We've all seen how hard you've worked to save the inn. Everyone wants you to succeed, Daniel included. He won't rush you."

"He'll agree to hold off on marriage?"

"If you set a reasonable timeline."

On a wave of hope, she returned to her chair. "Two years before we discuss forevers? We'll have the inn on sure footing by then."

"I'm sure he'll understand."

Drawing the discussion to a close, Linnie flipped to the contract's next page. Her eyes landed on the first paragraph. "Jada, check this out."

"What is it?"

"This is unbelievable." Her mood plummeting, Linnie ran her finger beneath the offensive section. "Freddie can buy *me* out. He must wait until we're both in our fifties, but he can force me to sell."

"*What?*"

Linnie read the paragraph with her hopes deflating. "This can't be right. Why would my parents force me to sell? Why let me assume control just to take it all away later on?"

"Hey, it's all right. You're only thirty-two. This portion of the contract won't become active for nearly twenty years."

"There's an 'out' clause?"

Jada's expression darkened. "More like a noose. The next section states if either you or Freddie don't abide by the contract's stipulations, the shares in question revert to the trust of Treat and Sarah Wayfair. The executor of the trust will then decide whether to gift the shares to the other sibling or sell them in a public offering."

The trapdoor beneath Linnie's world popped back open. "This *is* a noose," she moaned. "I'm ruined."

"There's time to fix this."

"How?"

"Look at the contract's date. This was written right after your Dad's stroke."

Catching on, she straightened in her chair. "Right after his stroke . . . when I wasn't thrilled about having the Wayfair dropped in my lap."

"Which you made patently clear. How many times did you call Florida pleading with your parents to sell the place? Freddie hadn't been gone very long. Your parents might have thought they'd lure him back to Ohio if they gave him half of the inn with a guarantee of becoming sole owner later on."

The theory had merit. "They *did* want him to come home."

"Talk to your parents. Freddie's back on good terms with them. Can't they sway him to let you buy *his* shares? With luck, he'll agree to a buyout over a reasonable amount of time—say, ten years."

Although the suggestion was sound, the familiar doubt surfaced. "You're assuming I *can* sway my parents. I can't recall one instance when I pushed for what I wanted. Cat's right—I'm gutless. I'm a lightweight, and my parents steamroll right over me." She pushed the contract away. "They want Freddie to own the inn. Not today or tomorrow, but eventually. That dumb tradition of leaving a man in charge. It's right there, in black and white."

"Situations change. They wanted him to take over when they drew up the contract. Look at all you've accomplished. Thanks to you, the inn *is* solvent."

"Barely. We won't see big profits until we reopen the south wing to guests. We have too many rooms sitting empty."

"At some point, we will open the south wing and the rest of the rooms in the main building. Think about it. If your parents had waited to write the contract, why wouldn't they have given it all to you? They drew this up when you were upset about being left in charge. Freddie hadn't been gone very long. They probably thought filmmaking was another one of his larks. They assumed he'd grow bored with it and come home."

"He didn't," Linnie supplied.

"No, he didn't."

"And I stuck around, made a go at running the inn."

"You've proven you deserve to own the place."

Was the observation correct? In the deepest part of her soul, Linnie wanted to believe. In the past, the inn passed from one male heir to the next because no daughters were born into the family. She was the first. She'd proven her qualifications, and her parents were enlightened people. If they supported her desire to become the inn's sole owner?

They'd convince Freddie to return his stake to the trust.

For the next two days, she searched for ways to force her brother out of the picture. Blackmail? She didn't have the funds. Open threats? She didn't have the heart. No matter how she chose to confront him, her actions were sure to dissolve the fragile ties of affection in her family. Even if he relinquished his shares to the trust, there was no guarantee her parents would give her sole ownership. Not if she hurt their precious son in the process.

Linnie was still ruminating on a solution when her cell phone buzzed. "Are you busy?" Daniel asked.

"Always." Completing the week's payroll, she pushed the ledger across her desk.

"Drop whatever you're doing," he remarked in an oddly jubilant tone. "Stop by my office. I have great news."

Mystified, she reached for her purse. "You've found a way to evict Freddie from Sweet Lake?"

"Just get down here. You won't be sorry you stopped by."

Two boxes, meant to hold bottles of Canadian whiskey, held a place of prominence on Daniel's desk.

"They're from your brother," he told Linnie. To spare her feelings, he added, "Leave it to Freddie to come up with a childish prank. We'll all be in the grave before he reaches anything resembling emotional maturity."

"Tell your client I already have a liquor supplier."

Fortunately she didn't follow the retort with a look of thunder. In fact, she seemed incapable of looking directly at him. Whenever her hazel eyes strayed in his general direction, spots of color warmed her cheeks. Daniel's body gave an eager response to her pretty flush of arousal.

If the pheromones building in the room got out of hand, he'd ask Kay for a bucket of ice water. He'd excuse himself and go soak his head.

He found the presence of mind to say, "Go on. Open them."

Peering inside the first box, Linnie released a startled breath. Dazed, she withdrew a pack of one-hundred-dollar bills from the top of the stack.

"I instructed Freddie to wire the money into an account I opened at Ohio Republic," he explained as she ran her thumb down the crisp banknotes. "Obviously he thought this was a more amusing idea."

"Is this . . . ?"

"I've counted each box. This represents everything he took from the inn plus interest. There's an additional twenty thousand. If I were you, I'd regard the extra cash as restitution for pain and suffering. If anyone paid for his reckless behavior, you did."

At last, she looked at him directly. "How did all this money arrive? Pony express?"

"I can't speculate. Your eccentric brother may have stashed greenbacks in his carry-on luggage."

"Wouldn't a wire transfer have been easier?"

"But not nearly dramatic enough." Daniel chuckled. "Freddie should run the trapeze act under the big top."

"When he was a kid, he *did* talk about running away with the circus."

"Will you accept the money? I don't keep a Glock in the office. We should ferry this over to the bank."

"Tell your client to haul the cash back to California." She returned the packet of bank notes to the box. "I want his shares of the Wayfair instead. If he's willing to sell, I'm sure my parents will bless the deal."

The announcement gave Daniel pause. "The shares aren't for sale," he replied, hating to disappoint her.

"You're not a mind reader. There's no harm in asking."

"I'm way ahead of you." Regret sifted through him. "Unfortunately."

"What do you mean?"

Succumbing to the urge, he came around the desk. "I've already made the offer." He declined to add he would've gladly paid for the shares personally. Hooking a tendril of hair behind her ear, he added, "I'm sorry, Linnie. Freddie won't sell his stake."

The apology sank into the heavy silence overtaking the office. Her attention lifted past his shoulder to a point that didn't exist. He nearly heard the gears shifting in her head, bringing her to the obvious conclusion. Air tightened his lungs when she finally spoke.

"The money . . . is this why you agreed to handle the mysterious legal work? Freddie pays me back in trade for your help on another matter?"

Torn between regret and relief, he nodded. Then regret took prominence as she removed his roving fingers from her hair. She clasped his hand loosely, her attention lifting to range across his face. Did she view his trade in a positive or a negative light? The signals flashing across her features came too quickly to assess with any certainty, which left him in a miserable state of confusion.

He'd only wanted to protect her. He'd never stopped to consider if Freddie was manipulating them both.

He said, "You're under no obligation to use the money for upkeep or to refurbish the inn." Tightening his grip on her cold fingers, he brought her closer. "You've been the general manager for seven years now. In all that time, have you paid yourself a decent wage?"

"Paying the staff, taking care of my parents—I make less than anyone else."

"Which is reason enough to put a portion of the money into a private account. Or all of it. Freddie has no legal recourse to stop you."

"I can't. There's so much to do. The longer a portion of the inn remains shuttered, the harder it'll be to refurbish later. Have you seen the carpeting in the rooms still in use? Threadbare in places—and what about the lobby? A fresh coat of paint would do wonders."

"What if your rush to make improvements plays directly into your brother's hands? Until now, he's owned fifty percent of a struggling enterprise. Your interests are best served by waiting to start improvements."

"I'm not waiting."

"Linnie, don't behave rashly. It's not like you."

"You're asking me to sit by while my family legacy falls into decrepitude." She stared at him stubbornly.

Obviously she wouldn't back down. "If you're determined to proceed, I should take another shot at persuading him to sell out," he suggested.

"You said he's already turned down your offer."

Clasping the threads of his patience, he kept a purchase on her fingers. "Humor me," he said, brandishing a smile. "If I can't get Freddie to see reason, so what? Let me take the shot."

"What's the use? My brother is self-centered, but he's only trying to respect our parents' wishes." She released a heavy sigh before adding, "Daniel, there's something else. Jada made me read the entire contract. We found a clause I should've known about long ago."

With growing anger he listened as she described the stipulation allowing Freddie to buy her out once they'd both reached their fifties. Her stake in the inn would revert to her irresponsible brother.

He liked Treat and Sarah Wayfair. Overall, they were fine people. Yet they'd put their daughter in an untenable situation. Although they viewed their son as a disappointment, they favored him. No amount of sacrifice or hard work on Linnie's part would alter the equation.

Doubtful Linnie grasped her brother's preferential treatment. She wasn't petty, the type of person to keep a scorecard.

Confident he'd do a better job championing her rights, Daniel said, "Contract negotiations, especially between family members, can get pretty dicey. There's always the chance of hurt feelings or saying something you'll wish you could take back later. I should talk to Freddie. I'll make a cash offer to buy him out."

Immediately she dismissed the idea. "Even with a bank loan and the money he's returned, I can't pay in full immediately. I'll need to make payments."

"No, you won't."

Her shoulders lifted to her ears, an indication of her eroding confidence. "There isn't a mountain of cash hidden in a forgotten vault inside the Wayfair," she sputtered.

Fully aware she'd view a gift as an insult, he treaded carefully. "I'm honored to loan you the money. Pay me back whenever you'd like." An elegant solution—after he won her over, he'd insist the money was a gift.

The offer quieted her expression. "Still trying to protect me?" She rested her palm on the side of his face.

The softness of her touch made his voice hoarse. "I'll always keep you safe, Linnie." Angling his neck, he brushed his mouth across hers.

A hypnotic gravity drew her closer. Once he captured her in his orbit, he longed to take her mouth fully. An unwelcome sixth sense warned him to hold back. Briefly she closed her eyes.

When she opened them, he glimpsed a world of sadness. "You can't protect me, not this time," she whispered against his lips. "This *is* a family matter. It's time I stood up for what's mine. Spineless and scared is no way to go through life."

Her pupils, huge and black, fastened on him. A gratifying discovery—she wasn't immune to their growing attraction. The moment unfurled like a ribbon on the wind. Finally she moved out of his arms. The distance she put between them came at a heavy cost to his heart.

She cast a sidelong glance, searching his face for the answers he yearned to give.

In an admirably neutral tone, she added, "I'll talk to my parents, ask them to reconsider. If they intervene, Freddie will sell."

Intuition warned she'd be sorely disappointed. The Wayfairs were careful people. They wouldn't alter the inheritance.

"Why don't we speak to them together?" he suggested. "I'll fly down to Florida with you."

"I can't do this in person, not with Freddie sticking around. We'll sort this out on the phone." The barest hint of amusement danced in her eyes. "Besides, it's not a good idea to travel with you. All things considered."

"Because I'd make good use of our time alone?"

"We'd both make good use of the time."

The bold statement sent elation winging through his chest. "Is that the first positive remark you've made about our relationship? Could be."

A tentative smile glossed her lips. "This is like driving without GPS."

"I'll guide you."

The conviction in his voice returned her eyes to his. At her waist, her fingers worked in a sudden display of nerves.

Rushing headlong, she said, "Daniel, this is nothing like relationships when we were kids. Most of the boys I dated? I chose them based on my parents' disapproval. The more they disapproved, the happier I was to continue a romance. My reasoning was immature, destructive. Why didn't I have more self-respect?"

"You were rebelling," he pointed out, wishing for the power to erase the past—wishing for the courage to tell her that he loved her completely and the past didn't matter. "Linnie, you have a first-rate intellect. Your parents never encouraged you to develop your gifts. I'd imagine you were bored. And angry."

"There *is* more to life than fashion and endless shopping." She shrugged. "Just don't tell my mother. She lives for Nordstrom."

"You're more like your father. Bright, driven, but without his hair-trigger temper. You inherited the best parts of his personality. Why spend so much time doubting yourself?" A lesson, he mused, he also needed to learn, at least when it came to winning her over. Nearing, he added, "You aren't spineless. You were born into a family with a history of larger-than-life men. You're an accomplished woman. If your parents fail to recognize your gifts, the problem is theirs, not yours."

The softly issued compliments seemed a burden. Tears welled in her eyes.

Impetuously, he asked, "What do you think of my house?"

Sniffling, she glanced up with confusion. "Your house is nice. Why?"

Running his thumbs beneath her eyes, he collected the tears. "Should we sell it, buy something larger? Don't ask me to move into the south wing. Jada and Cat may like the free digs, but we'll never get Puddles off our bed if we're camped out in a place without decent heating."

Grinning, she shook her head. "Are you planning our life together before the first date?"

"Just thinking ahead."

"Well, stop. You're intimidating."

The observation startled him. "In what way?" He viewed himself more as an oversize teddy bear.

She pushed lightly against his chest. "You're so sure about us," she replied, and he noted she'd kept her hands moving. He relished the sensation of her tentative caresses. "What if you're wrong? What if we date for two months and screw it up? Expect lots of missteps. This *is* my first serious relationship."

"And your last," he put in, bending slightly to tease her mouth with the hint of a kiss. "I'm not letting you go."

"Will you at least take it slow?"

"I'll do my best," he replied, certain he'd fail.

Her eyes strayed to the boxes. "Will you go with me to the bank?" she asked, steering them both back to earth. "Let's get the money into the Wayfair's accounts."

Chapter 12

Linnie's unpredictable brother wasn't finished with the surprises.

After toting the liquor boxes of cash to the bank with Daniel's help, she returned to find the inn abuzz with excitement. Three white vans emblazoned with the distinctive sea-green logo for Ballantine's were parked out front. From the vans a line of women carried dresses tucked inside pale-pink tissue.

Parking beside the vans, Linnie heard a shout.

Cat sprinted across the veranda. "You won't believe what your brother's doing now. He's offered to buy dresses for all of us."

The lobby rang with the excited voices of guests who were growing strangely accustomed to the unusual happenings. Behind the front desk, an overwhelmed Mr. Uchida muttered in Japanese. One of the guests, a sporty woman with a toddler on her hip, stopped the last Ballantine's clerk in the procession. The woman rooted through the dresses in the clerk's arms.

Linnie asked, "Why is my brother buying us clothing?"

"Mami thinks it has something to do with a conversation he had with Frances."

"What did they discuss?"

"Frances wouldn't give the details." Cat shrugged. "My mother is getting in touch with the rest of the Sirens. We'll all look fabulous for my parents' anniversary party."

She darted through the throng to direct the Ballantine's women up the stairwell. Linnie attempted to follow. A tap on the shoulder halted her pursuit.

She spun on her heel. Jada, picking flecks of icing from her curls, gave her a look of exasperation.

The icing dotting her hair wasn't the biggest problem. A large circle of goo stamped the front of her blouse. She looked like the victim of a food fight.

"What happened to you?" Linnie swiped her finger through the batter. "Wow. That's delish. Chocolate cake?"

Nudging Mr. Uchida out of the way, Jada hunted beneath the front desk. "It *was* chocolate cake. We're one dessert short for tonight's menu." She came back up with a rag to mop up the mess. "Our kitchen staff went berserk. I was on my way to the oven when the Ballantine's vans drove up."

"They heard about Freddie's offer?"

"Every female in sight stampeded to the lobby. I got a vision of water buffalo racing over a cliff."

Linnie's imaginary trapdoor joggled beneath her. "Wait. Cat's parents didn't invite the staff. Mostly because, you know, we need them to cook and serve."

"No, but Freddie did."

There wasn't time to digest the unsettling news. *Thump, thump, thumps* from above rattled the lobby's chandelier.

At her questioning look, Jada said, "They're in the unoccupied suite by the stairwell. Your brother turned the place into a mini department store. Bedroom, sitting room—Cat's helping with setup. Most of our female employees are up there tussling over formalwear. There'll be blood on the walls."

"No!"

Sure enough, women streamed through the suite, making grabs for dresses. The overexcited culinary staff were pushing the bed to the wall to make room for squabbles over the elegant selections. The house-keeping staff had hijacked seven or eight rolling coat racks from somewhere on the first floor. The Ballantine's saleswomen filled each rack to bursting.

Jada latched on to her arm. "Don't go inside," she advised. "You won't come out in one piece."

Linnie shook her off. "We *are* going in—after I take this up with my brother. Where does he get off raining chaos down on my establishment?" Stalking down the corridor, she threw a glance. "Are you coming or not?"

The door to Freddie's suite was locked. Inside, feminine giggling accented the rock music blaring from the stereo.

"Open up!" Linnie followed the command with fierce pounding.

With the sound of stomping feet, Freddie threw open the door to his room. His attire consisted of nothing but metallic-green boxers and a pink party hat with "Jumbo" stitched across the front in yellow lettering.

Repulsed, she stumbled backward. "Freddie, put on some clothes!"

The more levelheaded Jada took in the glam boxers and party hat with distaste. "Some people never change," she muttered.

"Jada, my fiery vixen." Leaning against the doorjamb, he gave her a look. "You're more beautiful than ever."

Linnie shoved him back inside the suite. "Put a sock in it," she growled. "The kitchen staff is *not* prepping tonight's entrees, and housekeeping has gone bonkers. How am I supposed to run this establishment with half the employees going AWOL?"

He poured champagne, then lifted the glass with celebratory glee. "What's the harm in letting them have some fun?"

"Is it true you invited the entire staff to Silvia and Marco's anniversary party? They're celebrating their fortieth with friends and family, not hosting a carnival for the town."

"How stingy of you. My sister, a modern-day Scrooge. Of course I invited everyone."

"Silvia will have you strung up and shot."

"For heeding Frances's advice? I doubt it. Besides, I'm footing the bill."

Frustration welled in Linnie. "I don't care about your generosity or what Frances advised—there's a problem. If everyone attends, who will cook, serve, and clear the tables?"

"A valid consideration."

"One that didn't cross your mind? Seeing as you're in a Mardi Gras sort of mood?"

"Never fear. I shall solve the dilemma." He regarded his orange-haired assistant. "Lexie, call the nearest temp agency. We need kitchen and waitstaff for Saturday. Don't forget to hire bartenders and a troop of busboys."

"You're not bringing in strangers to work at my inn. I don't have time to run them through interviews."

"*Our* inn."

"A stupid technicality."

"The agency will only hire qualified people." He patted her on the back with the detached sympathy of a psychiatrist. "Do you need a cookie? You really are unhinged."

"Freddie—"

"Oh, c'mon. For once, let's free the staff from dirty dishes and crabby guests. We'll give them a night to remember."

The familiar popping sound—her blood pressure skyrocketing—ratcheted through her ears. "Fine. Call a temp agency. I'll also call some of our past employees—the ones thrown out of work, thanks to you. Some of them will come through for me."

"Sounds good. If we host more events, you can hire them all back."

Maybe, but she wasn't about to give him points. "Consider this your last bright idea," she said. "Assuming Silvia doesn't mind, the staff can attend. But only because I don't want a riot on my hands."

"Is that all you have to say?"

"I'd add *leave Ohio immediately*, but I doubt you'd comply."

He smoothed the tips of his mustache. "Honestly, Sugarpop." He regarded her with feigned dismay. "Something along the lines of gratitude is in order."

Jada looked from one to the other. "What's he talking about?"

Linnie tugged her from the room. "Ask later." He meant the liquor boxes of cash, a topic not worth exploring. "Freddie, remember what I said. Keep any future generosity under wraps unless you clear it with me first."

In the spare minutes since they'd left, the department store suite had become more crowded. The place stank of a disorienting mix of perfume. In the corridor, a line of eager shoppers waited to enter.

A matron with a moon-shaped face shivered with anticipation. "A trunk show—how marvelous! My nephew's wedding is next month."

Jada bumped two girls from housekeeping from the line. "Please, go right in," she told the matron. "We're selling gowns for the bargain price of five hundred dollars each. Hurry before the best ones are taken."

The woman trotted inside. Jada blocked the tardy employees to let other guests follow.

Linnie hissed, "What are you doing?"

"Resist the urge to kill your brother. If we sell a few gowns, the money goes straight in the till. Where's the harm in profiting from his generosity?"

"Good point." Should she ask Mr. Uchida to slip announcements beneath guest room doors? From the looks of it, Freddie had ordered several hundred dresses.

They squeezed into the packed suite. In the sitting room, Daisy from housekeeping twirled in a pale-blue gown. Three members of the kitchen staff, all dressed to the nines, looked on approvingly. In the main room, the matron from the hallway stripped down to her bra and taupe slip, then directed one of the harried Ballantine's clerks toward a lavender frock. Near the windows, five waitresses from the Sunshine Room chatted animatedly in their party clothes.

One of the clerks gave Linnie and Jada an assessing glance. After searching through the racks, she came forward with two dresses.

Linnie stopped her. "Put them back," she ordered. "We're not interested."

A pained expression crossed the woman's face. "You're Mr. Wayfair's sister, aren't you?" Linnie nodded, and the woman rushed on. "We're under strict orders to fit you for the party. Do you like the red? It'll be perfect on you."

The glittery dress *was* gorgeous, but Linnie didn't care. "Tell Mr. Wayfair his sister says *no*."

"He thought you'd feel that way," the clerk replied. "If you won't accept a dress, he's asked us to leave five selections for you at the front desk. We'll also open up a personal line of credit for you at Ballantine's." Nearing, she whispered, "Please take the dress. There are other women waiting for help with their selections, and I really must get back to them."

"Fine. Go help the others." Linnie accepted the dress. She handed the gold lamé number to Jada. "And thank you."

She dragged Jada toward the bathroom.

"Out, all of you!" Jada shooed several maids from the john. She locked the door.

Linnie stepped out of her stretchy pants. "My brother is totally inconsiderate," she muttered, noting her selection appeared two sizes too small. Hopefully the fabric contained Lycra.

"Absolutely. Why would he instruct the best department store in Ohio to deliver party clothes without seeking your permission? He's turned the Wayfair into a zoo." Jada shimmied the gold lamé fabric up past her hips.

"I should call my mother, complain about Freddie." The red gown *did* have tons of give. "Why am I always afraid to talk to her?"

"She can't possibly know he's in Sweet Lake stirring up trouble."

Linnie paused before the mirrored wall separating the sink from the large whirlpool tub. "I'll fill her in. After, I'll beg her to ask him to sell his stock." The dress, cut daringly low, revealed tons of cleavage while detracting from her less-than-svelte waistline. She angled sideways for a profile view. "What do you think? I can't breathe, but who needs air?"

"Not any woman on the prowl. You're a bombshell. Wait 'til Daniel gets an eyeful."

Shivers of anticipation danced down her spine at the prospect of him glimpsing her in the skin-hugging number. "I hope he doesn't miss the party. He mentioned another trip out of town."

"More secret meetings on Freddie's behalf?" Jada threaded her arms through the spaghetti straps of her outfit. "I'd love an inkling of what's going on."

"Me too."

The night they'd met on the beach, why hadn't she pressed? The intel might give a clue to the length of Freddie's stay, not to mention the true reason for his visit.

The doorknob rattled. On the other side, Linnie found Silvia, Frances, and the effervescent Tilda Lyons. Tilda, the town's only realtor, had a penchant for texting the latest gossip, real or imagined.

Frances swept past. "Share the room, ladies. I refuse to undress in the midst of the cackling masses." In her arms, a charcoal dress with miles of taffeta rustled agreeably. "I can't wait to try this on!"

Linnie stopped her. "I heard an ugly rumor. Is it true you're behind my brother's generosity?"

The question stole the smile from the elderly Siren's face. "Are you upset? This isn't what I intended."

"What *did* you discuss?"

"I'm sorry, child. Our conversation is private."

"Gosh, Frances. You're beginning to remind me of Daniel."

Tilda edged past Silvia. "Did you hear the other news?" Latching on to Linnie's shoulders, Tilda forced her against the wall. For a woman the size of a nutcracker, the realtor possessed uncommon strength. "I'm so happy, I'll take back every insult I've ever flung your brother's way. Paying for Silvia's party and inviting your staff—what a lovely gesture!"

Linnie pulled herself free. "That's my brother, the epitome of grace."

The snarky comment went over Tilda's head. "I hope his film schedule doesn't call him away too soon. He's a perfumed breeze in the backwater of Sweet Lake." She shimmied her shoulders with glee. Then lightning appeared to strike her dizzy brain. "Should we beg him to stay the summer?"

Linnie gasped. "Are you serious?"

"Don't you think I should ask?"

Jada leapt before the realtor. "Bite your tongue," she said, "or I will."

Frances steered them apart. "Retract your fangs, Jada. We shouldn't give Freddie the key to the town, but he's done a kindness. Don't you like your gown? He's trying to make amends."

Silvia, stripping out of her capris and blouse, trembled with rage. "Are you insane? Paying for the party, agreeing to give the Sirens three percent of his next movie—it's a plot. Machiavelli couldn't beat Freddie Wayfair at deception. Mark my words. You'll all be sorry."

Frances regarded her with ill-concealed impatience. "You're a font of hypocrisy. You're letting him pay for your party *and* trying on an outfit."

"Only because it's Oscar de la Renta. How can I resist?"

"You storm his suite, and he shows kindness in return—Silvia, you're wicked to the core."

Tilda stepped between them. "Ladies, please! Can't we enjoy ourselves?"

Silvia swished her frothy gown. "Can we? I don't know, Tilda. Why don't we ask the lady of the house if she's in a celebratory mood?"

Her imperious gaze found Linnie.

"I think you're right," Linnie admitted. "Freddie's plotting my downfall." Unable to mask the despondency in her voice, she added, "I stopped by Daniel's office today and found two boxes on his desk. All the money Freddie took years ago, plus interest. There was also another twenty thou for pain and suffering."

"The bastard," Jada breathed.

Frances said, "You're mistaken. He's made some screwups, but he means well. Give him a chance. Your brother won't find his higher angels without help."

Linnie raised her shoulders to her ears. "I can't take the risk. The gifts, his sudden generosity—it's a Trojan horse. He'll wheedle his way into everyone's good graces and then strike. Daniel warned me not to use the money to fix up the inn. The more profitable the place becomes, the bigger the prize when Freddie pushes me out."

Silvia and Jada bobbed their heads in agreement. Frances pressed a hand to her throat, and Tilda sighed. Linnie peeled off the dress as second thoughts dove through her brain. Was it cruel *not* to give her brother a second chance?

Jada arched a brow. "You aren't going soft, are you? Call your parents and fix this mess. If you don't, I'll find the nearest brick. Time to knock some sense into you."

"Don't go hunting for a brick." Linnie swallowed down her doubts. "I'll make the call."

Chapter 13

The inpatient ward of the Devlin Institute hummed with subdued, orderly activity. There seemed as many nurses on staff in the world-class facility as patients recuperating in the long corridor of private rooms. The antiseptic scent Daniel associated with medical facilities was missing, and the walls boasted a cheery yellow paint. The color reminded him of Fancy, the bright strands of hair fluttering behind her whenever she raced after Puddles.

At the nurses' station, a brunette nodded in greeting.

"Has Mr. Wayfair arrived?" Daniel asked her. "We're here to see Bryce Reed. His surgery was this morning."

She typed in the name. "I'm sorry. He hasn't arrived."

Daniel glanced at his watch. Where the hell was Freddie? He'd promised to make an appearance. Bryce's surgery had gone well, and his parents were undoubtedly visiting. They expected to finally meet the benefactor responsible for their son's treatment. Disappointing them—and their son—was out of the question.

Retreating from the nurses' station, Daniel pulled out his cell.

Freddie picked up. "Ozzie, there's a limit to my patience. Are you sending the revisions or not?"

With effort, he tamped down his irritation. "Freddie, it's Daniel. I'm in Cleveland. Where are you?"

"Cleveland . . . at Devlin? How's Bryce?"

"Not sure. I'm about to go in."

"Why haven't you?"

The question was bizarre. "I'm waiting for you." Lowering his voice, he added, "I spoke with the surgeon on the drive up. The cornea transplant for the right eye looks good. Dr. Eriksson isn't sure about the left."

On the other end, the news created a heavy silence. At last Freddie said, "Bryce may lose the sight in his left eye?"

"I didn't get the impression Eriksson held out much hope."

"When will he have a firm prognosis?"

"Next week. He'll run more tests. Touch-and-go until then."

"How awful."

"Tough break for a young man." Tough break for anyone, Daniel mused, but a kid Bryce's age would take it especially hard. During their brief conversations, mention of a girlfriend never came up. Did the kid have a sweetheart, someone to reassure him if he needed a glass eye? Stowing the thought, Daniel got back on track. "All the more reason for you to put in an appearance, brighten his day. Are you still on the road?"

The offer to drive together had been refused. Freddie had mentioned stopping over in Columbus for the night. Something about a reunion with an old college buddy.

More silence, and he sensed the forming of a flimsy excuse.

"I never made it to Columbus. Obviously, Cleveland is out of the question." Someone murmured in the background, and Freddie muffled the phone. When he came back on, he said, "The film, the one I'm shooting in August? There's a problem with the script. One of the actresses will pull out of the production if we don't beef up her role. I'm trapped at the Wayfair discussing plot revisions long distance. Poor Ozzie. He's attempting to make the changes. He doesn't work well under pressure . . ."

Down the corridor, Janis Reed stepped from a room. Casually she thumbed through her phone before slipping it back into her pocket.

She peered down the corridor and then pivoted to speak with someone out of view. Daniel was grateful she hadn't spotted him.

"I have to go," he said, cutting Freddie off. "Sure you won't come?"

"Work before pleasure, I'm afraid."

A fine thread of fury worked through Daniel's blood. "You never planned to meet the kid directly. Hiring me to play intermediary, the excuses for skipping the visit to Medina—why didn't you level with me from the outset? Drumming up excuses for your absence is no picnic. Not with decent people like the Reeds." Without awaiting a reply, he added, "For the record, it's my impression you mean a lot to Bryce. Why, I can't fathom. Behind the wealth and peculiar generosity, you're the same self-serving bastard I remember from high school."

He hung up, and immediately his spirits fell. Three boys dashed out of the room to join their mother. Younger than their star-crossed brother, they paced in their cheap tennis shoes, awaiting the arrival of a legendary filmmaker. Their youthful expectancy, necks craned to catch a glimpse of magic, filled Daniel with sadness.

He strode toward them with a bitter sense of failure dogging his heels.

The next morning, Linnie woke with a craving for butter pecan ice cream and a sour stomach from bad dreams.

In the nightmare, she stood barefoot outside the Wayfair in the red ball gown. Rain fell in buckets, soaking her to the bone. On the inn's veranda—much larger in the dream than real life—Freddie regaled his guests with stories of his filmmaking career. The mud pooling around her ankles began sucking her down into oblivion.

A less auspicious start to the day was hard to imagine. Especially since she'd promised Jada and the Sirens she'd call her parents.

Resigned to the task, she padded toward the bathroom. From the hallway, snatches of conversation pinged off the walls.

A small miracle: Freddie wasn't roaming the inn half-naked. A few paces outside her door, he looked stylish in a blue suit with zigzags of yellow thread running through the sumptuous fabric. Why he felt compelled to conduct early-morning business in a hallway of the neglected south wing was a question for a sage.

She mouthed, *What do you want?*

He scowled at her and then resumed the call with saccharine patience. "Yes, Wheaties are jumpers. I have a trainer scheduled to visit tomorrow. Yes, he'll come as often as you'd like."

"What's a Wheatie?" she whispered.

He pressed the smartphone to his well-tailored breast. "A type of terrier."

"What? You're a dog breeder on the side?"

"A filmmaker of my stature does not have time for canine mating rituals." He paused long enough for her to fear his next disclosure. "I bought the pup for Mother."

Shock lanced through her. "You're chatting with Mother?"

With glee, he watched her jaw slacken.

"Hang up the phone!"

"Make me."

"Don't think I won't."

"Sugarpop, you're hyperventilating. Breathe. There's nothing attractive about resembling a guppy hurled from the sea." Returning to the call, he said, "Yes, Mother. Didn't I mention I'm with Linnie? Yes, in Ohio. Of course I've seen the Sirens. No, they aren't threatening to boil me alive. We've settled our differences . . ."

The implications jarred her brain. Freddie, with cunning aplomb, had called their parents first. And he'd bought their mother a puppy? A masterstroke of cunning. In comparison, the gowns brought in from Ballantine's was a minor ploy.

"Yes, I'll give Frances and Silvia your love. Oh, and Mother? Linnie thinks I should relinquish my rights to the inn. That's correct—all my shares. Certainly. Do whatever you think is best. Oh, and say hello to Dad."

Hanging up, he surveyed her sleeping costume—an old T-shirt and plaid knee socks. "I can't imagine why you cast aspersions on my party clothes," he remarked. "The ghoul in my latest sci-fi extravaganza has more sex appeal than you."

"Forget about my pj's."

"How can I? You're my sister and the daughter of the stylish Sarah Wayfair. You should have some fashion sense."

The zinger nicked her ego. Stupidly, she went back for more. "What's that supposed to mean?"

"I tremble at the prospect of you ending up alone. Old, grey, buying your clothing from a catalog with ducks on the cover and canoes in the center spread."

"There's nothing wrong with rural chic." She steered him back to the problem at hand. "Why did you call Florida at sunup? I haven't even seen a coffeepot yet. You never did play fair."

He adjusted his tie. "Oh, please. I chat with Mother daily."

Astonished, she stepped back. "You do?"

At best, she called once a week. The conversations left her convinced she didn't measure up. Or the stilted exchange left the impression she should acquire an allergy to sugar until the Grim Reaper pitched her pudgy frame into the grave. Whining about Linnie's sweet tooth was a favorite pastime of her mother's. Like Freddie, the emotionally fragile Sarah possessed an enviably trim figure.

Freddie jolted her from the reverie. "I suggest you pick up the call," he said, clamping onto her shoulders. He spun her toward the suite.

With dread, she detected the faint hum of her smartphone. By the time she launched back into the room, he'd sauntered down the hallway.

From the dresser she snatched up the phone.

Snuffling tears came across the line. "My poor babies!"

"Good morning, Mother."

"Are you having a spat with Freddie?"

"After seven years he shows up without warning—what did you expect? I'd roll out the welcome mat and throw a parade?"

"I'll settle for the barest courtesy you'd show a stranger. He's your brother!"

Linnie threw herself across the rumpled bed. "He's taken three of my best suites and installed his film weirdos inside. These are *not* nice people. One of his assistants gave me the finger. The rest drink heavily and don't sleep until dawn."

"Why, they're only having fun. Aren't you happy your brother has friends?"

Friends?

A humiliating memory accosted her. The fifth-grade swim team screaming at the top of their lungs. Freddie, sprinting through the locker room with a fire extinguisher, blasting the girls with the noxious white foam. Jennifer Meyers, the overexcitable star of the swim team, dropped in a dead faint. Linnie crawled through the foam to rescue the unconscious girl.

The heroics didn't matter. Freddie's prank earned her pariah status—none of the girls ever spoke to her again.

Freddie came up short in the friend department? She'd lost friends every time an evil whim popped into his head.

She pressed a pillow to her face, threw it back off. "Mother, let's not argue. We'll never see eye to eye when it comes to Freddie."

More snuffling. "Why wasn't I one of those lucky women with a devoted daughter? All my friends have grandchildren. Patty Freeland's daughter takes her shopping every weekend."

"Mother, I *am* devoted."

"Are you sure? I can't recall the last time we enjoyed a spa day together."

A spa day? "Definitely not within my budget," she said with rising agitation. *Or yours.* "If the situation changes, I promise to spend a weekend primping with you."

"Oh, Sugarpop. What makes you certain I wouldn't like to take you?"

"I don't know, Mom. Because you live on a fixed income?" At times her mother's grasp of reality was tenuous at best.

"No, you're right," Sarah croaked. "This isn't the time for a spat. Much better to let you break my heart in person. Don't worry about picking me up. Freddie promised to send a car to the airport."

Dismay yanked her upright. "You're flying in?"

No! Dealing with Mr. Evil and the Queen of Tears required the emotional dexterity of a politician. She'd never survive simultaneous visits.

"I'd come tomorrow, but I must see the dog trainer. I have a tea at the women's club the following day. Friday's out—your father's bridge tournament. I can't leave our new baby alone in the house."

In free fall, Linnie tallied the days in her head.

No, no, no!

"You're coming on Saturday?" The day of the anniversary bash. "Not a good idea. How 'bout a visit later this summer?"

A delicate honking carried across the line. Presumably Sarah was blowing her nose. "I'll take the red-eye Friday night," she supplied in a stronger voice. "Freddie booked first class. Isn't that sweet? I'd stay the weekend to catch up with the Sirens, but duty calls. The church bake sale is Sunday. I volunteered to man the cupcake station."

"You're only staying the day?"

"Only long enough to make you listen to reason."

The comment's subtext landed like a blow to her stomach. Her desire to push Freddie out of the family biz was unreasonable. Her mother would arrive to trail tears and guilt-inducing comments until Linnie relented.

She was screwed.

"Don't come." She hated the risk of trampling her mother's emotions. In person, her mother's histrionics were powerful enough to make her agree to anything.

In the background, a frenzied yipping sounded. "Enjoy the rest of your week, Sugarpop," Sarah remarked breezily. "We'll get you all straightened out on Saturday. Kisses, sweetie!"

Linnie hurled the phone across the bed. Enjoy the remainder of the week? The female employees were poisoned with glam fever. Plus her evil sib planned to augment Saturday's skeleton crew with temp workers. Some of the staff she'd let go after Freddie stole the money promised to work the night, but they'd all need a refresher course. They hadn't worked at the inn for seven years.

Now her mother was coming in on Friday's red-eye.

An equally pessimistic thought intruded. During the short conversation, the contract never came up. Desperate for reassurance, she recalled Jada's words. *If your parents had waited to hand over the inn, why wouldn't they have given it all to you? They drew up the contract when you were upset about being left in charge.*

The time had come to demonstrate who was best suited to own the Wayfair.

As if there was any doubt.

Thirty minutes later, she'd donned a sedate dress and steely resolve. The empty lobby glowed in golden light. Behind the front desk, Mr. Uchida dozed.

Leaning across the desk, Linnie poked him. His dark eyes snapped open, and she said, "Call up to Jada's and Cat's rooms. Tell them to meet me in the office at eight sharp." She moved off, reconsidered. Retracing her steps, she asked, "Why do you split your workweek between third and first shifts? Rotating between two shifts keeps you sleep deprived."

Mr. Uchida palmed his chin. "Cat makes the schedule. I work when she says."

"Have a preference?"

His gaze brightened. "First shift."

"Give me a few days to set it up." She'd hire someone younger to work third, or alternate between two people.

Happy with the decision, she waltzed to the kitchen. Sunlight arced through the windows. Pots clattered in the sink. Fragrant mounds of herbs nestled in tidy rows on the butcher block. By the stove, the day cook and several of his assistants were discussing the breakfast menu.

Calling the staff to attention, Linnie explained a few regulars were needed for Saturday night. Anyone willing to skip Silvia and Marco's anniversary bash would receive time and a half. Many of the staff members had families. They might skip the party in trade for a bigger paycheck. Besides, she refused to leave the Wayfair in the untested hands of Freddie's temp agency hires.

Ellis Leavey was the first to raise his hand. The raven-haired cook—considered the resident "hot body" by most of the female staff—sent his stern regard across the kitchen. A heartening number of his staff followed suit.

"I owe you one," she told him.

Ellis grinned. "I won't forget."

She turned to the holdouts. "Anyone else?"

One more employee volunteered. Not the best outcome, but good enough.

Entering her office, she jotted a note to make the same offer to the kitchen's dinner staff, as well as the waitstaff.

Five minutes later, Jada and Cat walked in. Jada, appearing fully awake in jeans and a blouse, leaned against the bookshelves. Stifling a yawn, Cat flopped into a chair before the desk. She'd pulled on jeans and a top, but had forgotten shoes. Purple nail polish gleamed on her toes.

Producing a rubber band, she pulled her long, wavy hair into a ponytail. "What's up?" She flung her legs over the arm of the chair.

On the desk Linnie folded her hands. "We're making changes, starting today. Cat, get in touch with your friend, the one with the ad agency in Cincinnati. Work up a campaign—print, digital, the works. When did we last update our Facebook page? Also get a quote on updating our website. We'll start advertising in tandem with the renovations."

"What renovations?"

She explained about the liquor boxes stuffed full of cash. Cat's full lips released a burst of air. Jada, in mute shock, listed like a ship unmoored.

Beaming, Cat wiggled her toes. "You're not spineless or gutless," she breathed. "You're *rich*."

"Hardly. Have any idea how much work the inn requires?"

The realities of hospitality management coasted past her dream-addled friend. "Bali," Cat murmured. "We'll go, just the three of us. Swim in the ocean and find hot bodies on the beach. Let's run away forever."

The comment nudged Jada from her stupor. She smacked Cat on the side of the head, drawing a yelp. "We're not running away to Bali. There's work to do." Taking a seat, she regarded Linnie. "Freddie returned all the money?"

"And then some."

"Did he explain why he waited so long?"

"Getting a straight answer from a toddler is easier than extracting the truth from my brother."

Jada grunted in agreement. "The washers and dryers are shot," she said. "Housekeeping will throw flowers at your feet if you replace them. I'll get quotes."

"Would you also look into an overhaul of heating and cooling in the south wing? No one local can handle a job this big. Talk to companies farther afield."

Ever sensible, Jada tempered the excitement in her voice. "You're thinking about reopening the south wing?"

Cat rubbed the side of her head where Jada had smacked her awake. "If guests occupy the rooms, where will we live? I don't like sleeping in long johns in summer, but my suite *is* roomy—and rent-free."

Linnie chuckled. "If we're pulling decent wages, we'll rent apartments. There's no rule that we must live on the grounds."

Her heart lifting, she recalled Daniel's question. He'd looked so earnest when asking if she liked his house. Waking up in his arms, sharing the evenings cuddling on his couch with Puddles at their feet—the notion *was* tempting.

And marriage? Later they'd talk about forevers. No sense jinxing the chance for happiness by jumping in too quickly.

A more urgent concern—dealing with Saturday's unexpected visit.

Would the plans for major renovations impress her mother? A tough call. Sarah wasn't easily impressed. She was more apt to forgo presents and pack her luggage full of criticism.

Jada caught the worry flickering across her face. "This is all thrilling, but I have the impression you're leaving something out. Care to share?"

"Freddie called Mother."

Jada shrugged. "Men call their mothers. So what?"

"She's flying in on the red-eye Friday night. Only staying through Saturday afternoon. Long enough to reason with me. Or, in her words, let me break her heart in person."

"That's bad."

"Gosh, you think?"

"You pressed the case for sole ownership?"

"Conducting a reasonable conversation was a no-go. She started crying."

Glumly Cat shook her head. "No offense, Linnie. Chinese water torture is less effective than your mother's tears. She should work for a government antiterrorism unit. She can get anyone to roll over. What did she talk you into this time?"

The question raised Linnie's defenses. "I didn't snap under pressure, all right?

"You're sure?"

"Yes, I'm sure. I'll reason with her when she arrives. Doesn't matter if she weeps throughout. I won't buckle."

"You always do."

"This is different. I've never told her how much I care about the inn. An oversight. I didn't expect Freddie to show up after all this time. Why does he want to hold on to his shares? They're meaningless to him."

"This isn't about his shares. He likes driving you to the brink of insanity," Cat supplied confidently. "You've never been close. When we were kids, you mothered him constantly. Kept his bedroom tidy so your dad wouldn't blow his stack, kept his book bag organized—he didn't like your meddling. Which probably explains why he likes making you squirm. Remember the time he tied you to a chair and made you eat brussels sprouts?"

The slimy veggies remained one of Linnie's most despised foods. "Not a high point of childhood," she agreed with a shudder, "and not a fair fight. How's a second grader supposed to take on a demon in sixth? This time, I'm ready to rumble."

Jada said, "The renovations . . . there's no guarantee a schedule of improvements will sway your mother. You're taking a big gamble."

"Hey, weren't you the one who suggested I talk to my parents?"

"Talk, not throw tons of money into the Wayfair. Freddie still owns half. Besides, I gave the advice before learning your mother is coming in. If she's worried you'll break her heart, she's using Mom Code. She wants her children to mend their differences."

"No problem. If Freddie sells, I'll patch things up." Not really, but she didn't like where Jada was headed with this.

"Get real. She's hopping the red-eye for one reason only. All your big plans for the Wayfair won't matter a damn."

Defiance fired Linnie's voice. "We're moving forward with the changes. For once I have enough money to make a real difference. I refuse to wait."

"Yeah, I'm getting that." Jada's eyes filled with sympathy. "Nothing about this is fair. I'm betting your mother will guilt-trip you into staying in charge while insisting Freddie stay in the picture. Are you sure she won't?"

Frustrated, Linnie chewed on her lip. No, she wasn't sure.

Chapter 14

The second meeting with the Stillwells proved more difficult than the first.

An angry vein pulsed in Duke Stillwell's neck. Carol, handling their supposedly amicable divorce no better, repeated her demands. The list included full custody of their daughters with only supervised bi-monthly visitation for Duke. Seated ramrod straight, she refused to look at the man with whom she'd spent the better part of twenty years.

Daniel retreated into a gloomy silence. A small-town lawyer was a jack-of-all-trades. Some work was fascinating, other cases simple. The only work he despised was divorce proceedings. No one came out a winner. Children lost the most, especially if their normally civil parents refused to compromise. He feared the Stillwells' three daughters would fare no better than most.

The couple resumed bickering, and Daniel stole a glance at his cell. For days he'd been trying to reach Linnie. With the Mendozas' anniversary bash slated for tomorrow, she was undoubtedly busy.

Earlier in the week, on the drive back from the Devlin Institute, he'd struck on a pleasant idea. Why not ask Linnie to accompany him to the party? A dozen red roses waited at the local florist shop for Saturday morning pickup. He'd present them with the dangly gold earrings that caught his eye in a jewelry store in Cleveland.

Rising to their feet, the Stillwells came perilously close to shrieking at each other. Breaking in, he said, "There's something I like to tell clients when they find themselves in your unfortunate circumstance. Care to hear?"

Carol pulled on her earlobe, mottling the skin. Duke frowned.

"You have three beautiful daughters," Daniel said. "Odds are good they'll choose to marry someday. Which means you'll become grandparents—together. Divorce won't change the facts. You'll remain a family."

The throbbing vein in Duke's neck relaxed. Carol released her ear.

In a firmer voice, Daniel added, "Do yourselves a favor. Go home. Make a list of demands. Separate lists, and be reasonable. At our next meeting, we'll sort through them to find middle ground."

Carol produced a tissue from her purse. "And if we don't compromise?"

"Then I'm sorry to say you'll each need a lawyer specializing in divorce. I only handle amicable cases. Bear in mind lengthy negotiations come with high legal bills. With your daughters nearing college, it's something to keep in mind."

Relieved to bring the meeting to an end, he escorted them out. He paused at Kay's desk on his way back.

"When does Joel Klein arrive?" A retired mechanical engineer, Joel was amending his will to include a new daughter-in-law.

Kay checked the calendar. "Three o'clock today."

"Great. I have time to head out to the inn."

"To ask Linnie in person?"

He grunted. "Think I should give her the roses early?"

"Save them for tomorrow." Kay regarded him with motherly concern. "Don't come on too strong. She has a lot on her mind. Unlikely romance is a top priority. And for heaven's sake, if you see Freddie, don't argue if she's within spitting distance."

Kay understood his upset over Freddie ducking out of the visit after Bryce's surgery. "I'll wait to read Freddie the riot act. He's back in California until the weekend. Something about a problem with the script for his next film."

"He's returning for Silvia's party?"

"I still have trouble believing she invited him."

"Who wouldn't? Freddie insisted on footing the bill. Wait until you see the outfits he sprang for. I hear Linnie's is quite stunning."

Curious about what she'd wear Saturday night, Daniel took to the road that wove around the lake at a leisurely pace. The breeze tickled his face as his thoughts returned to romance. He looked forward to dancing with Linnie in her pretty gown.

Pinkish-white clouds floated across the sky. Sunlight threw diamond brilliance on the lake. The beach swarmed with tourists. The Mendozas had chosen the date for their anniversary party well. The forecast called for temps in the eighties with no chance of rain.

In the busy lobby of the Wayfair, Jada handed a room key to the young couple at the front of the line. Silvia and Marco both came from large families, with relatives driving in from across Ohio. From the looks of the crowd, every room was booked.

Spotting Daniel in the crush, Jada said, "Check her office. She's buried in swatches. Prepare to offer an opinion. She can't decide."

Daniel hurried through the lobby. *Swatches?*

Jada's meaning became clear when he entered the office. Before the wall of bookcases sat a long table scavenged from the Sunshine Room. Books of fabric swatches and larger catalogs of wallpaper covered the surface. Linnie's desk was equally cluttered. Notepads filled with her familiar cursive shared space with neatly labeled folders. At the window, she stared absently at the brilliant blue day while finishing a call.

Hanging up, she came around the desk to greet him. Her steps were buoyant. Taking advantage of her high spirits, he steered her into his arms.

He kissed her deeply. She returned the kiss without hesitation, her lips tasting of the excitement she seemed keen to share. Setting her free, he grinned. "I can't recall the last time I saw you this happy." He inspected the table of swatches. "What's going on?"

"I'm getting together quotes and design samples for the south wing." She picked up a paint card he hadn't noticed. "Also getting bids from painters—the lobby is dreary, and half of the suites in the main section need perking up. Cat suggested I hire a decorator. I'd rather do this myself."

The disappointment he should've felt refused to materialize. "You aren't following my advice about waiting until Freddie is out of the picture?"

She eyed him playfully. "Sorry, Counselor. The once-conservative manager of the Wayfair is forging ahead. I have the funds to proceed, and I'm tired of acting like the caretaker of a dying enterprise."

"The Wayfair isn't dying. Didn't you reach breakeven last winter? You've turned the corner." Her good mood held other perks. She'd done up her hair. The heavy locks nestled in a loose chignon at the base of her neck. He imagined the pleasure of loosing each strand while placing lingering kisses on her neck. "This isn't like you. Plowing ahead with work on the main inn *and* the south wing—you never jump into action without careful thought."

Flipping open a fabric book, she fingered a swatch of moss-green fabric. "We'll never reach healthy profits with the south wing shuttered. Given the amount of work ahead, we must start soon. "

The cost of making the south wing habitable for guests was prohibitive. A twinge of worry swept through him. Was she getting in over her head?

Gently he said, "Will you accept my help? I'd like to study the quotes before you accept any bids. You're talking about everything from heating and cooling to work on the roof. You can't have bats in the hallways or raccoons showing up in the suites." Every year he offered to help patrol the attic. She insisted on evicting the vermin singlehandedly.

Lightly he added, "Redecorating sounds like fun, but deal with the structural problems first."

Her shoulders lifted to her ears. "I forgot about the roof," she murmured.

"Better make it job one."

"You don't mind looking everything over? I don't have all the numbers yet. Expecting two more quotes within the hour."

"Linnie, I want to help." Relief bloomed on her face, lending him the courage to add, "I didn't stop by to put a damper on your plans."

"Why are you here?"

"To ask for the honor of escorting you to the party. Normally I'd insist on picking you up. Since you're hosting the event, I'll settle for meeting you outside the ballroom."

The suggestion came out more stilted than intended. Linnie glossed over his clumsy speech with a smile on her lips. Taking her time, she returned the book of swatches to the table. Her cheeks flushed a sheer pink. As they did, an emotion that sure felt like victory brought Daniel to her side.

"Shall we go together?" He caught a stray tendril of hair escaping her chignon. He relished the softness between his fingertips. "I hope you're not planning to disappoint me."

"Will you take offense if your date occasionally disappears to check that everything's going smoothly?"

"I'll manage."

"Will you also manage to stop me from wringing my brother's neck?" she joked. "Freddie invited my regular employees."

"Who'll cook and serve? You don't just have the party to worry about. There are other guests staying at the inn."

"Not all of the staff will attend the party. Quite a few agreed to overtime pay. They'll skip the event."

"What about the people you let go after Freddie screwed everything up? If you're still shorthanded, I'm sure you'll get a few bites."

"I'm way ahead of you. Some have agreed to work the night."

"I'm sure they're hoping you'll reinstate them," Daniel said, well aware of how badly she'd hated letting staff members go. "Some of your previous employees have been out of work for a long time."

"I'd like to bring everyone back," she agreed. Irritation registered on her features as she added, "Freddie hired temp workers to fill out the staff. I'll need to keep an eye on them."

She began to add something else.

Compressing her lips, she focused instead on his tie, deftly repositioning the knot before smoothing the lapels of his blazer with painstaking care. He liked the way she straightened his clothing without seeking permission, the territorial nature of her hands moving across his chest, dipping beneath the blazer to warm the skin underneath. Intent on breathing him in, her nostrils flared the slightest degree. Pleasure rolled through his senses.

The pleasure receded as he noticed the anxiety thinning her mouth. What problem threatened her mood? He searched for a subtle way to ask.

He lost the opportunity. On her desk, the phone trilled. Another quote, he presumed.

Landing a peck on his cheek, she dashed off to answer.

Chapter 15

On the veranda, Linnie waited with her stomach in knots. As much as she missed her mother, she hated the prospect of a debate over the future of the inn. Sarah never raised her voice, but her tears and indirect censure were just as unbearable. Would she listen to reason? Linnie bit at her lip—in the past, she'd never once swayed her mother on any topic of importance.

In the distance, the limousine threw clouds of dust above the road leading to the inn. With jerky movements she smoothed down her dress, her lips dry and her muscles tense. Then she smoothed the anxiety from her brow and fastened a smile to her lips.

Dawn crested above the treetops as Sarah Wayfair stepped from the sleek ride.

In the peach-hued light, Sarah paused to appraise the new rhododendrons with an approving eye. Although she'd flown on the red-eye, she appeared fresh in a teal summer suit with threads as golden as the Wayfair's foundation stones knitted through.

Linnie came down the steps at a stiff gait. "How was your flight?"

"Pleasant, actually. Plenty of room in first class. I dozed for most of the trip." Her mother waved to the driver as the sleek automobile drove off. "Gerald was the high point of the journey. He whisked me out of the airport in no time. So kind of your brother to arrange the limousine to pick me up."

There was no sense favoring the comment with a response. "Where's your luggage?" She didn't have her brother's means to treat her mother to first class or a limousine. "Even if you're only here for the day, surely you want to shower and change before the flight out."

Her mother flicked a lock of platinum blonde hair from her brow. "I forgot my carry-on in the car when your father dropped me off. Lucy made such a fuss as I left, and he looked ready to blow his cork. There's no reasoning with the man when he's caught in a fit of temper."

Linnie tried to keep up. "You named the dog Lucy? Cute name."

"She's adorable. I've always wanted a terrier."

A wave of jealousy slid through her. Count on Freddie to butter their mother up precisely when Linnie most required her to remain open-minded.

Warding off the unbecoming emotion, she asked, "You weren't upset with the gift? Caring for a puppy sounds like a lot of work."

"I'm happy with anything that keeps your father busy. You know how irritable he becomes without enough diversions."

Linnie did indeed. Prior to the stroke, her father had possessed boundless energy. He'd managed the inn with military precision, demanding absolute perfection from everyone in his employ. He'd demanded the same of his children, and his arguments with Freddie over poor grades and overall appearance never abated. Linnie, with her attention to detail and love of schoolwork, never received the brunt of his fury.

Still, she hadn't been immune to the stress of a demanding parent. A fond childhood memory revolved around the soothing qualities of vanilla-scented shortbread. During stormy arguments between father and son, the kitchen became a favored sanctuary. She'd munch cookies while helping the staff with simple tasks, like washing vegetables or cleaning the counters.

In the lobby, Mr. Uchida shared a few words with Sarah. The interlude was welcome—the self-confidence Linnie tried to muster was quickly failing.

The pleasantries concluded, she asked, "Would you like coffee?"

"And a croissant. I'm famished."

Linnie stopped a waitress coming in for work. The girl trotted off to fill the order. When she had, Linnie ushered her mother toward the office.

Someone had brought order to a room cluttered with fabric swatches, wallpaper books, and the various job quotes still coming in. Jada and Cat? Leading her mother inside, Linnie made a mental note to thank them later. In her worry about the impending meeting, she'd forgotten the task.

Her mother said, "I spoke to Freddie on the drive in. He's switched to a later flight. Something about additional changes to the script for the August film shoot."

"He's not coming in this morning?"

Sarah lingered by the table, her fingers climbing the stack of wallpaper books. "An hour after my departure. We'll just miss each other."

"How can we discuss the inheritance without him?"

"Dearest heart, it's best if we chat alone." Having dropped the ominous statement, her mother assessed her from top to bottom. "Can't you find time to get to the salon?"

"I've been busy." She also lived frugally now, thanks to the difficulties the inn had experienced after Freddie took off,

"You shouldn't neglect your appearance. When you were younger, you were always beautifully turned out."

"You don't like the dress?" A summer knit, one of her best outfits.

"A necklace would do wonders." Nearing, Sarah drew her hand down the tangled hair framing Linnie's face. "You resemble a shaggy dog."

The light rap on the door felt like a reprieve. A waitress tiptoed inside. Linnie directed her to leave the order on the coffee table. The urge to follow her back out was difficult to suppress.

Painfully conscious of her posture, Linnie seated herself on the couch and poured coffee into china cups. An insistent drone carried across her eardrums. Her nerves stretching taut, she crossed her ankles. She managed to lift the steaming cup to her lips without clattering the saucer.

Concluding her inspection of the table, Sarah walked to the wall opposite the bookcases. She examined each photograph in turn, the private shrine of Wayfair men placed in chronological order.

Knitting together her jumbled thoughts, Linnie said, "I'm working on plans to update sections of the inn and reopen the south wing." She gave a brief explanation of the quotes already gathered. Summing up, she added, "By next summer, we'll book at full capacity. I'll run a small ad campaign this fall, print and digital. Next spring I'll increase the advertising."

Sarah joined her on the couch. "Should your father review the renovation quotes? Trades are less inclined to pad the price when negotiating with a man."

"I can manage."

"Sugarpop, you're unfamiliar with construction. The roof in the south wing needs repair, and what about plumbing and electrical? You don't know the first thing about either. Tradesmen *will* take advantage of your ignorance."

"If a price seems unfair, I'll talk to Daniel."

"Why ask Daniel for advice?"

"He offered to help."

The explanation thinned her mother's lips. "I'm not visiting long enough to debate minor points. If you don't wish to take advantage of your father's advice, then have Freddie review the quotes. There's no need to solicit the opinion of an outsider."

The comment felt like a reprimand. "Daniel is a close friend," she said, trying to brush it off. "I trust his judgment."

"Linnie, please. Stop pretending you're obtuse."

"Then speak plainly. I'm not sure what you're driving at."

Sarah pressed stiff fingers to her brow. "Forge ahead with improvements if you'd like, but do involve your brother."

Sarah picked up her croissant, tore off a corner. She ate slowly, and Linnie despaired at the fine mist gathering on her lashes. How much longer before she resorted to tears or suffered a nosebleed? The path into the conversation was rife with brambles. Yet remaining silent was the greater risk.

"Mother," she said with failing patience, "I can't involve Freddie. I won't. You and Daddy must recognize the facts. He's perfectly content in California. He doesn't care about the inn, not the way I do. This is my life."

The years working to save the inn, the long hours and low pay—none of the sacrifices made seemed to sway her mother. Sadness pitched through Linnie so quickly she stiffened in response. Her mother barely noticed as she set the plate aside with a hint of disapproval gathering in her eyes.

"Why would you make a career the sole focus of your life?" Sarah asked, and the hard tone of her query deepened Linnie's despair. "Work here as long as you like, although I hope you'll make room for more enjoyable pursuits. You're thirty-two. Don't you want to find a nice man and settle down?"

Linnie stared at her, astonished. "When would I have time to look for a husband? I've spent years keeping the Wayfair afloat."

"Your father and I appreciate everything you've done. We never meant to stop you from having your own life."

"What was I supposed to do? Freddie took the money, which nearly killed—"

"No, Linnie," her mother said fiercely, cutting her off. "Freddie did *not* cause your father's stroke. Good heavens, your father was a heavy smoker. I tried repeatedly to get him to stop. Oh, he learned to hide the habit well enough. It took the stroke to compel him to quit."

"I thought he gave up the cigarettes when I was in college," she murmured, adrift.

"There's a lot you don't know about your father."

The remark stretched tight the air between them. The secrets tucked in Sarah's memories brushed against her downturned lips. She closed her eyes.

When she opened them, she asked, "Do you have any idea how much your father once loathed the Wayfair?"

The question took Linnie off guard. "Impossible," she murmured, incredulous.

"I assure you, he did. Naturally you find the truth baffling." Reading the disbelief on Linnie's face, Sarah gave her head a weary shake. "Children rarely understand their parents. You come into our lives after we've found ourselves. After we're fully formed. You don't see the clay that shapes us."

"You're wrong. Dad loved everything about the inn." He'd lavished attention on the smallest details, his pride unmistakable.

"Not at the beginning." A hairline crack of sorrow appeared in Sarah's voice. Reaching for her purse, she produced a tissue to pat her watering eyes. "He regarded those years as a humiliation. As the sort of misstep only a man of weak disposition could make."

"What happened?" Linnie whispered, at sea.

"Why, he ran away—just like your brother. Fortunately for this grand house, Treat's love affair with painting didn't last long. He was eighteen, right out of high school. One short, sweet summer in Paris. Several art schools turned him down. I'm sorry to report his talent was limited at best. The money ran out, and he left Paris in time to begin the fall semester at Ohio State."

The revelation erased the boundaries of the known world. Her father had dreamt of becoming a painter? Dumbfounded, Linnie searched her memories for a clue to the hidden talent. Nothing came to mind. The father she remembered never doodled while taking notes or spent weekends photographing scenery. He certainly hadn't owned paints or an easel.

Sarah finished drying her eyes. "You might consider altering your opinion of your brother. Freddie's obsession with creative arts is hereditary, no different than the blue eyes from my side of the family. Which won't change the outcome. Eventually he'll take a man's path and claim his legacy. The Wayfair is a storied part of Ohio history. Treat understood. One day, Freddie will too."

Anger rippled through Linnie. "Why can't I claim the legacy?" Hurt followed in a scalding wave.

"Sugarpop, you know why."

She cringed beneath the loathsome sobriquet. "Because I'm not a man?"

A tear rolled down her mother's cheek into the waiting tissue. "Let your brother build castles. Don't you want children one day?"

Linnie waved off the speech. "Answer me. Will you pass me over because I'm a daughter and not a son?"

"We haven't passed you over."

"You can't do this."

"Without your efforts, we might have lost this grand house. No one will forget, dear."

"Thanks, but I'll pass on the accolades. Just treat me fairly."

"When your brother buys out your shares, he'll pay you handsomely. If he chooses to reassert control before then, you'll display the grace I'm certain you're endowed with and support him." Her mother laced the command with mock enthusiasm. "Keep in mind how quickly time runs out. Find someone to love. Marry and raise a family."

The incongruous statement was disorienting. "You act as if marriage and career are mutually exclusive. They're not."

"I'm saying if you live for your job, you don't have much of a life at all." Deepening the blow, Sarah pressed her hand to Linnie's thigh. "You'll have more luck winning a man if you watch your figure. How I wish you took after my side of the family. Well, no matter. There are dozens of eligible bachelors in Sweet Lake. If no one local suits, consider online dating. I've heard marvelous stories of couples meeting on those sites."

A terrible quiet swelled between them. A broken moment, and pain raced up Linnie's arm. She realized her nails were dug into the soft pad of her palm. Releasing her fingers, she stared unseeing.

She felt nothing. The enormity of all she'd lost was too great.

Her mother glided to the door, a ship on calm seas. "I should rest," she said, clearly eager to depart. "Shall we meet in the Sunshine Room at one o'clock?"

❧

Frances smiled at Jada, waiting for her in the busy lobby.

With more of Silvia and Marco's guests checking in for the party, the stress of dealing with the inn at full capacity showed on Jada's face. She looked harried, her curls mussed as she came around the desk where she'd been helping Mr. Uchida.

"Linnie doesn't know I called you," Jada said, steering her toward the stairwell. "I doubt she'd thank me."

Her loyalty was admirable. "Let's consider this our little secret." Frances looked past Mr. Uchida to the hallway leading toward Linnie's office. "Where is Linnie?"

"Holed up in her office."

"You haven't seen her since her mother arrived?"

"Only for a moment, in the kitchen. Mentioned she'll have lunch with her mother before Mrs. Wayfair leaves for the airport. She seems all right," Jada added, the doubt thick in her voice. "Did I do the right thing by calling you?"

"Not to worry," Frances assured her. "I'd hoped to visit with Sarah before she leaves. It's been ages since we've had a chance to catch up." She declined to add that Sarah had begged off, ostensibly because there wasn't time before the flight home.

Jada paused on the stairwell. "I didn't tell Mrs. Wayfair . . ."

"That I'm stopping by?" Despite the seriousness of the situation, Frances chuckled. Leaving the unexpected visit a surprise was an artful ploy. "Don't worry. I've been close with Sarah since before you were born. I won't make her late for her lunch date with Linnie."

The corridor, usually quiet on a typical Saturday, brimmed with chatter. Luggage sat in rows by the walls. Families checking in jingled room keys and corralled children, many of whom were undoubtedly eager to get down to the beach.

Jada said, "She's in room 117."

Count on Sarah to demand a corner suite during the Wayfair's busiest weekend of the year. "I'll take it from here." Frances gently nudged her nervous companion toward the stairwell. "You have more important matters requiring your attention."

Jada required no more urging. She retraced her path to the lobby.

On the third knock, Sarah opened the door. The terrycloth robe enveloping her trim figure seemed two sizes too large, and Frances quickly made the connection. One of Linnie's robes. Had Sarah's luggage missed the flight?

"Frances." Sarah donned a questioning look. "I thought we agreed there wasn't time to visit. I do wish I were staying longer."

"I won't keep you long."

An invitation to enter wasn't extended. Frances didn't care—she breezed past.

The door rattled shut.

"How's Treat?" Two chairs formed a cozy group, and she chose the one closest to the window. "Still driving you to distraction?"

An old joke, and some of the misgiving left Sarah's eyes. "Freddie bought us a dog, which helps keep Treat out of my hair. The stroke has slowed him down, but he still has more energy than the rest of us combined."

"I hope he can visit us soon."

"He misses the inn and all our friends." Sarah crossed the room to perch on the edge of the second chair. "Why do I have the impression you aren't stopping by to catch up?"

"Because I'm not. I'm concerned about your children."

"My children are fine." The statement carried a protective edge. "Freddie has finally returned—a relief for Treat and me both. We've been wondering if he'd reach middle age before showing an interest in his inheritance."

The comment revealed such insensitivity to Linnie's wishes, to her hard-earned rights, that Frances held her tongue until the anger left her blood. Pointedly, she said, "You have two children. Don't they both have a stake in the inn?"

"Yes, but my son is in charge."

An absurd notion, but she let it pass. "Did he lead you to believe he's returned to begin working at the inn?"

"Not in so many words. He does have his film company. I assume he'll wind down that hobby before moving home permanently."

"He's done well in California. I'm not sure I'd characterize his work as a hobby." More silence, and Frances steeled herself for what would come next. "Sarah, he isn't here for the inn. He's in Ohio for another purpose—one he won't reveal. And while I'd never dream of meddling in your affairs, I do wish to point out that there's more at stake than the future ownership of the Wayfair."

Sarah threw back her shoulders, her features brittle. "I suppose you feel compelled to set me straight?"

She did, but the task was a thankless one. Like many families, the Wayfairs had frayed the cords of love that bound them together by withholding forgiveness or making unreasonable demands—or, as in Sarah's case, by refusing to acknowledge the abundant gifts each of her children possessed. She clung to tradition, and it blinded her. If she couldn't see her children for the adults they'd become, she'd lose out on the love they yearned to give.

Which was a secondary consideration to the fear weighing down on Frances as she said, "Sarah, you and Treat have lost sight of the only real inheritance any of us leaves to our children. However you choose to dispense with the inn, you must stop setting your children at odds. You've made them competitors."

Bitter tears welled in Sarah's eyes. "You're mistaken."

Upsetting her was regrettable, but Frances pressed on. "None of us lives forever," she pointed out. "You won't, and nor will Treat. Once you're gone, Linnie and Freddie will only have each other." For emphasis, she stretched out the moment. "If their relationship breaks, each will lose something immeasurable."

∽

Cradling the phone on her shoulder, Kay stopped Daniel from leaving the office. He walked the client to the reception area, then retraced his steps.

"I'll tell him," Kay said, hanging up.

"A problem?" Not another salvo from the Stillwells, he decided. They were still negotiating the finer points of their divorce.

"Jada's trying to reach you."

Sheepishly he pulled out his smartphone. "Forgot to charge it this morning." He'd rushed out early to pick up the flowers for Linnie and his best suit at the dry cleaner.

Kay glanced at the calendar. "Were you supposed to pick up Fancy?"

"Going there now. She's playing at a friend's house." He'd promised Philip to deliver her home before dressing for the party. Philip planned to attend the bash after the babysitter arrived and Fancy went to bed.

"Don't bother. I'll collect Fancy." Kay's expression was grim. "Do you have tennis shoes in the car?"

He stowed a pair in the trunk for impromptu walks with Puddles. "Do I need them?"

"Linnie disappeared into the woods. Changed into shorts and tromped out." At his questioning look, Kay added, "Her mother came in."

"Sarah's visiting?"

"Only here long enough to see Linnie. On her way back to the airport now. According to Jada, Linnie seemed fine when the limousine departed."

"Not likely. The inn must be a madhouse with guests checking in and deliveries showing up for the party. She's not in the habit of shirking duties."

"Jada and Cat are taking care of the deliveries and helping the kitchen staff prep for the banquet. They'd like you to run down the boss."

He gave a quelling look. "The next time there's a crisis, barge into my office. I don't care how important the meeting—just get me."

On the road leading past the inn, families in bathing suits and shorts strolled in the sunlight.

Several of the faces were familiar. Relatives of Silvia or Marco, the newcomers were taking advantage of the beach and the water sports available on Sweet Lake before the night's festivities in the ballroom. Daniel parked away from the crowds, near the forest. Hurrying, he shrugged out of his suit coat, then pulled off his tie. The sun, pouring heat on the lake, beat down on his shoulders.

From the trunk, he grabbed tennis shoes. The wind kicked up, snapping beach towels on the sand.

With relief, he trudged into the forest's cooling shade. Birdsong carried in the trees.

"Linnie?"

Soft grooves from a thousand feet pocked the main path leading into the shadows. The trees grew dense. Thick limbs cradled the sky with a webwork of shivering leaves. Following a hunch, he took a secondary path toward the trickling melody of the ravine. Down a steep incline, he spotted Linnie perched on a boulder by the stream.

"Hey, stranger."

"Daniel." She tried to smile, failed. "You're early for our date."

"Don't worry—I won't show up in tennis shoes. Just thought I'd stop by." Sitting beside her, he took care to keep his voice light. "Aren't you hosting a party tonight? I'm betting you have better uses for your time than a hike in the woods."

"I should get back." Puffing out her cheeks, she released a sigh fraught with despair. "Needed to sort myself out first."

"You're all right?"

"Not yet. Working on it."

"Anything I can do?"

"I can think of something."

The breeze lifted her face. Boldly she allowed her gaze to drink him in without reservation.

A blatant appraisal. Daniel wasn't sure what he'd expected—anger, a crying jag, or the need for one of his countless "chin up" speeches. Not this.

Tossing aside propriety, she slid beneath his obliging arm and pressed her palm to his thigh. When he claimed her lips with slow, steady passion, she whimpered against his mouth.

The proof of her need stoked his surging emotions. Without conscious thought he drew her to her feet to better allow his hands to range freely across her back. She wasn't merely pliable in his arms. She met each caress with desire bordering on frenzy, her tongue dueling with his, her fingers dragging across the shuddering muscles of his chest.

He pulled away. "You're full of surprises," he murmured gruffly.

She ruffled the coarse hair skimming the tops of his ears. "I do feel reckless." Worry flickered across her face. "Do you mind?"

"Linnie, I spend most of my free time inventing ways to seduce you." But not in plain sight, he reflected. If they took this much further, they'd make love right here in the forest.

She pressed her mouth to his jaw. The fragrance of her hair filled his nostrils, an alluring blend of dusky roses and musk. A new perfume? It suited her. Breathing in the unabashedly feminine scent, he closed his eyes. Dimly he became aware of her hands sliding over his ribcage, testing the warm ridges of flesh, sensing the accelerating thrum of his pulse. An exploration he thoroughly enjoyed until her fingers crept beneath the tight leather of his belt.

On instinct, he stilled the movement before she went too far.

With a start, he opened his eyes. Everything about her behavior rang false. Sure, his male ego craved the notion that she found him irresistible. But she wasn't the type of woman to initiate sex on a whim. He took stock of her face, searching for clues.

This wasn't merely a reckless mood. There was more going on here. Following a hunch, he asked, "How was the visit with your mother?"

"Who told you she was here?"

"Kay spoke with Jada. They asked me to find you." He rubbed his nose across hers, savoring the silken texture of her skin. "Sarah doesn't usually jump on a flight for an afternoon visit. What did she want?"

"Oh, the usual. For me to lose ten pounds and get my hair styled." A shadow crossed her face. "My obedience in all matters pertaining to the family legacy."

"You mentioned the renovations?"

Impatience creased the corners of Linnie's mouth. "They didn't change her mind about the contract. She wants me to carry on, but only until Freddie buys me out. I'm playing the role of stand-in until he's tired of filmmaking."

It was astonishing how poorly the Wayfairs understood their son. "Freddie loves his work. Strange villains in outer space and fantasy adventures under the sea. Do they actually think he'll quit?"

"Oh, not right away." She slipped her hands free of his hold. Considering, she made slow circles on his shirt. "The weird part? My mother explained how my father pulled the same stunt—took off when he was young. Apparently he wanted nothing to do with the inheritance. He dreamt of becoming an Impressionist painter. Isn't that odd? He even spent a summer in Paris."

"Treat planned a career as an artist?"

The notion bordered on the bizarre. Her father was composed of stark lines and sharp edges. Nothing in his personality hinted at the softer attributes necessary for an artist. It was easier to imagine him choosing work in corporate negotiations or as a drill sergeant.

She read the incredulity on his face. "I'm not making this up," she assured him. "My father spent a summer painting landscapes, which is why my parents took Freddie's behavior in stride. I've always wondered why they weren't shocked when he took the money, why they forgave so easily. It never made sense."

"They won't rethink the inheritance?"

"Not a chance. My success running the Wayfair, small as it's been, doesn't factor in. I'm sure they've never debated if I'm better suited."

"You don't have to take this." He marshaled a list of options. "Let's fight them in court. It's one thing to demand obedience from your children, quite another to press your interests during a legal proceeding."

"You're shooting in the dark. I signed the contract. I agreed to the terms."

"You signed under duress and without legal counsel."

"I should've read the whole document."

"True, and judges don't like cases like yours. Not much grey area, and you were old enough to understand the nature of the agreement you'd entered into. All of which may prove immaterial. The *threat* of legal action may be enough. Call your parents' bluff. See if they fold."

"Daniel, the contract is clear. If I don't play by the rules, my shares revert to the estate. A bluff won't change anything."

"Then we argue for a settlement based on years of service and fair market value for your portion of the Wayfair. Or we simplify matters further and sue for lost wages. Given your responsibilities as general manager, your salary should near six figures. Aren't you the lowest-paid employee on staff? You deserve compensation."

She rested her cheek on his chest. "You're asking me to go to war with my family?"

He cupped the nape of her neck. "Is there a choice?" Treat and Sarah insisted on rigging the game. To Daniel's mind, they'd never see reason *without* the threat of a lawsuit. "Your parents assume you'll follow their directives because you have in the past. It's time to demonstrate you're playing by new rules."

The slightest tremor rippled down her spine. A fan of lashes hid her eyes as she drifted out of his embrace. Far above, the breeze jostled the leaves before dying down, leaving a pregnant stillness. In the green light dappling the shade, Linnie appeared small, defenseless.

Daniel nursed his own worries. Had the conversation with her mother undermined Linnie in some vital way?

Gingerly she stepped to the edge of the creek. "I won't tear my family apart." Her voice sank into the gurgling waters.

"There's nothing wrong with standing up for your rights."

"No, Daniel. They won't grasp why I'm forcing them to change, and it'll hurt them."

Impatience jolted through him. "Then walk away. Find a new career."

The suggestion started her eyes flashing. "What about the years invested in the Wayfair? Should I pretend they don't matter? Toss them out like yesterday's garbage and move on?"

The switch from passion to anger was unsettling. But understandable. Given the bind her parents had put her in, she needed to lash out. Only a fool would take the bait.

"If you enjoy hospitality management, put your skills to use at a national chain. Hilton, Marriott, Sheraton—take your pick," he said reasonably. "A dozen first-rate hotels would gladly hire a woman with your résumé. For years, you've managed an inn singlehandedly. Brought the enterprise back from the brink of bankruptcy, proven your mettle."

The compliments didn't erase the obstinacy from her expression. "In case you haven't noticed, none of the major chains put hotels in a town the size of Sweet Lake," she said. "I'd have to move to Columbus or Cincinnati. Pull up roots, start over."

"You wouldn't start over alone. You'd have me."

His sincerity moved her heart into her throat. "Daniel, I'm not ready to talk about forevers. You shouldn't be either." She glanced at him, hoping for understanding. He looked at her, unblinking. "We'll start dating and see where it leads. That's how couples begin—they date and hold off on the heavy stuff until later."

"What if I don't want to hold off?"

At the bullish light entering his eyes, she pressed her fingers to her temples. "I can't do this right now." Frustrated, she nodded in the direction of the inn. She tried grounding her emotions, but the frustration welling inside her was too strong. Needing to release it, she added, "Why do you keep pushing me? I just sat through an incredibly difficult meeting with my mother, and I'm about to begin service for two hundred guests in the ballroom. I've also got other guests at the inn, but they're getting short shrift tonight. Please, Daniel. Can you just *wait*?"

Oddly, he didn't answer directly. He didn't acknowledge her outburst at all.

"You're giving up on getting control of the inn?" he asked, his eyes hooded. "You can't reason with your parents, but you can't leave the Wayfair either. What exactly did Sarah tell you? I'm merely curious. I never thought you'd surrender without a fight."

His words cut her deeply. She was still searching for a reply when he approached.

"I need to know," he said, and she shrank back from the bitterness overtaking his features. "Can you ever love me as much as a piece of real estate that's caused you nothing but grief? The truth, Linnie. You've always rated second place with your parents. So tell me. Will I always rate second place with you?"

Chapter 16

Shrimp and chunks of ice skidded across the floor.

Joggling on her crimson pumps, Linnie stepped out of danger without a moment to spare. The tattooed youth masquerading as a waiter stared numbly at the mess he'd made.

At the stove, Ellis Leavey glanced heavenward for celestial intervention or, at minimum, the patience to avoid wringing the necks of the workers foisted on him for the evening. The cook rarely lost his cool. Losing five pounds of shellfish needed for shrimp cocktails might do the trick.

The sous-chef who'd arrived with the rest of Freddie's hires gave no reaction to the shrimp careening past her boots. She also turned a blind eye to Ellis's glowering regard and the onions on the chopping block. The buxom redhead pecked out another text message, snickered, then read the reply. Linnie made a mental note to increase the cook's salary for courage under fire. If he resorted to murder before the night was out, she'd back him up on a temporary insanity plea.

The waiter glanced from the platter in his clumsy hands to the emancipated shellfish at his feet.

Was the kid high? Linnie caught a pungent whiff of pot. The aroma reminded her of Freddie's third year at Ohio State. During his Greenpeace phase, he'd never been without a stash.

She snapped her fingers before the waiter's nose.

His eyes lurched to hers, and she said, "Clean up this mess before someone slips on the ice. You have one minute. Throw the shrimp away, and use the towels under the sink. Get moving."

The kid trudged past. Ellis, fed up with the texting, hurled the sous-chef's phone into a drawer. He slapped an onion into the woman's palm.

Satisfied when she began chopping, he turned his sights on Linnie. "When are the others coming in?" He prowled between his assistant and the stove with a panther's dangerous grace.

"Soon. Some of our former employees will also work tonight." She'd managed to pull together eighteen ready hands from the staff let go seven years ago.

He glanced at her swiftly. "Good of you to bring back some of the old help."

"Let's hope I can make it permanent. We'll see." Given the money Freddie had returned, she could reinstate some of them quickly.

Ellis picked up a wooden spoon. Whether he intended to smack his sluggish assistant or stir the pot bubbling on the stove wasn't clear.

"Just don't leave me in the lurch," he said. "We still have to finish dinner service for the inn's regular guests."

He moved toward the pot, and she exhaled with relief. "You'll have enough people." Eleven more employees culled from first and second shifts, plus the former employees who were coming in. "Jada also found several college students to help with service in the Sunshine Room."

"Yeah, she mentioned the Hail Mary pass. Most of the students are due within the hour."

"If you're still running short, we'll move several of the temp waiters to kitchen duty. I'd rather have slow service in the ballroom than no meals at all."

"You'll switch Freddie's pretenders to kitchen duty?" He eyed the kid chasing shrimp across the floor. "I don't mind giving the old employees a refresher course, but don't do me any favors with the idiots Freddie brought in."

"Your call, totally."

"I'll find a way to manage." He scooped up a chunk of ice, tossed it into the garbage. "I think."

The matter settled, she tiptoed away from the cloud of discontent forming around him. In the service corridor, the chatter of early diners in the Sunshine Room collided with the romantic notes of big band music drifting from the ballroom. Linnie followed the music toward the front of the inn.

The party hadn't yet officially begun, but the nine-piece ensemble on the dais was already playing. From the chandeliers, crests of light silvered the ruby-red bunting festooning the walls.

At the opposite end of the ballroom, Silvia and Marco stood at the head of the receiving line. Among the first arrivals were many of the Sirens and their husbands.

Guests clustered around tables frosted with white linens. The tables showed off centerpieces of ivory roses—Silvia's favorite flower. By the windows framing the grounds, several of the older Sirens shared laughter in a private circle.

Near the empty dance floor, Linnie came to a standstill. The ballroom's glimmering excitement stood in stark contrast to her mood.

Daniel's harsh words in the forest continued to haunt her. Somehow she'd led him to believe her attachment to the inn trumped her affection for him. She was falling deeply in love, her passions spurring her on without full consent of an intellect more prone to careful action. Why hadn't she revealed how much he meant to her? Since their first, fateful kiss, she'd done nothing but confide doubts in their ability to forge a lasting relationship. She'd asked Daniel to take it slow. She'd thwarted him at every turn. Not once had she admitted how completely she'd fallen for him.

"Why the long face?"

Frances drew Linnie from her musings. Waves of charcoal fabric rustled pleasingly as she came forward.

"Well?" she prodded. She carried a vintage fan, which she waved for emphasis. "Stewing alone won't solve the problem. Why not tell me what's the matter?"

"Nothing, really." Linnie inked her voice with false cheer. "Just have a lot on my mind."

"I imagine you do."

"Oh, I don't mean the party. We're short several pounds of shrimp, but everything else is going well."

Softly Frances chuckled. "I didn't think the party was the source of your distress. Is your mother's visit troubling you, or does this concern Daniel?"

Denying the truth didn't appeal, and Linnie admitted, "Both, I guess." The silence lengthened before she came to a decision, saying, "Frances, you've known my parents forever."

Amusement crinkled at the edges of her hazel eyes. "I certainly have." She drew Linnie close, whispering, "I have the impression you'd like to ask something important."

She recalled Daniel's parting shots in the forest. "This will sound infantile."

"Why don't you let me be the judge? Ask away."

"Do they love Freddie more?" The possibility was cold, foreign.

She expected the question to put surprise on the wealthy matron's face. Instead Frances peered down her nose with enough mirth to give Linnie the impression she'd asked the wrong question.

A suspicion Frances corroborated when she said, "You might consider if you're viewing your parents from the wrong angle."

"How so?"

"Although they love you and Freddie equally, they work to win his love. They take yours for granted. Any idea why?"

She lifted her shoulders in a careless shrug. "Got me," she admitted.

A secret amusement glittered in Frances's eyes. "I have a question for you," she countered. "But first, you must promise to answer from the heart."

"All right."

"Do you ever put yourself first? I don't mean horning in on another's good fortune or marching over the people you love for material gain. We're speaking of the spirit. On the ethereal plane, do you put yourself first?"

"Honestly, Frances. When you leap into the Siren lingo, I'm hearing gibberish."

"You hear well enough. You resist the message."

"About putting myself first?" She picked at her gown's tight bodice and screwed on her thinking cap. "I guess I'm not comfortable with the idea," she said, unsure if she was failing a critical test. "It feels . . . greedy."

"There's a world of difference between greed and abundance. Discovering your deepest needs and then fulfilling them has everything to do with self-love." As Linnie attempted to absorb this nugget of wisdom, Frances added, "Linnie, your parents take your love for granted because you're predictable. Everyone needs a shock to the system once in awhile. You, your parents—surprise them. Go against the grain. Surprise yourself."

"Got it." She didn't, but she spotted Cat rushing across the dance floor. Was she approaching with the first problem of the evening? Half of the guests hadn't even arrived yet. Linnie had assumed they'd get past hors d'oeuvres before the first snafus occurred.

Frances said, "This looks like trouble." She patted Linnie's cheek. "Try to enjoy the party."

She left as Cat bounded up. Sheer layers of royal-blue and ivory chiffon spilled from the waistline of Cat's gown. She resembled a sexy princess, minus the tiara.

"I was beginning to think you'd taken another hike in the woods. I've been looking for you everywhere."

"What's up?"

"The guests aren't receiving drinks." Cat motioned to the people milling near the receiving line. "Thank goodness my parents are still greeting people. If my mother notices, we'll all catch hell."

Linnie pointed to LaTasha Peale, a former employee who was already on the floor and hurrying between guests. "LaTasha's serving. I'm sure the others are too."

"The problem's with Freddie's hires. You have to do something. They're sneaking rum and Cokes."

And Frances wondered why Linnie didn't put herself first. How to find the time with all the fires she needed to put out?

"I'd like to check on dinner service for our regular guests in the Sunshine Room," she said. "Can't Jada deal with Freddie's so-called waiters?" Foisting the duty on her irritating brother was preferable, but his flight back had been late. He was probably still dressing.

"Forget about dumping the task on Jada. She didn't finish my parents' anniversary cake until ten minutes ago." Cat bounced a thumb toward the ceiling. "She's in the south wing getting dressed."

"Fine. Point me in the direction of the drunken revelry."

"Go through the lobby to the johns near the service corridor. You'll hear them."

Resigned to the task, Linnie slipped through the crowd. In the lobby, Daisy from housekeeping waved as she rushed past in her pretty frock. A family of four, tracking in sand from the beach, stopped to watch partygoers breeze to the ballroom.

Walking past, Linnie zeroed in on raucous laughter.

Sure enough, a group of workers stood at the end of the hallway outside the lavatories. Three women and two men—most held tumblers of liquor.

"I'm paying you to wait tables, not raid the bar." She nodded at the tumblers. "Drop them off in the kitchen and get back to work."

A man with caterpillar eyebrows threw a look of impatience. "What's the big deal?"

Employees never questioned her authority. Linnie bristled. "Do I need to spell it out? No drinking allowed. Break the rule, and you're gone without pay."

A girl with translucent skin glared. "We've had about ten seconds to get into our roles. We're working out the kinks. Is one drink the end of the world?"

"While you're on the job? Yes."

"Well, I'm having trouble with motivation."

"How's this for motivation?" Linnie growled. "Two hundred guests are filling the ballroom, and they're thirsty. You're a waitress. Serve them."

"I get that, but *what's my motivation*?" The woman flapped her arms, sloshing booze from her glass. "Am I angry or grateful for the job?"

Linnie teetered on her heels. Then panic seized her. Did Freddie come up empty at the temp agency? Evidently he'd brought in actors, which meant she should hand him off to Ellis. Let the cook roast his hide.

Footfalls thundered from behind. Freddie, looking glorious in a tux and bow tie, raced toward them.

"There's no rehearsal—we don't have time." Panting, he skidded to a halt.

The woman noticed her empty glass, grabbed Caterpillar's drink. "I want to renegotiate." She downed the booze.

"You'll do fine, my dear." Turning to the others, Freddie blasted a thousand-watt smile. "I'm looking for realistic interactions. Be spontaneous. Think of the golden age of television, when actors gave their finest performances live before thousands of viewers. You'll be marvelous!"

The group digested the speech with grumbling suspicion. Linnie, considering the ramifications of actors faking roles as waiters, tried to move her frozen larynx.

Her alarm went unnoticed by her dastardly brother. "I have every confidence you'll excel in your roles," he added, sugaring them with more encouragement. "Greet the guests, bring their orders to the bar, and wait for the drinks. My assistant will show you how to fill out the order slips." Patting his golden locks, Freddie craned his neck. "Lexie? Are you here?"

His orange-haired assistant jogged up. Evidently Lexie hadn't received the memo about dressing formally. Black leather pants, a biker's leather jacket over a plunging green top with tassels in unspeakable places—all she was missing was a leather whip.

With an executioner's grin, she herded the temps to the ballroom.

Linnie blocked her brother from traipsing after them. She took hold of his lapels, giving him a shake. "Why did you hire actors to work the party? I need waitstaff, not a bunch of second-rate talent. Are you completely out of your mind?"

Her fury bounced off his expensively clad shoulders. Pulling from her clutches, he tripped his attention down her outfit. Delight sparked on his mouth. Long fingers pressed to his chin.

"A marvel of nature," he murmured.

She wasn't following. "What is?"

"You, Linnie. The gown is exquisite. Make fire-engine red your go-to color."

The compliment was a forgery. Wasn't it? Never in their long and complicated relationship had Freddie proffered a compliment.

"And the cut of your gown!" He clapped his palms together. "Remember Marilyn Monroe in *Some Like It Hot?*"

"This dress will asphyxiate me before the night's out." She peeked in the mirror beside the entryway to the women's restroom. "I do like the style. I'm not sure about the heels. Jada insisted. Feels like I'm standing on a ladder."

"Beware of Silvia's nephews, the ones from Cleveland. They're on the hunt. Heartbreakers, both of them."

Linnie swayed on her dangerous pumps. It was a toss-up what was more disorienting—the protective tone in her brother's voice or his inability to recall the many hearts *he'd* broken in a long and inglorious career.

Softening beneath his genuine tone, she said, "Give it to me straight. Why did you hire actors to work tonight?"

"Culled from a theater in Columbus," he supplied. "They were in the second week of *Music Man*. An electrical fire closed the place."

"In your suite, you told Lexie to call a temp agency. I was there. I remember."

He ambled down the hallway. "She misunderstood. We were mired in screenplay revisions. The lead actress threatening to quit, the August film schedule in jeopardy—Lexie thought we were moving production to Ohio if we lost our leading lady."

She hurried to catch up. "That doesn't make sense. All your films are shot in California. Why would she assume you're moving production here?"

"I don't restrict shoots to California."

"What?"

He sighed with exasperation. "You *are* out of the loop. Last year, we shot in India. The year before, Brazil."

Her brother, a globe-trotting filmmaker? She *was* out of the loop.

"Don't blame Lexie," he said. "She hasn't been herself since the Sirens stormed my suite. She isn't used to middle-aged women employing craft store weapons."

"Okay, I won't blame your assistant. I'd rather blame you. What am I supposed to do? I can't have summer stock actors faking roles as waitstaff."

"They're serving drinks and dinner, not performing surgery. They'll manage."

"Consider yourself on bar patrol, Freddie. Your hires, your problem. Keep them out of my booze."

"Fine. I will."

Nearing the lobby, he stopped. She nearly collided with him.

"How was the visit with Mother?" he asked. "I'm sorry I missed her."

An authentic compliment about her gown wasn't the same as détente between siblings. "I'm sure you know exactly how the meeting went," she said, scaling the battlements.

"Hardly. I've been too busy to check in with her. I do hope the pup has stopped piddling on the floor."

"Give me a break. Did you book a late flight back to Ohio so she'd get me alone? I'm sure you've been laying the groundwork, making sure she knew you wanted control. Not today or tomorrow, but someday—and why not have Sugarpop run the place until you're ready to claim your inheritance?"

"You're under the impression I . . . *coached* Mother on what to do?"

The question didn't merit a reply. His rapport with their father bordered on nonexistent. There was no doubt he'd influenced their mother.

"Think I'll roll over and take this?" she demanded.

"You usually do."

The jab plunged into the ventricle recently bruised by Daniel. "Not this time. Plan on a fight to the finish."

"Don't bother with the ultimatums." He gave a devil's grin. "Get your own script."

"How's this for new lines? I'll hire the best law firm in the tri-state area." She didn't have the stomach to destroy her family. But sticking up for herself felt great, so she plowed ahead with the fabrication. "I'll get a legal team with lots of experience wading through messy family agreements."

"You're threatening legal action?"

"You catch on fast."

"A twist in the plot. And without a hint of foreshadowing. Intriguing." He narrowed his regard, a shark scenting blood in the water. "To clarify, you'd risk court without Daniel at your side? Did you have a spat?"

"Don't ask for details about my private life. We've never been close, remember? You're the last person I'd confide in."

They reached the lobby. Guests stepping in from the veranda stalled beneath the raised voices.

Relishing the attention, Freddie nodded at the audience. "Now I haven't a clue where the plot shall lead," he said, lifting his voice another octave. "Saint Daniel stumbles. What did he do to upset my normally placid sister? You look absolutely volcanic. Do you need a sword to cut him down? If there's a joust scheduled, I'll buy a ticket. Front row, please."

To her horror, Daniel materialized from the crowd. There was no telling how much he'd heard.

"She's not selling tickets." He towered over her brother. "Fair warning, Freddie. Stick around, and I'll make sure you wish you hadn't."

"Enter the Saint of Sweet Lake. Good evening, sir." Freddie sniffed the pain and fury colliding before him. "This *is* peculiar. Should I depart? My sister is beginning to resemble an incendiary device."

Linnie's hold on her emotions loosened. She wasn't prepared for Daniel, not with an apology forming on his handsome features and his eyes attempting vainly to catch hers. The bouquet of roses in his fist hung loosely, nearly skimming his polished shoes. He'd worn the charcoal-grey suit, the outfit he saved for court appearances. He looked dashing in a harried and visibly upset way.

"If you'll excuse me." She pivoted toward the Sunshine Room. "I should check on dinner service before joining the party."

Daniel stepped forward. "May I accompany you?"

"No. Go to the ballroom."

Freddie put in, "Another twist. I thought you'd tell him to go to hell."

Daniel gripped Freddie's shoulder, turning him by force. "Go. Away." He returned to her side. "Let's not ruin our date. We'll go into the party together. These are for you."

Flowers wagged in her face. "They're lovely," she said. "Give them to someone who cares."

She walked toward the Sunshine Room with as much dignity as three-inch heels allowed. With most of the staff working the party, service for the inn's regular guests was suffering. A skeleton crew of waitresses dashed between tables. A father with fogged spectacles and two boisterous toddlers flagged her down.

"Miss?" Swiping at his glasses, he appraised her formalwear with bafflement. "We've been waiting thirty minutes to order."

"Linnie, will you give me one—"

The apology stiffened her spine. Taking Daniel by the arm, she thrust him before the table. "Take their order," she commanded. "Give it to one of the waitresses."

"I don't have a pen or paper."

"Daniel, you made it through law school with flying colors. Memorize."

The roses hung in his dejected grasp. She took the bouquet and stalked off. A couple stewing at table nine, a family with three adolescent boys gripping forks with looks of starvation—let the service decline much further, and a slew of one-star reviews would pop up on Travelocity.

At table eleven, a waitress dealt out the orders on her tray like winning hands in blackjack. When she'd finished, Linnie pulled her aside. "Give these to our female guests." She handed off the bouquet.

"Gosh, red roses. Can I have one?"

"No."

The dash of hostility snapped the waitress to attention. "Right."

"If an order takes longer than fifteen minutes, tell the other waitresses not to charge for the meal."

"Sure thing, Miss Wayfair."

The kitchen. Was Ellis still waiting for regular staff? Best to check before heading to the ballroom. With a little ingenuity, avoiding Daniel all night was a no-brainer.

Strong fingers clamped around her waist.

Daniel half walked, half carried her out the French doors to the patio. Cool air swirled through the railing. The sun, weary from the day, pulled a carpet of stars across the firmament.

"What are you doing?" She wrenched free.

A bad sign: his eyes wore the intimidating hue of forged metal. Her stomach knotted beneath his tightly constrained anger.

Then a reprieve as his attention sank from her face. His eyes ranged across the silver screen–worthy dress. For a heart-stopping moment, he paused at her cleavage. He rubbed his chin, dazed. A thrilling emotion bounced through her ribcage.

"Daniel, I'm busy," she got out with a skinny dose of dignity. The way he was staring at her breasts, he'd need a cold shower before joining the party. "Whatever you have to say can wait until tomorrow. Call me. I might pick up."

The dismissal yanked him from his bedazzlement. "We need to talk now." He looked at her imploringly. "This afternoon, I didn't mean to lose my cool. I'd never intentionally hurt you. I was totally out of line."

A decent attempt at an apology, but she was too angry to accept it. "I didn't even know you had a temper," she tossed back. "Feel free to stow it in the future."

"Look, I'm sorry. I didn't mean what I said about your parents."

"Yes, you did."

He was no more comfortable with falsehoods than she. "Okay— you're right," he conceded, dragging nervous fingers across his scalp.

"I do think your parents should get their priorities straight, especially where you're concerned."

"Why don't you say what you really mean? You're convinced they don't love me." She backed up, sought the railing for support. The wood scratched against the thin material of her gown, catching the threads. She didn't care. "My parents have incredibly dated ideas about the inn and tradition, but they don't play favorites. They love me just as much as Freddie. For Pete's sake, when we were kids, you would've thought *I* was the favorite. They never had a decent word for my brother. The big disappointment with his lousy grades and poor manners—my father argued with him constantly."

Daniel moved in, careful not to touch her. "Were you scared?"

A non sequitur, the meaning unclear. "What do you mean?"

"Your father. Were you frightened when Treat argued with Freddie?"

"Yes," she whispered, and the admission drove straight through her heart.

"How often did they go at it?"

"Constantly. The warring didn't stop until Freddie left for California." The earth tilted on its axis. A stream of images followed, each memory more painful than the last. "You've never seen my father at full throttle. Cornering my brother, threatening to ship him off to boarding school if he didn't get his act together. Bad enough when we were little. So much worse after Freddie reached high school, learned to fight back. I thought they'd come to blows."

"They didn't?"

"No. Never." Loyalty compelled her to add, "My father isn't the sort of man who'd strike his children."

"Doesn't make his behavior acceptable." Daniel frowned. "Your mother's either. She should've asked him to tone down his temper."

Emotion rose inside her, threatened to spill over. "Stop talking about my parents."

"I'd rather talk about us. I don't think you're ready for the conversation." She tried to march past, but he stopped her, adding, "Linnie, I really need to know. Will your feelings for me always take second place to the inn?"

Sorrow wound through the query, and doubt. "Of course not," she replied, hating the quaver in her voice—hating how she'd given him reason to question her devotion.

"I want to believe you."

"But you don't, which is my fault. I want this to work with you—I do. That doesn't mean I can pretend the inn's not in jeopardy, and my future here as well. My mother's visit didn't go as planned, and I'm hurt. If you feel like I've been pushing you away, I'm sorry." She met his eyes with a look of entreaty. "I don't care about the inn as much as I care about you. Not even close."

"I'll do whatever you want. Stay in Sweet Lake, or leave. Tell me what you need."

A sense of responsibility to Silvia and her guests warred with the ache centering in her ribcage. "Let's not go into this tonight," she said, choosing responsibility. "I should check on the kitchen staff."

He let her go. A trivial concession. The soft greying of his eyes held her in place.

Softly he said, "I love you."

The moment ground to a standstill. The clink of water glasses hustled on a tray. The breeze fondling the hem of her gown. Daniel, assessing her face for a reaction, for any sign he hadn't lost her.

Finding none, he added, "I love you heart and soul. Maybe I'm the first. Maybe no one's ever noticed how special you are until I came along. Your parents don't. Freddie sure doesn't. But they're your family, and Lord knows you're devoted. You don't love easily, but you never stop once you make the leap. Can't you find a way to love me too? I'll never let you down."

"You never have. You wouldn't know how." She climbed out from beneath the raw emotion clouding her mind. "You've been my rock for as long as I can remember, as good a friend as Jada or Cat—but you're so much more, the best man I know, the man I want to spend my life with. I love you, Daniel. I'm trying to make this work, trying to understand this fierce, consuming emotion that's been hounding me since we kissed the night Freddie arrived."

The declaration thumped against Daniel. He stiffened, a tall man at risk of losing his purchase on gravity.

"But I love my parents, and my brother too," she added, refusing to sink beneath the passion rising between them. "I don't know how to fix everything wrong with my family. I'm not even sure how to forgive my brother, and nothing would give my parents greater joy." Without conscious planning, she allowed her heart to veer in a new direction. "The other day? I was talking to Frances. She caught me on her way out of the Sunshine Room. She'd just finished lunch with Penelope and Tilda."

"What did you talk about?"

"Did you know she's the oldest of five sisters? I never even knew she had a sister. Guess her family grew up outside Cincinnati."

"Linnie, I have no idea where you're heading with this."

"Frances has a saying about sibs. It struck me as corny when we were chatting. Now I feel differently."

"What was the saying?"

"A sibling carries your history."

She read the longing in his eyes, felt her bruised heart answer in kind. One of the busboys peered through the French doors but left them to their privacy.

"Beautiful, don't you agree?" She lifted her face to the shifting heavens, the orange day bleeding down to the horizon. "We only have our parents for part of the journey—friends too. But a sibling? Freddie remembers the stuffed bunny I dragged around until first grade and the day I got my first pimple. I remember the wild boy of the woods, the tree house he built without our parents' knowledge, and the summer he fell in love with filmmaking. It's the same with you and Philip. I've heard him talk about how you taught him to ride a bike while your dad was away on business."

"Philip told you about the lessons?" Daniel asked, clearly moved. "I wasn't aware he remembered."

"Well, he does. You watched your little brother fall in love—you carried him after he buried his wife. You've been part of each other's lives from the beginning. You'll continue to carry each other's history all the way to old age."

"Frances is wise."

"She is."

"With regard to siblings, she's damn quotable."

Tell me what you need.

Inside Linnie, a desire crystallized.

"Why did Freddie come to Ohio?" she asked, tacking deep into her heart, unaware of what she needed, precisely, until her voice added form to necessity. "This is one time you must forget attorney-client privilege. For me. For us."

Tears caught on her lashes. She let them clot the mascara she'd applied earlier. Daniel leaned closer.

Warding him off, she said, "Fixing everything that's broken in my family might be impossible. I might be wasting my time. But I can't try without all the facts. Whatever brought Freddie here matters. It matters a great deal. I've never understood the first thing about my brother—I'd like to start. So I'm asking. Don't say you love me and then pretend it's okay to hide the truth."

Regret burned in Daniel's eyes. "Linnie . . ."

Disappointment steadied her chin. She loved him, and so she waited. Ticking off the seconds, she hoped for a miracle. For proof Daniel prized devotion above all else.

His silence remained unbroken.

Head bowed, she brushed past.

Chapter 17

Dragging out a chair, Philip sat heavily.

"Man, I never thought I'd escape," he told Daniel. He murmured greetings to the others at the table, Marco's great-uncle and his wife, and a clutch of pubescent cousins who'd waited too long to grab seats. "Don't think I can deal with much more *Pretty, Pretty Princess*. Who invents these games? Fancy wouldn't go to bed until she'd covered herself in glitz."

Daniel grunted. "Why didn't you ask the babysitter to play? Would've made for a clean escape."

"She *was* playing. Fancy insisted on all three of us." Philip craned his neck, searched in vain for a waiter. He eyed Daniel's untouched meal. "You mind?"

"Go right ahead."

With relish, he dug in. "I love prime rib."

The cousins finished their plates, took off for the dance floor. The great-uncle rose next, led his wife toward the music.

Once they were alone Philip asked, "Why are we stuck in the back of the room? I thought we'd share a table with Linnie and Jada."

"Change of plans."

Philip accepted the explanation. A relief, since the lowdown would lead to a revelation of Daniel's true feelings for Linnie. His dreamy kid brother still wasn't up to speed. It was entirely possible he'd miss the obvious until a wedding invitation dropped into his mailbox. Of course, a wedding wasn't a done deal.

Not until there was a plan to patch things up.

Women. Whatever happened to his ability to read Linnie without error? For years he'd provided counsel and guidance, assessing her internal temperature with ease. He'd gauged her moods with unerring precision. Toss romance into the mix, and he was picking up so much static, he wasn't sure how to get a message through.

Or how to fix this. There was no clear indication of where to start. She'd professed her love—a thrilling development his miserable heart refused to celebrate—then backed off twenty paces. All night long she'd veered out of his path. He was beginning to feel like he carried some sort of plague. He'd given up trying to approach her.

Was it time to quit the battlefield and return home to his lonely mutt? He'd recite Linnie's name like a poem, give the dog over to tortured howls until the few neighbors not invited to the party called the police.

Philip elbowed him. "What's the matter with you?"

"Nothing."

"If you had a crappy day at work, put it behind you. Great music, lots of beautiful women—it's playtime." His brother swiveled in his chair. "Mind if I ditch you? I see a good target by the dance floor."

Daniel peered over the heads at the tables blocking theirs. "Better hurry. Silvia's got two nephews with 'sex maniac' written all over them. A third one too, but that chump can't be older than twenty-five. You can take him."

"Guess it's time to try out my dancing shoes."

Curiosity pulled Daniel from his fog. "Do you want to ask Jada to dance?" Since his wife's funeral, Philip hadn't so much as mentioned dating.

His brother shrugged, a clumsy ruse. "Think she will? I mean, if she's not busy?"

"Get moving. The Latin A team will crowd in if you don't."

His brother stuffed a last roll in his mouth, brightened. "Kay!" Swallowing, he waved her over. "Mind keeping a sulky bastard company? He's oozing bad vibes. I'm too busy to cheer him up. They're playing my song."

Kay adjusted the beaded shawl nesting on her shoulders. "We'll stay with him," she told Philip.

Daniel weighed the social call against a root canal. The dentist won out.

"I'm fine by myself, Kay."

"Pouting in public? So unlike you."

"I'm not pouting."

"You have a reputation to uphold. Besides, doom and gloom doesn't suit."

"We're staying," Frances added.

Nearing, she swished layers of charcoal fabric. The old dame looked good in the classic gown and diamond necklace. The Siren-inspired earrings ruined the effect. On each ear, white string wrapped around cobalt-blue feathers.

From a blue jay? Daniel hoped she wasn't picking off birds with her late husband's rifle.

Dredging up his manners, he held out chairs. The women hemmed him in.

Frances patted his hand. "Lovers' quarrel? The roses were beautiful. I'm sure the diners in the Sunshine Room appreciated them."

Hoodwinking the Oracle of Delphi was probably easier. "Yes, Frances," he admitted. "I'm quarreling with Linnie."

"How difficult." The old dame sipped primly at her martini. "Have you tried sex? Archibald, God rest his soul, mended hundreds of our quarrels with the heat of his loins. I never could latch on to my fury when he got that look on his face."

"Frances! I'm not comfortable discussing my sex life with you."

Kay muttered, "Or lack thereof." He glowered, and she shrugged, asking, "What happened?"

He waited a beat then admitted, "Linnie wants something I can't give."

Veering off point, Frances put in, "You *can* give her whatever she needs. There's nothing wrong with experimenting. Have you tried those devices? Some women need help reaching organism."

"I think you mean *orgasm*." Daniel peered at her closely. "How much booze have you had?"

Following up, Kay swatted her. "Frances, this is your last martini. For a woman who prizes her dignity, you cannot hold your liquor." Lowering her voice, she asked him, "Do you mean the matter with Freddie?"

"Kay, I can't disclose his business. I won't sidestep my ethics, no matter what my feelings want."

"You're a fine man."

"Linnie would debate your assessment."

"Why does she care about Freddie's business?"

"Curiosity, mostly. They don't get along, and she'd like to know what's behind this visit. She's aware the inn wasn't the real draw."

Frances said, "I imagine she craves what she's never had." He frowned, and she added, "Daniel, you've had your nose pressed to the glass for too long. You don't see the Wayfairs for what they are."

"Which is?"

"A family encumbered by history. Every first grader in Sweet Lake learns about the Wayfairs alongside stories of Johnny Appleseed. Their ambition founded this town. The Wayfairs spend more time protecting that monument of an inn than interacting like normal people. All the talk of their uncanny luck. Siring a son in each generation ended up being a curse, frankly."

He wondered if she was onto something. "Why a curse?" he asked.

"Until Linnie came along, they were never forced to choose between family and real estate. They'll hurt their daughter to protect their son."

The explanation tacked close to his own theory on the Wayfairs. Considering, he relieved Frances of her martini. "When we were arguing, I implied her parents didn't love her." He took a long sip, the gin scorching his throat. "I really messed up."

Frances sighed. "Don't be silly. Of course they love her. Sarah and Treat are traditionalists. From their perspective, running the Wayfair is a man's business. They'd rather Linnie found a suitable husband and made her personal life the primary focus."

In a frustrated gulp, he downed the martini. The notion of a woman with Linnie's intellect putting diapers and kiddie homework before her career was nuts. She'd do both—with his help, since he'd gladly perform the role of loving husband.

"They still believe Freddie will come back to run the inn," Frances continued. "It pains me to say this, but if they've failed either of their children, it's their heartbreaker of a son."

Daniel reeled at the ready defense. "How do you figure?"

"Freddie nearly flunked every year until college. How did he manage to do well at Ohio State? And he *did* excel. My late husband and I were friends with the dean of arts and sciences—Doug Williams. Right before Freddie enrolled, Treat gave OSU a substantial gift. Believe me, Doug kept watch over the boy." She paused long enough for Daniel to absorb the explanation. Then she added, "He's dyslexic."

The revelation startled Daniel. "You're positive about this?" he asked.

"Oh yes. Doug got him help without breathing a word to Sarah or Treat. A minor point, since they never would've sought help when Freddie was a child. A Wayfair in need of special education? Treat wouldn't have allowed it."

"I'll say one thing for Freddie," Kay remarked, breaking into the conversation. "He comes up with the most insane solutions. Yet they succeed. The workers he hired are actors. Every meal delivered has been cold, but no one cares. They've kept the guests entertained all night."

In his funk, Daniel wasn't aware of the impromptu entertainment. Now his attention veered to the center of the tables, where two waiters stood before a group of diners. The band paused, allowing the men to sing. They were good.

He asked, "Does Linnie know her brother hired imposters?"

The question was barely out when he caught sight of her near the dais. Silvia's nephew, the older one with the beard, whispered in her ear. She laughed, the gaiety forced. She swayed gently side to side. Daniel recognized the mannerism, an indication of nerves or distress. She did the metronome thing every year at tax season. It appeared the nephew had asked her to dance, and she'd halfheartedly agreed.

Frances swerved from the topic of special needs children to the indignities of YouTube videos. Daniel watched her lips moving with his anxiety rising. Silvia's husband, Marco, stood to toast his wife, blocking the view. Daniel craned his neck. Then Marco escorted his wife to the dance floor. The view cleared.

Sweat pearled in Daniel's armpits. The nephew took Linnie by the hand. She didn't look keen on dancing, but the bastard was persistent. She allowed him to escort her to the dance floor.

As if on cue, the chandeliers dimmed. The band resumed playing. "Dancing in the Dark."

A sense of urgency carried Daniel across the ballroom. Couples swirled through the shadows. The romantic music lured more people to the dance floor, a frustrating crush of eager bodies pairing off in the semidarkness. His eyes adjusting, he wedged past Silvia and Marco. They moved languidly, cheek to cheek.

Where was Linnie? Panic sent his attention darting through the crowd. *There.*

Near the edge of the dance floor, Silvia's nephew spun her in a slow circle. Daniel cut a straight path with the resolve of a linebacker in the fourth quarter. High heels screeched on the parquet floor. Men grunted warnings. There wasn't time for apologies, not with Silvia's nephew putting the moves on Linnie, and he kept going. He nearly clipped Jada. Philip pulled her out of the way.

The nephew spotted incoming. For cover, he swerved Linnie toward the safety of the crowd.

Bad move.

Daniel blocked him. "May I cut in?"

"Find another dance partner. Linnie's taken."

She frowned. "I'm not 'taken' by anyone."

The guy missed the warning in her voice. "You're with me." Apparently he mistook one dance for an all-night commitment.

"Guess again. In fact, why don't I take myself off the dance floor?"

She began swiveling away, but he pulled her back. "Hey, don't go." He nodded at Daniel. "He's the one who should push off."

A sizzling tension shot pain from Daniel's head to his gut. He had five inches and forty pounds on the interloper. Height and muscle were terrible things to waste.

"You want me to push off? How's this?" Grabbing the bastard by the collar, he pushed him to the ground.

The shriek of startled women careened through the music. From somewhere by the tables, a boy cackled. At Daniel's admittedly undignified behavior, Linnie went stock-still. He was still composing an apology when her eyes burned fury across his face. In five clumsy seconds, he'd managed to embarrass her in front of all her guests.

She pushed past an openmouthed Jada and hurtled off the dance floor.

The overload of sensation at her flight immobilized him. Beneath the emotion he detected a sizzling tension. He called out an apology, but she kept going. He wasn't aware he'd started after her until she spun around to ward him off.

They were done with conversation. He'd had his fill.

Lunging, he caught her by the waist. A collective gasp vibrated through the crowd as he lifted her off her feet. Then a smattering of applause from deep in the room as Kay and Frances leapt up. The clapping proved a catalyst, and Sirens across the ballroom came to their feet. Amidst the clapping, he caught sight of Silvia cupping her hands around her mouth and hooting a cheer.

Daniel might have taken a bow if he hadn't already flung a thrashing Linnie over his shoulder.

He marched out.

Chapter 18

"What do you think you're doing? Put me down!"

Daniel was thankful no guests mingled in the lobby or on the stairwell. It was one thing to pull a caveman routine in the party, quite another to perform for the paying guests.

Impotent taps of rage landed on his back. "Linnie, cool down." He took the stairwell quickly, then stalked past a row of suites. "There are kids sleeping."

"No kidding, Sherlock. This *is* my place of business. If you think abducting me is a good way to make up, you're way off. This isn't putting you in my good graces."

"Not what I wanted to hear."

He peered into the shadows leading left and right. Where were the stairs to the south wing? In a decade of unrequited love, he'd never asked for a tour. Imagining the mansion from a bird's-eye view, he took his best shot.

Swerving left, he shielded Linnie from bumping into the wall. Giving her a goose egg on the brow wouldn't earn brownie points either. She resumed thrashing with a rage equal parts distressing and titillating. She nearly rolled off his shoulder. Reaching beneath the gown, he latched firmly to the back of a smooth thigh. The move stabilized her—and hitched his temperature up another degree.

I'll get her upstairs to talk, and ditch my inner caveman.

Success wasn't guaranteed on either count. She'd given no indication of chatting calmly. Then again, her squirming femininity resting on his shoulder did amazing things for his libido.

"Daniel, I mean it!" Against his back, she grew still. "Where are you taking me? Wait. No."

The corridor emptied into a dusty stairwell. Fleurs-de-lis decorated the cast-iron banister winding into the air. Cobwebs laced a window dull with grime. Satisfaction spread through him. The south wing was one flight up.

On the walls, blown-glass lamps threw wisps of light. One of the oldest sections of the inn, the south wing was an elegant lady past her prime. Where the wall met the ceiling, yellowed strips of wallpaper peeled back to expose greying plaster. A patter sounded overhead. Squirrels?

Daniel gave himself a mental kick in the ass.

This is where Linnie crawled into bed at night? The air smelled of damp and the dust accumulating since the Eisenhower presidency.

Why didn't he sweep her off her feet long ago? At least she would've bedded down each night in comfort.

He butted his chin against the tempting curve of her buttocks. "Which room is yours?"

"None of your business."

Her arms swayed limply. "You're done beating me up?" He let his questing fingers roam higher on her thigh. She trembled, the response hitting his central nervous system like high-octane fuel. If he didn't stop roaming, his heart would shoot from his chest like a cannonball. "Damn. I enjoyed your angry-woman massage. I was hoping you'd get to my neck. Sitting at a desk all day long makes me stiff."

"Very funny, Daniel. I'm not giving you a massage."

"Will you at least give me five minutes to explain myself? I'm a lawyer, and 'succinct' isn't really my thing."

"Take me downstairs!"

"After we sit down and talk." He caught his fingers inching toward her panties. He pounded his inner caveman into retreat. "If you don't tell me which room is yours, I'll have to use my powers of deduction."

"Good luck. You'll never figure it out."

A game? He was eager to play.

She muttered unintelligibly as he ducked into the first bedroom. Fiesta colors. A disturbing blow-up man propped behind the chaise lounge, with "Happy Birthday!" written across his plastic torso. The antique dresser groaned beneath a trail of cosmetics, hairbrushes, Siren trinkets, and flamboyant jewelry.

He laughed. "I pity the man who falls for Cat. He'd better love chaos."

Linnie tried to wiggle off his shoulder. "You'll never figure out which room is Jada's or mine. We might as well be twins."

He hoisted her back in place. "Try me."

On the opposite side of the hall, a fresh evergreen scent led him in. A comforter the color of tangerines was smoothed neatly across the bed. A photo album rested on the nightstand. He'd begun to enjoy the game, so using the album amounted to cheating. Clothing ordered by style in the closet. A well-thumbed Bible on a settee from the Wayfair's glory days. The settee's walnut arms were polished to a gleam.

Still undecided, he crossed the room. His muscles strained from carrying Linnie, but he was content to keep her in place. He peered at the items on the dresser. A lace doily beneath a single bottle of perfume. A coffee cup with lipstick marks. Several job quotes for the renovation work. Three books from the library, with the due date slip on the top book in the stack.

A translucent green piggy bank, filled to the brim.

"Jada's room," he announced.

On his shoulder Linnie squirmed. "Bravo. You win."

"Do I get a prize?" He'd take a kiss, but thought better of the suggestion.

"No, you do not. Congratulations, you're more astute than antici-pated. But we're not going to my room. I don't bring men up here."

"I'm glad."

She gave him a thump. "Daniel, *you're* a man."

"I'm the only guy allowed up here—ever."

"Mind getting off your high horse before I kick you off?"

He reconsidered. "Cat and Jada may have guests, as long as I vet the guys first. Only the upstanding and responsible need apply."

"Think you're calling the shots? Forget it, pal."

"I'm not your pal. We left that port of call when you landed a kiss on me the night Freddie arrived."

"You'll never visit that port again if you don't listen up." She thumped him again on the back. "Downstairs. Now."

The command barely registered—the next door led into her suite. Daniel entered with the reverence of a man viewing a hidden cache of art. What wonders lay inside? Men occupied places; women possessed them. He was keen for a glimpse of the room where Linnie closed her eyes each night.

Kicking the door shut, he steered her feet to the floor. He aban-doned her to tread a slow circle around the room's perimeter, his hands coasting up and down his thighs with the intensity of his concentration. The first thing that struck him was her scent, layered faintly across the furnishings and drifting lightly through the air. He'd never been able to pinpoint why it stirred him so deeply. Just breathing her in settled his thoughts and gave him a sense of contentment.

Pausing before the rocking chair, he reached for the threadbare robe flung across the arm. With fascination he thumbed the fabric, com-ing across the careful stitching on the arm where Linnie had mended a tear. She knew how to sew? It seemed a charmingly dated pastime, but then he remembered her frugal nature, how carefully she cared for things—and people.

The book tucked beneath the bedside lamp snagged his attention. The pages murmured as he rifled through.

"You read Emerson?" Another discovery, and he felt like a kid on a treasure hunt.

"I like his essay 'Nature.'"

"What's it about?"

Linnie reached for the doorknob. Her hand fell to her side as the charged atmosphere struck her. At a leisurely pace, Daniel had moved off to examine the photos on the walls. Pulling off his suit coat, he tossed it aside like a man digging into work. He picked up her hairbrush and then the compact of blush she'd left out, examining each for a moment before returning them both to the dresser. His unvarnished curiosity moved her deeply.

At length, she replied, "'Nature' is kind of a spiritual look at the natural world. I've read it a dozen times."

He circled back around to the bed. "Sounds nice." Brows lifting, he retrieved the Magic 8 Ball partially hidden beneath a pillow.

"Not mine," she protested. "Cat was in here before the party."

"Divining her future in a kid's toy?"

"Not seriously. Well, her baby clock *does* tick incessantly. She'd convinced some of her cousins to bring friends to the party—all single men. She wanted a hint if she'd meet a nice guy tonight."

"Did she?"

"No idea. I was carried off before checking in with her."

Shrugging off the reprimand, he returned to a portrait hanging near the window. "Your parents look like teenagers in this one."

"Taken the year they married. They *were* young."

"They look happy."

"Not much to burn through their bliss in those days."

He spotted the photo on the end table by the chaise lounge. Jada beaming for the camera in an apron dusted with flour.

He asked, "When she owned the bakery in town?"

Sadness whispered through Linnie. "Opening day." Soon after business declined at the Wayfair, the bakery went under.

"Does she miss the independence?"

"She did. The year after she closed the place was hard for her." Prudence suggested it was time to return downstairs. Resisting the notion, Linnie wandered to the window. Older guests, the first to leave the party, were strolling to their cars. "Jada still handles most of the baking for the inn. She's begun delegating some of the work, leaving room for management duties. She's a natural leader. I'm sure she's aware I'd like to make her co-manager, assuming the Wayfair remains profitable."

For a long moment Daniel regarded her. "You're staying, even if Freddie won't sell?"

"I think so," she replied, hating to disappoint him.

Her emotions rebounded when he said, "Whatever you decide, you have my support. That's what I was trying to tell you earlier."

"I appreciate your understanding."

He'd taken care to give her a wide berth. Now he approached, his eyes solemn.

He dipped a hand into his pocket. "For you."

A jewelry box of blue velvet. What was inside? Worried, she clasped her hands at her waist.

"Relax, Linnie," he said, chuckling. "I wouldn't spring an engagement ring on you without dropping lots of hints."

His smile was contagious, and she felt the knotty tension leave her neck. She opened the box. Gold earrings with diamonds sparkling on fragile threads. Each earring boasted four diamonds. A soft gasp escaped her lips.

With touching concern, he searched her face. "Do you like them? If you don't, we'll return them."

"Oh, Daniel—they're beautiful."

Pleased, he took one and held it to her cheek. "They'll look good on you." He returned the earring to the box.

Grateful, she went up on tiptoes. "I love them," she murmured, kissing his cheek.

The sweet delight melted from his face, leaving behind something masculine and dangerously appealing. Her pulse tripped. She was suddenly aware he was doing his best to keep his eyes leveled on hers. He was determined not to drop his gaze to the gown that plunged daringly to show too much cleavage and caught so tightly at the waist she couldn't breathe. Or maybe it was the look in his eyes that made her breathless.

He slid a glance to the door, returned to an intense survey of her face. "Should I escort you downstairs?"

"Would you rather stay here?" she asked, putting voice to the longing thrumming between them.

He required no more encouragement. Cupping her face, he kissed her with a thoroughness that transformed her longing. Hunger dove to her core. She fumbled with his tie, undoing the knot. The strip of silk came loose from his neck, and she rushed forward in her quest, her fingers moving to unbutton his shirt. The task completed, she reached for the quivering muscles underneath, her caresses timid at first. Then his mouth quickened on hers, an undeniable catalyst that made her caresses brazen. Daniel groaned, a long, pent-up confirmation of need.

He broke off the kiss. "Slow down, Linnie." He nipped at her ear. "My turn."

Without seeking permission, he flicked the gown's straps from her shoulders. The command he took was a potent aphrodisiac, as were his breaths, coming in tight gasps to heighten her arousal.

Dizzy, she swayed closer. He reached behind her, found the zipper. Slowly he tugged downward, his attention locked on her face, gauging her every reaction as the fabric slid apart. Air shivered across her skin. With drowsy regard she watched him drop to one knee. He shimmied the fabric past her waist and hips, his pupils dilating and his breathing raspy. The gown fell in a puddle at her feet.

Desire flushed the sharp angles of his cheekbones. "You're beautiful." Rising, he peeled off his shirt, stepped out of his pants.

"You're not disappointed?" A humiliating query, one she couldn't stop from issuing.

"Linnie, most men have an ideal of the perfect woman." He rubbed his nose across hers. "You've always been mine."

She laughed against the tears catching on her lashes. "You're crazy."

"For you? Always."

Driving home the point, he placed a trail of kisses across her collarbone. She arched willingly, grateful for the love he offered without reservation, savoring the sensation of his rough hands on her skin, unclasping her bra and letting it drop to the floor. He dispatched with her panties as quickly. Her knees weakened beneath the onslaught of his lovemaking, the strokes heating every inch of her skin, his husky, barely discernible voice carrying through her ears with praise and the devotion of a man who'd loved her for more than a decade.

Scooping her into his arms, he strode to the bed. He settled on top of her. They grew quiet as their bodies merged together, muscle and bone. A profound contentment filled Linnie. Gently she traced the lines carved beside his mouth and the faint crow's-feet framing his eyes.

His mouth dipped to hers. His lips tasted of fire.

Sinking beneath the sensation, she clung to his neck, needing more, needing all the love he'd waited to give.

Chapter 19

On his shoulder, Linnie dozed.

Chasing shadows across the ceiling, Daniel snuggled her close. A deep stillness enveloped the Wayfair.

A full night of lovemaking would test any man's endurance, but his muscles sparked with energy. As did his mind, leaping through the last hours, replaying the memory of each minute. Linnie had given herself over. She'd given herself completely. Joy rolled through him in exuberant waves.

Beneath his arm, she stirred. "You're awake?" She eyed him with drowsy amusement. "After taking me to the moon and back three times, I assumed you'd sleep until noon."

"Baby, the rocket ship is ready for another trip anytime you'd like to jump on board."

Grinning, she struggled up onto an elbow. "Haven't you slept?"

"Too excited."

"What are you thinking about?"

"The past, the future. Mostly the future."

"Hmm. That sounds nice." Beside his calf, her toes wiggled. "What time is it?"

"Probably around four." Possessively he slid her thigh over his legs. She'd slept curled into his side in a habit he hoped would become permanent. "Why don't you catch some more shut-eye? I'll wake you before I leave."

"Daniel?"

She left his name hanging in the cool air. Her fingers wove a lazy trail through his chest hair.

"Yeah?"

"I was also thinking."

"While you were sleeping? That's a neat trick."

"I have many talents." She rubbed her chin across his chest, back and forth, her eyes following the moonlight shivering across the floor. "I'll never own the inn, will I?"

A trick question, and he weighed his reply. "Without a court battle?"

"There won't be a court battle. I'm not fighting my parents."

She'd experienced enough upsets. After their night together, he preferred steering her to more positive topics. But in good conscience, he couldn't lie.

And so he said, "Then your brother will take over someday."

The confirmation released a sigh from her lips. Gently he stroked her hair, wishing for the power to take on a portion of her disappointment.

It was a relief when she rallied with a smile. "He'll buy me out when he does. It's something, right?"

Resignation inked the comment. "Is that enough?" Needing to protect her, he steered her cheek to his chest.

"I thought so." Her breath scattered across his skin. "Now I'm not sure."

"I meant what I said. Whatever you decide is fine with me. I'm always in your corner."

"I know you are—and I really appreciate it." She ducked out from beneath his arm, her expression serious. "What do you think about the buildings on the other side of the circle?"

Another trick question, but he liked this one better. "They've been on the market for years. Any one of those buildings would sell for a song. I like the brick with the arched windows, the one that housed the savings and loan. Three stories—lots of room."

"The dark-red brick? Also my favorite. Sure would be nice if someone opened a business in there."

"Have someone in mind?" he asked. He wasn't sure where this was going, but there was no harm in tagging along.

"Me? If I get a business off the ground, maybe I can bring in Jada and Cat later on."

"Sounds like you have a plan."

She laughed, extinguishing the pain in her eyes for the briefest interlude. "Nothing comes to mind," she admitted, and he understood the tentative nature of the conversation, the difficulty of letting go. "I have the hospitality business mastered, but Sweet Lake can't support another lodging. I'm really not sure what I'll do."

"There are dozens of businesses worth investigating. You're smart women. Do the research." She bit at her lower lip, hastening him to add, "There's no hurry. Stay at the inn, don't stay—do whatever makes you the most comfortable. I'm in your corner."

"If you were in my shoes, would you walk away?"

He followed the shadows drifting across the ceiling. "I'm not you," he pointed out. "If my parents left a business to me and Philip, and I knew my brother would take control . . ."

"What?" she prodded.

"I doubt I'd enter into the partnership in the first place."

"At the party, Frances said I need to learn to put myself first. Something about self-love and the spiritual plane. I didn't get all the mumbo jumbo. That was the gist."

"She doled out different advice to me. How to help you reach orgasm, that sort of thing. She called it 'organism,' but I caught the drift."

"She did not!"

He chuckled. "Maybe it was the martinis talking. She'd had a few."

A secret lingered in the mischievous curve of Linnie's mouth, one she suddenly revealed. "I wonder if we're on the Sirens' agenda. You know, how they play matchmaker with people in town."

He'd take all the help available to win Linnie forever, but he wisely hid the opinion. "What gives you that impression?" he asked, feigning casual interest.

"Right before we served dinner in the ballroom, Penelope pulled me into a corner. She looked so serious. You know how earnest she is."

He'd always liked Penelope's bashful sincerity. "What did she say?"

"She informed me that she'd always thought I'd make the prettiest babies with you." Linnie rarely giggled, but she did so now. "That's exactly how she said it, 'make babies,' like all we need is a cup of flour and a dash of sugar to whip up beautiful children."

Mirth vibrated through Daniel's chest. "Hey, she knows what she's talking about. Last spring I was in the circle having lunch and overheard Penelope and the other Sirens discussing their success with love among the ancients."

"I'm guessing you're *not* referring to pyramids and ancient civilizations."

"You're close. Ralph Euchanhofer and Kelly O'Neill."

"Over at the retirement home? Ralph's closing in on ninety, and Kelly's older."

"Yeah, and it gets better. Ralph's sons were in my office last week. They wanted to know if his will changes once he marries Kelly." Daniel hesitated. "You'd think they'd be happy for the old geezer. Been decades since he lost his wife."

"The Sirens played matchmaker?" He nodded, and a warning flashed across her features. "Well, that's as far as they go. Pretty babies or not, I'll wait for a sit-down about having a family."

"Hey, don't wait on my account," he joked. "I like kids. When they reach the nasty teenage years, we'll ship them off to their grandparents."

"I'm all for the great sex, Daniel. No way are we discussing kids right away—or marriage."

"I get it, Linnie. You're not ready." Relaxing, she twined her fingers through his chest hair, and a feeling much like triumph coasted through him. Riding it, he added, "Let me know when you are."

"Okay," she murmured, and the emotion increased.

Pressing a kiss to her forehead, he changed track. "Are you really considering a new career?"

"If I do, I'm sure I'll have second thoughts. My parents won't approve, and Freddie will have to hire a manager. Even if I bow out, he won't leave California anytime soon."

"And if you stay?"

She huffed out a breath. "Same thing. Lose-lose situation. What if I start to hate myself for pouring my efforts into an enterprise I'll never own? I'll wonder about the opportunity costs, the career possibilities I passed up, the chance of owning something for real."

"Seems like you've come to a decision."

She stirred against his chest. "Maybe I have."

"Then here's a suggestion. Look into several business possibilities. After you've settled on one or two that make sense, it'll be easier to—"

"Daniel!" She launched upright.

He lurched up beside her. *"What?"*

She pointed to the clock. "It's four thirty. While I'm thrilled you spent the night, aren't you forgetting someone?"

The sheet rustled to her waist, leaving the top half of her luscious body exposed. For precisely ten seconds, Daniel let his inner caveman admire her second-finest attribute—her hazel eyes coming in first.

Then the practical side of his brain clicked on.

Puddles.

The beast hadn't been let out since dinnertime.

"You bail me out constantly," Philip said, dropping into a chair at the kitchen table. "I don't mind helping you. Where were you anyway? Why didn't you text for a rescue?"

Daniel tossed the rag back into the pail of sudsy water. "I had other things on my mind."

In the backyard, Puddles's barking punctuated Fancy's singsong laughter. The kitchen floor was again spotless and the house back in order, although Daniel needed to add cereal to the grocery list. For reasons unknown, when Puddles butted open the door to the pantry, three boxes of cereal had met their maker. The dog had finished them all.

Philip slung his feet onto a chair. "Other things . . . mind giving the details? No, let me guess. You went joyriding after the fight with Linnie, got a ticket, and spent the night in the pokey."

"Forget the landscape gig, little brother. You're on your way to a career as a detective."

"Okay, so you didn't spend the night in jail. Then answer this. Why did you carry Linnie out of the ballroom? Bro, your move was all people were talking about. The Sirens were placing bets."

He went to the sink, washed his hands. "Placing bets on what?"

"Whether or not last night was an aberration, or if you and Linnie have been dating on the sly. Are you?"

"We are now."

Philip took this in, his mouth curving wryly. "I feel clueless. I never suspected you liked her. Thought you were both happy with the buddy routine."

"I more than like her." He reached for a towel. "And you *are* clueless."

"Then elaborate."

The coffee finished brewing. Desperate for the stimulant, Daniel filled a mug. After calming down his forgotten dog, he'd grabbed two hours of sleep on the couch. It was nearing ten o'clock, but a morning nap wasn't in the cards. The plant stock for one of Philip's jobs had come in early. He needed a babysitter while he went in to Unity Design.

Daniel said, "I'm planning to ask Linnie to move in."

"Here?"

"No, into Mick Petersen's garage down the street. Mick's given up on adding a chicken coop to the garage, so there's plenty of room." He placed a mug of coffee before his brother. "Yes, here."

"Linnie. Moving in." Philip looked like he'd been hit by a stray ball. "Think she'll go for it?"

"She'll draw up a long list of pros and cons, and bite her nails down to the quick. But yeah, I think she'll make the leap."

"I'm sure you can persuade her."

The vote of confidence, mixing with his elation, compelled Daniel to say, "I'll give you the wedding date once my persuasive charms wear her down." From over the rim of his mug, he assessed his dazed brother. "Close your mouth, Philip. You look like you're catching flies."

"You're *getting married*?"

"Not today. Soon, I hope."

The chair groaned as his brother got to his feet. "Talk about moving fast. Sure about this?"

If not for his brother's concern, the question would seem comical. Getting Linnie over the first hurdle—admitting they were in a relationship—was the hard part. Last night's intimacy proved they were moving in the right direction.

"Am I sure about spending my life with her? Absolutely. She's perfect, at least from where I'm standing. Besides, I don't want to stare down my forties as a bachelor, coming home each night to a lonely dog and an empty house. What's the point of building a life without someone to share it with?"

"She'll want kids." Philip glanced out the window at his daughter and Puddles tearing across the grass. "I've lost count of the times she's mentioned how lucky I am to have Fancy. You'll make great parents."

A compliment, but Daniel noticed Philip's shoulders sagging. "Do you ever think . . ." The pain in his brother's eyes stopped him from completing the thought.

"About trying again?" Philip guessed. His brow furrowed. "Sometimes."

"It'll happen."

"We'll see."

Privately Daniel regretted the turn of conversation. "You won't have the same outcome," he said, picking his way carefully, praying he didn't tread upon the landmines encircling his brother's emotions. Considering the hell he'd been through, it was a good sign if Philip was beginning to think about trying again. "You didn't do anything wrong. Bad stuff happens. Sometimes the bad stuff happens to the best people."

Philip shrugged, his eyes distant.

Daniel nodded at the clock. "Don't you have shrubs to deal with? We'll talk when you get back."

"Yeah, I should go." His brother paused in the doorway, the sorrow ebbing from his features. "Man, I didn't see this one coming. You and Linnie. Incredible."

"I think so too."

"She's a great girl." A light blinked on in the attic of his brain. "Wait a second. Did you spend the night with her?"

Daniel bounced his thumb at the door. "Go. Don't take too long. Didn't get much sleep—I'm running on fumes." He took a last sip of coffee. "How long do I have Fancy?"

"Couple of hours, tops. Big delivery. I have to get the plants organized."

Meaning Daniel needed to devise a healthy lunch for a five-year-old. PB&J with carrot sticks on the side? There wasn't time for the grocery store.

Philip's pickup left a plume of exhaust billowing down the street. Daniel strode into the backyard shaking his head. His niece had arrived in one of her princess costumes. The puffy pink confection was now damp with canine affection.

On the grass, she rolled to a stop. Puddles left her side to race circles around his master.

Daniel helped her up. "How 'bout if we take the wild thing to the circle? He needs a run."

"I do too!" Fancy slipped her small hand into his grasp.

Traffic was heavier than usual. People were taking advantage of the balmy weather for a Sunday drive, and the service had just ended at the church on Willow Avenue. Parking behind the law office, Daniel waited with growing irritation as cars streamed past. The circle needed stoplights at each end. The zoning committee still hadn't tackled the issue.

Finally a young couple brought their Toyota to a stop. Waving in thanks, he skirted across to the circle's green spaces with his niece firmly in his grip and his dog tugging on the leash.

Leaves skittered across the empty picnic tables. "Looks like we've got the place to ourselves," he told Fancy.

On tiptoes, she patted his stomach. "Where's the Frisbee?"

He sighed. "Sorry, kiddo." He really was out of it. "I forgot the Frisbee at the house."

Her eyes registered disappointment. "You never forget," she said, and Puddles whined as if in agreement. She threw herself across the dog's back. "It's okay, baby. I'll find you a toy."

"Check under the trees," he suggested. "Puddles will fetch a stick."

"Okay." Fancy skipped to the nearest tree, a maple fluttering against the sky. She rounded the trunk, returning with a branch longer than her arm.

Unclasping the dog's leash, Daniel chuckled. "You'll never be able to throw that. Find a smaller stick." Puddles bolted after her.

She dashed to the next tree, and he shuffled to the nearest table. He sank down on the bench, glad to get off his feet. *Early bedtime tonight.* He'd call Linnie this afternoon and then call it a day. The fuel of excitement over their night together was wearing off quickly, leaving patchy dots in his vision and stiffness in his muscles. Why hadn't he thought to bring a thermos of coffee? Yawning, he decided to give Fancy ten minutes to play before suggesting they return to the house.

Beneath the third tree, she located a stick small enough to master. Spinning in a circle, she flung it farther down the grass. Puddles raced after, barking.

"Stay where I can see you," he shouted. She bobbed her head, and he added, "Throw toward the middle of the grass. Don't get near the street."

Fancy curtsied daintily. Then she laughed as Puddles butted her with the stick. Hiking up her princess gown, she spun again. The stick flew end over end.

The girl and the dog got into a rhythm, throw, retrieve, throw. Daniel let his thoughts drift.

He was unaware of his eyelids drifting shut until a horn blared.

The sound jolted him back to consciousness. He blinked once, twice. Then the moment stilled in a sickening jolt. The stick arced like a lance toward the streaming cars. Puddles galloped forward on autopilot.

Fancy bolted after him. Her attention fastened on the dog.

She raced toward certain death.

In a pump of desperation, Daniel hurtled across the grass. He heard himself bellow in warning. The sound was far off, like a voice shouting from deep inside a cavern. Miraculously Puddles darted past the hood of a Ford pickup. Streaking through the cars in the second lane, the dog reached the sidewalk.

Fancy was smaller—easier for the driver to miss—and the truck kept going. The bright strands of her hair flew high. Sensing danger, she came to a standstill directly in the truck's path.

At full bore, Daniel scooped her up. The exertion threw a sheet of blackness across his eyesight. He sensed he'd made it past the car. His vision clearing, he threw his attention over his shoulder.

It was a dangerous miscalculation.

In the second lane, the woman texting on her phone looked up a moment too late.

Tires squealed. The car met Daniel's leg with a crack of pain. The impact pulled Fancy from his arms and sent his body into the air. Pain seared him, a tidal wave.

With horror, he watched the pavement rise up to meet him.

Chapter 20

Linnie made the twenty-minute drive to Park Center Hospital in a fugue of disbelief.

Memories of her father's stroke punctuated the journey. She recalled the blue-and-red lights strobing across her bedroom walls. The clatter of wheels on the inn's veranda, and the urgent voices breaking through her dreams. How she'd stumbled to the lobby, where paramedics were strapping her unconscious father onto a gurney and her mother looked on, shaking uncontrollably.

More often than not, life strung together in an orderly fashion. Then the unthinkable happened. The string of continuity broke.

Not Daniel. Linnie swerved into a parking space. *Not Fancy.* She bolted toward the hospital entrance.

In the busy waiting room, Philip rocked with his head in his hands. Clumps of dirt formed a semicircle around his work boots. He was nearly invisible in the undertow of conversation vibrating around him, the people waiting for loved ones to check in or check out, a florid-cheeked toddler squirming in her mother's lap, a youth in tennis whites cradling his elbow. A busy Sunday, but most of the injuries appeared little more than inconveniences.

Linnie called out. He looked up with relief.

She hugged him and then asked, "How are they?"

He led her through the aisle of chairs to a corner near the entrance. "Fancy's doing all right," he said. "Broken arm, lots of bruises. Bump on the head, which doesn't look too bad. They'll keep her overnight for observation, make sure there's no concussion."

"Oh, Philip. I'm so sorry."

He waved off the comment. "She'll be okay. Could've been worse. A whole lot worse. Daniel got to her in time."

"You mean he caught her before . . . ?"

"Sure did. Frances said he came out of nowhere. He flew straight into traffic."

"Frances was on the circle?"

"Two cars back, coming from church. She saw everything." He made an effort to stop his composure from crumbling, and she noticed the tracks wending through the grime on his cheeks. He took a swipe at his eyes. "My big brother, a regular superhero. Fancy rolled out of his arms when the car hit him—she rolled off the hood. A miracle she landed on the curb."

"What was she doing in the middle of the street?"

"Chasing Puddles. Frances got the impression the crazy pooch was playing fetch. She saw something fly across the street."

"Where's Fancy now?"

"On her way to a room. We can go up soon."

"Where's Puddles?" Daniel adored the mutt. Was the poor dog forgotten in the confusion following the accident? If so, she'd scour the town until she found him.

Philip put her fears to rest. "Frances hustled the mutt into her car. Called me right after, which is how I found out about the accident. I'll pick him up later."

Dread over the next query chilled her skin. He'd only supplied the barest information on the phone. An accident. Both Daniel and Fancy hurt. In his tone she'd captured the impression Daniel was more badly injured. She was terrified of what she might learn.

At last she asked, "What about Daniel?" Nausea rolled through her. "How's he doing?"

She wasn't aware the question had loosened her knees until Philip grabbed hold of her waist.

With ease he helped her outside, his embrace tightening as she went limp.

"Let's try some fresh air." He practically carried her to a bench by the emergency entrance. "Work with me here. Breathe."

"I'm okay." She marveled at the clammy perspiration dotting her arms.

"Like hell. Take another breath."

She did, her lungs aching from the effort. "This is embarrassing. I'm supposed to be the one propping you up."

"Like a mouse propping up a giraffe? That'd be a neat trick." He clasped her shoulder firmly, his eyes canvassing her face. "Still feel like you're blacking out?"

"Good question." Beside the bench, the bed of impatiens wobbled in bands of pink and white. Her vision was spotty at best. "I feel seasick."

"Rescue's coming, sailor. Be right back."

Philip trotted off, a reprieve of sorts. She felt silly dropping her head between her legs and sucking in more air. What if she'd grown faint winging down the highway? As if the town needed a second accident on a Sunday. The thought was discarded before it played havoc with her stomach.

By the time Philip reappeared, her pulse had slowed to within normal limits. She still felt woozy, but her sight was clearing.

He handed over a can of ginger ale. "Bottoms up."

She took a sip, waited until he joined her on the bench. "Tell me about Daniel's injuries." He studied his mud-spattered boots with palpable unease, and she added, "I won't go into a swoon, I swear. Tell me."

Assenting, he rattled off the terrible list. "Nasty break to his left femur, some cracked ribs. They're doing X-rays, making sure his ribs didn't cause internal damage." He stopped to gauge her reaction. She lifted her brows, urging him on. "A slight crack to the skull, but no brain swelling—that was the first thing they checked. Lacerations on his face. Some are pretty deep. They were stitching him up when I got here."

The list of injuries put bile in her throat. "Can we see him?" she asked, swallowing it down.

"Once they're finished in radiology, the doc will let me know."

Hopefully they wouldn't have long to wait. "How fast was the car going?"

"Not too fast, thank God. Clipped him on the side. Launched him over the hood and onto the sidewalk, past where Fancy landed." Philip dropped his elbows onto his knees. "He was unconscious when the ambulance arrived."

Linnie pressed a hand to her stomach. She forced her thoughts on more pragmatic concerns. "Should I phone Kay? She'll rearrange Daniel's schedule. He won't see clients this week." In her haste, she hadn't even told Jada before racing out of the Wayfair.

"Doubt it's necessary. Frances will shout the news from the rooftops. Once all the Sirens hear, the whole town will know in ten minutes flat. We'll dine on chicken casserole for a month."

"At least you won't have to cook."

"I've never learned how. Lucky for me and Fancy that my brother picked up the knack." Philip glanced at her briefly before throwing his attention on the flowerbed. "I didn't call anyone but you."

She'd received the only call? The significance was impossible to miss. Before leaving the inn at daybreak, Daniel hadn't mentioned babysitting Fancy today. When Philip dropped off his daughter, did the conversation include the topic of a sleepover in the south wing? It would explain why she'd crossed Philip's mind during the ghastly morning.

He nudged the ginger ale closer to her lips. "Drink. You're three shades beyond pale."

She did before asking, "How long will Daniel stay in the hospital?"

"A couple days. If the break to his femur isn't bad, they'll splint his leg. They'll wrap his ribs, but the concussion is a bigger concern. They'll keep him under observation as a precaution."

"If the break to his femur *is* bad?"

"I didn't think to ask." Philip rubbed his unshaven jaw. "They were throwing so much at me, I was having trouble keeping everything straight."

She clenched her eyes shut. Only a few hours ago, she'd nuzzled in Daniel's arms. They'd spent the better part of the night making love, and the tranquil hours before dawn plotting out the future in bold sketches. What if he'd been killed?

What if the best portion of her life had begun and ended on the same day?

Philip read her face with concern. "Cheer up. He'll come through this in one piece. He's a tough guy. You don't have to worry."

A terrible thought intruded. "Am I to blame?"

"Geez, Linnie. You weren't behind the wheel."

She brushed off the comment. "None of this would've happened if he'd been alert." She rubbed her arms in angry strokes. "I kept him up all night. I knew he'd worked a full day, and naturally, Jada sent him to find me in the woods before the party. What's wrong with me? He didn't get any sleep. When I woke up around four, he was still awake staring at the ceiling."

It dawned on her she was rambling. Cutting off, she cringed. Why dump a confession on Philip, especially one sexual in nature? Like he needed a recap of the best night of her life. His precious daughter was inside Park Center being whisked to a hospital room.

Searching for an apology, she peeked at his face. Beneath the dried riverbed crossing his cheeks, his expression brimmed with mirth.

"Linnie," he said, trying for sobriety but missing the mark, "there's not a chance in hell my brother is upset because you kept him up all night. He's a monk. Hell, we both are. If you've broken his vow of chastity, let's tell the Sirens. They'll throw a party. At the least, they'll send over a month's supply of condoms. Just go easy on him until he's fully healed."

Despite her gloom, she smiled. "Will do."

They went back inside. At the desk, Philip checked on Fancy's progress. He motioned her over.

"We can go up now," he said. Together they headed to the elevator.

She asked, "Any news on Daniel?"

"Not yet."

In the semiprivate room, a stocky nurse fussed over Fancy. The second bed was empty.

The nurse checked the IV, nodded them in. "Look who's here to see you, Fancy." She came across the room, paused in the doorway. Lowering her voice, she told Philip, "Don't stay too long. It's been an exciting morning. She needs her rest."

"Got it."

Linnie followed him in. The bed dwarfed the girl neatly tucked beneath the blanket. A neon-pink cast covered Fancy's right arm. Scrapes and bruises dotted the fragile curve of her jawline.

She patted the cast. "They let me pick the color," she told her father.

"Pretty cool." He brushed wisps of hair from her brow. "How are you doing? Did the tears go away? You had me worried in the emergency room."

"I only have little bits of scared now."

"Don't worry, sweet pea. Pretty soon the cast will come off. You'll be doing handsprings."

She leaned close to her father's ear. "The lady said I can have ice cream after naptime. Can I have seconds?"

"Sure thing."

"I like the lady. She smells nice."

She meant the nurse, and Linnie said, "Should we bring in some of your dolls? I'm sure they miss you." Fancy prized her collection of baby dolls.

"Yes, I want my babies! They have bits of scared too."

Philip slid Linnie a glance. *Why didn't I think of that?*

To his daughter he said, "I'm allowed to come back after dinner. Which babies should I bring?"

"Jenny, Janey, and Tulip. Janey's playing in the closet. She likes my princess dresses."

"Anything else?"

"Will you bring Puddles?" Fancy did her best to ape a stern expression. The attempt only made her more adorable. "He's sad. Did you give him kisses?"

"I will when I see him," Philip promised. "He can't visit, though. You'll see him when you come home tomorrow."

Oddly, she looked past her father to pose the next question to Linnie. "Is Uncle Daniel scared? He got more boo-boos than me."

A dark sickness swept through Linnie. "Uncle Daniel doesn't mind the boo-boos. He'll get over them fast." She dredged up her most reassuring smile. "He's glad you're okay."

"Will you give him lots of kisses? They'll make him get better even faster."

Warmth brighter than sunlight spiraled through Linnie. "Of course, baby girl. I'll give him enough kisses to circle the world."

The nurse returned, motioned Philip into the corridor. The timbre of their voices, the low urgency and Philip's short, staccato responses, jiggled the trapdoor Linnie imagined beneath her feet. Warding off the panic before it caught her full throttle, she focused on Fancy, who was regarding her with the instinctual senses of a small child, that cord of self-preservation entwined with the love for special adults.

Give in to fear, and Fancy would too.

Linnie rose to the challenge. Opening her purse, she allowed the curious girl to investigate the tubes of lipstick, the stray bottle of nail polish, and the worn photograph hidden in a zippered pocket. The snapshot was taken when Linnie and Jada were seniors at Sweet Lake High and Cat was a sophomore. Returning the photo, Fancy rooted in the bottom of the purse.

She'd discovered a pack of gum when Philip trudged back inside. Linnie presented the gift before he pulled her out of earshot of his daughter.

"Daniel's in surgery," he said. "The bone was displaced in the break to his femur. They're resetting it."

She quelled her fear. Philip had enough to worry about without adding her fluctuating emotions to the mix. Daniel *was* a strong man. He'd pull through the surgery just fine.

"If you talk to him later, please tell him I was here," she said. "What about tomorrow?"

Philip gave a meaningful look. "Only family can visit." He squeezed her hand. "I told the nurse to add your name to the list."

By five o'clock on Sunday afternoon, the last relatives who'd come in for the Mendozas' anniversary bash checked out of the Wayfair. Housekeeping took over the ballroom, returning tables to storage and cleaning the parquet floor. The staff worked silently, their excitement over last night's party extinguished by the news of the accident. Even the revelry in Freddie's suite was more subdued than usual. On the patio behind the Sunshine Room, Linnie caught sight of her brother speaking with Jada. Undoubtedly she was filling him in.

With many of the rooms now empty, the inn seemed unnaturally quiet. Her energy waning, Linnie plodded to the check-in desk.

Tomorrow would see a flurry of new arrivals, vacationers taking advantage of the summer weather and the activities on the lake.

At eight o'clock Philip called. Daniel was out of post-op and doing well. Relieved, she decided to make it an early night, conking out within minutes.

Four hours later, a gentle nudge disturbed her dreamless sleep.

Jada flicked on the lamp. "Wake up, sleepyhead."

"Go away," Linnie garbled.

"The Sirens have invited us to a meeting on the beach. They're having an initiation, whatever that means. Aren't you curious?"

She rolled sideways, squinted at the clock. "Not even a little." It was past midnight.

"Don't be a party pooper."

After much cajoling, Linnie dressed. On the veranda, Cat bounced on the balls of her bare feet like a jackrabbit. As the daughter of a Siren, she'd dressed vibrantly for the occasion. She'd chosen the floral top of her favorite bikini paired with a beaded scarf tied sarong-style at the waist. Three necklaces swung from her neck.

Angling a hip, she asked Jada, "Should we give her coffee before getting her drunk?"

Jada brushed past. "Your bright ideas never cease to amaze. Who drinks coffee before booze?"

"Anyone planning to party hearty, that's who."

"Forget the coffee. We're already late."

"Okay, okay." Cat flipped a hank of wavy hair over her shoulder. "Don't get pissy with me. I just thought we should wake her up before dousing her with mojitos."

"I'm not getting drunk," Linnie mumbled. She couldn't see. It dawned on her that opening her eyes might help.

The warm breeze licked her face. With July's approach the humidity had risen, the air laden with droplets of moisture. The rolling song of the waters led them down the incline to the lake.

On the beach votive candles formed a circle around the twenty or so women who'd chosen to attend. The decision would ensure they'd begin the week groggy and perhaps hung over. Each woman resembled a hippie from the 1960s, with a feathered headband and a long scarf tie-dyed in shades of purple and burnt orange. As the leaders of the group, Silvia and Frances had added necklaces to their regalia. The long, roping affairs were decorated with shells, tiny stones, and pretty blue feathers.

Although Cat never admitted as much, Linnie assumed she'd attended Siren gatherings at one time or another. Linnie and Jada had never received an invitation—the gourd rattling to warn Linnie of danger didn't really count, since they hadn't stayed long enough to witness anything unusual.

Rumors abounded about the goings-on at the affairs. Some of the speculation was outlandish—Linnie doubted mature women possessed the stamina to climb trees to sing to the moon. She certainly didn't buy the stories about Sirens concocting potions they slipped into coffee cups at town meetings to influence decisions by Sweet Lake's mayor and the town's zoning board. But their established habits, like skinny-dipping in the lake, naturally led to more bizarre conjecture.

Frances spread her hands in greeting. "Welcome, guests," she intoned.

Across the circle, Penelope scooted to make room. The owner of Gift of Garb was a natural packrat who'd turned a yen for garage sale hunts into a prosperous enterprise. Tufts of white hair streaked auburn locks cut in a bob style. Add in the owlish glasses, and she'd always reminded Linnie of a cartoon depiction of a worm reading a book.

"Sit down, girls! Make yourselves comfortable." Penelope's double chin jiggled as she patted the sand. She regarded the diminutive Tilda Lyons to her left. "Pour them a drink, will you?"

A lime-infused mojito appeared before Linnie. Booze was a no-go for a woman half-asleep, but the Baccarat tumbler was a nice touch.

The heavy crystal glinted in the moonlight. Had Frances brought the tumblers? She was the wealthiest Siren by far.

Penelope lifted her glass. "I love induction ceremonies," she told Linnie. "Pity you can't stay for the whole affair. 'Hear the Siren's call and give kindness in secret.' Such noble words."

Silvia's gaze shot arrows. "Penelope! We do not discuss an inductee's task with outsiders."

Frances gave a regal nod in agreement. "Loose lips sink ships," she put in. Her father had fought in World War II, and the dictum was one of her favorites.

The dual reprimand sank Penelope's chins into the folds of her festive scarf. The other women twittered.

Linnie and Jada exchanged quizzical glances. *An inductee's task—to give kindness in secret?*

Tilda asked Linnie, "How are Fancy and Daniel? We all wanted to visit, but it's too soon."

"You can visit Fancy at home tomorrow. Philip expects the hospital to discharge her by the afternoon." She gave the details of Daniel's more extensive injuries. "He won't receive visitors tomorrow. Well, other than family . . . and me."

Frances smiled at the admission. "Has Philip called his parents?"

The elder Ketterings had retired in Dallas, where members of their extended family lived.

"They were planning to book a flight in the morning. Philip talked them out of it," she explained. "His mother had bunions removed last week. She's still in pain when she walks."

Frances winced. "Airport security after foot surgery?"

"They'll come next week instead. Philip thinks it's for the best."

Reflecting on the news, the women sipped their mojitos. Finishing hers, Silvia prodded the carafe from Yume Uchida. Mr. Uchida's older sister was a retired teacher. Yume riddled her yard with glass trinkets made in her garage-cum-art-studio.

"Where is she?" Silvia muttered.

Yume tilted her face to the moon. "Patience."

"I have clients in the morning. I can't stay all night." At Linnie's questioning look, Silvia added, "Our new member is tardy. Whenever we induct a woman into the Sirens, our combined hearts produce an abundance of positive energy. That's why we invited you, Jada, and my daughter. We didn't think you'd join us without their urging."

"I'm here to witness an abundance of energy?" Perhaps *energy* was code for *watch Sirens drink excessively.*

Frances cleared up the matter. "We'd like you to carry the energy to Daniel when you see him tomorrow."

A strange request, and she asked, "How do I carry the energy?" In a Baccarat tumbler? In her pocket? "You'll have to forgive me. I'm new at this."

"There's nothing to carry. We'll surround you with good vibrations."

Like in the Beach Boys song? Inquiring further didn't seem wise. "Will this take long?" she asked instead. Climbing back into her warm bed was tempting. So was sneaking into the inn's kitchen for a midnight snack.

"Only a few minutes," Silvia put in. She craned her neck. "What's keeping her?"

Frances said, "If we must wait, I want all the details. Linnie, why did Daniel carry you out of the party? It was terribly romantic."

"We'd had a disagreement."

"A man carries a woman off, he's more than angry. He's inspired." Frances toyed with her weird necklace. "Was the sex good?"

Linnie recalled Daniel's comment about the elderly Siren giving him advice on helping a woman reach orgasm. She discovered her tongue glued to the roof of her mouth.

Frances merrily raised her glass. "Look, she's blushing! Jada, if she's too bashful to fill us in, why don't you? Spare no details. At my age, a randy man would pose a danger to my ticker. But living vicariously is safe enough."

Cat stopped digging her toes in the sand. "Frances, what makes you think Linnie didn't spill the dirt to me first? I'm also her best friend."

"This isn't a competition, dear."

"It feels like a competition!"

"Only because you're guzzling your drink. I suggest you sip."

Cat demonstrated proper sipping, but she'd already emptied her glass. "I can keep secrets. Why does everyone act like I can't?" She poured another. "I'm not like Tilda."

The realtor choked on her mojito. "What are you implying?" she sputtered. A manufactured insult if ever there was one. She knew everyone in Sweet Lake feared her twitchy texting finger.

Frances shushed her. To Cat, she said, "I'm sorry. I simply assumed . . ."

Breaking in, Jada lowered her drink to the sand. "Forget the assumptions. Linnie's been mum since she got back from the hospital. Last night there was enough moaning and naughty language coming from her bedroom to scare cats into trees. But do I know if she's finally in a relationship with Daniel or was just using his big, hunky body for the night? Nope. I don't."

Linnie recoiled. "Give me a break. I wasn't in the mood to chat when I got back from the hospital."

"Then let me fill *you* in on news you haven't heard. Your brother is checking out soon. Would've already, but he wants to make sure Daniel is on the mend. Best guess, you'll have him out of your hair by Wednesday."

"He's leaving on Wednesday?" Relief battled the regret inside her. The regret made no sense. Wasn't Freddie's departure cause for celebration? "You're sure?"

Snatching the pitcher, Jada sloshed booze into her glass. "Gosh, I thought you'd do the happy dance."

"I am happy," she retorted, succumbing to sadness. "I guess I thought . . ."

Jada heaved out a sigh. "What?"

This wasn't the place to discuss quitting the inn. Linnie wasn't sure about leaving, and the Sirens had her trapped with avid stares. In fact, several of the women were peering beyond her, into the darkness.

Curious, she was about to follow their line of sight when Frances said, "You're safe inside our circle of love. Tell us what's bothering you."

"I'm not sure exactly." She set her drink aside. "Since Freddie showed up, I've put pressure on Daniel to explain why my brother came back. At some level, I assumed the reason for the visit would help me understand Freddie, maybe even connect with him. I've only recently become aware of how much I'd like to connect. And if we did start acting like family, would I find a way to forgive him? I'd like to think so."

"Forgiving him will heal you both. You *are* family."

Silvia glowered. "Frances, I can't believe you're peddling forgiveness. If you made a voodoo doll of Freddie and impaled it with sewing needles, there isn't a woman here who'd find your behavior mean-spirited."

Frances eyed her friend closely. "The psychological term for your outburst is *transference*. Silvia, have you been making voodoo dolls of our favorite scoundrel?"

"What if I have? And he's no one's favorite."

"Perhaps I'm also on the road to forgiveness."

"You have more exit strategies than a cat burglar."

"Oh, drink your mojito and be still. If I never speak to Freddie again, where's the harm? He's not a member of my family." Her sympathetic gaze found Linnie. "I'm not the one with much to lose."

Linnie hung her head. "I can't lose what I've never had. We're practically strangers. Add in this bottled up attraction I've uncorked with Daniel, and it makes for trouble—especially now."

Jada frowned. "Why now?"

A hush fell across the women as they awaited Linnie's reply. The compassion flowing toward her was an emboldening force. Never had she enjoyed a heart-to-heart with her own mother. A bridge of expectation separated them—Linnie's, built on her desire to have her ambitions taken seriously, and her mother's, erected with a thousand damaging comments about a woman's role as keeper of home and hearth, as if outward goals didn't matter. Was it any wonder she viewed Sarah more as an adversary than a mother?

The sad observation brought a startling conclusion. At their essence, Siren meetings weren't about Silvia's mojitos or Frances encouraging the group to swim naked beneath the moon. The women supported each other. They were a sister league prepared to buoy each other up.

They were also a mother league willing to support her too.

Tossing caution aside, she looked to Jada and Cat. "If I left the Wayfair and started a business, would you quit the inn once I got the new enterprise off the ground? I'm just asking. I haven't made a decision. That's part of the reason why I'd like to patch things up with Freddie. If I go, I won't feel right unless I tell him first. Once I'm out of the picture, he's in charge."

Softly Jada asked, "You're considering giving up your share?"

"Leaving will be hard, but my parents won't give me control. I need to decide what's best for my life in the long run."

"You're seriously considering this?"

"I am." Her chest throbbed, but she dredged up a cheerful tone. "So, will you both think about it? Daniel suggested I look into businesses Sweet Lake needs, but aren't available in town."

Jada trailed her fingers through the sand. Her love for the inn equaled Linnie's.

Cat, more impetuous by a yard, said, "Why don't we quit with you? Start the business together?"

Jada read the answer in Linnie's eyes. She told Cat, "Linnie won't gamble with our futures. When Freddie took the money way back when, you lost your event planning business and my bakery went under. How long did it take for us to dig out of debt?"

"Ages."

"Which *is* the point."

Cat's face fell, prodding Linnie to add, "We'll see how it goes. Assuming I come up with an idea, I'll ask both of you to join me the moment the business is profitable." She looked off into the starry night with a sense of hopelessness invading her bones. She really didn't want to leave the inn. "But let's not get ahead of ourselves. I'm still working out if I can bear the thought of starting over."

Jada said, "Whatever you decide, I'll give you brownie points for even thinking about patching up your relationship with Freddie. You're a good person, Linnie."

"Thanks."

Again the women began peering into the darkness. Linnie started to turn, to investigate, when Frances cleared her throat.

"I wonder," she said, drawing all eyes, "if Linnie does quit the inn, will Freddie ask Jada to take over? It would seem logical."

The suggestion drew a disapproving grunt from Jada. "He could double my salary, and I wouldn't take the job. Frances, do you have any idea how much Linnie handles in a given week?"

"Then what about Cat?"

At her name, Cat flinched. "Table the idea right now. Jada and I help out, but we don't have Linnie's expertise. All the accounting, ordering just the right amount of food every week, payroll for fifty employees—and dealing with bitchy guests when something goes wrong. I don't mind pitching in, but I don't want to run the place."

Taking this in, Frances sipped her mojito. Then she said to Linnie, "Replacing you may put your brother in a bigger bind than Silvia's voodoo doll."

"Definitely one of the reasons why I'm still undecided."

"And a good reason for your brother to think before attempting to replace you."

"Freddie, *think*? He's more apt to shove me out the door and then realize he needs to scare up a new manager."

Frances pursed her lips, her eyes glittering with another one of her private amusements. "Well, I wouldn't fret. Your brother won't face such a dilemma. You'd never act out of character or give up your post after all the hard work of saving the inn. You're a predictable soul, as constant as the seasons. There isn't a spontaneous bone in your body."

Was this a compliment? Politely Linnie murmured, "Thanks," thinking, *for nothing.*

Oddly, the edge of insult in her voice made Frances more animated. "Steadfast Linnie Wayfair—a veritable anchor throughout the years. I applaud you for putting your brother's needs first. You wouldn't dream of leaving without giving ample notice. You certainly won't do anything rash, like give Freddie the typical two-week notice. Good heavens— what would he do then? You'd put him in an impossible bind."

Silvia muttered, "Do it, Linnie. I'll loan you the rope."

Frances shushed her. Then she regarded the Sirens.

As if on cue the breeze stirred, gaining strength to whirl around the circle of bowed heads. Answering the wind, the surf crashed, louder now, a ready companion to the sense of wonder converging on the beach. Goosebumps rising on her arms, Linnie sensed a strong cord of the sacred binding the women together. One after the other, the Sirens reached out and clasped hands.

To the night, Frances said, "The moment has been selected for you. Let the initiation begin."

The women lifted their faces to the stars winking overhead. "To kindness given in secret," they said in a beautiful blending of voices.

From the darkness, out stepped Daniel's secretary.

"As you wish." Kay adjusted the feathered headband cocked on her hair. "Oh, and please forgive my delay."

Chapter 21

On the third floor of Park Center Hospital, an aide directed Linnie to room 312.

A privacy curtain hid the farther half of the room, a soft mechanical whirring drifting from underneath. Only the glow emanating from the bathroom broke the darkness.

Her eyes adjusting, she surveyed the quarters. In the first bed, Daniel slept.

An IV line snaked past the gauze covering the left half of his head. A cumbersome device elevated his leg, which was hidden under the sheet. A bitter scent assailed her nostrils. On his jaw, neat stitches were visible beneath translucent surgical tape. Her heart overturned.

His eyelids fluttered. "Love . . . your . . . perfume."

"It's soap," she replied, and her voice broke.

In a marvel of sheer will, he lifted his eyelids to half-mast. "Hello, darling. How are you?"

The first time he'd used the endearment, and her throat tightened with gratitude. "Hanging in there," she said. "How are you holding up?"

"Dopey from the painkillers." His head listed slightly. He flinched, and his discomfort sent a twinge of sympathy pain through her. "Is there a light? They've kept me in dungeon darkness since yesterday's surgery."

She found the switch, put the dimmer on low. It was early, and the patient in the other bed was undoubtedly sleeping.

"You just missed Philip," Daniel said. "He checked in on me before heading to Fancy's room."

"I'll stop by her room before I leave." She pressed her lips to his unmarred cheek. "I'm sorry about this. If I hadn't kept you up all night—"

"I kept *you* up all night. When you woke up and caught me staring at the ceiling? I was thinking about persuading you into another round."

His pirate's grin nearly took her hostage. "Wouldn't have taken much persuasion." Despite the injuries, he was in a playful mood. A relief, and she added, "You'll never guess where I was last night. The Sirens inducted a new member." An interesting evening, although Linnie still wasn't sure about Frances's comments regarding her steadfast nature. A compliment or a veiled criticism?

"You're kidding. The Sirens invited you to one of their meetings?"

"Not to watch the actual ceremony. I did chat beneath the summer moon, but skipped the mojitos. The invitation was nice." With the expansive gestures of a circus performer, she twirled her hands through the air. "I hope this helps. I'm supposed to carry healing energy to you. Feel anything yet? If this works, I'll bring more good vibes tomorrow."

"Tell Frances and the other lunatics I said thanks."

"They aren't lunatics. The meeting was sweet. Like a slumber party for grown women, without the sleeping bags and with much deeper— and lewder—conversation." She'd left the festivities in a better mood. Still, she was miles from a decision about leaving the Wayfair, and oddly blue regarding Freddie's upcoming departure. "Cat and Jada also tagged along."

"Who's the new member? Not McCready down at the drugstore— she's been trying to join since the world was new. She must carry bad vibes."

"She *is* cranky."

"Are they hunting for younger members? They did give you, Jada, and Cat a glimpse of their inner workings."

"Beats me."

"Let me guess. Did they induct the Galliard sisters? They sure meet the quirky requirement to join the Sirens. I heard they've come into money and are planning an Internet venture in their old Victorian mansion."

"They'll have to get back into Silvia's good graces first. She's still furious with them."

"Tamron Pereira, over at the greenhouse? Awfully young for Siren membership, but she'd fulfill the earth mother requirement. Given all the bad luck she's encountered, she could use the emotional support."

Linnie silently agreed—she liked Tamron, who'd suffered one tragedy after another. "I doubt the Sirens would induct anyone her age," she replied. "She's younger than Cat."

Daniel wagged his brows. "So who's the new member?"

Her smartphone buzzed. In a grand coincidence, it was Kay.

"Linnie, are you with Daniel?" she asked. "I hate to bother him. This is important."

She put him on. Nodding, he listened intently. "No, it's fine," he finally interjected. "Kay, I'm not battling death—I have a broken leg. They did? When? That's great. No, don't bother. I'll ask Linnie to stop by."

Handing back the phone, he said, "I'm working on a divorce settlement. The couple dropped off an agreement. You wouldn't believe the difficulty I've had getting them to find common ground. Would you mind playing errand boy?"

"You're in no shape to draft a divorce settlement today. Tell your clients to wait."

Warmth sparkled in his eyes. "I like your protective streak." He glanced at the privacy curtain. "Why don't you lock the door and slip into bed with me? Granted, the painkillers will slow me down. That's not necessarily a bad thing."

"And you call the Sirens lunatics," she said, smoothing the hair from his brow. "I'll play errand boy on one condition. You promise not to work today."

"Deal. Can you drop off the document tonight?"

"No. If I do, you'll work until the wee hours of the morning."

"You're a hard taskmaster, Linnie."

"Consider yourself warned. I'll fetch the agreement, but no work until after you're released." Giving in to the urge, she trailed her fingers across the stubble on his cheek. Nuzzling his ear, she whispered, "Besides, what makes you think I'll return tonight?"

"You find me irresistible."

"You've got me there." *And everywhere else,* she thought wryly.

"Last chance." He waggled his brows. "Sure you don't want to go for a quickie?"

"In the shape you're in? Get some sleep." She tiptoed to the door. "I'll see you later."

"Linnie."

"Yeah?"

With effort, he lifted his head from the pillow. "Who's the new Siren?"

Relishing the expectancy in his voice, she drew out the suspense. "This you won't believe."

◦⃝

"I left the envelope on his desk. Go on in."

Having issued the statement, Kay adjusted her azure-blue eyeglasses and glared at the blinking phone. Linnie hurried past. She'd hoped to inquire about the mysterious induction ceremony. The Sirens were notoriously tight-lipped, and the odds weren't good that their newest member would share state secrets. Even so, she'd promised Jada and Cat she'd try to get the skinny.

Although it wasn't yet ten o'clock, several bouquets and get well cards were arranged on the credenza inside Daniel's office. Linnie made a mental note to check his house too. If more gifts were coming in, leaving bouquets and confections baking in the June sun was *not* a good plan.

In the center of the desk lay a manila envelope. She picked it up. The efficient Kay had removed just about everything else. No doubt she was organizing Daniel's cases in order of importance to better help him wade through the backlog once he returned to work. If he insisted on working from home while he recuperated—a distinct possibility for a dedicated lawyer—Linnie determined to do her best to keep the hours short. They were both committed to their jobs, but he *did* need time to heal.

She tucked the envelope into her purse.

In Kay's area, the phone rang again. Picking up, she launched into an explanation of the accident.

Linnie was about to leave Daniel's office when her eyes strayed to the corner of the desk, to the tiny shells and stones threaded on a short length of twine. The fanciful object sat atop a file the same dark-green hue as the blotter on the desk. If not for the Sirens' handiwork, the file would've escaped her notice.

The guilty thrill of discovery sent her hand across the desk. This was private business, one of Daniel's cases. She slid the file close.

WAYFAIR—REED

Who was Reed? A business associate of Freddie's? Anxiety tumbled through her belly. The contents detailed the reasons for her brother's visit. There was no doubt.

Indecision gripped her. It was wrong to look inside. This was confidential business—Freddie's business. She'd fought with Daniel and nearly lost him, thanks to the contents of this unassuming file.

Vacillating, she picked up the twined shells and stones. Slowly she rolled them across her palm. She recalled last night's meeting on the beach. Excitable Penelope Riddle had scooted sideways to make room for her to join the circle of women. What had Penelope revealed about the induction ceremony before Silvia barked her into silence?

Hear the Siren's call and give kindness in secret. Such noble words.

An inductee was tasked with giving kindness without the receiver's knowledge. Who was the newest member of the Sirens, the woman charged with embarking upon this noble task?

Kay.

She'd performed an act of kindness in secret because she was the only person able to do so. At minimum, she knew the basics of why Freddie was in Ohio. As Daniel's secretary, she was familiar with all his cases. Her kindness provided Linnie with a more complete picture of her estranged brother.

Her pulse jumping, Linnie slipped the folder beneath her arm.

The copy machine, located in Kay's area, sat ten paces behind her desk. Feeling like a felon on a crime spree, Linnie scooted to the machine. Kay, talking on the phone, pretended she was oblivious to the whining fury as copy after copy spit out. Statements from the Devlin Eye Institute. Correspondence with Janis Reed of Medina, Ohio. Notes in Daniel's handwriting, and a photograph of a young man, a sweet-looking kid. Linnie copied every document.

On wobbly ankles she walked back to the office. She deposited the original file on the desk.

What was the protocol after theft? A metallic taste filled her mouth as she crept past Kay.

The phone slammed down. "Hold on," Kay said to her back.

Linnie's stomach clenched. The enormity of her error placed a stinging wash of crimson on her cheeks. Kay hadn't left the file out with the intention of Linnie making off with confidential information.

She hadn't meant to reveal a mountain of medical bills for one Bryce Reed of Medina.

Searching for an apology, she retraced her steps.

Kay shuffled through the papers on her desk. "The address and driving directions," she said crisply, handing over a typed sheet. "Mrs. Reed and her son are expecting you. I've informed Jada you won't return to the inn until tonight—she thinks you're running errands for Daniel. If you aren't back until after visiting hours at the hospital, I'll cook up something to tell your beau. I'll make it good so Daniel isn't upset."

Relief flooded her bones. "Thank you."

"Save your gratitude. If our favorite attorney finds out, I'm pretending you riffled through his file cabinet without my knowledge." Behind rectangular eyeglasses, Kay's eyes grew stern. "I have a suspicion he'll forgive you . . . and I have no intention of losing my job."

"I won't breathe a word."

"No, you won't. But your brother will burst like a piñata if he finds out." Kay patted her silvered head with temperamental dignity. "Let the chips fall where they will." She pointed to the door. "Better hurry. You have a three-hour drive to Medina."

∽✈

A tangy kick of adrenaline quickened Frances's stride as the Honda peeled from the parking lot.

She breezed into the reception room with the sweet nectar of success brightening her mood. Let Silvia stew in her juices and make voodoo dolls until her fingers ached. They were Sirens. Their energies were best used helping their younger brethren wade through the seas of stupidity. There was more at stake than old grudges and lost dignity thanks to Freddie's deplorable YouTube video. If Silvia ever discovered what she'd done and blew sky-high, well, Frances would take on the volcano.

Kay gave the thumbs-up. "She took the bait. On her way now."

"Perfect."

The secretary regarded her with clear admiration. "Frances, I had no idea you're this devious. Are we all puppets on your string?"

"I'm stunned you must ask."

"In any case, I'm happy to help. I'm sure you haven't told Silvia. She adores Linnie, but we'd find igloos in hell before she'd lift a finger to help Freddie. Am I the only one privy to your delicious plot?"

Tilda burst in, a smart azure briefcase swinging at her side. "Did it work?" Gleaning the truth on their faces, she leapt in the air. She reminded Frances of a pixie discovering flight. "Oh, I'm so excited—I love happy endings!"

Frances sighed heavily. "No one knows but our favorite realtor," she informed Kay.

"She was lurking in the bushes when you and I met on the circle?"

"When you agreed to join the Sirens and I detailed my mad plot."

"I wasn't lurking!"

Frances pointed at the briefcase. "Is your cell phone inside? If you text any gossip regarding this, I shall smash the device to smithereens."

Kay began rocking in her chair. "Speaking of cell phones . . . isn't there a call to make?"

Tilda stopped jumping and stared expectantly at their leader.

Snapping open her purse, Frances withdrew her phone. She winked at the others.

"Hello, Freddie? Yes, this is Frances. I'm sorry to bother you. Linnie isn't picking up. I suppose she isn't taking calls on the drive to Medina. What? No, she didn't explain, other than to say she had a meeting with a family by the name of Reed . . ."

Chapter 22

At every stoplight and while getting gas, Linnie gleaned the basics of Freddie's involvement with the tragic Bryce Reed.

The file was a house of mirrors, unveiling images of her brother that were surely distorted. Freddie, coming to the aid of a kid grievously injured while setting off fireworks. Freddie, packing up the boy's apartment in San Fernando and shipping the contents first class. Freddie, putting Daniel in charge of the affair, leaving Bryce Reed's mother to pen sweet notes to her benefactor's attorney.

The notes, which she read in snatches, were embellished with the highest praise for Sweet Lake's most disreputable son.

Fitting the pieces together was like working a jigsaw puzzle blindfolded. Nothing made sense. She pulled into the Reeds' driveway more perplexed than ever. In her purse, her cell phone hummed.

Another call from Freddie. Whatever he wanted, it could wait until tonight.

She'd barely cut the engine when a woman trotted out of the house. Janis Reed waved enthusiastically, as if they were old friends.

"How lovely of you to stand in for your brother," she said in greeting. "Such a busy man—Bryce was disappointed, but his father and I understood. With all those films to make, who could expect Freddie Wayfair to find time for a visit? You're sweet to see Bryce on his behalf."

"My pleasure," Linnie said, playing along. So Freddie was covering all the boy's medical expenses but refused direct contact? A plausible reason didn't come to mind. "Thank you for allowing a visit on such short notice."

"Nonsense! Bryce is so pleased. I asked a neighbor to watch my younger boys to give you some privacy." At the steps leading into the house, Janis lowered her voice. "Try not to stare at the glass eye. He's not used to it yet. A tough situation for all of us."

"I'm sorry. This must be very difficult."

"Some of Bryce's friends offered to visit. They'd like to cheer him up. He's refused everyone."

"He won't see his friends?" She wondered if the youth was seriously depressed.

"Just sits in his bedroom all day long. We consider ourselves fortunate he's willing to join the family at dinnertime. Then he goes back to his room."

Sympathy for the youth steeped her. "He won't accept visitors because he's embarrassed about the glass eye?" If she was the first visitor, she'd been presented with a compliment—and a burden.

Janis bobbed her head. "We've tried to explain he has nothing to worry about. Like talking to a wall. He's barely left his room since coming home from the institute. Drives my husband batty."

"Staying cooped up alone isn't healthy. Can he talk to someone?"

"Some of his past teachers from the high school offered. They all loved Bryce. Our minister tried too." Absently Janis plucked at her fuzzy sweater. "Dr. Eriksson at Devlin suggested a psychologist. I like the idea, but my son refused."

"Perhaps he needs time to sort himself out."

"I hope so. We're dropping hints about Bryce returning to college. We'll see. I'm sure your visit will perk him up. "

A daunting task. "I'll do my best," Linnie promised.

With misgiving, she followed Janis inside. She'd craved an understanding of her brother's motives, not a swim in choppy seas. Not
gale-force winds and an injured boy caught in the maelstrom. Freddie
collected people and then discarded them just as easily. He surrounded
himself with sycophants and a tribe of weird and dislikable employees.
In the fantasy world of film, he found himself most at ease because, she
presumed, the glittery lights of make-believe placed no demands on his
heart or his conscience.

How did an injured kid fit into a life so shallow?

In the living room, Janis paused. "Can I get you anything?"

"No, I'm fine."

"Then you might as well go in. Last door to your right."

"Thanks."

She abandoned Linnie in the dim light of the hallway. In her wake,
the secrets Freddie kept vibrated through the murky air.

Needing answers, Linnie strode forward.

Chapter 23

Bryce Reed didn't occupy a bedroom. He lived in a shrine to Freddie Wayfair.

Light slanted through the hastily drawn curtains. The thin beam arrowed to the movie posters lining the farthest wall like oversize stamps in a collector's album. The titles were all in English, but not all of the promotional copy—Linnie recognized Spanish and Japanese and what she presumed was Hindi.

To her right, a lamp bowed low on a sturdy desk that had undoubtedly presided over the room since Bryce's first years of school. The tight circle of illumination showed off carefully arranged movie paraphernalia, swords and strange crowns bristling with thorns, ghoulish masks, and a mason jar stuffed with ticket stubs. On the wall behind, magazine clippings and news garnered online formed a wallpaper of sorts. Astonished, she crossed to the desk. The clippings were arranged in chronological order, beginning with the humble inception of Bad Seed Productions and finishing with the more recent successes, including a host of independent film awards. Freddie had won awards on five continents?

"Weird," said the young man lurking in the shadows. "You don't look like him."

Startled, she turned toward the voice—behind the bed, a silhouette. Apparently the meager sunlight and the desk lamp were a clumsy attempt at stage lighting. Bryce was doing his best to show her the room without showing himself.

She motioned to the light switch. "May I turn on the overhead?"

The query rolled across the uncomfortable silence.

Trying again, she said, "How 'bout if I open the curtains?"

"Leave the curtains shut." A finger pointed through the shadows. "Want to check everything out? Start in the closet. There's some really cool stuff I bought on eBay."

She angled the desk lamp, found the closet. "Like what, exactly?"

"The best of Bad Seed Productions. Costumes, props—whatever I can get my hands on."

The disclosure took her off guard. "You have *more* stuff from my brother's movies?"

"Are you kidding? If I don't set alerts on my phone, I miss the best deals. Lost out on a trident from *Sea Warrior* last week."

Linnie wasn't sure what she'd expected from the visit. Certainly not a phantom hiding behind a bed. Not a brightly heartbroken mother, and a task impossible to fulfill.

Following the suggestion, she walked to the closet and opened the bi-fold doors. A stench rolled forward to greet her—a blend of cumin, cinnamon, and chili peppers laced with mold. She sneezed.

Bryce laughed. "Pretty gross, huh?"

"Nasty." She pushed aside a black cape reeking of the scent. Thankfully the other costumes hanging in the closet were less odorous. "How do you tolerate the stink?"

"I should throw the cape in the washing machine. Guess I've smelled it for so long, I'm immune."

Or his olfactory sense was DOA, she decided.

"It's from *Space Demon Revenge*," Bryce offered, his reticence melting beneath excitement. "I read about it on a blog—*Avinash's Mad Moviez*. The blog's in Delhi. Avinash is a major fan—covers everything

Bad Seed produces. During the *Space Demon* shoot, Freddie made the cast wear this nasty perfume. Really pissed off the actors."

"Why did he spritz them with stinky perfume?"

"To keep them in character. See, the space demon attacked the Paladin home world to steal the spice they mined. The demon needed the spice to feed the time shifters he used to destroy planets. If the inhabitants of a planet wouldn't join his death league, they were goners. Kind of a *Dune* motif, but with more fight scenes and less rain. Actually, I don't think it did rain on the demon's world."

"Interesting," she replied, caught up by his zeal.

"*Revenge* won the Green Duck in Sydney."

From the closet she removed a less pungent costume. The gown was surprisingly heavy. "What's the Green Duck?"

"An indie film award. Really big deal. Freddie's won three."

Surveying the costume, she muffled a gasp. The creepy plastic bodice resembled lizard skin. Leave it to Freddie to add shoulder padding that looked like gouged flesh. The skirt was less repulsive. The drape of silver fabric featured long glass beads trailing to the hem. How did her brother dream up this stuff?

Her heart shifting, she recalled her mother's comments about the hidden creativity of the Wayfair men. It was plausible Freddie's vision appealed to adolescents the world over. Was Bryce an example of the fervor reserved for the creations of a man who was, in many ways, more adolescent than adult?

She returned the garment, selected another. "You like my brother's films?" she asked, hoping to draw Bryce out. He remained trapped behind the bed in a self-imposed prison. How to perform a rescue operation wasn't clear.

"Like them? They're fantastic." He drummed his hands against the wall with a child's enthusiasm. "No one beats Freddie at crazy plots and disturbing characters. First movie I saw, in fifth grade? Scared the shit out of me. *Maze of Misfits*. Freddie doesn't do gore—he's a purist, and there are never slasher scenes—but the *Misfit* hero summoned really creepy ghosts from other planets. The guy looked so much like my school principal, I was sure there were space phantoms hiding in the gymnasium. I was hooked. I've been collecting his stuff since I was a kid."

She laughed. "Bryce, you're still a kid."

"I'm twenty-one," he said with mulish pride.

"You have your whole life ahead of you."

He grunted unintelligibly.

Which was when she tired of conversing with a mystery host. "I'm opening the curtains," she announced, "mostly because I'm beginning to feel like Christine in *Phantom of the Opera*. Want to dive into bed, pull the covers over your head? Better leap fast."

A garbled protest followed her steps to the window. She flung open the drapes, pouring sunshine into the room. There was no sense coddling Bryce. His desire to flee the uncomfortable proof of his injury was no different than Freddie's sure-footed flights into the woods long ago, the desperate escapes to avoid the indomitable Treat Wayfair whenever he came down too hard on his son. Linnie suffered an ache of regret. She'd been too young to help Freddie when he'd needed her most.

Bryce was another matter.

Training her eyes on the desk, she gave her anxious host time to compose himself. She read one of the magazine articles tacked to the wall. Freddie, in Stockholm, receiving a gold medallion at the Indie Magnet awards. He looked rakish in faded jeans, a yellow tie, and a nubby blazer.

Behind her back, feet shuffled. Then the squeak of the mattress giving as Bryce sat on the edge.

"May I turn around?" she asked, steeling herself for what she might find.

There was a pregnant delay, then, "Sure."

A smattering of burn marks covered his forehead. There were scars too, and a starburst of pinkish skin stretching across his left temple. Around large, oval eyes, maroon bruises lent the impression of a raccoon. Peach fuzz on a sweetly pointed chin. A wide mouth with full, sensual lips. He grimaced, drawing into relief high cheekbones.

Bryce Reed was good-looking.

"You aren't half-bad," she joked. "Get out more often. A nice girl might hunt you down."

Pleasure darted across his face. Quelling it, he lowered his attention to his lap. He was doing his best to conceal the glass eye.

Approaching, she held out her hand. "Nice to meet you. I'm Linnie Wayfair, proud manager of the historic Wayfair Inn. I know exactly zip about the movie business, although I do have a crush on Benedict Cumberbatch. I never can decide if I love him more in *Star Trek* or *The Imitation Game*."

"Tough call." Beneath the weight of his gloomy thoughts, Bryce rolled his shoulders. "Guess I'd choose *Star Trek*. I love anything sci-fi. Cumberbatch was also great as Alan Turing. Did you know Steve Jobs idolized Turing?"

"I did not," she said, aiming for peppy interest. "Pretty cool."

An overblown gambit, and her enthusiasm drooped his head lower. "I know you mean well," he said with a cool resignation hinting at maturity. "I'm not ready for anyone to see it just yet."

"What if I want to see?"

The instant the words left her lips, she saw Jada instead.

Jada in third grade, pushing the students back with her baby-plump arms. Her wild hair bouncing as she stooped before the girl who'd tumbled from the swing set. The tough cherub's voice explaining she fell down too—but she got back up. How she'd reached past Linnie's hiccupping sobs to pull her to her feet.

The best lessons come when our hearts are broken open. Bryce was broken too.

There was time for him to heal.

"We all have something," Linnie said, sitting beside him. "Look at my thighs. A day doesn't go by when I wouldn't like to take a chain saw to them. I'm not even going to discuss my butt."

He shifted to glance at her jean-clad legs. "They're okay."

"So is your eye."

He regarded her. His left eye tracked slowly behind his right.

"Not bad." She smiled.

"It's plastic."

"Not glass?"

"Mom calls it glass, but she's a dope. They've been using thermo-plastics for about fifty years." Bryce regarded her for as long as he dared. He looked away, saying, "Can I ask you something?"

"Anything."

"Why didn't Freddie visit?"

"I'm not sure."

"It's no big deal. He begins filming a new movie this summer. I read about it on *Avinash's Mad Moviez*. There's a rumor he'll shoot in Australia, but it's conjecture. He keeps lots of stuff under wraps until he starts filming. Good PR, if you ask me. Keeps the fans guessing."

"I imagine it would." She glanced at him swiftly. "I don't have much of a relationship with my brother, a situation I'd like to remedy. If not for you, we probably would've gone another decade without running into each other. Longer, maybe. So, thanks."

"He came to Ohio for me? I figured he was here for speaking engagements."

"Nope. You're the reason."

As was the shrine he'd built, a monument to the achievements of an eccentric filmmaker. Which, Linnie mused, might explain Freddie's absence. A die-hard fan's unconditional love glossed over the warts we all possess, the less-than-admirable behavior. Bryce viewed his idol as perfect. Did Freddie avoid contact to protect a young man's fantasy? Linnie couldn't blame him if he did.

Through the window, the sun slid toward the horizon. Conscious of the long drive back to Sweet Lake, she drew the visit to a close. In the living room, she shared a few words with Janis before walking to her car.

She'd driven to the stop sign at the end of the street when an unfamiliar Ford zoomed up from behind. The horn blared, nearly shocking her out of her skin.

A rental, obviously, with Freddie at the wheel.

Another blast from the horn, and he stuck his arm out the window. He pointed at a grassy field to her left.

By the time she climbed out of the Honda, Freddie was in full lather. "What are you doing here? My sneaky, meddling sister. Snooping in other people's business, going where you're not invited—what's the matter with you?"

"Nothing's the matter with me!" The insults hurt, and she balled her fists. "Stop yelling at me."

"Who told you about Bryce?"

"No one told me, Freddie."

"Yeah. Right."

"I was picking up stuff for Daniel and saw the file on his desk." Better to take the fall alone than drag Kay into this.

The answer didn't satisfy, and her brother stalked closer. "You're lying. Did your boyfriend break a confidence?"

"Daniel, break a confidence? You've got to be kidding."

"I'll have him disbarred. You had no right coming here."

"Then again, you have *every* right to come here—but you haven't. What are you afraid of?"

Ruddy color peaked on Freddie's cheekbones. He appeared immobilized—by shame or the blunt nature of the question, it was impossible to tell. In that instant, she pitied him. Freddie had invested heavily in his bad boy reputation. Lend the opportunity to display goodness, and he was quickly out of his depth.

Wanting to steer him, she said, "Bryce is a sweet kid. You've made a real difference in his life."

"How is he?"

"Why don't you go see for yourself?" She'd already deduced he wouldn't have come at all if not for her visit. But he was here now, and Bryce deserved the courtesy. "Freddie, there's nothing to fear."

"But fear itself," he said, putting gravel in his voice to ape Winston Churchill. Immediately he sobered. "You shouldn't have come."

A comment doused with petulance, and she laughed. "You're a pain in the ass, big brother. Must you make everything difficult? If you're peeved because I've looked behind the curtain and discovered you aren't Lucifer, I swear to take your secret to the grave."

"Don't get any ideas, Sugarpop. I haven't signed up with the Random Acts of Kindness League. And let's not pretend we'll become friends because you got it into your head to drive to Medina after snooping around Daniel's office. If this one arbitrary event leads you to believe you've glimpsed weakness, guess again."

An allusion to their battle over the inn, and she wondered if she was witnessing an actor deep inside his role. "We're still enemies?" she asked, taking care to mask her disappointment.

"We're adversaries. You want what I have, and I'm not inclined to hand over my shares. Why should I?"

She recalled Frances's remarks at the induction ceremony. "I guess you shouldn't," she replied, trying her hand at spontaneity. "I've treated you like a dirtbag—mostly because you act like one, but you've probably had your reasons."

"Keep laying on the sugar. You know how I like it." Freddie studied his nails. "Oh. Wait. You're the one with a penchant for sweets."

She ignored the bait, needing to get this out before second thoughts intruded. "Here's the bottom line," she said, the emotion glossing her voice coming as a surprise. "I have no right to push you out of the family biz. It's your family too."

"I'm astonished you noticed."

The droll retort emboldened her to say, "I don't expect a puppy for Christmas, but I would like to get along better. You *are* my brother." Her throat tightening, she added, "Despite all your maddening qualities, I care about you."

"Ah—more lies!"

"Freddie, I mean it."

Clearly unconvinced, he said, "Did Saint Daniel suggest you try buttering me up? A stealthy maneuver, but I'm on to you. Tell your boyfriend he can't sit on both sides of the negotiating table, not when he's already agreed to represent me." Freddie stopped abruptly to regard the field where they stood, the weeds up to his ankles and the crumpled soda cans strewn about. "Who lives in a place like this? There's more excitement in the Tibetan wilds."

"Good people like the Reeds. If you hurry, you won't interrupt their dinner."

"Oh, go home, would you?"

Climbing into the car, she brought the engine to life. Freddie hadn't budged from the weeds, his eyes vacant, his expensive sport coat flapping and his beautiful hair tufting in the summer wind like horns. The horns didn't call to mind Lucifer.

More than anything else, Freddie resembled a lost boy from *Peter Pan,* a perpetual adolescent for whom maturity would never arrive.

Sticking her head out the window, she shouted, "Are you going to visit Bryce or not?"

Chapter 24

Inside the suite, the music droned at an acceptable volume. For the last twenty-four hours, Freddie had remained holed up with his staff.

On a steadying breath, Linnie rapped twice.

The ill-mannered Lexie opened the door. "Yeah?"

"May I see my brother?"

"He doesn't want to see you."

"Please. It's important."

His assistant chewed over the request. Finally, she said, "Hold on."

The door creaked partially shut. A good time to flee, Linnie mused, or dash to the kitchen for a sugar injection. There wasn't much chance of a friendly reception. For strength, she pretended Siren vibes, a charming fiction, were surrounding her now. She imagined the energy forming ribbons that were purple, silver, and a clear hazel shade, which, come to think of it, described the eye color she shared with Frances. A mere inconvenience that she didn't also possess a dose of the old dame's majesty, the habit Frances had of peering down her nose as if surrounded by commoners she accepted with benevolent patience and a large dose of affection.

After long minutes Freddie sauntered up. An unfamiliar brunette hung on his arm. At his side, his assistant glowered.

"Lexie, I'll take care of this." She stalked off, and he gave the brunette a squeeze. "Sasha, do you mind? I prefer to cross swords with my sister in private."

Linnie waited for the woman to move off. "I'm not here to argue." He regarded her suspiciously, and she hastened to add, "I'm sorry about Medina. I shouldn't have gone without asking first."

"You're admitting your behavior was deplorable?"

Hear the Siren's call and give kindness in secret.

"Absolutely. Really bad move on my part. I hope you can forgive me." She eyed him questioningly. "So. Did you see Bryce or not?"

"I did."

"How did it go?"

Faint satisfaction wove through his features. "Better than expected. His bedroom is a bit much." Freddie gave an elaborate sigh, but she wasn't fooled. "Bryce owns enough memorabilia to open a museum. He's taking fandom to a whole new level."

"Oh, c'mon. You got a kick out of it. He's crazy about your movies. Your number one fan."

The observation left him slightly mollified. "I suppose." Adding a touch of kindness to his voice, he asked, "What do you want?"

"To show you something. It's a beautiful night. Let's take a walk."

"You're inviting me for a nighttime stroll?" He knit his hands together, presumably as he searched the offer for subterfuge. "Planning to have your stealthy friends change the locks while I'm off the premises? Don't bother. I'm checking out soon."

The words nearly spilled out. *I'll miss you.* Then she remembered the bar in the Sunshine Room was still leaking booze, and his late-night parties had drawn complaints from several guests. Although she wanted to patch up their relationship, he'd stayed long enough.

Lightly she touched his arm, a peace offering. "You'll get a kick out of this," she promised.

Intrigued, he followed her downstairs. She picked up the flashlights she'd deposited on the veranda and handed one over. She'd already stowed the neatly typed letter in the pocket of her loose summer sweater.

A light rain had fallen earlier in the day. The skies were now clear, and the moisture had lured swarms of lightning bugs. Pinpoints of light bobbed over the damp grass like sparklers waving in an unseen hand. A good omen, and she felt the jangling nervousness cede to her lifting spirits. Taking the lead, she strode toward the lake and the forest beyond.

Slowing his pace, Freddie curved his palm through a swarm of lightning bugs, taking care not to touch the fragile insects. "Where are we going?" In childhood, he'd found them fascinating.

"To the forest."

"You don't have an ax hidden behind a tree, do you? Knives buried in the dirt?"

"I don't do murder."

"You would if there was sugar for incentive," he remarked testily. "If Jada promised a lifetime supply of her brownies, you'd take out anyone who caused her the least irritation."

"She hasn't suggested I tie bricks to your ankles and throw you in the lake." She sent him a backward glance, adding, "Not yet, anyway."

Although it was nearing eleven o'clock, several couples strolled the beach, kicking their feet in the surf and gazing at the moon. They were among the week's new arrivals. Bypassing them, Linnie ducked onto a secondary path guests never used, one she'd forged with her brother during childhood. The sands merged with the much darker earth at the forest's edge.

Trailing behind, Freddie asked, "How's Daniel? I presume you spent the day tending his every need."

"Doing great. Will you visit him before you leave?"

"If Daniel doesn't mind."

"I'm sure he'd love to see you."

"Linnie, have you found some high-grade weed? I don't know what to make of your cordial tone."

"The cordiality is genuine." The path ended in a patch of rocky ground. To get her bearings, she arced the flashlight through the trees. "This way." She charged through heavy brush.

Freddie caught up. "What's this about?"

At last she found the spot. In the small clearing, an oak tree thicker than three men stretched toward the open heavens. She sent the flashlight's beam up the knotty wood. The intense ring of illumination came to rest on the third limb.

"Look."

Starved of light, the ponderous limb had grown horizontally before forming a nearly perfect ninety-degree angle. A tree house was tucked into the nook. The small structure boasted walls of mismatched lumber and a makeshift roof fashioned with dowel rods.

Freddie drifted back on his heels. "My tree house is standing? Remarkable."

"No one hikes this far into the woods. It's remained unmolested."

"Should've come down in a storm." A pile of new lumber caught his notice, and his face tensed. "Why do I have the impression repair work is about to commence?"

"Because it is." A sweet heaviness pulled in her chest. "Earlier today I asked Philip and his men to bring the necessary materials. I'll patch up the loose boards and fix the holes in the roof. Nails, a glue gun—easy peasy."

"Why perform this amazing feat?"

"Freddie, it's your tree house," she said, astonished by the need to explain. "You loved coming here when you were a kid."

"Still, this is an odd kindness," he replied, impervious to her attempt to make amends. "You've been angry with me for years."

"I'm not angry now."

"You were. Whenever I tried to get in touch, you refused my calls. Marking my e-mail as spam was a particularly hostile move. I assumed you'd write to the governor of California next, ask him to put me on death row."

She laughed. "Now that's a punishment I didn't think of."

Abandoning him in the moonlight, she approached the tree. Eyes drifting shut, she settled her palms on the trunk. The scratchy texture bit at her skin. She wasn't sure about carting energy around as the Sirens presumed, but she'd always respected the power of trees. She imagined the grand, outsize life force pulsing beneath her fingertips.

His expression in flux, he appeared at her side. "I can't deduce a logical reason why you'd repair my childhood sanctuary," he muttered sulkily. "This makes no sense."

"A secret kindness."

"What?"

"The Sirens have a practice . . . never mind."

He drew tall with wavering dignity. "Tell me why you're doing this," he demanded, and she caught the subtle change in the tone of his voice, the edgy filmmaker persona coming to the fore. "So unlike you, and an unnecessary gesture. Call the raccoons and let the forest take the shack. What do I care?"

"C'mon, Freddie. You *do* care, and I don't want to see the best part of your childhood fall apart," she said, aiming past the façade to the child cradled underneath. "A boy's greatest triumph and a marvel of inspired engineering. While you were putting this contraption together, I used to sneak out here to see what you'd added next."

The affection she offered drew him closer. "You followed me?"

"You were my big brother."

"And your greatest tormentor."

The statement's accuracy made her smile. She grew serious, asking, "How *did* you manage this? I've always wondered how you got the supplies past Dad."

The query put unmistakable pride in his eyes. "Stealth planning, at night. Remember the guy who worked third shift at the front desk? He retired before Dad's stroke."

"Max? Wasn't he Greek? No. Armenian."

"Albanian," Freddie corrected. He warmed to his story. "I'd sneak out of bed in the wee hours, dig around for supplies in the oldest sections of the basement. Unbelievable the whatnots our ancestors left behind. I have a tin of letters written to our great-grandmother during the Roaring Twenties—remind me to show you sometime. Anyway, Max helped drag the supplies to the beach. Clapboards, a bundle of dowels, flooring left over from a renovation in the 1950s. He'd dump everything on the sand and leave me to carry on alone. I spent most of junior high putting this mess together."

"Not a mess. You did a good job." He'd stepped back, presumably to entertain the notion of climbing up. The lack of artifice on his features, the genuine delight residing in his eyes, gave her the courage to say, "There's something else I've been wondering about. Are your movies on Netflix? I'd like to catch a few."

"I knew it. You're on hallucinogens." He stared with mock horror. "Should I perform an intervention?"

"I'm serious. I'd like to see your work." She swallowed around the lump in her throat. "I'd also like to offer an apology. Most of us don't have the guts to dream, but you did. You took your vision and built something wonderful for thousands of people to enjoy."

"Millions, in time." The tiny lines framing his eyes relaxed. "Watch and learn. I'm on the upswing."

"I'm proud of you."

The compliment bestowed more sincerity than he appeared ready to accept. He lifted his attention to the starry night, but not before she glimpsed a flicker of warmth in his eyes.

"Are we becoming friends, S—" He stopped from issuing the loathsome *Sugarpop*.

"A good plan . . . assuming you're not upset. You won't like what I have to say."

"Here it comes."

Rhythmically she swung the flashlight's beam across the mossy ground, needing to occupy her nervous hands. She'd only come to the decision yesterday, on the drive back from Medina. Meeting Bryce and gaining an appreciation of Freddie's artistry, the accident with Daniel and Fancy—the crush of unpredictable events had steered her heart to what matters. Family, love, and the forgiveness she owed not only Freddie, but also her parents. She wouldn't waste another day nursing her bruised pride. She didn't have to like their choices.

She wasn't obligated to live by their dictates either.

Before second thoughts might stop her, she withdrew the envelope from her sweater. "I'm giving notice," she got out, stuffing the envelope into his fist. Recalling Frances's remark about her lack of spontaneity, she added, "I was planning to give a month's notice, but what the hell. Mom and Dad want you to have the Wayfair, so consider me out of your hair. I'm gone in two weeks."

His attention jogged from the envelope to her. "You're surrendering your shares?"

"Effective immediately." Never had she chosen an unpredictable course of action, and her brother's astonishment made her giddy. "Should I call the 'rents, or do you want the honor?"

"We're not calling Florida. You aren't quitting."

"Want me to stay? Then tell Mom and Dad you're out completely unless I receive majority ownership. Tell them you'll return *your* shares to the estate if they don't agree with our plan."

A mulish light entered his eyes. "Resorting to the subterfuge of repairing my beloved tree house, softening me up—the webs you weave, Sugarpop."

"One has nothing to do with the other. I'm fixing up your child-hood sanctuary even if we can't come to terms."

"Well, we can't. I'm not giving you majority control."

She smiled through her sorrow. "All right," she conceded. "I'm gone in two weeks."

"Fine—go. But what, may I ask, am I supposed to do? Manage the ancestral home from the Great Victoria Desert? I leave for Australia in six weeks!"

The gambit had failed, but the loss wasn't total. There was time still to repair their relationship.

"Freddie, I'm staying in Sweet Lake. If you have problems at the inn, I'll pop over to give advice," she offered. "Hire someone with experience in hospitality management. If you bring in an unemployed actor to 'channel' the role, I *won't* lend a hand."

He began pacing, his blond locks silvered in the moonlight. "This is unfathomable. You love the inn. How can you leave?" Rolling to a standstill, he scoured her face with confusion.

"Aren't you pleased?"

"I'm not, damn you. We've been running a perfectly adequate script since I dumped the inn on your shoulders and left for California. This is utterly out of character. Who am I if not the evil brother?"

His distress edged a smile onto her lips. "You're not evil, Freddie. Self-absorbed, irritating, careless—why don't you treat people better? Free ball gowns are nice, but common decency is better."

He swatted away the sincere advice. "Why change? I've been typecast for years. Mother sees through the façade, but you and Dad wrote me off long before I took the money and left for California." He toyed with the tips of his mustache. "I like the role," he admitted. "The fiery rebel of the Wayfair clan."

"Find a better role."

"We'll see." He began tearing open the envelope. His courage evidently fleeing, he tried handing it back instead. "I won't allow you to surrender your shares."

She waved him off. "Like you can stop me."

"Another cheap ploy." Rallying, he added, "Fine, Linnie. I'll call your bluff. Want to leave? I'll have Jada installed in your job in precisely two weeks."

"Sorry, big brother. She doesn't want the job. Cat, either, if that's your next move."

The bravado left his face. "Then you're bluffing. This must be a bluff." Desperation laced his voice. "What's happened to your dreary, responsible nature?"

She gave him a quick hug. "Two weeks," she repeated. "Better cancel your flight. You can't leave until you find a new manager."

Freddie opened and closed his mouth like a guppy tossed from the ocean. Doing a secret kindness felt good. No matter how events shook out, she'd repair his tree house—and she'd given him a dose of strong medicine by forcing him to acknowledge he needed her at the helm.

Sticking up for herself? *That* felt even better.

She gave him a peck on the cheek, then sauntered out of the forest.

⁓

Daniel asked, "Did you get the mess straightened out? Kay said you lost most of the July reservations during the system crash."

Avoiding his attentive gaze, Linnie finished straightening the blanket across his chest. Concocting a cover story to hide Monday's trip to Medina wasn't the smartest move, and she felt more than a little guilty. Yesterday she'd only visited for a short while because the painkillers the doctors prescribed had made it difficult for Daniel to keep his eyes open. He was much more alert today.

There was the additional problem of Freddie—what if he lodged a complaint with his attorney? Quickly she discarded the possibility. After last night's conversation in the forest, he was more apt to brood in isolation while considering his options—scramble to find her replacement, or back down and hand over majority control. Unlikely that blowing her cover was at the top of his agenda.

"We lost tons of data," she improvised. "Luckily Mr. Uchida prints out each reservation the moment it comes in. Cat helped input the list."

"All the data's restored?"

"Took hours, but they got everything done."

She'd just dragged a chair to the side of his bed when her cell phone buzzed.

Her mother.

"Mom, hello. Thanks for returning my call. No, nothing special. Just wanted to hear if you and Dad are managing with the new puppy. Oh, that's wonderful. I'm glad the trainer is working out . . ."

Over the next five minutes, she listened to the trials and successes concerning the puppy. Midway through the call, her father got on to regale her with the list of tricks he'd taught Lucy. Not once during the conversation did she mention work or the notice she'd given Freddie.

A salient bit of news she hadn't yet shared with Daniel either.

She hung up to find him gaping in puzzlement. "You called your parents *to chat*?"

An unexpected twinge of pride drifted through her. "I sure did."

"You *are* making changes."

"More than you know." He arched a brow, and she rushed on. "Last night I gave Freddie my resignation. A crazy gamble, but one I don't regret." She covered the high points of the conversation, adding, "He insisted he won't agree to my terms, but we'll see. As of this morning, he still hasn't flown back to California."

Daniel's eyes widened. "You gave notice, just like that? Definitely not like you."

"I'm trying my hand at spontaneity. Follow the bold impulse, and logic be damned."

"I've never thought of you as spontaneous."

"Time to revise your thinking."

"Happy to do so." Concern filtered through his gaze as he asked, "How'd your staff take the news?"

She felt her shoulders creeping higher, to her ears. "I'm not telling them, at least not until Freddie decides his next move."

"They have the right to know if the boss is heading out the door."

"I'm not leaving—at least I hope not."

"Linnie, you have to stop holding your employees at arm's length. You've kept them at a distance ever since you were forced to lay off half the staff. Stop underestimating their affection. They care about you. They'll take it hard if Freddie calls your bluff."

Did she keep the staff at a distance? Unsure, she remarked, "Sometimes you give the impression you know me better than I know myself."

"Maybe I do." He rested his hand on hers.

"Well, let's hope I won't need to upset the staff. If there's ever a time for my brother to grow a brain, this is it. He should back down. I *am* willing to let him keep a hand in the business."

Daniel looked unconvinced. "You're asking a lot. He must return his shares to the trust, forcing your parents to give you control. Then he must trust you to return a portion of his shares. What are you aiming for?"

"I'll give him thirty percent," she supplied, hating the doubt clouding his eyes. A real blow to her confidence. Determined to stay optimistic, she added, "I did tell Jada and Cat about my gamble. They agree—threatening to leave is the only move left. They promised not to tell the staff. However, since Cat's aware of the situation, I'm sure the Sirens have learned all the gory details. Maybe they'll hold a special meeting, conjure positive vibes so good fortune smiles on me."

Daniel shook his head in bemusement. "I'm sure they'll applaud your gambling spirit. If this works, remind me to take you to Vegas."

"Guess I'll know soon if I'm holding all the aces."

"Might be, if your brother hasn't checked out of the inn."

"Nope. Still hiding behind locked doors."

"Knowing Freddie, he'll brood for days. Stay in his room, pray this is all a bad dream."

She didn't care if he did. Taking the gamble was exhilarating and somehow freeing. High on the emotion, she followed an equally bold impulse, saying, "Speaking of changes, I've been thinking about something else."

Daniel chuckled. "This must be a doozy. You're inching your shoulders toward your ears. A big giveaway that you're nervous."

She tried to relax. "About us." The casual note she attempted failed, and she added quickly, "Why don't I move in with you? I know this is fast, but mostly I can't wait to wake up every morning in your arms."

Obviously he didn't trust his ears. His jaw grew slack as his brows lifted to his hairline.

"You don't need to think about it?" he asked. "Draw up a list of pros and cons, anything like that?"

His surprise wasn't unexpected given that she wasn't in the habit of making snap decisions. Then again, she'd made quite a few lately.

She kissed his cheek. "Daniel, I've been scared about making the leap, rushing in too fast. After everything that's happened recently . . . living together just feels right."

A sweet astonishment glazed his features. "How 'bout we start today?"

⌒の

Daniel's comment about Freddie brooding proved accurate. During the next days, he roosted in his suite as the members of his entourage checked out, one by one. The hostile Lexie was the last to go. On a sunny Friday morning she thumped her suitcase down the stairwell in thigh-high boots and a leather jacket. The jacket had "Hell's Angels" embroidered on the back in angry red stitching.

From the veranda, she flipped Linnie the bird. Linnie resisted the urge to respond in kind.

Behind the lobby desk, Mr. Uchida did not show equal restraint.

At the Wayfair, Lexie's eccentric boss remained behind, stewing in his suite and slipping out late at night after Linnie drove home to Daniel's place. Whether Freddie spent the hours interviewing potential managers for the inn or hooking up with women in out-of-the-way bars was anyone's guess.

Obsessing about her brother's decision wouldn't affect the outcome, so Linnie kept her thoughts focused on the positive changes in her world. Daniel returned home from the hospital. As she packed up her belongings in the south wing, the stack of boxes in his living room grew in size; in the evenings, Jada and Cat helped unpack and sort. In equal parts, her closest friends mourned losing her company for late-night chats and celebrated the start of her new life with Daniel.

On Saturday night, Frances called to inquire if the recuperating patient was well enough for a barbecue the following day, compliments of the Sirens. Linnie suspected the offer wasn't just about Daniel—no doubt the women thought the get-together would keep her occupied as she awaited Freddie's impending decision. The gesture was appreciated, and she suggested holding the festivities in Daniel's backyard.

Jada offered to skip the affair. She agreed to work the evening shift at the Wayfair instead.

On Sunday afternoon, the crowd began gathering for the cookout.

Linnie waved as Tilda, among the last to arrive, came into the backyard. "I heard a rumor about a trick you've taught Puddles," the realtor said of Daniel's mutt. "What is it?"

In the days since she'd moved in, Linnie had discovered Puddles cried out whenever her name was uttered. Seeing a dog in agony didn't suit, and she'd hit upon a solution—teach the pooch a new trick.

Silvia, ferrying steaks to her husband at the grill, looked up. "I'd also like to see the performance."

Cat giggled. "Kookiest trick I've ever seen." She regarded Linnie, seated on the grass and ruffling Puddles's ears. "Do it again."

From the grill, Cat's father shook his head. "The dog's tired," Marco told his daughter. "Your mother needs help setting the picnic table. Why don't you pitch in and stop making the poor mutt perform?"

"But he loves performing!"

Maneuvering carefully on crutches, Daniel came across the lawn. He exchanged amused glances with Linnie. "Once more," he suggested. "Then we give Puddles dinner and call it a day."

Tilda bounced on her heels and clapped her hands. Her enthusiasm drew Frances and several other Sirens near. An air of anticipation surrounded the small crowd.

Linnie whistled. In response, giddy anticipation shivered across the dog's mop of fur.

"Here we go." She motioned *sit.* Puddles dropped to his haunches on the grass. The onlookers quieted down.

She drew out the singsong command:

Linnneee . . .

Puddles lifted his snout and howled at the stars.

. . . loves . . . Daniel . . .

Leaping up, the dog pranced across the grass with his large tail wagging.

. . . and Puddles too!

Rolling onto his back, Puddles released a joyous wave of barking. Linnie crouched, made the signal. He leapt up and flew into her arms.

Daniel said, "And I thought he was my best friend."

She let the dog push her down on the grass. "Not anymore," she replied from beneath the mountain of fur. Waking up each morning in Daniel's arms was everything she'd expected. Canine adoration? A bonus she hadn't anticipated.

Fancy, salivating at a burger sizzling on the grill, heard the commotion. She raced over to join the lovefest. Her arm was still in a sling, and she danced carefully around Puddles as the pooch slathered Linnie with kisses. Little-girl laughter resounded across the yard.

From the picnic table, Frances called for everyone to take seats.

Daniel lifted his nose to the savory scents. "You coming, or planning to play with the beast all night?" he asked Linnie.

Cat added, "Jada sent over a batch of her brownies for dessert."

"Go ahead," Linnie told them. "I'll be right there."

They didn't require further urging. When they'd gone, she crawled out from beneath Puddles. Relishing the summer night, she curled her toes into the grass. Above the flowerbeds, the dancing flicker of fireflies gave the approaching night a magical quality. Contentment flowed through her. Growing up in a mansion that rented rooms by the night, she was unfamiliar with the simple pleasures of a home where privacy was plentiful and the living spaces were shared by only two people. If she walked around in her birthday suit, she drew wolf whistles, not complaints; if she dozed on the couch, she'd awake to find Daniel smoothing his hand across her hair.

In all the years of friendship, she'd rarely visited his backyard. A half-acre deep and nearly as wide, the tree-dotted vista was now one of her favorite haunts. With Philip's help, she'd begun clearing the flowerbeds of weeds and salvaging some of the perennials.

He'd also surprised her by offering to help with the repair work on Freddie's tree house. Although Philip pronounced her crazy for proceeding with the plan, he insisted on handling all the heavy lifting, his off-key whistling carrying through the forest as he taught her the basics of carpentry. Yesterday they'd spent the better part of the afternoon patching up the roof and replacing several of the rotting floorboards. Daniel wanted to tag along to watch their progress, but negotiating the forest on crutches was out of the question.

Tomorrow, assuming she cleared the work from her desk by five o'clock, she planned to repaint the structure. Until Freddie came to a decision, keeping busy proved a balm for her worried heart.

Would the gamble pay off? Unease pooled in her belly. Freddie hadn't left town, but he hadn't given in either. If he hired a new manager, what then? She wasn't ready to begin the difficult task of plotting out an alternative career, not until he came to a decision.

Frances materialized at her side. "Aren't you hungry?" She closed the sun parasol used to protect her still-flawless complexion. "They're starting dinner without you."

"Guess I'm not very hungry."

"Still no word?"

"Not yet."

Frances squinted into the sun, dipping toward the horizon. "Whatever happens, I hope you and Freddie don't remain on bad terms."

"We won't. If I lose, I'll lick my wounds for a month or two, no more. I won't shut him out of my life a second time." Linnie toed the grass. She'd begun to build a new life with Daniel—one that wouldn't feel complete until she mended old wounds. "Doubt he'll accept an olive branch right away."

"He may, in time."

She hoped Frances was correct. She hadn't expected Freddie to waltz back into her life. Now that he had, she couldn't bear the prospect of losing him again. He'd returned to Ohio to fulfill a private obligation to Bryce Reed, but Linnie viewed the event as an undeserved gift: a do over, a chance to create a lasting relationship with her brother. She didn't want to fail.

"Putting things right with Freddie is my best-case scenario." Recalling the elderly Siren's advice, she dredged up a smile. "Seeing that we're siblings and he carries my history."

"He does. And you his."

"With luck, we'll keep doing so. We've already lost seven years. I don't want to lose the rest."

The remark clearly pleased Frances. "You're a brave girl."

"Thanks."

Frances studied the night, creeping toward them. Changing track, she said, "This afternoon I ran into Daisy at the grocery store. We had quite a chat. She mentioned none of the girls in housekeeping have cleaned Freddie's room in days. He's barred them entry."

This wasn't exactly news. "I told housekeeping not to bother. I could send them in when he sneaks out at night, but what's the point? Freddie won't stay cooped up forever. He's got a film shoot later this summer. At some point, he must return to California."

"Daisy also seemed unaware you've given notice. You may leave your post in one short week, and your employees haven't a clue."

Disapproval colored the statement. "Don't make me feel guilty, okay?" she told Frances. "I've already been over this with Daniel. I'll inform the staff if Freddie pushes me out."

"Honestly, dear—shouldn't you apprise the staff immediately?" Frances made no attempt to hide her censure.

"And worry them for no reason? I won't. They're hardworking employees. If I don't win this battle? They'll have a hard enough transition, getting used to a new boss and all the changes sure to come. It's doubtful Freddie will move forward with the inn's renovations—he'll oversee his inheritance from California, and the Wayfair will take a backseat to his film company. The inn will decline, and some of my employees will lose their jobs in a year, maybe two. I'm not making them anxious a moment sooner than necessary."

"In a situation so dire, the good people working for you *should* have all the facts."

Was Frances correct? Indecision swamped Linnie. She only meant to do right by her employees, to protect them from upsetting facts until the outcome became clear. With nearly a week gone and Freddie still at the inn, she may have acted in error.

Gleaning the uncertainty in her eyes, Frances said, "No one in Sweet Lake ever held you responsible for the inn's troubles. You aren't your parents, following a tradition that should've died out long before you were born. You certainly aren't your brother, a reckless man carting around the lonely heart of a child—a child, I might add, who was pushed and prodded to become something he is not. Linnie, the whole town loves you, your employees most of all. You should tell them."

Linnie's mouth trembled as the words unhitched her composure. Tears leaked from the corners of her eyes. The gamble and the waiting, and now the affection Frances offered—the roller coaster of events threatened to career her off the tracks.

Nearing, Frances brushed the tears away. "This is no time to fall apart," she murmured. "Have faith, child."

"Conjure some of your good vibes, will you? I need them for strength."

"You don't need anything you don't already possess. You have character, which will see you through."

The timing of the pronouncement seemed uncanny as the back door to Daniel's house banged shut. Jada strode across the patio with her brows lowered. Intuition splashed Linnie with cold fear. She'd left Jada in charge of the inn, a responsibility she wouldn't shrug off without good reason.

Evidently Frances sensed the same omen. She placed a steadying hand to Linnie's back. A welcome kindness as Jada paused at the picnic table to whisper in Daniel's ear. The others fell silent.

Together Daniel and Jada started across the grass.

Linnie's shoulders curved forward. "He made the wrong choice," she whispered, her heart emptying out.

Frances patted her gently. "I'm such a fool. I truly believed your brother would make the right choice."

"So did I."

Confirming the terrible news, Jada told them, "Freddie instructed Mr. Uchida to call everyone on staff. We're all to report to the Sunshine Room tomorrow morning at seven to meet the new manager."

Daniel, unsteady on his crutches, muttered under his breath.

Absently Linnie wondered what he'd paid to convince someone to take over the inn, sight unseen. "Who is it?" she heard herself say. Oddly, she felt nothing.

Jada sighed. "His name is Dutch Stevens. Freddie said the guy managed a Hilton in Columbus."

"He's leaving the Hilton without adequate notice?"

"Not exactly. Freddie pulled him out of retirement."

Excusing herself, Frances left them discussing the inn's new manager. Philip was still at the picnic table, urging his daughter to finish her plate. Marco sat beside him, forlornly sipping a glass of wine. The Sirens who'd attended, clustered by the patio, brought their gloomy conversation to a close as Frances joined them.

Silvia's eyes flashed daggers. "We should've run him out of town the minute he arrived," she snapped. "Now look what he's done."

Penelope's eyes watered. "Poor Linnie! How can he take the inn from her? There must be something we can do."

"There is," Frances assured her. She turned to Silvia. "Tell Cat we have a mission for her, but she mustn't breathe a word to Linnie. Have her run up to the inn to get the phone number of every employee. Tell her to meet us at my house."

Silvia gave her a sour look. "We're calling the employees? To do what, wish them bon voyage on an early retirement? With Freddie at the helm, the inn will run aground in a matter of months."

"Hardly. This isn't over." Contrary to Silvia's assessment, there was time enough for the Sirens to work their magic. To the others, Frances said, "Round up the rest of our comrades. We're getting to work, ladies."

Tilda frowned. "Doing what, exactly?"

"Lobbying the staff to stand with their leader." Frances ushered them toward the door. "I'm astonished you need to ask."

Chapter 25

For a man in the winner's circle, her brother looked decidedly unhappy.

After spending days sulking in his suite and only slipping out at night, his skin wore a dull pallor. He'd dressed in a nice enough suit, but the coat sported wrinkles. Linnie spied a stain on the canary-yellow tie. With all the hiding out, he'd clearly forgotten a trip to the dry cleaner's.

In the doorway to her office, he wavered. A hint of apology filled his eyes.

"You're here?" He stepped inside. "I assumed you'd skip the meeting."

Although it was nearing 7:00 a.m., none of the employees were assembled in the Sunshine Room. Linnie was certain—she'd checked.

"I work here, at least until next week." She looked past his shoulder, to the empty hallway. "Where's my replacement?"

Even though she was heartbroken, she wished the mysterious Dutch Stevens no ill will. In fact, she planned to show him around personally. The sadness at losing out wouldn't abate anytime soon. Still, as the inn's manager, she'd accept her replacement with grace.

Fiddling with his tie, Freddie noticed the stain. "Stevens took the wrong exit off the highway." He buttoned his blazer, hiding the stain. "He called from a pay phone. I wasn't aware pay phones still exist. Apparently they do."

"His phone's on the blink?"

"He doesn't have a cell phone. He promised to get one soon."

She recalled Jada mentioning her brother pulling Stevens out of retirement. "Gosh, Freddie. How will you introduce the new manager to the staff if he's out roaming the highway? How old is he anyway?"

"Eighty-one."

She arched a brow. "You're joking."

He grimaced. "I wish I were. As it turns out, locating proper help on short notice isn't easy."

"You're a goofball, big brother."

"Says you."

"Call off the meeting." Despite the gravity of the situation, she chuckled. "Better yet, call off this nonsense. You don't want the inn. I've offered you a fair deal."

For a tantalizing moment, Freddie weighed the suggestion. The contrition on his face tugged loose a memory of him at age nine or ten, his untended homework scattered on the floor of his bedroom and their father stalking a raving path around his browbeaten son.

"You're digging in your heels because of Dad?" she guessed.

His shoulders began lifting toward his ears in a mannerism she hadn't been aware they shared.

"You're afraid to tell him you're never taking over," she said, amazed it had taken her so long to arrive at the reason for Freddie's obstinacy. "That's it, right? Mom you can handle. But Dad? For Pete's sake, Freddie. You've been running from him your whole life."

The pronouncement, harsh though it was, lured her brother across the room. He sank into the chair before her desk.

"I'm not scared." His attention drifted to the photographs on the wall, the line of Wayfair men who'd steered the inn. "Don't you see? This isn't about fear. I'm a grown man. I stopped letting Dad intimidate me ages ago."

"What, then?"

His gaze found hers, then slid to the floor. "I can't stand the thought of disappointing him. Not anymore."

An odd statement, but then she remembered another bedroom—one she'd recently visited. The movie posters on the walls, a shrine for an eccentric filmmaker.

Freddie had visited too.

Unable to resist, she asked, "How did it go with Bryce? You never did share the details."

"Better than expected. We talked for an hour. I promised him a job if he returns to Ohio State and completes his degree. He only has three semesters to go."

"You encouraged him to finish school? Nice move. Keep it up, and people will suspect you're becoming responsible." He shrugged off the compliment, his expression in flux, and she added, "I've never been anyone's hero. Not in the way Bryce looks at you."

"Being viewed as perfect isn't easy. A strangely transformative experience that makes you wonder if . . ."

His voice trailed off, and she supplied, "If you try hard enough, you'll deserve the adoration? You don't have to, you know—try so hard." Her heart shifted. "Most of the time, Dad is a royal pain. But he loves you. He loves us both."

"We won't see his more affectionate side if we derail his grand plan. Mom will be equally furious."

Their reaction no longer concerned her. "Let me talk to them," Linnie said, the awareness blooming that she was stronger than Freddie, had always been stronger. "Sure, they'll pitch a fit. They'll get over it."

He was mulling this over when her ears caught the murmur of voices outside her office. Cat dashed past, disappearing from sight. A louder chorus of voices followed.

"Hello?" Linnie called. "What's going on out there?"

Mr. Uchida walked in, the natty carnation on his lapel sparkling with dew. Without acknowledging Freddie, he strode to her desk. With a bow, he laid a typed letter before her nose. His signature was affixed at the bottom.

She'd only begun to read the contents when Ellis walked in, the kitchen staff trailing like goslings behind a mother goose. More letters fluttered to the desk. Daisy, the rest of housekeeping, the staff in the Sunshine Room, and finally Jada and Cat. Within minutes, Linnie's desk brimmed with snowy-white sheets.

Resignation letters.

A dizzy joy sent her attention across the stack. If she was booted out, they'd go with her. Every last employee.

Flying high, she motioned Freddie near.

"Want to give me the go-ahead to call Mom and Dad?" She handed over the stack. "I'm betting you do."

∽

"Your brother," Daniel said, "is slippery like a snake. Didn't he agree to thirty percent?"

"First thing this morning." Linnie helped Daniel to his feet. "In my office."

"He's vying for a higher percentage."

"I'll give him the evil eye, make him back down."

Alone in the kitchen, they'd hashed out the details of what to say to her parents. At the inn, Jada was baking a batch of cakes. Several girls on the waitstaff were hanging party streamers in the ballroom. Linnie was looking forward to the impromptu celebration with her employees.

She glanced at the clock. "It's time."

"Go get 'em, tiger." Daniel brushed his nose across hers. "Have I mentioned how proud I am of you? You had the courage to roll the dice, and got exactly what you wanted."

She breathed him in for strength. "I love you." The conversation with her parents would be difficult, and she was grateful to have him by her side.

Daniel kissed her, grinned. "I know you do."

"I don't want you to forget."

"Not likely. You tell me every time I bring you to . . ." His expression devilish, he feigned confusion. "What did Frances call it?"

"When she'd had one martini too many? 'Organism.' And yeah, I like telling you then too." Leaning in, she brushed a kiss across his jaw. "I figure encouragement will keep you bringing your A game to bed."

"You bet."

They walked into the living room. At the bar Freddie was pulling down the bottle of Smirnoff. He poured generously.

Linnie made another note, then set the pad and pen on the coffee table. "Is that a good idea?" She motioned to the glass.

Her brother gulped some down. "I'm nervous. Don't badger me."

"I *will* badger you if you keep trying to renegotiate." She helped Daniel to the couch. "We agreed on thirty percent."

"Highway robbery."

"You think? Then my resignation stands." She wiggled her shoulders with uncontained triumph. "And the staff walks out with me."

"Stop dredging up my worst nightmare. If everyone bolts, I'm stuck with an empty mansion and no one to run it. Am I supposed to live alone in the backwoods of Ohio? There isn't decent sushi in a thirty-mile radius. Let's not even discuss the absence of nightlife." He gripped his skull. "I don't have the constitution to live like a pioneer."

Daniel, enjoying her brother's distress, put in, "Then stop playing around."

"Fine." Freddie swirled his drink, sipped. "I'll retain forty-five percent. Nonvoting shares."

Daniel's eyes silvered. "In your dreams."

Freddie's cheeks blazed. "Forty."

Linnie, fed up with the antics, took the drink from his hand. "Thirty—and that's final." Stalking around the bar, she poured the booze down the sink. "Nonvoting shares. You'll receive annual profits at my discretion. But not soon. I need to get the inn back to full capacity."

Her brother waved a cocktail napkin in surrender. "Oh, all right. At least you aren't demanding I give away all of my inheritance. You win."

"Hold on. I've just thought of something else."

"*Now?* You said we're done negotiating!"

She made a quick note on her pad. "Before we entertain discussions regarding profit taking, you'll make a goodwill investment."

Daniel, flipping open the laptop, looked up approvingly. "Nice," he murmured.

Freddie gulped down air. "I've made an investment. I returned the money I'd taken and threw in an extra twenty thou!"

"Which I appreciate, but you can do better." She named her price, adding, "You're managing a lucrative film company and won't miss the cash. Besides, I shouldn't have to secure bank loans to cover the bulk of the renovations."

"A film company now *less* profitable because I promised the Sirens points on my next film. Or have you forgotten those devious women have their claws in me?"

"They're not devious. More like inspired."

Linnie was well aware of how much she owed them. Did the Sirens know about this morning's events at the inn? She had a sneaking suspicion they not only knew, but were instrumental in encouraging the staff to hand in resignation letters en masse. A kindness done in secret she'd never forget.

Absently she wondered if Frances was home this afternoon. Her gorgeous colonial lay on the street behind Daniel's. After the Skype meeting with her parents, Linnie decided she'd walk over and thank Frances in person—for all the wisdom imparted over the last weeks.

Including, she thought wryly, the protection delivered with rattling gourds.

Returning to the matter at hand, she told her brother, "You have until August to make the goodwill investment. Wire the money before leaving for the film shoot. If you don't, I'll hunt you down in the Australian outback."

Freddie gripped his heart. "Where's the rack? The iron maiden? Impale me now!"

"After everything you've put me through? Don't tempt me."

The theatrics were getting him nowhere, and he dropped the act. Or had the sense to stop stalling before she came up with more bright ideas.

Either way, she felt pretty damn good.

"All right, I agree to your terms. My sister, the hard bargainer. Never thought I'd see the day."

Catching the amusement in his eyes, she said, "I love you, big brother."

The endearment lifted his brows. "I love you too." He waved the napkin sulkily. "Sometimes."

Daniel laughed. "Aw, you big cream puff. You love her all the time."

Ducking the observation, Freddie sat on the couch. The barest hint of happiness played on his lips.

Replacing it with mock disdain, he regarded her outdated laptop. "How do you log onto Skype with this thing? I can almost hear the chipmunks racing around inside. Ah. Here we go." He motioned for her to join them, asking, "You told Mom and Dad to await our call?"

Anxiety bounced through her. "Sure did."

"You explained why we're calling?"

"No."

He stared longingly at the bar, then frowned at her. "Was that wise?"

"We'll see." She sat on Daniel's opposite side.

Skype jingled, and her parents logged on.

The indomitable Treat Wayfair looked slightly less intimidating with the puppy on his lap bouncing in and out of view. Sarah appeared nervous, her fingers scaling the collar of her blouse.

Treat glared at the camera. "Linnie, what's going on?" Without awaiting a reply, he looked to Daniel. "Hello, son. What are you doing at a family meeting?"

Freddie patted the perspiration from his brow. "Dad, we need Linnie's boyfriend at the meeting." He dropped his head into view. "We'll sort this out faster with an attorney present."

Treat scratched his balding head. "Now, hold on. Daniel is dating Linnie? When did this start?"

Daniel grinned at her. *They don't know we're living together?*

The anxiety in her belly morphed into a beehive of discomfort. "Dad," she said through parched lips, "I'd characterize my relationship with Daniel as more than dating. We're living together."

The news drew a gasp from her mother as she dipped out of view. "You're living with a man after a few dates? Why would you do anything so impetuous?" She came back up blotting her eyes with a tissue.

For reasons unknown, the response melted Linnie's anxiety. "Yes, Mother," she said firmly, "I've become impetuous. I'm living in sin and rather enjoying it."

Freddie said, "Might we discuss sin at a later date?" He readjusted the laptop to put Daniel center stage. "I'm giving Linnie control of the inn. Daniel will explain."

He didn't get a chance. Glowering, Treat said, "You aren't giving anything away. You have a responsibility as my son—"

Daniel cut him off. "Mr. Wayfair, your son is returning his shares to the trust. Since your daughter is prepared to do the same, you *are* in control. When should we expect you to take over the operations?"

"Hold on just one minute. I'm not taking over. I'm retired."

"Since your heirs won't succeed you, would you like the name of a real estate agent? I assume you'll sell the mansion."

Daniel's eyes turned steely. An impressive sight, and Linnie squeezed his hand. When he glanced at her, she used all her energy to transmit the silent message. *I adore you.*

He winked before returning his attention to the screen. "Mr. Wayfair? Would you like my assistance in locating a realtor? If not, I hope you'll hear me out. I have a solution both your heirs will sanction."

The resolve Daniel conveyed altered the trajectory of the conversation. His persuasive charms altered the future of one of Sweet Lake's founding families. Within minutes, Linnie's father grudgingly agreed to the new terms. His daughter would receive seventy percent and full control of the Wayfair. Freddie gladly agreed to thirty percent in nonvoting shares. With the inheritance complete, the trust would dissolve.

The Skype call ended, and Freddie snapped shut the laptop. "About the goodwill investment." He appeared visibly relieved. "Will you take a rain check until next year?"

"August—you'll put it in writing." Giddy relief swam in Linnie's veins. "I'd like to get crackin' on the renovations."

"So soon, Sugarpop? We're not talking about a few greenbacks."

"As if you'll miss the cash. You're rich." She opened a bottle of wine, poured three glasses. Setting down the bottle, she pulled out her cell phone and sent the text. "And don't call me Sugarpop."

"As you wish, *Linnie*. I'll have the money wired before I leave on the film shoot."

"No excuses." Her cell phone pinged as Frances responded. "Call from Australia begging for an extension, and I won't be amused."

"Oh, go and find a doughnut. I said I'll have the money, and I will."

Daniel cut into the bickering between siblings. "Congratulations, sweetheart. You did it." He kissed her before sending Freddie a teasing look. "Shouldn't you go now? Pack your luggage, book a flight home? I'd like to celebrate with my woman."

Playing dumb, Freddie lifted his glass. "I thought we *were* celebrating. The meeting went exceedingly well. Let's get drunk."

Linnie handed Daniel a glass of wine. "Keep him on a short leash," she said. "I'll be right back."

He reached for his crutches. "You're leaving? I thought we were celebrating."

"We will, shortly." She took the crutches, set them aside. "Hang tight. I'm walking over to see Frances. I'd like to thank her in person."

"For what?"

The question lingered in the air. For what, indeed. Companionship and wisdom, and advice delivered over the rim of a mojito on a moonlit night. Other advice too, about how a sibling carries your history, all those memories, which begin flooding your heart early in childhood and carry you forward as you collect people to love and dreams to follow on a journey beautifully twined, the sorrow with the sweet.

She blew Daniel a kiss. "I'll explain in twenty."

She nearly danced out of the house. The door clicked shut, and she paused on the front stoop with her good fortune sinking in, warming her beneath the clear summer day. Overhead the maples rustled. The melody of gears shifting reached her ears as a girl bicycled past, her arms lifting from the handles to cup the wind.

A crunching beneath her shoes halted Linnie's descent. The sharp fragrance of lavender bloomed in the air.

On the stoop, and the steps too, dried herbs made a fine layer. She was still inhaling their promise when she noticed the small gift. Beside her feet, a feather, blue like the ocean, clung to a length of twine.

Linnie tucked the feather into her pocket.

ACKNOWLEDGMENTS

WITH HEARTFELT THANKS

To my wonderful editor, Kelli Martin, for believing in the Sweet Lake concept from the outset.

To my agent, Pamela Harty, for her generous advice.

To my developmental editor, Krista Stroever, for all her brilliant suggestions, my copyeditor Jessica Fogleman, for her careful edit, and my author relations manager, Gabriella Dumpit.

To the fabulous Liberty Ladies for beta reads in a pinch, stimulating book chat, and most of all your friendship.

To KindleWorlds editor Sean Fitzgerald, for my first experience with Amazon editorial, which showed me how much the company values authors.

To Barry, for reading every review throughout the years and believing even when I entertained doubts. I love you, always.

ABOUT THE AUTHOR

Photo © 2016 Melissa Miley Photography

Award-winning author Christine Nolfi writes heartwarming and inspiring fiction. Her debut novel, *Treasure Me*, was a Next Generation Indie Awards finalist. Many of her novels have enjoyed bestseller status and have been listed as "highly recommended" by the *Midwest Book Review*. A native Ohioan, Christine currently resides in South Carolina with her husband and four adopted children. For the latest information about her releases and future books, visit www.christinenolfi.com. Chat with her on Twitter @christinenolfi.